CONFIRMATION:
INVESTIGATIONS OF THE UNEXPLAINED

BARNA WILLIAM DONOVAN

This is a work of fiction. Names, characters, places, and incidents are products of the author's imagination or are used fictitiously and are not to be construed as real. Any resemblance to actual events, locations, organizations, or persons, living or dead, is entirely coincidental.

World Castle Publishing, LLC
Pensacola, Florida
Copyright © Barna William Donovan 2018
Hardback ISBN: 9781629899503
Paperback ISBN: 9781629899510
eBook ISBN: 9781629899527
First Edition World Castle Publishing, LLC, July 16, 2018
http://www.worldcastlepublishing.com
Licensing Notes
Cover: Alisha Moore Damonza.com
Editor: Maxine Bringenberg

Table of Contents

CHAPTER 1

*Incident on Scenic Lane. The Globe. Just
Around the Corner. What the Doctor Saw.
A Hint of Success. And the Point Is....*

1.

Rick Ballantine drove through the inky darkness of the forest alone, just as he had been instructed. A confirmed city-dweller, having lived his entire life in Los Angeles, only now could he appreciate how truly *dark* the night could be when one ventured far enough into the Northern California wilderness.

Aside from concentrating on this road that seemed to lead further and further into nowhere, Rick had a script to recite. "As an ex-cop," he said, "I appreciate the valuable information confidential sources can provide. But you *have* to be skeptical. The Mount Shasta area has been a hotbed of unexplained phenomena for centuries. Native American tribes have seen strange lights in the skies, and legends claim the mountain is the center of all creation. Are they talking about true supernatural events? Or is there a scientific explanation for what's going on here? I have been contacted by a local who insists that I come and talk to her alone, so the rest of the crew has to stay back at our hotel. She claims she has some answers. And I certainly hope so, because that might take us one step closer...to *confirmation.*"

Mention you're an ex-cop. Check. Rick crossed an item off his mental to-do list. *Mention name of the show. Confirmation. Check.*

As nervous as it made him, he even cast the occasional glance into the SainSpeed F198 night-vision camera on the dashboard as he spoke. No matter where he was, no matter the circumstances, a performer had to try and make some eye contact with the camera.

Following the directions on the car's GPS device, it turned out that the address he had been given by Eunice Stevens, his publicity-shy local contact, was almost literally off the beaten track. The "Scenic Lane" she lived on was a gravel road, rising and dipping through the dense forest ten miles east of Mount Shasta City. Although in theory it seemed to pass for a two-lane road, Rick dreaded coming upon every blind turn that suddenly hooked out of the darkness. Then he hit a stretch of road that ran straighter than the previous mile and a half. The only obstacles in his way now were the sharply elevating hills. Every time he came upon one, he strained to see any lights on the peak, any indication that another car would come barreling at him from over the top.

It was only *after* he negotiated one such hill with no oncoming traffic that he found disaster flashing out of the darkness.

From one split instant to the next, there was no more road in front of his headlights. He kicked the brake pedal, felt the car skidding to a halt, but it was too late. There was some immense dark—circular?—obstacle blocking the entire road and no way to avoid colliding with it. The nightmare sound of crumpling, shattering metal and glass rang through the Pathfinder. Then the airbag exploded in Rick's face and the world blinked out of existence.

2.

Rick couldn't decide what was more incredible, the object that had totaled his SUV or the fact that he and his crew were being treated like criminals.

"Can you believe how many people came out here so early?" Cornelia Oxenburg asked quietly as she stepped next to him.

Rick noticed that for the first time since they had arrived in Mount Shasta City she wasn't clutching her iPad. And she knew that he noticed because she returned a thin little smile before saying, "There are no new developments from the hijacking story this morning. But even if there were, the health and well being of my colleague is first and foremost on my mind." She punctuated the sentence with a quick wink.

Rick, of course, couldn't blame her for her distraction over the past two days, over the fact that she looked like she probably wanted to scream, "I'm a real reporter. Get me out of this miserable place and off this ridiculous show!" A journalist by training, Cornelia had five years of on-air experience. Young and beautiful with blonde, cheerleader looks, she should have been in the prime of her career. She should have been making a name for herself with a major story breaking in San Diego right now. Yet here she was, standing among a crowd of new age enthusiasts on a dirt road in the middle of a forest, her career as a reporter most likely over, shooting a yet-unsold pilot for a "paranormal reality" television series. If he were in Cornelia's shoes, Rick thought, he would have been looking to do much more than scream. He would have been looking to sink down to the bottom of a very deep bottle of bourbon and live there for a long time.

"I appreciate that," Rick said, and returned the wink. "But as I was about to say—"

"Look at that!" Someone's ecstatic voice rose from somewhere among the crowd of onlookers. "It's incredible. I don't see any explanation for that. None whatsoever."

Rick looked over his shoulder, but he couldn't be sure who had spoken. Aside from the *Confirmation* cast and the police chief and five of his officers, the local spectators must have numbered around two hundred people or so. But the real show was just about to start now that an excavator had been brought out here, and a flatbed from McIntyre's Towing and Body Shop, which had removed the Pathfinder last night, arrived.

"*Again*, as I was about to say," Rick reiterated, "word of the unexplained spreads very fast around here."

"In that case," Cornelia said, "how *do* you explain...*that?*"

"I think I know how the local cops will."

That was what appeared to be a solid stone globe measuring some fifteen-feet across. It sat nearly square in the middle of the Scenic Lane gravel road. Making a rough estimate, Rick would have pegged the enormous object as weighing anywhere between fifteen and twenty tons. The perfectly smooth monolith hadn't even budged when he slammed the SUV into it last night. While the front end and engine compartment of the vehicle had been completely obliterated, the giant globe sustained little more than a few minor scratches along its curving face.

What had, in fact, amazed Rick after he regained his bearing last night, after he staggered out of the trashed car and proceeded to try and make sense of what he had run into, was how perfectly, flawlessly smooth the object was. Whoever had chiseled this thing out of an enormous slab of rock must have applied every polishing technique available to masonry to make the face of the globe feel almost glassy smooth.

Furthermore, looking at the object in full daylight now, he realized that aside from the meticulous polishing job, whatever engineer had created the globe made sure that his or her — or *their* — job was flawless in every possible way. The monolith appeared to be a perfect sphere.

Rick couldn't fathom what purpose anyone might have had for carving this gigantic object…or how they managed to place it out here in the middle of this stretch of road.

Apparently neither could the locals. With the area being a magnet for paranormal — and spiritual-phenomena buffs, many people in the gathering crowd had imaginations that were more fertile and adventurous than average. Phrases like "unexplained," "supernatural," "a sign," "a portent," "the government," "strange lights," "cover-up," "spirits," and "aliens" rose from the conversations all around.

And those comments would sound great on the air, Rick knew. Luckily, the entire spectacle was being documented by five of his good-looking young colleagues with cameras and sound equipment, all the while the globe itself was being closely scrutinized by the oldest member of the cast.

Rick had been repeatedly told to think of and talk about all the members of *Confirmation: Investigations of the Unexplained* as "team members," but as far as he was concerned, they were all in showbiz here; they were a "cast" — entertainers, all of them.

Confirmation, according to Rick's agent, was conceived as a "scientifically rigorous reality show about the unknown, bringing together the most seasoned field investigators ever assembled. A journalist, a noted academic, a no-nonsense street cop, a special effects wizard, and their crack team ready to find the truth behind America's greatest legends." Rick was the "no-nonsense" cop. In truth, what they had been shooting here in Mount Shasta City for the past two days was shaping up to be more like a gauche exploitation of unverified claims by the unstable and unscrupulous for the entertainment of the gullible and those desperately in search of some form of faith and a sign that something bigger and more mysterious existed outside of mundane, ugly, and hopelessly screwed up reality.

"Tell Jerry not to bother with his Viagra prescription. This thing'll give him a four-month-long hard-on," Dan Knight, the "noted academic" of the group, associate professor of Anthropology at Bakersfield State University, standing next to the globe said. Then, after a calculated, theatrical beat, he glanced toward one of the video cameras aimed at him and added, "Oops. Can I say that on television?" His voice had the taunting edge of a schoolyard bully who tripped you on purpose, then mocked with something like, "Ooh! I'm *sooo* sorry. Did I hurt you?"

Jerry Peretti was *Confirmation's* creator and executive producer. Rick knew that Knight had been unhappy with his salary for the pilot episode they were filming almost from the moment he signed his contract. In turn, he had taken this sort of malicious, juvenile pleasure in taunting and antagonizing Jerry ever since. Most of it he had been doing on video footage like this, footage that would later be sent to Jerry himself.

Rick noticed the young techies barely suppressing grins and chuckles. The prickly Dan Knight had become the "cool old guy" of the cast.

Their team, Rick knew, had been assembled not only with an eye toward their expertise but their demographic appeal as well. *Confirmation* had to draw a broad cross-section of audiences interested in supernatural phenomena. Rick and Cornelia, thirty-seven and thirty-one years old respectively, had been cast to appeal to those on the very late tail-end of Generation X. Cornelia, according to the show's publicity materials, was an "uncompromising, empowered female reporter. She took on the powerful and the corrupt as an investigative journalist. She backs down from no challenge and she is tough, skeptical, and ready to ask the hard questions when confronted with claims of the paranormal." As an ex-cop, Rick was envisioned as the show's real-life action hero. He found out that the producers had written in their casting memos that their cop needed to be a "dangerously mischievous Johnny Depp-type." He wondered if someone forgot to wear his glasses when they looked at his audition tape. The oddest comparison to someone famous Ballantine had ever gotten was being told that he looked like Patrick Duffy in the 80s soap opera *Dallas*. Knight, at sixty-two, described as "the controversial author of over twenty books on folklore and claims of true paranormal experiences," had to appeal to baby boomers. He would be the leader figure of the team. In each episode, he would present the team with a supernatural legend to investigate. Knight, of course, would also join the team in the field. He, according to the press kit, "embodies a generation that made its own rules and is not ready to step aside."

The rest of the team members rounded out the proper diversity of what Rick liked to think of as the "youth quake" half of the cast.

Tony Griffin, the twenty-four-year-old cameraman covering Knight at that moment, looked like a pouty teen idol with his perpetually tousled hair and somewhat melancholy cast to his eyes that resembled the soulful gaze of a young Elvis Presley. Rick was sure all the girls Tony ever glanced at found that look to be irresistibly dreamy.

The second cameraman, getting shots of the crowd all around the globe, was twenty-five-year-old Matt Cooper, a handsome African American who had been ordered to shave his head after casting to look like a "Tyrese Gibson type."

Twenty-seven-year-old Lacy Anderson, snapping pictures of the globe with her smartphone, was their surveillance and audio analysis expert. With her boyish, short haircut, jogging pants, and a *Star Wars* T-shirt reading "Han Shot First," she looked like anyone's tomboy little sister. Rick recalled Jerry's jaundiced characterization of the "type" he was looking for in the techie as being Cornelia's exact opposite. "If Cornelia's the ex-beauty-queen, the tech specialist should be total 180. She goes to *Star Trek* conventions and doesn't wear too much makeup. They'll say we're providing a great role model for sensitive little girls who don't fit in." Rick wondered if the final cut of the pilot would also mention that Lacy got most of her tech specialization in the army.

Their audio engineer, twenty-three-year-old Melinda Rowland, hovering close to Knight with a large boom microphone to record all of his cool-old-guy *bon mots*, was cast in the tomboy mode as well. The first thing one noticed about her was her strikingly muscular shoulders. A former college swimmer, Melinda had briefly competed as a natural—or steroid free—bodybuilder three years ago.

Ian Durfy, twenty-seven, was the team's "special effects wizard," a former designer of visual effects for the low-budget science fiction and horror films Jerry Peretti used to produce before he decided to branch into reality television. Ian's job would be to stage the recreations of all the alleged alien, ghost, and monster sightings the show was planning on documenting. With his six-foot-five-inch physique and flowing mane of dark brown hair, Durfy looked like a male model off the cover of a bodice-ripper romance novel. Behind his back, Knight had taken to calling Ian "Fabio." At the moment, Rick saw Ian talking to a couple of local men who were vigorously gesticulating with their hands, as if imitating mysterious objects flying around in the sky.

"You were saying about the cops?" Cornelia leaned closer to Rick and asked quietly.

Following her gaze, he noticed the local chief of police, James Carpenter, approaching again. He and his entire cadre of officers had been getting ever more antagonistic as the morning wore on and the crowd of gawkers kept building up.

"It looks like this is going to take a while," Carpenter said a moment later. "So why don't I ask you a few more questions? No problems, I hope."

Rick thought that Mount Shasta City's top cop looked and carried himself like an aging football coach, someone old enough to have been mimicking John Wayne with a saddle-sore, hip-swinging amble, but with the quietly insinuating questions of Lieutenant Columbo. Carpenter, Rick knew, was about to ask him yet again about the message from Eunice Stevens. He wondered why the chief was not acknowledging that he was dealing with a former cop who was clued in to the ploy.

Rick saw Cornelia tensing as Carpenter approached. As an ex-reporter familiar with interrogation techniques, she must have been getting increasingly agitated with the repeating questions.

"What's that, Chief?" Rick asked curtly.

"You're sure that the one message you got from Eunice Stevens yesterday is the only time she communicated with you?"

"And the reason I decided to drive out here in the middle of the night after that one and only message is because we're on a tight schedule and a tight budget. We came here to interview locals about their paranormal experiences and she was offering information. And it was nice and theatrical and melodramatic the way she wanted to conceal her identity."

When Rick paused, he saw the surprised look on the chief's face, one marked with transparently feigned indignation. It was the Columbo look of, "Have I said something to offend you? Because, gee, I really didn't mean to do that."

"I came over the top of that hill and didn't see this...this *thing* until it was too late. It *was* nearly pitch black, after all, and because of the rise in the road it's impossible to see it until you're smacking right into it. Does that make sense? I had an accident because I was driving down this road for the first time in my life, in the *dark*, and I didn't expect the road to be blocked by a giant stone ball."

The chief watched Rick with a sort of slack, tired expression now — except the cop's eyes looked sharp, focused, and skeptical. Somewhat hostile even, as Rick estimated.

"Look, I had an accident. And I don't understand why I'm being treated like a suspect."

After a beat, Carpenter said, "Is that what you think you are…?"

"I had twelve years on the L.A.P.D. and I know how interrogations work. I've told you — and *we* all told you — the same story like, God, I don't know, ten times already since last night. So why don't you tell us what the problem is here?"

His rising voice, Rick noticed now, had attracted Knight's attention. The professor had been intently examining the globe again, running his palms over its surface, no doubt looking for chinks and flaws in the carving. But now he stepped away from the monolith and started ambling toward the fray with Carpenter. Catching sight of the taut, veiny muscles rippling in Knight's forearms as he quickly clenched his fists in and out, Rick's adrenaline spiked. It wasn't just their executive producer Knight enjoyed mixing it up with. As Rick had learned since *Confirmation* had been cast, Knight enjoyed fighting *any* opponent *any* opportunity he got. Looking at his steely hard bearing, Rick was sure Knight was capable of much more than just verbal confrontation and battles of wit. He could, no doubt, still easily put many disrespectful younger men in their place. One of Knight's favorite stories, and one he had already repeated more than a dozen times — usually after imbibing an immense quantity of hard liquor — was of the time he threatened to punch out the father of one of his students demanding that a D final exam grade be raised to an A lest the well-heeled family stop its generous donations to Knight's school. "I wasn't always the man of peace and intellect you see educating America's youth today," Knight had also joked several times. Looking at the old man's face, somewhat resembling that of a retired boxer, with a nose that must have been broken several times and some scar tissue around his eyebrows, Rick thought the story about threatening that student's father was probably more than just a tall tale for the pub. Nevertheless, escalating the tension with the local police chief was probably a very bad idea right now.

Rick also noticed Carpenter's face tightening as Matt with his camera and Melinda with the boom microphone followed Knight.

"Here's the problem…*Officer* Ballantine? Is that it?" Carpenter nodded toward the excavator and the flatbed. "The equipment, the manpower it takes to clean this up…this is costing the city quite some money. And this…what else would you call it but *stunt*, is the reason for it. Since you're right in the middle of it, you're bound to know more about it than anyone else."

"Come on," Cornelia said. "You're suggesting we had something to do with this?"

"I'm not suggesting anything," Carpenter replied. "I just have questions about things that don't seem to make too much sense around here. And again, right now your team seems to be closest to all the weirdness."

"We're not *close* to it," Knight snapped, then took a slow breath. "We're in the middle of this because of an accident."

"If this is some sort of stunt, we're as much victims of it as your city's budget," Rick said. "We just had a car totaled. That's a rental our company now has to pay to replace. I got the living daylights knocked out of me when I got plastered all over the thing last night. So I think we're on the same side here. We just want some answers."

Carpenter didn't reply immediately. Instead, his gaze shifted to Matt and his camera, then over to Melinda and microphone.

14

"Here's one of the problems," he said at length. "You're looking for answers that'll look good for the cameras. I want the truth. I'm just worried, see, because the two are not always the same thing."

Before Rick could reply, Cornelia asked, "And you think *we* planted this enormous stone out here for our show?"

"Yeah," said Rick. "How could we possibly do all this?"

"Little some movie magic can't create today, isn't there?" Carpenter came back without missing a beat. "And now your cameras are rolling and you're in the middle of a real unexplained investigation. Not the same old mystery light and Sasquatch sightings."

When Rick noticed Knight's nostrils flaring, he could imagine the old professor sifting through a checklist of the most insulting retorts he could snap at the cop. Before Knight could say anything, Rick quickly asked, "How about we turn the cameras off right now? All of them."

Matt looked reluctant to do so, but he did as Rick suggested.

"Everything!" Rick said, glancing at Melinda.

"Everything's off," she said.

"Whatever you might have heard about multimillion-dollar film productions," Rick said, looking at Carpenter, "ours is not one of them. We're shooting a low-budget TV pilot."

"Right," Cornelia added. "Where would we get the moving equipment? Here in town? You could check that, couldn't you?"

"Listen," Rick said, and waved at Carpenter. "Let's just watch that globe getting moved, all right? I think we can prove to you that we're not behind this. Trust me. I'll explain everything later."

Loading the gargantuan stone sphere onto the flatbed took nearly an entire hour. The wreckage-hauler from McIntyre's shop had to position itself on one end of the globe—the one facing roughly west, the side opposite from the one Rick had struck—while the excavator stood on the other. The big earth-mover needed to use its shovel to gingerly maneuver the stone onto the flatbed. With unerring precision, the excavator's operator needed to make sure that the giant sphere moved onto the truck without tipping it a mere inch to either the right or the left. The smallest slip, what would amount to an imperceptible error to the untrained eye, could set the giant globe rolling off the truck and off the dirt road. By the same token, the tilting of the flatbed had to be maneuvered with the virtuoso skill of a surgeon. With the road descending on the west side, placing the flatbed back on the truck's chassis in its perfectly lowered position could make the globe roll forward and crush the driver's compartment. Then, once the monolith had been moved onto the truck, the McIntyre crew took another half an hour to secure it in place with a latticework of chains and cords.

"You can see the tread marks, can't you?" Cornelia asked triumphantly as the flatbed truck started backing up Scenic Drive, carrying its unstable cargo toward the spot where the dirt road connected into Signal Butte Road.

She was right. All could see it. The removal operation left deep, treaded gouges in the soft gravel surface of the road. There was no mistaking the marks of heavy machinery having been in the area.

"There was nothing like that on the gravel before," she said, studying Carpenter for any reaction.

For the moment, the cop remained stoic.

"And make sure you take a look at something else that wasn't there," said Rick. "Look at that globe very closely when it gets back into town. Look at the scratches all over its surface. Look at those deep, jagged grooves the earth-mover put all over its face."

Knight nodded vigorously. "Exactly! That thing was polished as smooth as glass before it was moved. How did they move that ball in here—from wherever they carved it—without a scratch on it? What kind of heavy-hauling equipment leaves no marks on the ground?"

"And look at the exact spot they put it," said Rick. "On a natural step on a sloping road. One foot this way and it would go rolling down the hill. One foot that way and it goes rolling down the hill. Someone knew the precise spot—to the *inch*!—they had to—"

"Wait a minute!" the chief cut him off. "Let's hold on a second here before we all go jumping on the supernatural bandwagon. There are easy explanations for everything you're saying. I'm sure museums have moved priceless statues, art treasures, without putting a mark on them."

Rick noticed Knight's brows pinching into an angry frown. "And you think we used a helicopter for this? Because that's the only way—"

"Look, Chief, you're right," Rick jumped in, then paused. Raised eyebrows and squinty, skeptical looks came from his own colleagues. "I mean, let's take a nice, logical, rational approach to investigating this. You're absolutely right in that. Someone flew a what—fifteen? twenty?—ton globe in here. Well, someone must have seen it. Let's all go to Eunice Stevens's place. She's got to be close by. Maybe *she* saw it. Maybe *that's* why she contacted us in the first place. Maybe she knows something. And who else lives out here? Let's get all the addresses and talk to *everyone*."

3.

The drive the rest of the way to Eunice Stevens's cottage had, indeed, been a short one from the site of Rick's accident. He, along with Knight, Cornelia, Ian, and Melinda, had piled into their remaining Pathfinder and followed Chief Carpenter's cruiser to the Stevens residence. The drive took exactly eight minutes, according to Rick's watch. He was glad for that.

"She lives almost literally around the corner," Cornelia said, turning around from the front passenger seat. Dan Knight was behind the wheel.

"Interesting, isn't it?" Rick replied.

"Yeah," said Knight. "I think she'll nicely torpedo most of the chief's theories."

"Like the one about the helicopter?" Melinda asked with a

perfect deadpan.

"Maybe," Rick said, unable to overlook a need to stay cautious.

"If getting that stone ball in there took the sort of construction project Carpenter's describing," said Cornelia as Knight brought the Pathfinder to a slow roll and a stop behind the chief's car, "Eunice Stevens should have seen and heard something. Especially if they used a helicopter."

"No kidding," said Ian, and chuckled. He sat sandwiched in between Rick and Melinda.

"Makes you wonder," Rick said, once again tentatively. There was something troublesome in what his colleagues were implying.

But Knight picked up on it now. "About what? Think there's something wrong?"

"This woman should have had some clue as to what was going on up here last night. And shortly before I got here at that. There's no way that stone thing was placed in the road much earlier. This may be a gravel road through the forest, but others have houses out here. This road is being used all the time. Someone would have seen it. But if Eunice saw something...."

Rick saw the proverbial glow of realization lighting up Cornelia's face. "Why didn't she come out to the gathering this morning, or try and do something to contact us again?"

"Wow. Yeah," Ian said slowly.

"She's a recluse," Melinda added.

Knight turned off the Pathfinder's engine now. "And that's a problem."

"Recluses can be weirdoes," Cornelia said grimly. "Know what I'm saying? *Highly* unstable."

"Instead of clearing this whole thing up," Rick said, "she can help muddle it."

"Do we think the chief's explanations make any sense?" Cornelia asked as Rick opened his door.

"I don't know," Rick said.

"Yeah," Cornelia said, "because if they don't, then what are we left with?"

Knight opened his door and got out. "Let's find out."

4.

If he would have decided to switch careers yet again, Rick mulled, going from ex-cop reality-TV star to author, he would want to start with buying a country cottage like Eunice Stevens's. His mysterious contact lived in the kind of tree-shaded little abode every writer dreamed of moving into and writing the Great American Novel. Although the place looked smaller the closer his group got to its tidy, freshly painted porch, a thicket of towering pine trees seemed to surround the house like a phalanx of bodyguards shielding a particularly vulnerable charge. With the glimpse of the snow-capped Mount Shasta visible through the forest, Rick thought he was looking at the sort of scenery no painter could resist putting on canvas.

The sense of guarded frailty Rick felt as he studied the house amidst its protective perimeter of trees perfectly represented Eunice Stevens herself.

It took a three-minute discussion between Stevens and Chief Carpenter before the woman allowed the entire *Confirmation* crew to enter her home. As per her previous written request to Rick, the cameras and recording equipment had to be left outside. Eunice Stevens was ready to "give direction about the mess on Scenic Lane," as she put it, but she wanted to stay at "just arm's length from the spotlight."

"Something's been all over that road," Eunice explained when the entire party had settled into her living room.

The cottage, as far as Rick could tell, looked every bit as well kept on the inside as it did on the outside. More than just being clean and orderly, the entire home looked like no expense had been spared to keep it looking new and elegant. An orderly house, more often than not, Rick had often concluded, was a sign of a sane and orderly mind. There were exceptions, of course, but

Eunice Stevens, in Rick's estimation, struck his cop's instincts for human nature as being normal and in full grasp of her faculties. That impression helped her delivery of a story that turned ever more fantastic.

"Something *had* to happen sooner or later. It was obvious. That's why I needed to get your attention when I heard that you were filming in town. An unbelievable coincidence, I know, so I needed to take advantage of it." Stevens explained calmly, her attention focused on Rick and Dan Knight throughout the conversation more than on any of the other people in the room.

The woman gave Rick a strange contradiction of impressions now. Much like her home, there was a sort of patrician elegance about Eunice's appearance. Her casual dress looked new and pricey. While pegging her age somewhere in the early sixties, Rick thought Stevens must also have at one point undergone some cosmetic procedures to subtract about a decade or so from her face. She had the kind of tight, slightly frozen features of the face-lifted, chemically-peeled, and Botoxed aging matrons one saw around Beverly Hills and Malibu. Soon after their brief acquaintance, though, Eunice told her visitors that she was a retired general-practice physician from Santa Barbara. She had moved to the Mount Shasta area soon after her husband's death. He had been an ophthalmologist. That accounted for the money, Rick realized, but the information had to serve another purpose in this conversation. Eunice Stevens must have been telling her guests so much about her background in such a short period of time to make sure they understood that she was an intelligent, sophisticated woman of a respectable background and social circles, not given to telling wild stories about the paranormal and the unexplained. If she was talking about strange goings on in the woods, Rick attempted to decode her intentions, then *her* stories could well be taken to the bank.

"You know," Eunice said, her large brown eyes focusing in on Rick, "I'm just so sorry you had to discover what all...all the *strangeness* added up to in such...well, such a violent way."

This time he noted something else about her manner and delivery. She radiated a sort of tautness of the nerves, like someone who had struggled long and hard to manage the assault of chaos on her life. Rick couldn't help but think that Eunice reminded him of a cornered cat rearing up on its hind legs and desperately clawing at its assailants. He could now start to try and understand some kind of a reason behind her theatrics of speaking only off the record.

"Did you know that globe was going to be in the middle of the road?" he asked.

"Oh, no!" Eunice's reaction was quick. "Oh, absolutely not. I mean if I knew you would have an accident, I would have warned you about it."

"Sure, of course. I believe you. What I meant was, did you know a globe was going to show up *somewhere*?"

Before Eunice could reply, Cornelia jumped in with, "Do you know what that globe is?"

"No," Eunice said tightly, her gaze calmly shifting now between Rick and Cornelia.

Again, Rick was sensing the tension beneath her veneer of cool composure.

"I didn't know what would happen. I didn't know where it would happen, or that it would be…well, the appearance of this giant stone. I mean, I have no idea what the meaning of this strange object is…except that I had seen some strange things in the area and I was suspecting something was going to happen for real this time. That's what I wanted to talk to you about. The reason I sent you that message."

"*This* time?" Dan Knight asked.

"Well," Eunice said cautiously, but with an equal thrust of determination in her voice. "Some of the…what I've seen in the woods, well, they've been going on with enough of a frequency lately, I could sense that it was all building up to something."

When she paused, Chief Carpenter cleared his throat. "Mrs. Stevens. Can you just give us the details? Exactly what have you been seeing in the woods?"

"Well...for one, lights. And yes, I know it's something scores of people can always be counted on to say. Lights in the skies, UFOs, flying saucers — what do they like calling it around here? — *ghost lights.* But it was always near that same area." She paused and looked at Rick. "By the road. Where the stone showed up."

Where I smashed into it last night, Right thought. Did she have a glint of satisfaction in her eye? he wondered. Had she spoken of this to others before? Only to be rebuffed? Ridiculed? Rick again considered that the Mount Shasta area was perhaps one of the safest places in the world to openly talk about paranormal experiences. It was akin to talking about UFOs in Roswell.

"All right," said Carpenter. "Can you describe these lights *exactly*? When did they start showing up? How often did they come? What color were they? We need as much detail as possible."

"About two weeks ago. I first started seeing them about two weeks ago. Sometimes as early as sunset. Then throughout the night. Lighting up the area. Shining beams of light through the trees."

"Did you ever hear anything?'

"No," Eunice said with a firm resolve in her voice. "Just the lights. No sounds like helicopters or airplanes or anything like that."

"Not even last night?"

"No."

"Just the lights? Like usual?"

"I've been seeing the same lights every night."

"Now the way these lights moved," Knight suddenly jumped in. "What were they like? I mean, was it all *one* light source?"

"No, not just one. It was like...*things.* I don't know — whatever it was that was emanating the beams...I mean, it looked like multiple objects shooting beams of light from the sky. I don't want to say *craft* because I didn't hear anything that sounded like a helicopter or aircraft engines of any sort, but what else can fly through the air and light everything up?"

22

"Forgive me," Carpenter exclaimed, "but can you be *absolutely* certain you didn't hear anything?"

"Last night," Eunice snapped at him forcefully, "while I was waiting for Mr. Ballantine, I had the TV on for a while. It was running an old episode of *NCIS*. But I do not blare the TV loud enough to drown out the sounds of *multiple* low-flying aircraft. My hearing is *perfect*, Chief Carpenter."

When Eunice fixed the cop with an indignant, withering stare, Ballantine nearly laughed. This was a smart woman, well aware of the sort of skeptical traps Carpenter was trying to guide her into.

"Furthermore," Eunice said, "when I saw the first lights outside, I put the TV on mute. I want to know exactly what this is all about. I tried to listen to anything out there. Other than the lights, I could see nothing else and hear nothing else."

"All right, I understand," Carpenter said, definitely placating her now. "But let me ask you another question. You said that you wanted to talk to Mr. Ballantine and his group because what you saw was unusual even by the standards of...well, all the other strange things people have claimed to have seen in the area. How do you mean?"

"Chief," Eunice said with a deliberate emphasis in her voice; more than a bit condescending, in fact, Rick thought. "I saw bright, blue-white rays of light coming through the trees. They looked like spotlights shining out of the sky. I've never heard of anything else like that around here. These weren't lights that blinked mysteriously in the distance or flickered over the horizon or zigged this way when they should have zagged that way." She paused now, looking around the room, as if trying to make eye contact with everyone. "When was the last time anyone ever said anything like that around here?"

That, actually, was a very good question, Rick thought. He and the group would need to look for others who might have seen anything like the intense aerial beams Eunice was describing.

"What can do that?" she asked. "What kinds of aircraft fly in the sky and shine such powerful lights and make no noise? And come out of nowhere and disappear in seconds?"

"And now you think this has a connection to the stone globe?" Cornelia asked.

Eunice arched a pencil-thin eyebrow as she looked at her. "It does seem like there are *two* unexplained mysteries here now. I *am* wondering about a connection."

"Well," Chief Carpenter said, "it does seem like it. Although let me just ask you something about this stone business."

"Yes?"

"You said there were no sounds coming from the air, from the lights. And you heard nothing from the road? From the ground? Anything that might have sounded like trucks or heavy machinery?"

Eunice shook her head emphatically. "No, I did not."

She was right, Rick thought. As far as her claim about two mysteries was concerned at least. There was no easy way of explaining either the lights or the stone. If they took her words about the lights at their face value, if she indeed saw what she said she saw, it was difficult, if not impossible, to account for how multiple beams of brilliant light just suddenly appeared in the middle of the night. But the globe was even more difficult to wrap one's mind around. It was an enigma that wasn't about to let one take the easy way out. There was no way of writing a fifteen-ton monolith off as a hallucination, as misidentification, or the trick of some freakish atmospheric condition.

"Mrs. Stephens," Carpenter said at length. "I'm curious as to why you did not want to be identified by Mr. Ballantine's program."

"Why?"

"Well, you do have quite an astounding story to tell."

"Astounding," Eunice slowly, as if feeling the weight of the word. "I've told an astounding story publicly before," she added, then paused.

The silence hung in the air.

Rick wished that at least one of their cameras could be rolling right now.

"It's the reason," Eunice went on after drawing out a long, dramatic beat, "I moved up here after Stanley's — my husbands' — death. As I said, I was a doctor before retiring. I, however, had the misfortune at one point of seeing an unidentified flying object hover over, then quietly drift away from, Leadbetter Beach. That's by Santa Barbara." She paused, then allowed herself a tight, rueful little smile. "Then after I agreed to be interviewed about it by a local TV station, the harassment started. It was a group called the Rational Investigations of Unidentified Aerial Phenomena. They wrote article after article on their blog about how a doctor could give credence to talk of green men and alien invaders. They said I was mentally unstable and shouldn't be allowed to practice medicine. Probably no abortion doctor had ever been harassed and threatened by any group of evangelical nuts as viciously as I was."

As Eunice spoke, Rick noticed a strange light in Knight's eyes. Several times he nodded — at first ever so slightly, then more and more vigorously — as the woman's story unfolded. "Unbelievable," he said emphatically.

"Oh, believe it, Dr. Knight," Eunice replied. "Then they sent their letters and emails to my patients, telling them that their lives were in danger every time they walked into my office. They hounded me out of my practice. I had enough money at that point so I could afford to close my office and retire. I would have liked to have been able to work a few more years…but it just wasn't worth putting up with this anymore."

"Trust me," Knight spoke again, "I've been an associate professor for over twenty years, Eunice. I tried for a promotion to full professor time and time again. No luck. All because I once wrote that phenomena may exist that we simply do not have a measurement device for, the technology to quantify. And mind you, once I even published a paper on the mythology of the Loch Ness monster, where I very clearly wrote that there is not one iota of evidence to suggest—by *any* stretch of the imagination—that the monster exists or *ever* existed."

Eunice chuckled bitterly. "Doesn't matter, does it?"

"Nope."

"Well, you do have everything I can tell you about the lights I saw. You know, I didn't move up here, by the way, because of all the new agers and paranormal buffs. Stanley and I had bought this house three years before his death. But, nevertheless, please understand that I really don't want any more public attention when it comes to unexplained mysteries."

"Sure," Knight told her, that odd, elated look of joy at having found a kindred spirit, Rick thought, beaming off his face.

5.

"I think Jerry will forgive you for wrecking the SUV if we just stay on this story," Knight said and pocketed his cell phone, all the while slapping Rick on the back. "Another round for me and my friends here," he then told the bartender with a grin.

"No problem, Doc," the girl behind the bar confirmed.

Rick was surprised by how quickly the particulars of their group had gotten around the Mountaintop Vista Hotel. He was also amused by the way the spirits of the two people the most ambivalent about their roles on *Confirmation* had risen throughout the day. Perhaps Cornelia was starting to sense the emergence of a real news story around this globe, he guessed. And Knight might have seen the possibility of getting more money out of Jerry. Until now, Rick was certain he was the most appreciative of the show among the three senior members of the cast. He, unlike Knight, had no best-selling books to his name, so he considered his payday adequate. Moreover, Bigfoot sightings, UFO reports, and mystery globes beat having to deal with the L.A.P.D.'s Internal Affairs division as he had done in his previous life.

"Whoa!" he said. "It's been a long day for a third round of whiskeys...."

"Come on!" Knight said with that giddy tone that had been

getting more and more ebullient throughout the day. "Don't embarrass yourself by letting the old man drink you under the table."

The pretty brunette bartender, a local college coed, Rick would have guessed, slid the shot of JB in front of him and winked.

"If you put it that way," Rick said with a mock sour expression as Knight was handed his own drink.

"We might as well get smashed and have a good time," Cornelia said, and turned off her iPad. As she sat next to Rick at the Happy Hour Tavern's bar, she had snuck a glance at the latest updates on the San Diego terrorist situation. Since she said nothing about the story, Rick assumed there were no new developments. "We're not getting arrested, and this stone globe thing just might make *Confirmation* a hit."

As Cornelia glanced at Rick and smiled, holding eye-contact for a drawn-out beat, Rick suddenly realized that there was no amount of alcohol he could drink that would make him feel as warm as that look in her eye.

"*That,*" Knight said, and raised his shot of whiskey to Rick and Cornelia, "is *exactly* what Jerry said. So pick up your drinks, kids, and let's start acting like grownups. You can sip if you want, but a toast is in order." He then proceeded to drain the shot glass in one swift swig.

Cornelia winced.

"To Jerry, I suppose," Rick said, and tipped his glass toward Cornelia and Dan.

"He can be a pain in the ass, but he *is* perceptive little prick," said Knight.

Despite whatever anyone might ever say about Jerry Peretti, he was, Rick had been told, an unusually decisive producer—by Hollywood standards, at least, where years usually passed between a project's conceptualization and its actual filming—but he was also notoriously tight-fisted. Jerry had produced three ultra-low-budget films about, respectively, giant time-traveling spiders, a beautiful female FBI agent partnered with a T-rex dinosaur to solve a string of serial killings, and a vampire who gets elected president of the United States, for the SyFy network. When paranormal-investigation reality shows hit the ratings stratosphere, however, Jerry was, as usual, fast to jump on the bandwagon. Rick was lucky, he supposed, that his agent, Wilt Kamen, played poker with Jerry every Tuesday night at the producer's house in Malibu. It had been over three years since Rick saved Wilt's life from the crossfire during a bank robbery in Sherman Oaks. It had also been over a year since the CBS network canceled Rick's first reality series, *Hollywood Justice*, after ten episodes. Wilt Kamen, still grateful for Rick's act of off-duty heroism, set on repaying the favor by establishing him as a "real life action hero," had recommended Rick for the *Confirmation* team when Jerry Peretti's paranormal brainchild was conceived during a five-hour poker-and-beer-bender.

"Of course," Knight said as he winked at the bartender and cast a glance at his shot glass, "as we all know, Jerry, he's a cheap little bastard, too. But, since he says — and I quote — 'I'm sensing a thirteen-episode commitment from one of the cable networks, so I won't deduct the price of the totaled SUV from Rick's salary' — we stay right here and see where this whole stone ball situation is going to go."

"To Jerry's benevolence. My salary's very important to my ex-wife and her lawyer," Rick said, and drained his whiskey while Knight was getting a refill.

Cornelia merely toyed with the shot glass in front of her. "But what if it goes *nowhere*?"

"Good point," Rick replied. "But think about this: where do you think our original investigation of the mysterious portal to otherworldly dimensions under Mount Shasta was bound to go?"

There was a sly, cynical hint of a smile somewhere in the right corner of Cornelia's mouth now.

"We would've talked to locals," Rick continued. "Gotten some interviews with wide-eyed, serious-looking people talking in a serious-sounding whisper. We get the night vision gear and wander around the woods at night...." He paused and looked at Knight. "We have a CGI budget for this thing, right?"

"As far as I know."

"OK," said Rick as Cornelia licked the whiskey in her glass. "So our special-effects wiz-kid, Ian, and some college tech-geek Jerry's going to screw out of a payday will go and make up some special-effects footage of what the mysterious subterranean dimension's supposed to look like, based on all the *reliable* and *unimpeachable* eyewitness testimony."

"You know, you *do* need to keep a degree of an open mind when you investigate the unexplained," said Knight, with a tone that was both somewhat serious and ironically self-mocking as his glass was refilled

"I stand corrected," said Rick. "But it doesn't much matter what we find or don't find over the next few days here. We just keep shooting footage, talk to people, and then Ian will turn it into a coherent narrative."

"I just wish someone else would have seen something," Cornelia said at length after sipping some more whiskey. "Some of those lights Eunice Stevens talked about."

After the Stevens interview, Tony, Matt, Lacy, and Melinda had accompanied a pair of squad cars to check the cameras at three local toll booths. The digital recordings, the *Confirmation* team had been told, would be sent to police headquarters. They wanted to see if the police chief's hoax theory had any credibility. Was there any evidence at all suggesting that some mysterious party of hoaxers had transported that globe through the area and up to Scenic Lane? But just as Rick suspected, there was no sign of any vehicles sneaking a gargantuan globe into Mount Shasta City.

Rather than tagging along with the police for the rest of the day, Rick, Knight, Cornelia, and Ian chose to do some of their own canvasing of locations that a truck of any sort carrying an enormous stone globe might have passed by. They had found no one claiming to have seen anything out of the ordinary.

"Goddamn, this stuff tastes like shit," Cornelia exclaimed after downing her last swallow of whiskey, just as Rick noticed the incoming text message alarm of his phone *blang* to life.

"Come on!" he said, fishing his phone out of his jeans' pocket. "You gotta act your part. Doesn't your press release say you're the tough, kickass action girl of the show? You're supposed to be able to drink any man under the table."

"Are you trying to intoxicate me so you can take liberties, Mr. Ballantine?" Cornelia asked, and even surprised Rick with a little wink.

The heat spreading through the middle of his body reminded Rick of something he hadn't felt since before he got married.

"The men wearing the uniform of the Los Angeles Police Department have unimpeachable integrity, ma'am," Rick said, and winked back.

"Yeah, and do you see any uniforms?" Knight quickly exclaimed with a leering chuckle.

Glancing at his phone's display, Rick saw that the text was from Lacy Anderson.

"Well, on the show they can have me drinking iced tea, and we'll pretend it's whiskey or bourbon or something," Cornelia said. "Who is that?"

"Lacy. She says we should meet the rest of the team at the Indie Voices bookstore. Right now. It's very important, she says."

"I think that's two blocks from here," Knight said. "What's going on?"

6.

"A chance for us to get our names in the paper. How's that for raising our profile?"

Knight chuckled. "Nice going. *Very* nice. What's happening?"

Lacy kept glancing over her shoulder as they walked toward the inner recesses of the large and very tightly shelved bookstore. "Remember that crowd of people from the globe this morning?

It looks like they got word to the local newspaper. A reporter's nosing around."

"Jerry will love this," Cornelia said. "Let's get us written up in the local paper. Start spreading the word about *Confirmation*."

"So what's the reporter doing here?" Rick asked. He was trying his best to get a sense for what the store specialized in. Aside from the general genre fiction and nonfiction sections, Indie Voices, not surprisingly for Mount Shasta City, was well-packed with occult, paranormal, and new age literature.

"Checking out a discussion group," said Lacy. "Some locals usually hold a book club meeting in here. Mainly talking to Mount Shasta authors. Except for tonight. Tonight's all about the globe."

"And what do you think those locals'll have to say about us?" Knight asked. "Any of 'em think we set this whole thing up?"

Lacy gave him a pointed look over her shoulder, then a sly grin. "Are you kidding? They think we're rock stars."

The group found Matt, Tony, Melinda, and Ian in a sort of meeting space in the back of the store. The space, Rick thought, looked somewhat like a college dormitory lounge from the seventies. Situated in front of a fireplace, the clearing amidst the bookshelves had a thick blue-green shag carpet on the floor, and most of its occupants sat on a mismatched collection of chairs, a futon, three beanbag chairs, a ratty recliner, some uncomfortable-looking ottomans, and a wooden bench. Five people sat on the floor.

When Rick and the team joined the gathering, they were glad to see that Matt, Tony, and Melinda were recording a vigorous exchange among the locals.

"...We can't fall into the same old trap!" Rick noticed a woman taking her turn in the discussion when he and his partners situated themselves on the periphery of the meeting. "Do you understand what I'm saying?" she said. About fifty-years-old, the woman was wearing an ankle-length, hippieish linen skirt and a sweater with very bright—mainly orange, red, and green-based—Native American designs. She made him think of a junior-high-school art teacher. "We can't react to this phenomenon with fear. I see all the long faces here, all the worry...you know, all the stress already, and I'm like, 'what are we automatically afraid of?' Why are we even having a discussion of whether or not this object's something we have to worry about?"

"Because," a man called out from the bench, "none of us've ever seen anything like that thing." He paused as abruptly as he'd first spoken, his eyes sweeping the crowd.

Rick wondered whether the man was gauging the crowd to see how many potential allies sat nearby. There appeared to be a very strong, fundamental difference of opinions about to surface between this man and the woman with the bright sweater. The man appeared to be somewhere in his late fifties, with a headful of perfectly white hair. With his sturdy-looking face and clear, resolute intonations, he resembled either a retired businessman, Rick pondered, or a career politician on vacation. Although dressed casually in khakis and a bright purple denim shirt, Rick thought the man's outfit looked high-quality, expensive. He appeared to be a man of means bedecked in top-shelf designer wear well-cut to look rustic and casual.

"So what?" the woman in the sweater answered quickly.

"So what? We only have something that appears to be a completely impossible object placed in an impossible location, *causing an accident,* and we haven't the faintest clue yet—*no one* has—as to what it is or who placed it there...or why. Now no one's going to pull something like this off without some kind of a major agenda. I'd just like to know what that is and why the perpetrator is still in hiding."

"I think...." A man of about thirty, sitting on a folding plastic chair and wearing a light green T-shirt with the logo "Life is Good," cargo shorts, and hiking boots, spoke up next. "That we might not even be asking the right question if we're asking *who* put that big globe there. Do you know what I'm saying?"

"We need to ask *what* put the globe there. I don't think it's manmade at all," the woman in the colorful sweater said.

Rick thought he saw Cornelia wincing next to him. When they made eye-contact, he saw her mouth the words, "They're jumping to completely wild conclusions."

"No way it's manmade," someone else said from the crowd.

"OK!" the man in the loud purple denim shirt said. "That worries me even more."

"But why the worrying?" the woman in the bright sweater challenged him with a pleading tone. "I mean, that's my whole point here; why the negativity? I'm just bothered by all the distrust. Maybe this is a completely positive, transformative phenomenon. Maybe we need to get ready to embrace it."

There were a lot of nods in the crowd. But, Rick realized upon a closer inspection of the group, there were just as many looks of quiet, edgy concern.

"Lois, I'm not quarrelling with you in theory," a slightly paunchy man with a perfect jet-black beard—somewhat reminding Rick of the late infomercial pitchman Billy Mays— said from one of the beanbag chairs. "But the thing is that I'd like to know what I'm embracing first...."

"Well, this is interesting," Dan stepped closer to Rick and said quietly.

"Isn't it?"

Cornelia leaned toward both of them. "Is this turning into some kind of hawks and doves debate?"

"Probably," Knight said. "I'm not surprised, though."

"Where do you think this is gonna go, Doc?" Rick studied Knight's expression.

Apparently he wasn't ready to render a verdict yet because he said nothing more, only studied the gathering.

"Of course, it's all about what is *behind* that globe," the woman in the bright sweater, Lois, said. "I want to know that. Everyone wants to know that. But why are we starting out here with the same old assumptions? Why are we so quick to worry about some kind of a threat?"

"Because," said the man in expensive purple denim,

"whatever made that globe has some pretty impressive resources at its disposal."

"Yeah," the man with the black beard said. "The last I heard, the cops have absolutely no idea how anyone could have gotten the giant thing onto that road. Know what I'm saying? Totally impossible if you're using any known earthly technology."

There were murmurs in the crowd. Rick thought he heard some references to the Egyptian pyramids and South American ruins.

"So why are you saying the unearthly technology is a threat?" Lois asked.

"I'm *not* saying that," replied the man with the beard. "It's only that—"

"That you need to consider the possibility that whoever has that kind of technology could do anything he wanted to you," Purple Denim exclaimed.

Rick noted how the man's voice rose ever so slightly.

"And that automatically means that they want to harm you?" said a twenty-something man wearing a Homer Simpson hooded sweatshirt.

Rick saw the look of satisfaction on Lois's face. At least one of her clear allies was speaking up.

"Well, at least there's a consensus that we're dealing with something out of this world," a man's voice spoke up quietly from behind Rick and his partners. When they turned to see who it was, they saw a man in jeans, a green plaid shirt, and a light brown blazer nodding at them. He appeared to be somewhere in his mid thirties, of a somewhat average build and nondescript face, but with probing, quick, inquisitive eyes. "Hey," he said, and nodded at the group. "I'm Joe Lansing—"

"The Mount Shasta Herald?" Lacy asked quickly.

"Yeah, the local press," Lansing replied with a slow grin and a nod. "So you're covering all this as well, I see."

"Just at the right place at the right time," Rick said.

"For a TV show, right?"

"Hopefully," Rick said before Cornelia jumped in.

"We didn't come here to do a story on any mystery stones," she said. "Just the town and its legends."

"But *are* there any legends of mystery stones up here?" Knight asked.

"No…no, there aren't," Lansing said in a tone that might have been either concern or amusement. "It looks like you stumbled onto a brand-new mystery."

"Lucky for both of us, I guess," Rick said, but snuck a quick glance Cornelia's way.

"Exactly," Lansing said with a grin stretching the right side of his face. "So let's see what the locals are making of the whole thing."

As the debate veered into such high-strangeness territory as whether or not earth spirits were telepathically communicating through the globes, a loud, not quite shrill but taut, stressed voice nearly yelled over the crowd, "Wait a minute!"

The debate came to a halt.

"I think," someone said — still very sharply — from the crowd, then paused for a beat. "I think we're all missing the *fucking* point here."

Rick was sure everyone was startled by the obscenity itself, since no one else said a word.

"We're all missing the big picture, all right?"

The source of the interruption stepped forward. He was, Rick thought, the most startling contradiction of impressions. The man, somewhere roughly in his mid to late forties, held and carried himself with something of a hard, attitudinal swagger that matched his commanding tone. Yet he looked like the vision a lazy hack writer — one content to rely on easy stereotypes to populate a story — would have of a geeky, awkward small town male librarian. Tall, gangly, and narrow-shouldered, with a head of thinning, short, curly brown hair highlighting a narrow head and wedge-like face, the man wore a baggy pair of dark brown corduroy pants, topsider shoes, and a red-and-black-patterned buttoned sweater. As the man walked into the center of the gathering, his gaze flittered about the room in quick birdlike flashes. His narrow, pallid, somewhat cheese-like complexion and face with its probing agitated glances made Rick think of an angry librarian yet again, one prowling the common reading areas and looking to reprimand someone for making too much noise.

"What do you mean, Hank?" someone spoke at last.

"I mean we're all wasting our time arguing about ridiculous trivialities here!" Hank, the agitated man, replied. His voice was again hard, resolute, and commanding. There was nothing nebishy in his behavior, Rick realized. Whoever this guy was, no matter how rowdy the debate was going to get, he was going to stand his ground and not hesitate knocking some heads.

"Oh, him," Joe Lansing mumbled as he leaned toward Rick. "Hank Adler. We did a story on him two years ago. He's a UFO abductee and *activist*."

Rick caught the accent on "activist."

"Oh?"

"Claims the aliens did torturous experiments on him...."

"And the government knows all about it?" Cornelia cut in.

"Of course. He leads petition drives and tries to get a million people to march on Washington to demand *answers*."

"I hope he succeeds," Lacy said with a perfect deadpan. "That would make for a great episode of *Confirmation*."

Rick glanced toward Dan Knight, noting the professor's intense study of the crowd and Hank Adler's performance.

"Hank!" Lois suddenly spoke up. "I don't see how you mean trivialities...."

"Who made the globe?" Hank replied. "Why did they make it? Are they good? Are they evil? Listen to yourselves, people!" His voice seemed to rise in volume and resolve with every word.

With his thunderous vehemence, Rick was actually surprised that Hank hadn't yet been able to marshal at least the Mount Shasta area for his march on Washington.

"Can't you realize the most important thing here?" Hank boomed. "What we're all saying? Look, people, the point here is that we *all* agree on one important thing!"

This time Hank paused ever so dramatically. Rick noticed some heads starting to nod. Realization appeared to be dawning on the crowd.

"The *point*," Hank said, "is that we *all* agree that we have solid, tangible evidence of an unexplained event. We have the real thing, folks. An unexplainable, paranormal event. And this time...." Hank almost shouted, his right index finger stabbing forward several times, stabbing toward unseen enemies perhaps. "...*This* time, no one's gonna explain this away with some *bullshit* about mass hysteria and hallucinations and cloud formations and stars and hoaxes. Can't you see the significance of all this?"

Affirmative mutterings rose from the crowd. Nearly everyone was nodding now.

"We are entering a whole new world. Finally! All of us! This entire world is on the edge of something new. Something that's gonna change all of us. And let's just see someone tell us that we're crazy, that we're delusional and can't tell a fifty-ton stone ball from swamp gas and car headlights. Let's hear a *scientific* explanation for this one...."

"Oh, yeah! Scientific!" a disdainful voice rose from the crowd. "You're all crazy and you don't know what you see. Science in the twenty first century. How nice."

"Exactly!" Hank replied with bile in his voice. "Let them come and tell us that we're crazy this time. Bring it on! We're not letting anyone make fools of us any longer — you got that, folks?"

Loud, raucous, angry, affirmative responses rose from the crowd.

Then Hank turned toward Tony Griffin's camera, stabbing a finger toward it. "You got that?"

"Wow," Cornelia said quietly. "I think what he meant was that this is payback time."

"That's exactly what I was thinking," Rick replied.

"Interesting, isn't it?"

"What *I* was thinking," Cornelia said, then paused, apparently looking for the right words, "is that it's kind of...frightening."

Rick's attention was demanded by the vibration of his cell phone. He fished it out of his pocket and glanced at its display. The call, it indicated, was from Jerry Peretti.

He took the call and listened to their producer's breathless, harried revelation.

Cornelia and Lacy gave him questioning looks.

"What's going on?" Knight was the first one to speak, though.

"It was Jerry again. They found another one."

7.

Front Page
"THE MARBLES OF THE GODS?
MYSTERY GLOBE BAFFLES MOUNT SHASTA"
By: Joe Lansing, *The Mount Shasta Herald*

For a place used to its share of mysteries, speculations about the unknown and the extraordinary, the Mount Shasta area is now left to wonder about the origins of a massive stone globe that appeared seemingly overnight on a stretch of Scenic Lane.

The mystery globe, measuring fifteen feet across, was discovered overnight by Richard Ballantine when he crashed his Nissan Pathfinder into the object. According to Ballantine, a cast member of a new paranormal reality television show, *Confirmation: Investigations of the Unexplained*, he was unable to avoid a collision with the globe as he came over a rise in the road.

Since numerous people living in the vicinity had used the road during the afternoon and the evening prior to Ballantine's accident, how the object could have been placed there without anyone else noticing is, as of yet, beyond explanation.

"We examined [the globe] as best we could before the police removed it," Ballantine said, "but we couldn't come up with any ideas for how a perfect sphere that big could have been placed out there."

While speculations of the globe's supernatural origins have been spreading, Mount Shasta Chief of Police James Carpenter insists that there are bound to be perfectly down-to-earth explanations for the enormous object.

"It is absolutely not outside the capabilities of any number of powerful moving tools and lifting equipment to place a giant object like that on that road," Carpenter said. "There is no reason at all to think that aliens or any kind of magical or mysterious forces put the globe there."

The police department insists that the globe must be the work of an unusually creative practical joker.

For many others in the area, however, the mystery globe is all too similar to what they see as unexplained ancient stone constructions around the world. Some compare the globe to Egyptian pyramids, England's Stonehenge, or the enormous stone statues known as Moai on Easter Island. One witness said that the globe looks like a marble left behind from the toy set of a giant alien child.

What makes the Mount Shasta globe so intriguing to everyone, however, is the fact that no mystery globes like this have ever been found before.

"I definitely think this is a sign of something very positive," said Lois Mackenzie, a webpage developer who went to see the removal of the globe. "I think some elemental force is trying to communicate with us. I think it's speaking on behalf of the earth, on behalf of nature, and I think it's saying that it is peaceful. [It's significant that] the object is round and that we have never seen anything like this before. It represents the spirit of the planet, I think. It might represent the real dawn of a new age for all of us. The more I think about it, the more I believe that I just somehow, you know, felt that this was going to happen. There was almost a vibration of positivity, I guess, in the air before the globe showed up."

Whatever the explanation for the globe might be, it is certainly bringing new attention to the Mount Shasta area. According to the police department and the chamber of commerce, reporters from Japan, Germany, Spain, and England have all arrived in town to cover the mysterious phenomenon.

CHAPTER 2

Dr. Knight Returns to New Jersey. Rutgers
Geology. Logic. Scotland. The Peter Rollins Show.

1.

"It looks pretty tightly developed up there," Ballantine said. "A lot of houses. A lot of driveways."

Following his gaze, Knight saw that he was looking at the upper reaches of the valley they stood in.

"Yeah," Cornelia replied. "Upscale neighborhood. The kind of people I would guess would quickly ask questions and make phone calls if strange machinery came rumbling through here in the middle of the night."

"Like helicopters?" Ian asked.

"Right on all counts, ladies and gentlemen," Knight replied. "This forest preserve is surrounded by a seven and eight figure income neighborhood."

Tony let out a short whistle. "I guess we're on the right side of the tracks. So is this the part of New Jersey you're from?"

"No," Knight replied. He almost left it at that, but felt his teammates' eyes on him. For whatever reason, they seemed to think he owed them more information about his background. "I'm from north of here," he said, feeling a spike of irritation surge through him. "Newark."

"All right, guys," Cornelia said at length after surveying the terrain, thankfully breaking an uncomfortable silence. "So are we going to get a local explanation again for how the globe was trucked in here?"

"Without a trace on this muddy ground?" Lacy added.

41

The globe was found by a pair of hikers in the Watchung Reservation, a nearly two-thousand acre forest preserve in the hilly terrain of the central New Jersey township. The elevation of their position was four hundred feet. The reservation was nestled in the middle of one of the wealthiest communities in the state, accessible only through a winding network of narrow, two-lane roads. Like many millionaire neighborhoods, the Watchung residents liked to keep their town hard to navigate, just to dissuade too much through traffic. It was a geographically ideal spot to buy seclusion and privacy in one of the most populous states in the country.

Just trucking such a globe to this height, traversing the roads — presumably at night — would have been hard enough. But once — *What would you call them?* Knight wondered. *Mystery Masons? Globe-Planters?* —*whoever* was behind the bizarre enterprise got to the forest preserve, unloading the object in the narrow valley where they did had to have been much tougher than what they'd accomplished in Mount Shasta. There the globe had been placed on a dirt road. True, it was a descending dirt road, Knight recalled, and the placement of the stone object would have required an impressive bit of surveying work to make sure it was placed in just the right spot to avoid rolling away. But the Mount Shasta globe was still on a *road*. Here, the globe showed up on a footpath next to a river — well, a stream more like it, Knight considered — and in a spot that could in no way be approached by the kind of massive hauling vehicle required to move such a tremendous object.

"Only by helicopter," Knight muttered.

"Say that again," he heard Melinda calling to him.

Knight glanced up at their athletic sound-specialist.

"We're rolling," she said.

Both Matt and Tony were covering him with their cameras. It was time for a little performance.

"A helicopter," he said in more pronounced tones this time. "Just like you said, Ian. A helicopter. The way the globe was removed."

In fact, the crew was only left with a wide indentation in the ground to survey after they arrived in Watchung.

"It took local authorities...who was it, by the way?" Knight asked, and glanced at Ballantine and Cornelia.

Ballantine shrugged. "Yeah, good point. The cops? The forest service?"

Cornelia, on the other hand, was already tapping away on the screen of her iPad. "State police, I believe."

"The immense stone globe," Knight continued narrating, "could only be removed from this secluded spot by a helicopter. While there are access roads into the reservation, this spot is so remote, so hilly, so dense with trees and forest vegetation, that it could only be reached on foot or horseback from the reservation stables three miles to the north of here. When the globe was finally removed, it took a helicopter to get the job done." Knight paused, looked around for dramatic effect, then glanced at Matt's camera. "Our investigation's just beginning here, but I'd be willing to bet on a number of things. One: There were plenty of people who heard and saw that helicopter removing the globe. Two: Not so many people saw any kind of aircraft around here two nights ago."

"Nice one," Matt said, and panned his camera around for more footage of the rest of the group walking around the globe's indentation in the ground.

"Do we know where the globe was taken?"

Cornelia's fingers were sliding around the iPad before he finished the sentence. "To Rutgers University. Over in New Brunswick. Earth and Planetary Sciences Department. I think we'll need to look for a guy named Alvin Spangler. Professor of Geology."

Knight said, "Rutgers is not far from here."

2.

"Technically, the globe is made of granite," Alvin Spangler

explained in quick, clipped tones. "It weighs exactly twenty tons. A circumference of fifteen feet. And, to answer your first question, yes, it does appear to be a perfect sphere. How could it have been created? No reason to suspect anything other than the usual cutting and sculpting methods. Diamond wire saws, hydraulic drilling, water jets. They could have been—most likely were—used to create this thing."

"These *things*," Ballantine said before Knight could have.

Spangler's gaze shifted back and forth between them. The professor made little attempt to disguise his taut, impatient dislike for his guests. Although he'd allowed Knight and the *Confirmation* group to bring their cameras into the Wright-Rieman building of the Earth and Planetary Sciences Department, neither the scientist nor the rest of his staff hid their animosity from Knight and his team.

"Right, these *things*," Spangler said with a frustrated sigh. "From what you're describing, the sphere in California sounds like it's an exact duplicate of the one we found here."

"Where *is* the globe that was found in Watchung?" Knight decided to press on with the questions. He had dealt with Spangler's sort of hostility before. The team was on a time budget right now, and Knight didn't particularly feel like trying to win the officious scientist over to their side, to make him realize the groundbreaking importance of uncovering the origins of the giant globe. Knight had, after all, spent years dealing with the Spanglers of academia. As long as the man was willing to give them an interview and the information they needed, Knight really couldn't give any less of a shit about Spangler's feelings.

"It's at our Core Repository building," Spangler said. "About two miles from here."

Rutgers University's New Brunswick campus was, Knight knew, a collection of four campuses situated in two towns on the two sides of the Raritan River in central New Jersey. The science departments are located on the Busch campus on the northern, Piscataway side of the river. The Livingston campus, originally added to the university in the 1960s, incorporating the old Fort Kilmer Army barracks and storage facilities, lies just East of Busch, bordering the town of Highland Park.

Spangler paused. Knight thought the man looked like he was carefully weighing his next words.

"I'm told," Spangler said at length, "that if you can make it brief, we can let you shoot some footage of the globe if you'd like."

"That would be great," Knight said.

"Yes," Spangler replied slowly, with another one of those condescending sighs. "It's a nice warehouse we've got there. I think it would be very...let's just say photogenic."

"Really?" asked Cornelia. Knight could hear her trying to make the question sound upbeat and friendly. "How so?"

"We have a lot of wooden crates there," replied Spangler, as unctuous as ever. "It will look a lot like the big warehouse in Indiana Jones."

Just then Knight would have been willing to sacrifice anything for the chance to punch Spangler in the stomach. Instead, he turned to Tony. "All right, I think we're good in here."

He also noted a moment's eye contact with Ballantine. The ex-cop nodded at him ever so slightly.

"Matt," Ballantine said, "how about you guys get some footage of the grounds outside? And...uh, let's start getting the SUV ready for the ride over to the other campus."

As Ballantine, Matt, Tony, Cornelia, and Melinda decamped, Knight stepped closer to Spangler. "Have you guys been given a lot of hard time by the local media?"

Knight had merely gotten the word from Jerry that an interview with the Rutgers geologists had been set up. Whoever had made the decision to let the *Confirmation* team in here, it wasn't Spangler. Knight could imagine him vociferously objecting. Spangler had probably sputtered something angry and self-righteous about the trivialization of scientific research. The fact was, Knight often admitted, that the news media were for the most part laughably ill-versed in science, medicine, or the world of research and academia. One merely had to listen to the absurd oversimplifications of health and dietary medicine on the nightly news when trying to lose ten pounds to realize that most of what reporters said about science was complete bullshit born of ignorance. But the granite globe matter had nothing to do with life and death science. Alvin Spangler was merely enjoying the chance to let his ego run wild, throw a bitchy-fit, and dress it up as his defense of scholarly integrity. Of course, school bureaucracies being what they were, and the thirst of said bureaucrats for good PR and media coverage, an "idealist" like Spangler was quickly overruled. Someone above him must have decided that it was good to have the Rutgers University Earth and Planetary Sciences Department get referenced in the local and — *possibly* — national news, not to mention a new television series.

Spangler appeared to be weighing his words before speaking, but not for long. "We've been getting inundated with ridiculous questions fit for a cheap supermarket tabloid. I was asked about whether or not there were UFO sightings over Watchung. So, sure, I was nonplussed for a moment by a question like that. UFOs? Have they lost their minds? But then I read the stories coming out of California."

"Of the Mount Shasta ghost-light sightings?"

Spangler shook his head derisively. "Ghost lights.... For God's sake, what a load of garbage."

"It might sound odd, sure," Knight said, ever so conscious that he keep his tone well-controlled and neutral for now. "But we *did* find another one of those globes."

"You found one," Spangler said with a contemptuous sneer. "And isn't that good for your new TV show...*Doctor*?"

"Aren't you even curious what's behind this? Two identical twenty-ton objects like this showing up in remote locations. On opposite sides of the country. Within days of each other."

"As far as my expertise matters, these are giant pieces of granite someone shaped into perfect globes and planted in two forests. Period. Why they did it, I have no clue. But, as I said, I'm a geologist. I tell you what the object is. I tell you how it can be made. By whom and for what reason is not my concern." Spangler paused and took an angry breath. "However, let me also add that what does concern me—*personally*, totally on a subjective level—is the sort of absurd irrational speculation that's already cropping up. UFOs and ghost lights and aliens and nonsense like that. The sort of idiocy the media likes to glom onto and run with for days and weeks on end."

"You have to admit, Doctor—"

"No!" Sangler snapped. "I do *not* have to admit that we need to keep an open mind about any of that pseudo-scientific tabloid *horseshit*! Those globes could have been carved with existing technologies. There is nothing mysterious or supernatural about *any* of it."

"I was about to talk about the placement of the globes."

"In those remote locations? Please! Just like the globe, it might take time to figure it out and get it done, but it's *not* impossible."

"Don't you think it would have taken an incredible number of people to—?"

"Sure, it would have!" Spangler nearly growled at Knight. In fact, Knight could have sworn there was a raspy, barely perceptible animal *growl* to the geologist's voice. How could such rage build up in this man, Knight marveled, over a couple of simple questions? Sure, not innocuous questions. Perhaps provocative even. But such rage....

Except, Knight realized, it might not have been rage in Spangler's voice at all. But perhaps something else....

"It would have been an incredibly hard and expensive and time-consuming exercise," Spangler continued fuming. "But that does not give anyone the justification to jump to the conclusion of aliens or ghosts or—"

"I'm not jumping to *any* conclusions."

"Isn't that what would make your TV show more successful?"

"Believe it or not, *Doctor*, what would make my show the

47

most successful would be to actually solve this puzzle and come up with some real answers."

As Knight spoke, he couldn't help but notice how he took a couple of steps closer to Spangler. But Spangler, in turn, started backing away. Knight liked that just fine.

"Oh, would it now?" Spangler shot back with a jagged, unsteady cackle. "Forgive me if I don't believe you."

"What's your problem, huh? That you didn't want to appear in front of the cameras and — who was it? Your dean? The school's PR people? — someone forced you to do it? But whether you believe it or not, and whatever all the other investigative shows've led you to believe, we really do want to put this whole phenomenon under real, complete, rigorous *scientific* examination. We didn't need to come here. We could be running around out there speculating and jumping to conclusions already."

"You got some footage and you got your quotes, all right? And you can shoot videos of the Core Repository and compare it to Indiana Jones and Area 51. And you can tell everyone...." Spangler paused suddenly, stared at Knight for a protracted moment, and stabbed an index finger in his direction. "...And you can tell *yourself* that you're doing something that amounts to real science. And then your producers and editors'll go ahead and cut and manipulate all your videos to give the superstitious and paranoid and fantasy-prone nuts and rubes and conspiracy theory yahoos exactly what they want to see. So, I'm sorry, Doctor Knight, if I sound like the ivory tower elitist who's dismissing the popular media. But what you're doing — despite what you want to make yourself believe — is not science and not the search for the truth. It's a *perversion* of science and a betrayal of the truth. And by lending your name to this reality TV circus, you're betraying everything and everyone in your own field. You've sold your scholarly credentials to the highest bidder. Frankly, I find it disgusting and disgraceful. So if you don't mind, please leave my lab. I'm quite busy."

Knight backed away from Spangler, studied the frenzied

look in the man's eyes for another moment, then turned and left.

He had been right, Knight realized as he exited the Wright-Rieman building. It hadn't been anger in Spangler's eyes after all. It was something much more disturbing.

It was fear.

3.

"What an asshat!" Lacy said, and shook her head.

Knight glanced toward the farthest seats in the back of the Chevy Suburban they were driving back to the Heldrich Hotel in New Brunswick. Tony and Matt had, just as he hoped, stowed their camera equipment in the cargo bay of the big SUV. He knew the two men had to have realized it was wise not to record this conversation. For all the *Confirmation* viewers would know when they got a chance to see the edited final cut of the adventures of Jerry Peretti's merry band, the intrepid investigators had just gotten valuable tips for solving the granite-globe mystery from Rutgers University's friendly geologists.

"I think he's just scared," Knight said simply. He was still trying to figure out Alvin Spangler's strange, hysterical behavior back at the lab.

"What?" Cornelia asked. "Of the globe? The thing that made the globe?"

Knight strained his back and neck, twisting further around to make eye contact with Cornelia. She was sitting next to Lacy. Luckily, the massive, tank-like Suburban was big enough to carry their entire crew.

"No," he said. "The fact that he can't explain the globe and he knows it. He's going through the motions. The whole boilerplate logical explanations. But I think he knows it's about something else."

"And that's scaring him?" asked Lacy.

Ballantine, driving the SUV, spoke up this time. "Dogma's a powerful thing. Especially since he's hitched his wagon to skepticism and scientific explanations. Dogma and ego."

"Aren't they good?" Cornelia quickly replied. "I mean at least to a point? Come on, Rick! A cop like you has to be in favor of those rational explanations."

"It's not just ego," Knight corrected them both.

"Oh yeah?" Lacy asked.

"Yeah. And I think I know where he's coming from…because I've felt like that a million times myself."

Ballantine gave him a quick, surprised sideways glance. "You thought you had the world all figured out? Then realized you were way off the mark?"

"That's probably the best way of putting it."

"You were as skeptical as all your *asshat* critics, right?" Lacy asked. "And then…where was it? Your research in Haiti made you reconsider?"

Knight almost had to bite the side of his mouth to keep from laughing. Lacy was reciting part of the copy from his press-kit biography. He loved her indignation over the asshat critics. *Thank God for those wonderful, unyielding asshat skeptics!* he almost yelled. He had said those words many times over the years himself. But now it was so endearing to listen to Lacy and her childishly naïve, dialectical thinking. This wonderfully simple-thinking girl couldn't quite imagine that if people like Alvin Spangler, the people who attacked his books, and the zealots who pressured Bakersfield State University to deny his promotion application time and again didn't exist, he would probably have invented them. He would have had to hire these pompous, closed-minded gas-bags and pay them off to criticize him, to personally instruct them to petition college libraries to pull his books off their shelves. Knight had been denied a promotion to full professor three times…and the rejections had helped him cement his reputation as a "maverick" scientist, made his books bestsellers, and earned him enough money in advances, royalties, and speaking fees to live in a community as wealthy and insular as Watchung.

"Listen," he said at length. "There's no way you grow up in a toilet like Newark after your old man runs out on you and your mother and not be a bit skeptical. Know what I'm saying?" When he glanced at Lacy, he saw her pretty face cloud over with unease and something akin to embarrassment. "Not to make this the Dan Knight, Sad Soul Show or anything, but I never really had much time to try and put stock in the existence of invisible forces that had to be obeyed and placated, because if you didn't say the right words or ate the wrong food on the Sabbath, the magical being got angry."

On the streets of Newark, Danny O'Malley had been level-headed, cunning, and intelligent enough to survive and thrive as Dan Knight, then smart enough to see when he was hurtling headlong into a dead-end life, and to get out the moment he might have prospered as a newly-minted trigger-man for a street gang. But in all of his decisions, from the car thefts and the burglaries to the heroin-dealing and the small-time pimping to the moment he decided to walk away from cutting the throat of the shooter of a best friend, Knight's decisions had been motivated by clear, quickly crystalizing logic.

Ever since Jack O'Malley, his shiftless, habitually unemployed bum of a father, left to pick up the family's welfare check and never came home, Dan's life had become a chess game. At stake was his day-to-day survival, and his decisions were made by spur-of-the-moment reflexes about effects and causes, the repercussions of actions taken and not taken. He recalled his decision to drop his father's name after Jack O'Malley disappeared and it was obvious he would never come back. Dan was twelve at the time and left alone with his mother. She had been sixteen when she got knocked up by O'Malley, and her parents kicked her out of the house. The daughter of Hungarian immigrants living in Cleveland, her maiden name had been Ildiko Huszar. The English translation of Huszar was "knight," and that, on the streets of Newark, Dan had decided, sounded more bad-ass than O'Malley. Being as bad-ass as possible in that time and place was the only key to survival. Cementing that reputation with purse-snatching, heroin-dealing, and busting a school security guard's knee to hell with a brick—eventually to hook up with the neighborhood's toughest gang—had all been the most logical decisions given the time, the place, and the circumstances. Knight never felt the hands of fate, or higher powers, spirits, gods, or demons guiding his actions. It had always been logic. It had been logical to be a thief, a con-man, and a drug dealer when that was what it took to keep from starving. It had been logical to become a thug, to strike first, to crush would-be assailants in a world ruled by thugs, in a world divided among predators and victims.

Eventually it had also been logic telling him to turn his back on the streets, even at a moment when he was on the cusp of making a small fortune. It had been logic, along with the birth of his daughter and a couple of well-chosen words from Harris "Smoky" Washington, the head of the Essex County Youth League where Knight had been sentenced to perform community service after nearly putting a man's eye out in a drunken brawl in Hoboken. "I seen your evaluations, you asshole!" Washington had said, getting in his face and hammering him in the chest with a calloused forefinger. "An IQ so high it just about goes off the charts, but you don't got sense enough to see where you're heading? You'll make some money on the streets, sure! You'll blow some money all over the place like the hotshot you think you are, sure enough. Then you'll die. And you know it! A bullet don't care how smart you are when your back's turned. And that bullet's out there. And then what? You'll become your old man, that's what. You'll be the same piece of shit he was because now you've left your kid and her mother to fight for themselves in that same sewer out there where your white trash piece of shit daddy left you."

Logic every step of the way, as far as Knight was concerned.

"I know what you're saying, Doc." Lacy's voice snapped Knight back into the moment. "With all the crap in this world... if the great invisible being gets angry because you eat meat on Saturday...well, I think the great being should just try a little harder."

Instead of naivete, Knight saw something knowing and mature in that impossibly youthful face of hers now. But he also needed to remind himself that underneath the young, tomboy-punk looks, Lacy Anderson was also a veteran. When she talked about the "crap" of the world, it was more than rhetorical. She, too, had seen her share of it.

Ballantine cut in, "I don't recall those details from your bio."

Knight was glad to have to shift his body and glance at the ex-cop. Having been forced to twist around and look at Lacy and Cornelia in the seat directly in back tried his hip and lower back.

Ballantine cast a look his way for a moment, then returned his eyes to the road. "What happened in Haiti? You saw something, right? And now the facts seem to be pointing toward something invisible putting those globes out there."

Knight didn't reply right away. There was something lurking under Ballantine's words that bothered him. No...it pissed him off. Sure, Knight admitted, he could just as well have been paranoid, but there had always been something subliminally irritating about Rick Ballantine. Knight wouldn't have said that he disliked Ballantine, only that he didn't entirely care for the man.

He knew for a fact that it had nothing to do with Ballantine having been a street cop, whereas Knight had grown up as a hoodlum. He was too old to get caught up on that most basic of their differences. Knight had, on occasion, tried to give some analytic thought to his feelings about Ballantine. Perhaps it was just the fact that Ballantine always appeared to be too sure of himself. While Knight appreciated confidence, he had also learned to be wary of people who believed they were always right. Perhaps it was the academic in him, Knight pondered, that stoked the animosity for those who felt they had all the answers. The fact was, in Knight's estimation, that the more one learned about the world, the more an intelligent man became convinced of his own smallness and inadequacies. Ballantine, as far as Knight suspected, based on his very short acquaintance with the man, seemed to lack that quality.

Furthermore, at that very moment Ballantine's words felt like a subtle…jab. *A jab!* the thought flittered across Knight's mind. That was it, he pondered now. He didn't like being jabbed by Ballantine. Sure, on the surface Ballantine looked like a tough guy, a hard guy, the ex-cop, former high-school or college football-player type, no doubt, based on his muscular physique. But Knight also sensed that there might have been a weakness inside Ballantine. Despite his years on the streets of L.A., Ballantine was the product of the suburban middle class. He had first been schooled in the worlds of crime, violence, and depravity out of books in some criminal justice class in some college. Ballantine had seen, had become acclimated to a world that could be brutal, but Knight couldn't believe that Ballantine could be a truly brutal man himself. He was perhaps *afraid* of the recesses of his psyche where brutality lived. Certainly, Knight was aware of the sketchy basics of Ballantine's troubles with the L.A.P.D. Internal Affairs division, but those were troubles he could have fought. But Rick Ballantine was not as tough a fighter, Knight estimated, as his rugged, tough guy exterior suggested.

And how many jabs did you let that lazy bitch of an ex-wife of yours take at you? Knight wanted to say. *Probably a lot. Just as many as those bottom-feeders and bureaucrats jabbed at you in L.A. when you let them end your career without fighting back.*

"My bio didn't get into that," Knight said evenly. "But, if everyone's curious, I saw the exorcism of a kid in Haiti. The son of a French doctor working in a charity hospital. Up until that moment I was, as you might imagine, skeptical about possessions and exorcisms. You hear a million stories of little kids or average people being possessed by Satan or demons or dark forces or some such dire, apocalyptic beings. So what's wrong with that picture?"

Knight paused and looked around the SUV. When no replies came, he realized how pedantic he must have sounded, as if he was delivering a lecture in the classroom.

"OK," he went on. "So it's kids and all these so-called *average* people, right? So think about this: these demonic beings are possessing people because they want to destroy humanity. Or at least that's what most religions that have this sort of a light-and-dark duality tell us. Well, aren't the demons underachievers? You want to destroy humanity, so you possess a fifteen-year-old girl and make her scream some obscenities? Is that the best the devil or the great deceiver or the prince of darkness can do? Why not possess the pilot of a fighter jet carrying enough bombs to wipe out a small town? Why not possess the guy with the nuclear launch key in the silo?"

Knight caught a rueful grin on Lacy's face, and knew his reassessment of her was on the money. She indeed had seen too much bad shit in Afghanistan to believe in simplistic black and white, angels and demons fairy tales.

"But something made you change your mind," Cornelia said.

"Not about whether or not gods and devils control us. Or tempt us or expect us not to eat real dairy ice cream on the Sabbath lest they get pissed off. But that there's something out there no one's created a measurement device for. You see objects move on their own, levitate across the room around this supposedly possessed kid in Haiti…well, you get scared real fast. And no, not scared of the wrath of gods or the attack of demons. If there are forces in the great beyond—"

"The great beyond?" Lacy cut in. "The place you can't measure?"

"That's exactly it. The place you can't measure, you can't experiment on, and can't replicate in the lab. But if there are places like that…out there—outside of, I don't know, our known dimensions, our consensus reality—well, whatever lies in a place like that probably doesn't give a damn about how we live and which way we face when we pray. It probably doesn't care whether we keep our heads covered any more than you care about the mating rituals of mosquitos in a pond."

But before he was finished speaking, Knight noticed the

ever-darkening look on Melinda Rowland's face. "That's very pessimistic, isn't it?"

"Pessimistic?" Knight asked.

"Sure," said Melinda. "If you have some higher—I don't know—power, I guess—"

"Wouldn't he try to save us the way we save endangered species?"

"Yes, that's exactly right."

This is interesting, Knight thought. *So we find the cast-iron traditionalist in the girl bodybuilder of our group? And it turns out to be a woman who likes to challenge conventions...or at least conventions of traditional gendered appearances.* "Then why hasn't he—*it,* whatever—done it already?" he asked her.

"It wants us to help ourselves," Melinda replied.

That, of course, was what he'd expected her to say. It was the standard retort of the religiously inclined. Knight had heard that kind of argument coming from people like Father Petrocelli, the Jesuit priest occasionally teaching writing classes at Essex County Youth Activities Center and working at the soup kitchens in Newark in the mid sixties. God calls all people to service to combat the injustices of the world, Petrocelli used to explain, and God looked long and hard at those who shirked their duties to their fellow man. There is plenty of work to be done on the streets and in the trenches, Petrocelli would say, and there was plenty of praying and confession to be done to keep one's soul clean and well-managed. To Knight, that seemed to suggest that God was as much of an underachiever as the demons who wasted their time possessing teenage kids for no other reason than to make them throw cursing tantrums. And what was the point in managing one's soul and confessing all the time if it was to please a being who didn't seem to care a whit about all the garbage, bedlam, and destruction polluting his marvelous creation?

"Sounds like a pretty useless higher power then, doesn't it?" Knight asked, keeping his tone neutral, theoretical rather than confrontational.

"Well, if it did everything for us, it would...well, it would take away—"

"Our free will?"

"Exactly!"

"So instead it lets us torment and kill each other? You know your free-will argument only goes so far, don't you? Sure, some fanatical nut can exercise his free will to try and blow up an entire ship full of people. But where do his victims' rights to exercise their free will kick in?"

"But what about all the people who choose to do the right thing when they don't have to?" Melinda insisted.

"What about them?"

"Well, there are plenty of people out there in horrible circumstances who choose to do good when they could just as well profit from evil. Don't you think their conscience might be a sign of...you know, something trying to guide the world in the right direction?"

An old question, Knight pondered, an old question he had asked himself a million times when taking stock of his own life and his own choices. "That's the biology of good and evil. Evolution."

"Say what?" Cornelia spoke up this time.

"Most people have a conscience and an inborn sense of empathy because it was evolutionarily advantageous," Knight replied. "The morality gene, if you will. Our species needed it to survive.

"Well, Doc," Ballantine said with an exhale after a beat of silence hung in the car. Knight wondered how many of his companions' Sunday school upbringing he'd just stomped all over. "So that may explain a lot of things, right? Except now we have these big globes out there. And some power is sure making its presence felt."

"Yeah," Cornelia jumped in. Knight noted the force in her voice as she did so. "And it certainly wants something from us," she added.

"I know," Knight said. "And how does it fit into a cynical rationalist's world view? It doesn't. It scares the hell out of him. Because that big granite ball exists and it makes no sense. That's why someone like Spangler is scared out of his mind right now."

"And what about you?" Cornelia asked. "How does it fit into your—what?—modified cynical agnostic point of view?"

Knight's gaze drifted out the windshield in front of him as they crossed the Albany Street Bridge from Highland Park into New Brunswick. "I'm trying to figure that one out. And it scares me too."

4.

Knight thought that Jerry's voice and delivery usually sounded like he had just stepped out of some 1940s film, perhaps a screwball comedy or a tough-talking newspaper melodrama. It was amusing up to a point, but also easily irritating. Now that staccato, machinegun delivery of Jerry's was screeching out of Knight's cell phone. With the device on speaker phone, the producer's voice felt like sharp pin pricks along the auditory nerves.

"Yeah, there are mysterious forces at work, my friends, and right now those forces are grinning at us, ear to ear," Jerry said.

Knight and the *Confirmation* team stood around the breakfast table in Knight's corner king suite in the Heldrich Hotel the morning after their visit to Rutgers, listening to Jerry's update of the latest twist in the story of the granite globes.

"So, Jerry," Knight interrupted. "Does this mean that we can renegotiate our contract?"

"That's very funny, Dan," Jerry's words slashed out of the speaker phone. "I like that. You're a character—all you guys are—and the audiences will love it as well."

"I wasn't kidding. And yes, since you asked the first time we met, you *can* call me *Doctor* Knight."

"Your whole team has been in the middle of the story since the beginning," Jerry said. "You know more about this than any one person now."

The truth of the matter was that Knight and his group might have been in the middle of the globe situation from the beginning—or from the beginning as far as they knew, since they couldn't be sure if the Mount Shasta globe was the first of its kind—but they knew as *little* about it as everyone else. Knight had said as much last night when he got a call from a reporter working for the *LiveScience* online newswire service.

"It might all appear unexplained," Knight had told the reporter, "but we must put it under the most rigorous of scientific tests. There are things out there we can't explain, but we should not look at science as an enemy, and science should not look at people who have unexplained experiences as some kind of a threat. Let's work together to find the truths of this mysterious, unexplained universe."

By this morning, according to Jerry's breathless phone call, the quote had been picked up by a dozen papers and online news services, including *The New York Daily News*, the *New York Post*, the *Los Angeles Times*, and the *Miami Herald*. In each article, *Confirmation* was also prominently mentioned. Jerry's ecstasy was understandable.

"You guys need to discuss this with everyone who asks you a single question about it," Jerry yelled across the line. "You understand that? And, needless to say, make sure *Confirmation* is every other word that comes out of your mouth."

"We'll be sure and do that," Ballantine deadpanned.

"I got meetings with ABC and NBC," Jerry shot back, "Forget cable and syndication, my friends. *Friggin' ABC!* Can you get a load of that? And right now, it's CNN for you, *Doctor* Knight."

The whole point of Jerry's call was to relay the news of an invitation for Knight to discuss the globes on CNN's all new *Peter Rollins Show*. Once word of the Watchung globe had hit the New York media, and the fact that the Watchung globe was the *second* of its kind, newspapers and news stations started perking up. But most importantly, when the national media wanted to talk about the globes, they wanted to do so with the stars of *Confirmation.*

"And you realize that the best part of the CNN interview will be that chance for you to pound on that old nemesis of yours, the Amazing Pike," Jerry screeched across the phone line. "That's gotta be better than even a pay raise, right Doc?"

"I think I prefer the pay raise."

Jerome "The Astounding" Pike was Knight's counterpoint when it came to unexplained phenomenon. Calling himself a "warrior for rationalism, reality, and radical common sense," the former stage magician had made almost as good a living writing books debunking the paranormal as Knight had advocating the reality of the supernatural. The two had already debated about ghostly phenomena on Fox News and MSNBC on a couple of Halloween night "special editions." *The Peter Rollins Show* apparently was more interested in a verbal professional wrestling event than a reasoned discussion of an unexplained event.

Jerry said. "Go knock that bum out."

The complimentary paper slipped under the door that morning had yet another front-page globe story. But this story made Knight wonder about why The Astounding Pike would want to debate the issue on television. From the way events were shaping up, it looked like it would be harder and harder to tack on yet another one of the standard hoax/misidentification/crazy-people explanations to the phenomenon. According to the paper, the Mount Shasta and Watchung globes were not the only ones of their kind. A third one had just been found outside of Edinburgh, Scotland.

5.

The crazy fact was that Knight actually liked a lot of what The Astounding Pike had written about belief systems and people fabricating elaborate fantasy scenarios to explain how unseen forces accounted for the way the world worked. He, of course, would never tell Pike that. It had been too good for business to be attacked by a rationalist fanatic like him. One only built a loyal readership, a dedicated fan base, if one presented himself as a hero, a crusader for a cause, a man with a message. And what every hero needs to make him look good is a villain.

Pike had no problem acting as a caustic foil to Knight. Despite the fact that he liked to talk a good game about rationality and common sense, Pike was a high-strung, wild-eyed fanatic down to the core of his being. He was just as obsessive and blind in his zeal as any snake-handling fundamentalist preacher. He would have wagered extravagantly, would have been ready to fight to the death for the idea that no phenomenon existed that was beyond the explanatory capacity of known scientific measurement devices.

But now, sitting just a few feet away from Pike on the set of the *Peter Rollins Show*, Knight could imagine a sudden spike in the sales of at least his last two books. Pike had come in his best bombastic mood, and it looked like he would spare few words in attacking the superstitious scourge of the world.

"You know gentlemen," Peter Rollins said in his smooth, East Coast Brahmin tone, "I think you might agree on more things than you disagree."

Rollins, sitting between Knight and Pike under the glaring lights of the CNN New York City Time Warner Center studio, glanced back and forth between the two men. There was something about the host's minimal movements, his mannequin-like ramrod-straight bearing, that made Knight think of a Disneyland animatronic puppet that looked stunningly lifelike, but not quite natural enough to pass for the real thing.

Pike spoke first, the words rolling deliberately off his tongue with all the measured theatricality of a veteran stage performer. "That would happen in an unbelievably fantastic world where fallacies are fancied over facts."

The man, in both his writings and public performances, was passionately in love with alliteration. He liked to slosh his words and phrases around his mouth, seeming to savor them like fine, aged wine. But Pike's entire appearance was geared toward powerful visual impact. Fifty-five years old and with a rotund physique—along the lines of comfortable, well-fed middle age rather than obesity—Pike's main trademarks were his shaved, gleaming head and his very large, ostentatious handlebar mustache. The ex-magician also favored brightly colored outfits, as he did today. His burgundy suit looked like it could have been tailored from the drapes of a Louisiana whorehouse. Underneath the jacket he was sporting a vest with a red and green Scottish tartan pattern. Knight wondered if Pike had chosen that vest in honor of the globe found in Scotland, a setup for explaining how the globe was nothing but a trick of the light at sunset.

When Rollins let out a muted, mechanical chuckle, Pike arched an eyebrow and paused before replying.

"In other words," the phrase oozed sarcastically out of Pike, who then stopped again. He held his pause for yet another melodramatic beat before tagging on "Absolutely not."

"Oh, come on," Rollins said with a thin, plastic smile. "If some red-staters and blue-staters can get along in harmony, why can't you find a common ground?"

Before Pike could say anything, Knight jumped in with "I don't know, Peter. I don't think I've ever said anything other than we need to look for a scientific explanation for these globes."

Knight knew well enough that he would, like usual, have a low tolerance for Pike's bullshit theatrics. Before the interview would even be half over, he would be itching to smash the magician's nose in. But Knight knew better than to appear ruffled and angry. As long as Pike seemed to think his foppish obnoxiousness was amusing, Knight could actually look like the more reasonable of the two, no matter the fact that he was arguing the reality of supernatural phenomena.

Rollins looked at Pike. "Well, isn't the professor making a good point? What's wrong with a scientific investigation with an open mind?"

"As long as the professor leaves the door open to the possibility of the globes having been carved by dancing troops of feathered fairies flittering about on flying unicorns, I don't think there can be *any* common ground because—"

"Since when has the scientific process," Knight shot back, "ever included making up your mind about an outcome before gathering the facts and looking at data that support your preconceived notions, and ignoring everything that contradicts those preconceived notions?"

Rollins leaned toward Pike. "Isn't that what you're doing when you rule out the existence of something that's out of the ordinary? Are you not being unscientific?"

Pike's head was shaking vigorously even before Rollins finished speaking. "I'm doing something the good professor in his ivory tower might have run across once or twice. It's called having a hypothesis based on existing data—"

"Is that what it's called?" Knight couldn't help interjecting and laughing.

"Since there is absolutely *no* preexisting data whatsoever in the history of all of science to suggest that goblins and rock-carving beasties exist now or have ever existed, I think I can be fairly sure of myself when I refuse to find common ground with Dr. Knight."

"If we had a longer show, I would be happy to discuss an embarrassment of riches in unexplained aerial phenomena, as well as phenomena that have no known rational explanation—"

"You couldn't do that in a *ten hour* show and be convincing," Pike almost yelled.

"But these phenomena *could* possibly have an explanation one day, correct?" Rollins asked.

"Absolutely," said Knight. "And not in the sense that it was all caused by ball lightning and swamp gas. But I want to make a point about these globes...."

"Sure."

"The point is that you have these giant granite globes appearing in impossible locales. The only way they could have been placed where they were would have included an airlift by a helicopter. And there is *no* way a helicopter cold have been behind the placement of these stones."

"Hog...*wash!*" Pike yelled at full blast now. "Absolute, unadulterated, ninety-nine proof hog—"

"You really think a helicopter was used?"

"Of course."

"In Watchung, New Jersey?"

"Yes!"

"Have you even bothered to visit Watchung?" Knight demanded. He knew Pike's fast-and-loose record of visiting the actual sites of paranormal events he debunked was a good weakness to attack.

Pike snorted in derision. "I didn't visit anything."

"Just like you never bothered to visit most of the UFO landing sites you regularly dismiss."

"I didn't visit Watchung—a wonderful neighborhood, I'm quite certain—because there was simply no reason—"

"And an *unscientific,* preconceived conclusion you didn't bother to test."

It was Rollins' turn to arch an overly melodramatic eyebrow as he glanced at Pike. "You know, Mr. Pike, many of your critics would have a major problem with you refusing to even look at a place where the globe appeared."

"There are ways of making two—*two* mind you, *two,* and not one—full-grown elephants appear in this studio right here. Not by supernatural incantations and magic spells, but illusions. Trickery, gentlemen. And if I could make those elephants appear in here, some enterprising hucksters could conjure up one of these magnificent, mind-bending globes on each side of the country for people whose malleable brains like to bend too easily."

"Dr. Knight, some magicians have, indeed, pulled off some seemingly impossible tricks on stage. I've seen some incredible stuff in shows in Vegas and Atlantic City."

"That's not the same thing, and Mr. Astounding knows it. A magic act on a stage, in a controlled environment—"

"It doesn't have to be on a stage." Pike yelled, and flailed his right arm. "I can do street magic for you with those animals. I can do close-up magic. Right in your face. I'll swallow razor blades for you. Right here in front of you. Not on a stage. I'll put a blowtorch in my mouth. I'll eat fire."

"Then, by all means, tell us how you can put a twenty-ton piece of granite in someone's backyard overnight."

Rollins' attention snapped to Pike. "A fair question?"

"Maybe it wasn't put there overnight," Pike replied, his demeanor melting from outrage into haughty, pedantic condescension. "Quite a prickly possibility, isn't it? What the eye thinks it sees is not what it sees."

"Come on, Mr. Astounding," Knight shot back, "let's cut to the chase! How would they get these stones out there? Tell us *exactly* how these phantom pranksters move these giant stones to all the places they show up. And now we have them in Scotland, I understand."

Pike gave a dismissive shrug. "Just look for activity in these areas where someone was *supposed* to have been doing something that—"

"The chase, Mr. Pike," Knight couldn't help himself. "The *chase*."

"Doctor, if I may finish...."

"Just give us the facts."

"The *facts*, if you care to listen, are very simple. What might have appeared to have been a forest crew in New Jersey, or a truck making deliveries in California and Scotland, was our squirrely perpetrators delivering the globes, unloading them when no one was looking, camouflaging them, then *presto!* as the arcane saying in my trade goes, you have a globe that appears out of thin air."

"Let me just repeat myself. Perhaps what you need to do is go out and actually visit these places you debunk. I'd like to hear a magical explanation for how a twenty-ton globe can be camouflaged in the middle of a road. So that way you won't need to substitute character assassinations and personal attacks for a scientific examination."

"All right, gentlemen," Rollins suddenly cut in. "We'll need to hold that thought while we go to a quick break."

"Let me just say one thing," Pike interjected. "My message to all the hoaxers: you tell tall tales and you get the acid test! And that one can burn."

A moment later, by the time he thought the broadcast would likely have cut to a commercial, Knight couldn't help but smirk in Pike's direction and say, "So how about we get some of those elephants in here before the ads are over...?

The magician, however, didn't get a chance to respond. His attention, along with that of Rollins and Knight, was distracted by someone running toward the set. A young man wearing an earpiece, Knight noticed. A production assistant of some sort, no doubt.

"OK, we gotta go to some live coverage when we come back from the break, Peter!" the man yelled, breathless, agitated.

"Excuse me?" Rollins said, irritated sarcasm edging his voice. He was not about to stand for this sort of a disruption to the routine without a damned good explanation, the look on his face said.

But then Rollins appeared to stiffen. His hand went to the tiny earpiece in his right ear. He must have been getting instructions of some sort from the director's booth.

"There's more of them out there," the production assistant blurted out, apparently concerned that the director was not yet telling Rollins the true gravity of the situation. "They're everywhere. The globes. They've just found them in Russia, in Italy, in Singapore...."

Knight couldn't help but notice his own pulse quickening now. Everything he and his team had seen over the last several days was incredible, but this was....

"Hold it!" Rollins said sharply, raising his left hand to quiet the production assistant. His right hand was still pressed against the earpiece. "Jesus," he gasped at length, then looked from Knight to Pike and back again. "Well, gentlemen, it looks like we're doing this interview at the right time. There are breaking stories from all over the world. They just found one in a back alley in Portugal. There's one in Cairo. Unbelievable...one in... right here in *Central Park*."

Knight couldn't help letting his next words slip from his mouth. "Maybe we have a global conspiracy to camouflage giant granite globes all over the world."

When he glanced at Pike, he saw the magician's face look something like a frozen, waxy mask of tension.

6.

"GRANITE ARTIFACTS STUN THE WORLD AND LEAVE EXPERTS BEWILDRED."
By: Jennifer B. White, *Newsweek*

As the appearance of mysterious globes has taken over the headlines around the world and trends faster than the latest celebrity scandal on social media, Dr. Jonathan Mercer is not a happy man.

"I don't think that's wise," Mercer explains. "I realize that we're experiencing what appears to be some kind of a global phenomenon, but let's not just jump to the conclusion that this is the most important thing in the world. Or even that it's as mysterious and inexplicable as many people are saying."

The professor of astrophysics at the California Institute of Technology has often been invited to offer commentary on such paranormal topics as UFOs, ghosts, and lake monsters. But unlike many skeptics, Mercer typically sticks his well-sharpened debunking pins into such claims with grace and charming good humor.

These days, however, Mercer is up against a mystery that resists most of his pinpricks. Around the world, the appearance of enormous stone globes—each weighing precisely twenty tons — is baffling some of the most brilliant minds of our times.

"Sure, granite balls this size could be reproduced in any reasonably well-equipped stone-mason's workshop," argues Boston University professor of archaeology, Martha Selby, "except that does not explain the mystery. In fact [it] raises more and more unanswered questions. Just where is the mason's workshop? And, of course, how were those globes delivered all over the world without anyone noticing? And for what conceivable purpose?"

At press time, five globes have appeared in the United States, three in Italy, three in Russia, one in Scotland, two in Egypt, one in Singapore, one in Portugal, two in Poland, two in Romania, two in Brazil, three in China, one in Switzerland, four in Denmark, six in India, two in Ethiopia, one in Bolivia, three in France, one in New Zealand, three in Australia, one in Malaysia, and one in South Africa.

For those given to attaching numerical significance to the globes, or any kind of geopolitical meaning, New York University professor of political science Herbert Tudor advises patience. "These are all the globes that have been found so far. So there is really no reason at this point to speculate why the U.S. has five globes and India six, whereas Russia only got three and South Africa only one."

University of Chicago history professor Harry O'Brien remarked, "In truth, we still know absolutely nothing about this phenomenon, except that whoever, or whatever, is responsible wants our attention."

For that reason, O'Brien does not believe that other globes are hidden and undiscovered in the Colombian jungle or covered in snow somewhere in the Siberian tundra. To date, all the globes have turned up in the middle of populated areas or very near populated areas.

For University of Hawaii professor of comparative religions, Thomas Kelekolio, this is the very core of the mystery and the reason to believe that the world is witnessing the work of something that will offer no easy, prosaic explanation. "The skeptics, the debunkers, the people who explain things like this away as a hoax, are very nervous right now," Kelekolio says bluntly, "and they probably have every right to be. We are on the verge of discovering something that will shake all of science, all of our understanding of the natural world to its foundation."

Dr. Daniel J. Knight, a professor of anthropology at Bakersfield State University, who has been at the center of the globe phenomenon since his TV production team discovered the first globe at Mount Shasta, California, agrees. "Of course this is going to be frightening to a lot of people because we are witnessing the handiwork of someone, or something that seems to be toying with us. How many thousands of [surveillance] cameras are all over New York City? It's probably impossible to walk down any street in Manhattan without being seen by at least one camera. So how did one of these globes get placed in the middle of Central Park? Whoever is behind this has just demonstrated that they can do anything anywhere and not get caught if they don't want to get caught. So sure, I think that's a pretty frightening idea."

While Knight wouldn't speculate about who or what is responsible for placing the globes all over the world, plenty of other people are willing to give their theories. According to Don McKay—and the two million readers of his Global Conspiracy Exposed blog—there is significance in the fact that the mysterious artifacts are made of granite. For him, the culprits behind the phenomenon are the favorite whipping boys of conspiracy theorists everywhere: the Freemasons.

"The ancient secret society of the stonecutters," writes McKay, "that has become one of the most powerful, secretive, and destructive forces ever to have plagued humankind, is now sending a signal about their global end-game. They're here and they're taking over."

The world, according to McKay, is a heartbeat away from a fascist takeover. Others, like New Mexico's Church of the Universal Dawn, believe that the globes are signaling the return

CHAPTER 3

Invitation to San Francisco. An Altercation.
The Powell Street Incident. Tell It Like It Is!
Bruce Cheung. Conspiracy? An Invitation.

1.

Cornelia kept forgetting that she was not supposed to break the fourth wall. Her gaze skipped to Matt Cooper's camera once again. Then she noticed his left index finger pointing back toward the notepad on the desk in front of her.

Their job had mutated into something other than the production of a speculative reality show, but Jerry kept insisting that they maintain the documentary-style coverage of everything happening to them. Since they now sat in the conference room of his Beverly Hills suite of offices, Jerry hovered over and stage-managed each of their recorded movements.

So Cornelia forced herself to shift her gaze away from Matt's camera and look only at the phone and her notes.

"Look, Sarah," she said, "obviously if some government conspiracy is behind all this, it wouldn't place a globe so close to a military installation, right?"

"I know that," Sarah Robinson's voice came through the speaker phone. "And I think Dad does, too."

Cornelia glanced toward Jerry sitting on the far side of the conference table. The producer could barely contain his glee, despite the fact that he, too, as per his own directions, tried to act as if cameras were not in the same room. Over the last two days, it began to look like the national security question was about to emerge as the newest angle in the globe phenomenon. Rick, in fact, had made a passing mention of it after Knight's coup of a debate on the *Peter Rollins Show*. Once the show had been interrupted by incoming news of all those new globes, Pike seemed to unravel. His hoax explanation could withstand three globes, but with so many of those things turning up in so many places, seemingly overnight and without anyone seeing or hearing anything, the magician had run out of skeptical straws to grasp for. But then the next logical question was whether or not any government officials anywhere in the world might eventually speculate about a truly unexplained phenomenon that respected no borders or boundaries. "Imagine if one of these things appears inside a military installation," Rick had wondered.

The globes even overwhelmed the biggest security story of the past week. Cornelia, of course, appreciated the irony of it all. She had been trying to follow the story on her iPad and phone whenever she got a free moment, all the while taking the ribbing of her *Confirmation* costars. When they had arrived in Mount Shasta City, news broke of an oil tanker's hijacking by an Al-Qaeda-affiliated Indonesian terrorist cell. The hijackers had planned on turning the ship into one immense bomb, sailing it into the Port of San Diego, and blowing it up. Incredibly, the plan was thwarted by one crew member who managed to elude the terrorists and feed information to the Navy's SEAL Team Six. The ship had eventually been taken by the SEALs and the hijackers killed well before the vessel could be a threat to San Diego. Headlines blared "Die Hard on the High Seas" for days afterward.

Then the day after Knight's appearance on the *Rollins* show, during the president's press conference about increased seaport security-measures in the wake of the hijacking, the globes pushed everything off the agenda again. The word spread that getting someone from the military or intelligence circles to talk about the globes would be a major news coup. No one had yet managed to do it, but Cornelia thought she had a good shot at it via Sarah Robinson. They had known each other since high school, and now

Sarah's father, Air Force Lieutenant Colonel Garret Robinson, was stationed at Travis Air Force Base outside of San Francisco. The globe mystery, coupled with the installation's connection to the foiled San Diego attack, was now attracting the attention of some conspiracy theorists.

"Now we just need to convince his bosses, right?" Cornelia said. Out of the corner of her eye, she thought she saw Jerry drumming his fingers on the armrest of his chair in what looked almost like childlike exuberance.

"I think we can eventually do that," Sarah replied.

Cornelia almost wanted to breathe a loud sigh of relief. "I've seen military personnel talk to cheesy investigative shows before...unlike our show, of course."

Sarah chuckled from the other end of the line. "I trust you totally. And yeah, they've spoken before to like a million documentaries about UFOs and Roswell and all that stuff...but you know how it is now. The whole system's on edge. Hardly a day goes by without another one of those things turning up."

"And the speculation will keep getting wilder and wilder. I'm sure your dad knows that."

Sarah didn't respond immediately. "Cornelia," she said at length, then paused once more. A nervous beat later she added, "Do you know anything? Have you guys talked to anyone who has...you know, *any* clue about what's going on?"

Cornelia was taken by the tension in her voice. "One professor's or *expert's* guess is as good as the next."

"Oh, God...."

"Nobody knows. Aliens? Angels? Demons? Earth spirits? A hoax? The CIA? The end of the world? Take your pick, Dr. Robinson. Someone who graduated at the top of Stanford med school's bound get as close to the truth as a bunch of tin-foil-hatted conspiracy geeks chaining themselves to the gates of Travis and Coronado."

The latest globe appearance had unleashed chaos on the Internet. The object appeared on Silver Strand beach in San

Diego, barely a hundred feet from the waters of San Diego Bay. With the globe in the middle of the sand, no one could see any possible tracks that could have been left by transport equipment. For many, however, the San Diego area had been of even greater importance since it was the site of the thwarted terrorist attack. It was also in the vicinity of the state's biggest concentration of military installations.

From a navy training center to the Marine Corps Recruit Depot and the Coronado Naval Amphibious Base where four SEAL Teams are headquartered, the area is a virtual naval stronghold. The amphibious base had deployed the SEALs for the assault on the hijacked oil tanker. But despite this concentration of state of the art military preparedness-hardware and the navy's most elite fighters, yet another globe appeared seemingly out of thin air. For many conspiracy theorists, the military connection was impossible to ignore. Speculation had spread that the globes were the result of government experimentation on everything from camouflage techniques to mind control. Moreover, shortly after the raid on the oil tanker, one of the SEAL intelligence officers involved with the mission had been reassigned from Coronado to the Navy's Fleet Reconnaissance Squadron next to Travis Air Force Base. Now roving groups of conspiracy theorists had taken to camping out near Travis, the navy reconnaissance complex, as well as the navy and marine corps installations in San Diego.

"Oh, come on," Sarah said with an embarrassed chuckle, "I wasn't at the *top* of —"

"You were close enough."

"You guys don't need to inflate me like this in your final cut of the show. So go ahead and edit all this stuff."

Cornelia knew that Sarah's modesty wasn't false at all. Her friend had always been exceedingly down to earth, no matter how good she was at what she did and how far her career as a cardiac surgeon had rocketed her. But now Cornelia wondered about a feeling of discomfort somewhere deep in her core. There was a palpable sense of dread spreading among all the people she spoke to and interviewed about the globes. That dread was spreading through the world now. Yet for her a stronger feeling was...a promise of *opportunity*. She wouldn't lie to herself about it. She looked at the globes as a career opportunity, and even more so as she spoke to her childhood friend. Her phenomenally *successful* childhood friend. Cornelia wanted to use these globes badly. She wanted to use them to salvage her career, to get back what others had unfairly taken away from her during that accursed "Blogging Avenger" scandal in Florida.

And Cornelia also couldn't deny the bitter satisfaction she got out of thinking about how her career could thrive as a result of the globes, while that of Stewie Corcoran remained in its local-level — "hyper local" as they call it in the news business — stagnation. *Stewart* Corcoran — no one called him Stewie to his face — was the producer who had thrown Cornelia to the wolves five years ago, during the "Blogging Avenger" incident at Tampa's All Saints' College. While Stewie might have ultimately been trying to worm his way out of a firing when the Avenger case blew up into a P.R. disaster for the station, Cornelia suspected that he was also trying to get revenge for her rebuff of his drunken advance at a Christmas party.

In the Blogging Avenger case, Cornelia's TV station, WRND, had been pointed in the direction of someone who sounded like a faculty member of All Saints' College, blogging anonymously and accusing several high-ranking school administrators of some financial slight of hand. With WRND uncomfortable with reporting on the anonymous accusations, Cornelia's intern, Roger Pryce, took the initiative to hack the blog and reveal an All Saints' professor as the Avenger. At that point, one bad decision led to a worse one, with Stewie Corcoran, over Cornelia's vehement objections, airing the story. After the outed professor's firing and heat within the news industry coming down on WRND while the state attorney's office considered filing criminal charges for the hacking, Stewie managed to convince his bosses that not only was Cornelia the only one at the station who knew about Pryce's hacking, but she was the one who encouraged him to do it. The ax instantly fell on her.

The best Cornelia could do after her firing was announcing the weather under the nickname of "The Stormy Chick" on a Laguna Niguel, California, classic-rock radio station. That was until a year ago, however, when she was invited to a party thrown by a coworker's brother-in-law in Los Angeles. The brother-in-law produced commercials for ad agencies, and he knew Jerry Peretti from their days of producing music videos.

But even as her professional life took a turn for the better, some malicious force of destiny just had to balance it with a turn for the worse in her private life. Her real-estate agent boyfriend, Barry, despite having worked the topics of engagement and marriage into as many conversations as he could, suddenly turned frigid at the thought of the resurrection of her TV career. When she had told him that she accepted Jerry's offer to be a *Confirmation* cast member—and explained that her work on the show should not be a major issue for their relationship since L.A. is so close to Laguna Niguel—Barry threw a tantrum in the middle of their dinner at the Seaside Vista Grill and stormed out, accusing her of wanting to prove her superiority by "fighting tooth and nail" for a better paying career than his.

Cornelia shook off these memories of fate making a plaything of her life, and her gaze darted toward Rick. He, too, sat at the conference table, his handsome features set in stony concentration, his eyes intently staring at the phone while he sipped a tall cup of coffee. Rick was perfectly happy to use *Confirmation* to turn his own life around.

"This is frightening, Cornelia," Sarah's voice snapped her out of her momentary reverie. "Isn't it? You don't think they're right about a massive hoax, do you?"

"No. I mean, I don't think it's a hoax," Cornelia said, and her thoughts jumped to what Knight had been saying about the angry skeptics since their interview with the Rutgers geologist. "Probably a lot of people talking about hoaxes don't believe it's one either. Maybe it makes them feel better to ignore the obvious."

"I don't know what's more disturbing then."

"Yeah…I guess we have no choice but to go along for the ride."

There was a heavy beat of silence in the room, Sarah taking a few protracted moments to respond. "I'm going to talk to Dad. He'll trust you. And I'm pretty sure he's tired of hearing all the local conspiracy loons talking about the air force's time-fractal displacement experiments. He'll probably love to set the record straight…that neither he nor anyone he's working with have a clue as to what's going on."

Cornelia felt like she had been taken off guard by something truly bizarre. "Wait a minute. A time fractal what?"

Sarah let out a hearty laugh. Cornelia thought there was a nervous edge to it. Her friend sounded like she was really blowing off some tension.

"I have no idea," Sarah said. "It's something I read on a harebrained website. They probably got it off an episode of *Star Trek*. But how about you guys head on up to San Francisco as soon as you can? I'll meet you and hopefully we can set up one hell of an interview. I think Dad's superiors will appreciate a chance to respond to some of this conspiracy craziness that's been going on around here."

When Cornelia saw Jerry pumping a fist, then give her a thumbs up, she said goodbye to Sarah with "Will do, sweetie. And thanks a lot."

But just after she turned off the phone, Cornelia noticed that Jerry was no longer the person making wild hand gestures in the room. Now it was Ian's turn. He was waving one hand around, trying to get everyone's attention. His other hand clutched his iPad, something on the tablet riveting his attention.

"You guys've *gotta* see this!"

2.

"Someone beat the crap out of the Astounding Pike," Ian

yelled before anyone could ask what he was talking about. "From what it says, it looks like they went nuts and really messed him up."

"Because of something he said about the globes?" Jerry blurted out.

"It looks like it. Check it out!"

Cornelia was the first one to look over Ian's shoulder. The story of the Pike assault had a video link embedded. When Ian clicked the link, they saw a ghastly close-up of the magician's battered face. Not only was most of Pike's face obscured by the bandage covering his broken nose, but his left eye was still swollen shut and his right one overtaken by a purple/black bruise. There were blood-encrusted abrasions lining the tip of his chin and the left side of his jaw.

Cornelia felt embarrassed to think that there was a grotesquely comic touch to the way Pike's usually jaunty handlebar moustache now drooped walrus-like around the two sides of his mouth.

"What kind of a world do we live in when this can happen to you for the words you speak?" Pike mumbled as the video stream started.

There must have been some bad fracturing to his jaw or teeth, Cornelia guessed. Perhaps wires inside the magician's mouth had to remedy whatever damage had been done.

"Maybe it wouldn't have happened if he wasn't such a douche all the time," Ian said in a weird matter-of-fact tone. "It says the whole thing started after he called a guy in Florida a con man," he muttered, skimming over the article and pointing out the highlights to the *Confirmation* team.

In fact, Cornelia discovered as she read the piece, Pike had been getting ever more aggressive in his insistence on a worldwide hoax as the number of globe discoveries increased. One of the recent American globes turned up on the property of a man in Homestead, Florida. That man, George LaPlante, a former construction worker who had been unemployed for over a year with a debilitating back injury, was enterprising enough to charge visitors to take pictures with his globe and start printing and selling globe-souvenir T-shirts.

After the *Miami Herald* profiled LaPlante in a lengthy article, Pike responded in a blog post, denouncing the "crass, cash-grabbing con men and charlatans who are the key to the true nature of this global circus." When Miami's NBC affiliate invited both LaPlante and Pike for a debate about the issue, blows were almost traded on the air. *Almost,* but not yet. Pike insisted on calling LaPlante a part of a massive, money-making swindle. LaPlante, who was less facile with the alliterative phrases, merely called Pike a moron who enjoyed being blind to the facts, and an asshole (bleeped out during the broadcast) in need of a good ass-whooping. The ass-whooping itself only came when a congregation of the Atlantis-seeking Church of the Universal Dawn followed Pike to his hotel and started chanting "blind fool" at the tops of their lungs outside his room. The magician at that point should have been wise enough to wait for hotel security to come and take care of the problem. He, however, was not. Instead he confronted the group, suggesting they look for a good group-rate on psychiatric treatment. In a quickly ensuing melee, Pike, aside from head injuries, sustained one broken rib, a broken collar bone, and a broken wrist.

Knight cast a cool glance toward Ian. "Wow. Like you said, man. If he wasn't such an obnoxious ass *and*—"

Cornelia couldn't believe what she was hearing. "What? Are you saying he deserved this?"

"No," Knight replied in very calm, unruffled tones. "I was about to say that if he wasn't so arrogant, he could have waited in his room quietly and let security take care of those Universal Dawn idiots. But when you're the Astounding Pike, I guess you have to be a tough guy even when you're surrounded by psychotics like this."

The old professor said the right things, Cornelia had to admit, but she still didn't like the distant, nonchalant callousness on his face. For a moment, she could see a shade of the stone-cold teenage hoodlum from Newark in him.

Then, with a harder inflection, Knight added, "Pike might have been an asshole, but he didn't deserve getting beaten up for it."

"Well, folks," Jerry's voice cut a swath through the tension between Cornelia and Knight.

When Cornelia glanced at him and saw him smiling, she found his look just as unpleasant as Knight's.

"How about we move on to the next challenge, shall we? Let's see what kind of psychotics are protesting outside these military bases near Frisco," he said with ghoulishly chipper tones.

Cornelia couldn't help but detest Jerry's change of topics more and more with each word out of his mouth.

3.

The globe's path of destruction down Powell Street had started with a car crash. A crash somewhat like Ballantine's collision with the globe at Mount Shasta, Cornelia mused.

She wondered if her own thoughts had now come to resemble those of the conspiracy theorists and UFO buffs they had come to the Bay area to interview. She was making every kind of haphazard, convoluted connection between events and places as they popped into her mind:

The first globe was discovered in California.

A car crash started the chain of tragic events on San Francisco's Powell Street.

The discovery of the first globe was a major turning point for the world.

What kind of a turning point would this *become?*

The noise certainly didn't help her think straight. There were the sounds of the crowds all around; the onlookers trying to get as close to Powell street as they could, the police trying to contain them, the press on the ground as well as the news helicopters hovering overhead.

"This incredible chain of events started near the top of this hill we're looking at," Rick narrated as Tony's and Matt's cameras covered him. "From most accounts we've heard so far, it was the intersection of Powell and California Streets."

She should probably have been in front of the camera and doing the talking herself for this segment, Cornelia knew. But when Ballantine had offered to take over the segment, she didn't argue. Yes, a part of herself hated that she gave in, but she needed a moment right now to step back from what had happened here. Neither Ballantine nor any of the other team members were affected the way she was.

"It is just another example of the completely unexplained nature of this phenomenon that has been sweeping the world," Rick said solemnly.

Cornelia could hear the tension, the rawness of nerves in his voice.

"In broad daylight, on busy streets," Rick went on, "a globe appeared. At just the right moment, at just the right precise spot no one was looking, a twenty-ton granite globe somehow shows up. Again, at a precise spot on a street where no security, traffic, or surveillance cameras are looking, at a time when no pedestrians are walking nearby, one of the mystery globes somehow appears. The closest person to the globe, from what we've heard so far, was a motorist who took his eyes off the road for a moment to adjust the radio in his car. The next moment, when he looks up, the street in front of him is blocked by a globe. He hits the brakes, he just about misses a collision...except he gets rear-ended."

And then he hits the globe, Cornelia almost whispered.

"Just imagine how perfectly this massive object was placed at just the right spot, down to the exact square inch, where it could stand still in the level intersection, yet close enough to the extremely steep Powell Street to start rolling once that car made the slightest contact."

Matt Cooper was getting a long-shot of Powell, Cornelia noticed. The street climbed up one of San Francisco's many precipitous hills.

"From what police investigators could tell from the damage

to the car," Rick explained, "its driver was barely moving at the speed limit. He had, just as he told the investigating officers, almost completely avoided a collision had he not been struck from behind and his vehicle not pushed forward and into the globe. Yet that slightest impact started the globe rolling down the hill."

Where it derailed a cable car, putting twelve people in the hospital with critical injuries, Cornelia recalled the latest report of what had ensued an hour before she and her *Confirmation* teammates landed in San Francisco. After crashing into the cable car, the globe pinballed off to its left, crashing nearly head-on into a sedan. The car's driver managed to survive the accident with only a sprained shoulder. But the globe then smashed two parked cars and nearly killed a bike messenger who had been speeding down the street. Startled by the destruction just a few feet behind him, the biker lost his balance, wiped out, broke his arm and his nose, and received a concussion as he rammed head-first into the ground. From there, the globe rebounded toward the right side of Powell, striking yet another parked car. This one inexplicably exploded. The car's driver was killed. Two pedestrians were burned as a result. Five more people were showered and badly lacerated by flying glass and metal debris. Then the globe rebounded yet again....

Cornelia's pulse pounded as she imagined the chain of events.

...The globe rebounded toward the left of the street and into another row of parked cars. One of the cars belonged to Sarah Robinson. She had just parked moments before, and was still behind the wheel when the globe struck. She would die from her massive head-injuries at San Francisco General Hospital.

The globe eventually came to a rest at the bottom of the hill, at the Hallidie Plaza cable-car turntable.

4.

Cornelia and her group were granted access to the San

Francisco General Intensive Care Unit waiting room by Sarah's father. With the rest of the media clamoring all over the hospital, security was keeping as tight a seal on access as possible now.

Cornelia had told her partners not to bring any of their cameras inside. They all agreed. Now was not the time.

They had all been taken by the throngs of reporters down in the lobby, Cornelia knew. They saw all the news vans in the parking lots. San Francisco had just seen the first serious injuries and the first two deaths attributable to the globes. Everyone was looking for a scoop. Cornelia and her partners were lucky to get this access. But none of them said it out loud.

When they got to the waiting room, they were surprised to find Colonel Robinson and another air force officer in the small, bare-bones enclosure. The room's furnishings consisted of two couches, a table with four chairs, and a TV set on the wall. Cornelia wondered if the relatives of other patients had somehow been persuaded to leave.

"Cornelia," Robinson said simply as she walked into the room.

Garret Robinson had the sort of sinewy, strong-chinned, masculine features of a soldier who would have looked perfect on a recruiting poster. But now he looked haggard, spent. With his uniform jacket removed and loosened tie, he was but another grieving father, not a tough leader of men.

"Garret," Cornelia said softly. "I'm *so* sorry."

She noticed Robinson's gaze sweep over her colleagues as they entered behind her. They all said their quiet greetings solemnly and respectfully. But Cornelia wondered if Robinson might have been trying to figure out the capacity in which she had come to see him. Was she there as a family friend? he might have been thinking, or as an opportunistic journalist? She didn't blame him, of course. It made her feel unclean, disloyal. Moreover, no matter that the globes had now become *the* number-one news story around the world and they were working on pursuing information the public had a legitimate right to know, Cornelia still had a hard time thinking of herself as a journalist again.

Nonetheless, Robinson came up to her and gave her a hug. "I know," he said.

Cornelia noticed the other man nodding at the *Confirmation* team members. Around thirty-years-old or so, he had the sort of ex-prep-school look of a yuppie. Cornelia wondered if he might have been the air force version of a P.R. man, watching over Garret to make sure he said the right things to the media. His name tag read "Burns." His rank insignia was that of a captain.

"I think we all better get out of here," Robinson said after a beat. After another pause, he glanced towards Burns for a moment. "I know your team has a lot of questions for me...."

"I'm here because I've known Sarah and I've known you since I was fifteen," Cornelia said as delicately as she could. "I'm a friend now. This isn't show biz."

"I appreciate that," Robinson said firmly. "But the fact is that I have a lot to say. About Sarah. About the way she died. And about these clowns running around out there claiming we, the air force, the military, the government, the force of the great global conspiracy, are somehow behind this."

Cornelia was taken by his candor. But she could see that it was a cold, hard, furious candor.

"Let's go," he said, and grabbed his jacket off the back of one of the chairs.

Hospital security provided them a way out of the hospital through a series of utility corridors that would take them first to an ambulance garage and then on the shortest path to the parking lot. That way they stood the best chance of avoiding the news crews.

"If the military's behind this, we're obviously not doing a good job of protecting ourselves, are we?" Robinson said bitterly as their service-elevator doors slid open on the first floor.

So the colonel really was as eager to talk as he claimed, Cornelia realized with some surprise. His grief was obviously mutating into anger and indignation. Although they couldn't record the moment, Cornelia let him talk.

"I don't know what the hell is going on," Robinson continued, striding out of the elevator, "and I don't know *anyone* who does. But seeing how these things keep turning up virtually every day now, all over the world—in the middle of a goddamned city street, for Christ's sake—I guess we'd better start figuring it out."

Cornelia thought she noticed the other air force man, Burns, nodding ever so slightly as Robinson spoke. She guessed he looked *glad* that Robinson said what he did, rather than glad that he was following some prearranged script. The words coming out of the colonel still carried the tone of a grieving, angry father. And besides, for as long as Cornelia had known the man, he had never struck her as the type who could be easily cowed by the bureaucratic party line.

"Do you understand what I'm saying?" Robinson said, and shot a look at Cornelia. "Whatever is going on here.... Well, someone who's a lot smarter than I am—some physicists or mathematicians, or astronomers at Harvard or MIT or Princeton or wherever we can get a hold of those people—had better come up with some real answers real soon, and we'd better listen to them instead of pretending we know all the easy answers about conspiracies."

Cornelia was about to tell him that she was interested in the truth as Robinson saw it and not some confirmation of prefabricated conspiracy theory narratives, but Dan Knight beat her to the punch. "That's exactly what we're interested in, Colonel," he said quickly. "*Your* story, not another *X-Files* flashback."

"Oh, and one more thing," Robinson said curtly. "Don't expect me to look for a greater purpose behind Sarah's death," he added a short beat later. Cornelia noticed the bile tingeing each of his words. "It's only been a couple of hours since that globe rolled down that hill, and we already have some assholes out there talking about a greater purpose."

5.

"What greater purpose?" Lacy asked when they were back at the Omni San Francisco Hotel.

Jerry had them book their rooms after Sarah's invitation to San Francisco, yet none of the team had set foot inside their suites yet. Even now they sat around two tables that had been pushed together in the Omni's steak house. They were close to crashing from exhaustion after the day's events, and they needed some food to reenergize and time to get some perspective on what they found themselves in the middle of.

"They're referring to that exploding car," said Knight, and glanced up from his laptop.

Both the professor and Rick had their computers in front of them, and ceaselessly surveyed the Internet for every development, analysis, and commentary on what had happened on Powell Street.

Knight's gaze almost drifted to the camera on the tripod on his right side by the far end of the table. Matt had secured one of the cameras on one end of the tables, while Tony held the other one in his hand, covering the discussion at the table.

Cornelia had her iPad in front of her, but could no longer focus her attention well enough for effective net-surfing. Exhaustion, which had hit her like a body-blow the moment she sat down, coupled with the orange/red glow of a fading twilight bathing them through the restaurant's windows, was having its way with her, and she knew better than to fight it right now.

"It was a bomb," Knight exclaimed.

Everyone's gaze was fixed on him in that instant. The old man, though, stared at his computer screen as if he couldn't believe what he was reading. "The driver of the car had a bomb with him," Knight said a moment later, then paused once more. He met no one's eyes.

Cornelia wondered if she heard a strange, inexplicable taint of bitterness in his words.

"Yeah," Rick mumbled before Knight could say anything

else. They, apparently, were looking at the same information. "Because the guy was an enforcer for a Triad boss," he said with louder, more pronounced words this time.

"Triad?" Melinda asked. Since Lacy sat between her and Rick, she quickly tried to crane her neck to get a glimpse of his laptop. "As in…?"

"As in Chinese organized crime." Rick paused and cast a quick glance at Knight, as if to see if he had anything to add.

Knight was perusing his laptop screen too intently to say anything.

"We seem to be dealing with a hitman who was kept from his target," Rick said, and took the time to look at everyone around the table. He even afforded a glance at Matt and his camera. "Cops say the target was Judge Ronald Belknap."

"Was this guy in the car on trial or something?" Ian asked.

"His boss was," Rick said. "But our hitman," he continued, pausing only for a moment to refresh his memory off the computer screen, "is the late Johnny Lo. Real nasty piece of work. Loan shark. Extortionist. Suspected in at least four gangland killings. Two of them went to court, but he beat the rap on both. Until this morning he was in the employ of the man standing trial in Judge Belknap's courtroom for heroin smuggling: one-time star of the silver screen and the bottom of Hong Kong pop charts, Philip Cheung Chen-Sun. In case the name doesn't ring any bells, he *is* better known by his stage name from the late seventies: Bruce Cheung."

"Sorry, it still doesn't ring any bells," Cornelia said. She wasn't sure where Rick was going with the organized crime trivia, but she was too tired to even try and guess.

"Hey, wait a minute!" Ian exclaimed with something between real and mock astonishment. "*The Seven Fists of Death.*"

Lacy cocked an eyebrow with a confused look. "Dude! What are you talking about?" Cornelia could tell that Lacy, too, was too drained by the day for these guessing games.

"Classic Bruceploitation grindhouse cinema," Ian shot back

brightly, then looked at Rick. "Am I right, man?"

"Impressive. Bit before your time."

"Bro, I'm a classic-film buff."

"Cheung used to be an actor," said Rick. "One among dozens of Bruce Lee imitators. And yes, *The Seven Fists of Death* was his big-screen debut. Financed by his father, a chieftain in Hong Kong's Shadow Tiger Triad."

"And now Bruce Cheung is a gangster in San Francisco?" Melinda asked.

"Well" Rick said. "As lavishly as his father spent on the production of *Fists of Death* in seventy-seven, Junior didn't quite become — as he was billed — 'The New King of Kung Fu.'"

"Despite the numerology?" Knight asked sardonically.

Ian laughed. "*Seven Fists of Death* released in seventy-seven."

"Despite that," Rick said, "*Seven Fists of Death* didn't set the world box office on fire."

"Or even the Hong Kong box office," Ian chimed in.

"Yeah. It was a bomb. As were *Bruce Lee's Vengeance, Dragon Master* — "

"*Bruce Lee's Vengeance?*" Lacy asked, incredulous. "You can *not* be serious."

"Don't knock it!" Ian shot back. "The quality of the martial arts was much better than you'd expect."

After a long, rueful look, Lacy repeated, "*Bruce Lee's Vengeance?*"

"Bruce Cheung played a champion race-car driver who stumbles onto a Japanese conspiracy behind Bruce Lee's death."

"I guess I better get the DVD for that one," Lacy said. "So how do we go from Hong Kong chop-socky to San Francisco?"

"Well," Rick said, "as you might guess, Bruce Cheung's show biz career didn't really work out. This despite the fact that in 1978 he tried to jump on the post-*Star Wars* sci-fi craze and made *Interdimensional Kung Fu*. Costarring fellow Z-grade leading man, Hong Kong Lee."

"I'm not gonna ask what that one was about," Lacy said,

glancing at Ian, barely suppressing a grin.

"Something tells me you're about to find out," Melinda said, and chuckled.

Although Cornelia was just about on the verge of frustration with their banter, she could understand it. They had all been worn down by this day. Kidding around like this helped cut the tension for everyone.

"Bruce Cheung and Hong Kong Lee together in one picture?" Matt said, and laughed. "Dude, that's like Pacino and DeNiro in the same film."

"It was an unappreciated classic, right?" asked Knight.

"Hong Kong Lee was an alien bent on world domination," Ian explained, "but he first needed to eliminate all of the greatest martial artists who might stand in his way. And he almost succeeded, were it not for Bruce Cheung mastering a secret style of fighting. The interdimensional kung fu technique!"

"Why am I so nervous sitting at the same table with you?" Lacy asked with the perfect deadpan.

There were laughs all around.

"Sadly," Rick said, "not only was Cheung's acting career a bust, but he didn't fare much better as a Canto Pop singer."

"That's too bad," Knight said with mock pity.

"I bet," Cornelia said, and looked at Rick, "the entertainment world's loss was the underworld's gain, right?"

"You got it. When Bruce Cheung crashed and burned, Philip Cheung Chen-Sun did just fine in the family business. Heroin smuggling, prostitution, loan-sharking, gun-running. He was a virtuoso hood his father could always count on. Then, in 1992, shortly after taking full reigns of the Triad, he started relocating the organization's investments in fear of the 1997 takeover of Hong Kong by mainland China."

"And he seems to have made out well in San Francisco," Knight added, then paused with a graven, uncomfortable look on his face. At length, he said, "Until we get some supernatural intervention."

No one replied for several moments.

Finally, Melinda said, "So this globe starts rolling down that hill, hitting things, bouncing left and right like a giant pinball, and then it hits Johnny Lo's car and blows it up. We've got some incredible odds in play here."

"Yeah, don't we?" Knight said with a bitter edge to his voice.

"Because," said Melinda, "Johnny blows up with the bomb intended for the judge. And now Bruce Cheung's trial will go on...."

"And maybe justice will be done," Cornelia cut in. While she paused, no one said a word. They all knew what she was implying. Nevertheless, she made it explicit. "Criminal mastermind Cheung might go to prison at last...except Sarah dies in the middle of all the destruction."

"Yeah," Lacy replied quietly. "And dozens of other people are injured and maimed in the process too. There sure seems to be a benevolent force at work here, don't you think?"

Cornelia saw Knight giving Lacy a long, knowing look.

Once again, a grim silence hung in the air.

Until Rick cleared his throat and looked up from his laptop. "There are a lot of people who seem to think so."

"Not Sarah's father," Cornelia said, noticing how her words only came out as a near whisper.

"I know," said Rick. "But there was a guy interviewed by the *Chronicle* who called this globe the 'engine of destiny.'"

"Jesus," Lacy said. "How fucking ridiculous is that?"

"You know," Rick said, "along with Colonel Robinson, we'll have to talk to people like that as well."

"Well," said Melinda slowly, ruefully, "whatever these globes are, they *are* the engines of something. Even if we don't like what they're doing."

"Right," Ian said. "*We* might not, but plenty of people do."

"Until they get smashed by one of these things?" Cornelia asked, her words coming out sharper than she had intended.

"Yeah, well, I think that's the point of the problem," Rick

said. "What kind of a purpose is behind this whole thing if it puts one murdering scumbag gangster in jail, kills another one, and wrecks the lives of dozens of people in the process?"

"I think we're going to have a lot of fantastic opportunities to record some heated debates," Ian added.

"But if something like this happens again," Tony asked, "how heated do you think the debates will get?"

"Ask the Astounding Pike," Knight replied.

6.

A professional keeps doing her job, Cornelia told herself, and let her interviewee speak, as much as she found most of what he had to say tasteless and absurd.

"First of all, you need to understand that there are *no* coincidences," Bill Canyon insisted.

As he paused, Cornelia thought there was a strange, pedantic sort of a glint in his eyes. He looked like a teacher satisfied with himself when a student looked like she might have been understanding the point of a lesson at last.

Then again, the glint could just as well have been a momentary trick of the morning's sunlight. They were conducting the interview with a quintessentially San Francisco backdrop. Sitting at the Crissy Field waterfront park of the Presidio, the Golden Gate Bridge loomed behind them.

"Coincidences belong in fairy tales," Canyon said. "Coincidences are part of the propaganda designed to blind you from the truth in front of you."

Canyon had the sort of youthful, clean-shaven, guileless look of someone who should have been selling Bibles door to door.

Bill Canyon ran the *Apocalyptic Times* blog and hosted the *Millennium Survival* biweekly podcast. The former insurance agent and one-time coast guard reservist had burgeoned as an online broadcaster and independent documentary producer since 2003. According to Cornelia's research, Canyon had gotten very effective mileage out of his coast guard experience, regularly billing himself as a "military-industrial-complex insider" who was answering the call of his conscience and blowing the whistle on the "power elite's knowledge of the coming apocalypse." Canyon had been one of the first people on the September-11-was-an-inside-job bandwagon. He had also produced DVDs about the existence of an interdimensional portal under Denver International Airport, along with his podcast series about the Freemasonic shadow government's knowledge of the 2012 apocalypse. Although no apocalypse materialized in 2012, Canyon's cottage industry of paranoia was affected not in the least bit. In a four-part "research monograph" on his blog, he explained that December 21, 2012, was not an overt apocalypse, but merely the start of a "sinister new age of darkness."

Cornelia's mind reeled not so much from what Canyon said, but by the bright-eyed, earnest way he said it. "So you believe this granite globe rolling down Powell Street, injuring dozens of people, causing tens of thousands of dollar in damage, was merely a plot to kill *one* person?"

"Absolutely."

"That hardly seems efficient."

"I'm just saying that the perfect way of killing someone is to make it look as much like an accident as possible."

"But you're suggesting the real target is—"

"Colonel Garret Robinson. They were sending him a message."

"About what?"

"That he should keep his mouth shut about the globes."

"Why not just kill Colonel Robinson himself?"

"Because he's probably important for some reason to the successful completion of the conspiracy's end game."

"You realize, Mr. Canyon, that people would still have problems accepting what you're saying. That somehow it doesn't seem to make sense that—"

"Oh, sure. They have been conditioned to think that way. I understand."

"Your critics would say, 'if you want to kill Sarah Robinson to send her father a message, why not do it in an easier way?' Something that doesn't involve rolling a twenty-ton boulder down a busy street and hoping it hits the right person."

There was an infuriating little grin on Canyon's face now. He looked like he was being asked an embarrassingly obvious question, something so simple that he was given no choice but to make his interviewer look like a fool. "The murderers never had the slightest doubt that boulder would hit Sarah Robinson."

"How do you know this?" Cornelia snapped, even though she could hear from Canyon's inflection he had more to add to the story. But she couldn't help it. Could this man really be that cool, that confident, or just dangerously insane enough to sit in front of a camera and recite the most staggering line of absurdity without even trying to offer a single shred of evidence to back anything up? "Can you understand what bothers me, what would bother skeptics so much about what you're saying? Just how do you *know*? Can you prove any of this?"

"We've known for decades that the government, that *world* governments, an interconnected cabal of insiders, have had access to secret technology that defies anything we have been taught about physics and the very laws of nature."

"Have we, Mr. Canyon? *We've* known this? Who exactly do you mean? Where is your evidence for any of the claims you're making?"

"Insiders, whistleblowers, people who have been leaking information about the government's experiments on weather control, mind control, anti-gravity technology, interdimensional travel, and even time travel."

"You mean your network of conspiracy theorists believes that it has been getting reliable — ?"

Now Canyon shook his head, his calm demeanor only slightly rankled. "We prefer *alternate history* to conspiracy theorist. Conspiracy theorist has taken on such a negative connotation."

"But who are these sources?" Cornelia pressed.

"Well, I discuss them on my podcast—"

"You never identify them, correct?" Cornelia cut in once again. It had never been her style to badger interviewees, but trying to get a straight answer out of Canyon was starting to feel like an attempt at handling a drop of liquid mercury.

"I *can't* identify them," Canyon said matter of factly. "But I can assure you that I trust them, and I know they have access to the highest levels and their information is absolutely reliable."

"But you *do* understand why we remain skeptical about the veracity of these sources."

"Sure, I understand skepticism," Canyon said. "And skeptics have long been dismissing everything outside of the ordinary— things like the UFO sightings, cryptids like Bigfoot and the Chupacabra sightings, flying humanoids—as being nothing but lies and hoaxes and mass hallucination. But the fact is that we now have twenty-ton granite globes showing up all over the world, virtually every day, and no one can explain them. Can we seriously look at what happened on Powell Street and say it was a mass delusion? Did a mass delusion kill two people and injure all those—how many people were there?—injure all those other people and wreck those cars and that cable car?"

Cornelia didn't reply immediately because she now felt the distinct sensation of Canyon having kicked her ass with that comment. He was, she knew, mostly right. She still thought the government conspiracy he was peddling was nonsense, but the fact of the matter was that no skeptical argument held water either. The world had spiraled into the *Twilight Zone,* and perhaps an *X-Files*-type government conspiracy explanation was as good as any.

"Well," she said at length, "if you think the government *is* behind this—"

"I think a shadow *world* government is behind this," Canyon cut in this time.

Cornelia heard something harder in his voice now. He must have noticed that she had hesitated, been left without a self-assured retort to his claim. "First of all, if this shadow world-cabal you believe exists is creating and placing all these globes all over the world, then what is their purpose?"

"Cornelia," Canyon said, and paused to look her square in the eyes. His knitted eyebrows made him appear to be worried, but the sound of his voice came across as patronizing. "I have several theories, and they *all* make me very nervous."

"What theories?"

"I think these globes might be symbolic. I think they're sending us a message. I think they're saying, 'Make no mistake about it. The world is ours, and we're making a move to consolidate a hold on the entire planet.'"

"You think we're about to face some kind of a takeover?"

"I absolutely believe it."

"And what else do you believe about the nature of the globes?"

"I think that the technology used to create them will be turned on the world."

"What kind of technology do you think created this?"

"Any number of things the global cabal has been developing for decades, if not centuries," Canyon replied with a weird, eager glint in his eyes.

But the first thing Cornelia thought about was how much footage they were bound to get before this interview was over. It seemed like every sentence to roll off Canyon's tongue was packed with so much unverifiable, over the top nonsense that it couldn't be allowed to go unchallenged. *Just how in the hell,* her mind screamed, *could this global cabal have been working on their super high-tech granite-carving interdimensional technology without anyone finding out?*

"It could involve invisibility cloaks, small black hole and singularity-generating technology, anti-gravity and dark-matter technology, time travel even!"

7.

"So what do you think?" Rick asked after taking a sip of his coffee.

"I think it's bullshit," Cornelia replied without hesitation.

She glanced at her watch, wondering if they were going to get the clearance to proceed to their next interview at the Berkeley campus of the University of California. Dr. Marcus Gunderson, a professor of engineering, had agreed to speak with them today, except his school was now swarming with police. Someone had phoned in a bomb threat early that morning, and now no one was allowed in or out of the university. Gunderson, unfortunately, had already been in his office when the campus lockdown began.

According to the news, word was filtering out that the professor himself might have been the cause of the bomb scare. It wasn't confirmed, but Gunderson had given several interviews about the need to approach the globe phenomenon from a more reasonable and scientific perspective. The point of view, in fact, was what had caught Jerry's eye and what made him want to get the professor on the record. Gunderson conceded that the world was facing a series of events that were beyond the current abilities of science to explain. He had often used the phrase "inadequate scientific measurement devices," Cornelia recalled from the online editions of the *San Francisco Chronicle*. Rather than latch on to preconceived beliefs in supernatural forces, angelic manifestations, or demonic signs, Gunderson was asking for the patient, detached, objective scientific process to offer some sort of empirical accounting for the globes. On the feedback forum of the *Chronicle*'s online page, someone calling himself "Anunnaki Rebel" suggested that "Gunderson and the other tools of the scientific **REPRESSIVE**!!! regime that wants to stand by and see us enslaved by a coming ARMY of off-world CYBORG WARRIORS!!! should be put on a raft and floated out into the middle of the ocean and left to die of thirst and rot for SELLING OUT HUMANITY." Annunaki Rebel, Cornelia wondered, might have been a kindred spirit of the people who beat the Astounding Pike into a bloody mess. Perhaps when beatings no longer sufficed in the effort to save the world, bombs might be the next important step.

"Which part?" Rick asked, snapping Cornelia out of her musings.

"Huh?" Her sleep last night must have been more restless than she recalled. Plus, they had been up at the crack of dawn to prepare for the interview with Bill Canyon. Maybe Rick had the right idea with the coffee all along. She had been content to sit on the park bench and wait until Melinda, Matt, and Tony packed the gear away. Ian and Knight had originally decamped to get everyone who asked some coffee.

"I said which part of Canyon's story is the biggest load of bullshit," Rick repeated. He sat next to her on the bench. "The supernatural part or the conspiracies?"

A sudden trace of the morning breeze swept the aroma of his coffee toward Cornelia.

"I see your point," she replied at length. Although she knew it would be a tough question to answer.

"Something...."

"Something supernatural *is* making these things."

Rick nodded slowly. "And that globe showing up in the middle of the city the way it did just seals the deal, doesn't it?"

Every time she attempted to try and draw the implications of what was happening all around her to their natural conclusions, Cornelia felt the most uncomfortable jolts of adrenaline. She had felt it a lot the previous night, during and right after their discussion of Powell Street and the Hong Kong crime connection. It was adrenaline inspired by fear and dread.

"Yeah," she said. "It's not from around here. But which one of the theories explains it?"

Rick sipped his coffee before replying, "Exactly. What if we find out that the number of cars hit by the globe is the square root of the distance between Bill Clinton's forehead and his chin?"

Cornelia found herself smiling, despite another one of those adrenaline surges. "And that proves it was an inside job orchestrated by a brotherhood of space vampires from Area 51?"

"Whatever it is, it's excellent theater, if nothing else."

"You think?"

Rick raised an eyebrow under a rueful little glance. "It's *profitable* theater."

"How many people do you think are writing books about Area 51 aliens carving these globes?"

"Probably the biggest publishers in New York are fighting over every book with a globe explanation."

He was probably right, Cornelia thought. "No doubt about it."

"No, I don't think there is. It's very profitable theater for everyone." He paused and glanced at her.

Cornelia knew what he was about to say next.

"Including us," he tagged on, not disappointing her. "But I *am* sorry about what happened to your friend."

"Thanks," Cornelia said slowly. "But you're right. It is all good — *and profitable* — theater now…giving air to every crazy speculation."

Rick shrugged with a distant look in his eyes. "That's all everyone's got." Then he glanced at Cornelia again. "Like you told Sarah. One idea is as good as the next."

He was right, she realized. Perhaps the thin line between sensationalism and reason had now disappeared. "And we have a journalistic obligation to get all the ideas out there?"

Rick chuckled. "Journalists? Is that what we are? But yeah, whatever we are, it should be our job to, you know…."

Cornelia recalled old theories from journalism school. "Let the marketplace of ideas thrive?"

"Marketplace of ideas, yeah." Rick gave her an easy grin and nod. "I like that — you should coin that phrase."

Cornelia wasn't sure if he was joking or not, but she couldn't help but realize why he was such a perfect choice for all the shows his agent tried to cast him in. His lack of theatrical training and performing background accented his natural likability. Rick didn't affect charisma, he just had it.

After they both chuckled, in a more somber tone Rick added, "But it's all good enough to get you back in the spotlight. To get your career back."

Cornelia felt something she would have called a *different* type of adrenaline surge. This wasn't motivated by fear, but by the anger she had long worked on suppressing for the sake of her health and sanity. It was the adrenaline surge of resentment, of helplessness, of the rage she felt for being robbed of her reporting career.

"I've thought about that a lot," she said evenly.

"You should," Rick said. "You should take advantage of all this to take back what belongs to you."

If only it didn't involve Sarah, she thought. "Well, it made me feel lousy back there in the hospital yesterday. Like some kind of a mercenary."

"Hey, the colonel has a story to tell. He wants to talk to you. And do you think that piece of crap who got you fired back in Florida's getting the kind of access we are? Jerry's making the play for a possible network deal. Did you hear about that? Get what material we have on the air right away. Either that or turn this whole thing into a theatrical documentary. Let those bastards back in Tampa get a load of that."

The bastards in Tampa were probably trying to mine every angle of the Homestead globe story, Cornelia guessed. They certainly didn't have the opportunity for the kind of exposure and nationwide distribution she had now.

For a moment, though, Cornelia allowed herself to indulge in recognizing another type of adrenaline rush she was feeling. It had been triggered by Rick's words, and it filled her with pleasure. After her breakup with real-estate-agent Barry a year ago, it was so good to hear Rick being so supportive of her career. Although she had long dreaded the idea of being involved in a romantic relationship with a coworker, Rick's words made her reevaluate the concept of karma.

Except she couldn't keep her mind from wandering back to the "globes as engines of fate and karma" stories that had hit the papers and the web since the destruction on Powell Street. Could this have been her *real* share of karma? Cornelia turned the thought over in her mind, but didn't like it. She wanted to push the idea away as forcefully as she could, hoping to focus on the feelings Rick stoked in her instead, but circumstances wouldn't allow it. Cornelia had never believed in the concept of karma until now anyway, and she didn't want the Powell Street incident to change her mind. She would have preferred to have her proximity to Rick make her a believer. What forces of destiny would want to reward her by killing Sarah?

"Theatrical documentary, huh?" Cornelia said at length, and cast a glance at Rick with a dramatically raised eyebrow. "But do you know what *I've* heard?" She paused and teased him with the silence.

"Huh?"

"Book deals for us as well! You ready to write a book?"

Rick coughed forth a sudden burst of laughter. "Me? A book? Come one, I'm just a street cop."

"Back in L.A. you got shafted as much as I did."

Cornelia saw some of the good humor melting off Ballantine's face, just as she'd thought it might.

"I was fired from my show. It happens, right?" he said with cool understatement. But Cornelia knew for a fact that he, too, had gotten cheated out of jobs twice already. Yet he refused to complain about it.

"It was more than that," she said. "The L.A.P.D. turned its back on you as much as Stewie Corcoran and WRND screwed *me* over."

As Cornelia had learned, Rick's life had started veering from law enforcement to show business when his squad car had been summoned one night to intervene in a fight—and possible rape—at one of the cottages of the Chateau Marmont on Sunset Boulevard. When he and his partner, Steve Gaines, arrived at the hotel, they overheard chaotic noise inside the locked cottage. The Marmont staff and security had been afraid to intervene, as the instigator of the ruckus inside might possibly have been holding his victim at knifepoint. It was best to let the professionals disarm the situation.

The melee inside was a college graduation party that had gone to hell. As subsequent news stories would reveal, the head partier — and suspected rapist — was one Llewellyn Barclay of the Beverly Hills oil family. Young Llewellyn had previous run-ins with the law, stories would later elaborate, ranging from a series of drunken fistfights to a "possession with intent to distribute" drug charge against him during his freshman year at Pepperdine University. But not only had the law never punished him beyond a couple of hours of community service (for the drug charge), neither did his family. Kids in the Barclays' social circles, a *People* magazine cover-story would detail, didn't get punished; they were sent to therapy. Thus, after the drug incident, Llewellyn was once again sent to a clinic in Palm Springs where a psychologist was supposed to help him analyze his feelings. As the Chateau Marmont incident demonstrated, Llewellyn Barclay had still not yet understood his feelings for vicious antisocial behavior even by his senior year in college.

After Rick and Steve kicked open the door of the cottage, they found Llewellyn in a hysterical fit and swinging a chair around the room. His victim, a fifteen-year-old Hollywood High School sophomore, was cowering naked under a table, her eyes swollen shut from a couple of Llewellyn's punches. By then, his three Pepperdine-grad friends, who had originally been partying with him, had decamped. One of them, it would later be revealed, had enough of a troubled conscience to call the police when it looked like a drunken and PCP-fueled Llewellyn was going out of control.

Llewellyn's arrest itself was not difficult. Rick could easily subdue him and was just about to put the cuffs on him. Except Rick's problems began when Llewellyn did not exercise his

Constitutionally guaranteed right to remain silent. Instead, the scion of the Barclay family unleashed a string of taunts at *his victim*, promising her that he would not spend a second in jail because of his money and his family's connections in both Sacramento and Washington D.C. A moment later Llewellyn took a clumsy swing at Rick. Reacting purely on instinct, Rick jabbed a fist into the middle of Llewellyn's chest. That jab's precision delivery was ensured by Rick's boxing skills and strength he had built up as a competitive weightlifter in college. The kid, in turn, went down from the punch like a sack.

As the L.A. County Coroner's Office later reported, the punch stopped Llewellyn's heart on impact. The reason it was so easy to fell him, the report explained, was a combination of an undiagnosed heart condition and previous damage done by his drug use. But even before the coroner released his findings, Rick's fate was sealed by a mistake on his part...and then by the Internet.

Going into Llewellyn's cottage, neither Rick nor Steve Gaines had turned on their body cameras. In sexual assault cases, the concern over the victims' privacy had come to trump the public's demands for oversight of the police in the field. No cops had ever gotten into trouble for not turning on their body camera when dealing with a rape victim.

So the only person recording and broadcasting the confrontation with Llewellyn was Llewellyn himself. When his body had arrived at the coroner's office, his smart phone was found in one of his pockets, the device set to a live-streaming app. The phone had recorded and broadcast audio, but not video. The kid's taunts were all recorded, but there was no evidence of the punch he had thrown. His cursing and taunting rant made it sound as if he had provoked Rick until his patience snapped and he slugged Llewellyn. And as the entire incident unfolded, it was shared over and over again on social media.

Seemingly from one moment to the next, the L.A.P.D. did feel the full clout of the Barclay family. The chief of police was notified that the governor himself was interested in a very thorough Internal Affairs investigation, and proving as quickly as possible that the Los Angeles Police Department did not protect rogue, brutal cops.

Then, while Rick was on a paid leave during an I.A. probe, he had his run-in with talent agent Wilt Kamen and a gang of bank robbers in Sherman Oaks. Although suddenly finding himself hailed as a hero, the L.A.P.D. and the district attorney's office urged him to resign with a full pension and benefits in return for them not attempting to prosecute him.

Rick took the deal, and just a little over a year later his television career was under way, thanks to Wilt Kamen. "The producers of this new reality series CBS is interested in, *Hollywood Justice*," Wilt had told Rick, "see this whole Llewellyn Barclay situation differently than the bureaucrats at the L.A.P.D. And guess what? So do many other people out there. People with TV sets. People who think this spoiled little affluenza kid got exactly what he deserved. That perverted little creep was trying to live-stream his rape of that girl. What a piece of garbage! *Many* people out there believe that. And they believe that *you* got unfairly punished."

And for a while, Wilt Kamen was right. *Hollywood Justice* hit the air and Rick was introducing weekly recreations of crimes among the rich and beautiful of Southern California. Not only were the ratings solid to start with, but steadily increasing from week to week. Almost immediately there were talks about spin offs, more *Justice* shows set in exciting, glamorous places. *Hawaii Justice, Miami Justice,* and *New York Justice* were all fast-tracked for development.

And then another cop was accused of taking the law into his own hands.

After a Seattle homicide detective was exposed fabricating evidence against a college football player who had been accused of beating and choking a coed into a coma, the Barclay family resumed its crusade against "rogue police officers acting like judge, jury, and executioner when they happen to run across people they don't like." At the core of a "widespread crisis of police corruption," they argued on every cable news program, radio talk show, and social media platform, was popular culture that kept glamorizing vigilante behavior. The worst such program was *Hollywood Justice*, "hosted by a murderer like Rick Ballantine."

As the barrage of attacks went on for weeks, then months, then more months — the Barclays drawing the support of various anti-police-brutality activists — *Hollywood Justice*'s ratings started to soften. Although the show was still not suffering the kind of dismal viewership that usually got a program cancelled, CBS decided it had enough of the controversy and fired Rick.

But Wilt already had his next move figured out. Getting Rick involved in a paranormal reality series like *Confirmation* was sure to keep him away from any more controversies, Wilt reasoned.

Rick glanced at Cornelia now for a moment before looking off into the distance with a bittersweet smile. "Hey, as Doc Knight would say, getting a smash hit TV series — or whatever all of this is going to lead to — beats the hell out of getting cancer any day."

Sure, it was clever, Cornelia mused, and exactly the sort of leathery, put-upon macho humor Knight would use, but there was something weighty they needed to address right now. "Rick?"

"Yeah?" he said, and sipped his coffee.

"Our guess is as good as another, right?"

Rick turned back to her, a sober, piercing stare beaming out of his eyes. "So what do I think about where all of this is going? I don't know. But…something big, *obviously*."

"Our world as we know it might be ending right now."

Rick raised a skeptical eyebrow, just as Cornelia guessed he would. "Ending? Well, that's a little drastic, don't you think?"

"No. I mean that life, the world — you know, *reality*… everything we thought we knew about how things work — well, it's all going to be turning on its head."

"It's turned on its head already."

"Yeah, with Pike getting beaten up. People like this Canyon guy. Where do you think all this is taking...*us*?"

Rick didn't reply. He just gave a slight, cautious shake of his head and stared off into the distance. Then, at length, he gave her a weary grin and fished a folded-up piece of paper from his shirt pocket. He shook it open with one hand while sipping his coffee. As the paper flapped open, Cornelia recognized it as a copy of the email she, too, had been sent by Garret Robinson. It was an invitation and schedule outline for Sarah's wake and funeral services.

"What?" she asked as she took the paper from him.

"If we want more opinions about what all of this is leading to, let's keep talking to every point of view out there," Rick said with an odd, sour expression on his face. "No matter how nutty they might sound."

"What do you mean?"

"From what you told me about Sarah, she didn't sound like any kind of evangelical."

That was odd, Cornelia thought. "What do you mean? She wasn't. Her religion went as far as putting up a Christmas tree."

Rick pointed at the paper in her hand. "It says the services will be performed by the Reverend Nelson Prouty of the Reconstructionist Faith Chapel."

So it did, Cornelia read on the paper. "I guess her father set all this up. Who are these people?"

"I'm sure they'll have some colorful theories about the globes. So let's try and keep the cameras handy."

"Do you know this Revered Prouty?"

"No. But I know of his church."

"From where?"

"From my ex-wife. Well, I guess my wife-at-the-time some years back. When she left me for a pastor in this group."

8.

"RIOT AFTER FRENCH GLOBE APPEARANCE RAISES

NEW FEARS"
By: Dennis Clemmons, *The New York Times*

The French city of Marseilles witnessed the first acts of violence tied directly to the globe phenomenon sweeping the world.

One of the mystery globes appeared outside an apartment complex in the early morning hours of Saturday, September 8. Once local police forces arrived on the scene, gunfire erupted from the immense complex. Officers reported that snipers had fired on them as they examined the globe.

According to Jean-Pierre Faucheux of the Surete, the French national police, the snipers were members of an ISIS-affiliated terror cell that had been using the apartments as their headquarters.

"This group saw the arrival of the police," Faucheux explained "and they must have assumed they were being raided."

French authorities had been actively pursuing Kamal Aghmati, Issam Battuta, and Tarik Hamed, all three of whom were killed in the five-hour-long firefight.

Aghmati and Battuta were Moroccan nationals wanted for gun-smuggling and the attempted murder of a Toulouse police captain. Hamed, an Algerian, the police believe, was linked to the murder of Andre Bernheim, a Jewish doctor in Paris.

This incident, said Clotilde Pelletier, a reporter for *Le Monde* who has written extensively about terrorism and France's large Muslim immigrant community, just puts the accent on what many see as a powder keg that will keep exploding in that country.

"France, much like the rest of Europe, despite the violence it has seen over the last several years," Pelletier said, "keeps a very tolerant attitude toward the massive influx on African and Middle Eastern and Asian immigrants and refugees. But that, right or wrong, also raises fears of terrorism."

As Paris police commissioner Claude Paget said very bluntly in an interview on the popular *We're on the Record* show,

106

"European countries need to realize some hard truths. Many of these immigrant communities often shield radical elements. Terrorist cells, gun and drug smugglers, and anarchists have easily infiltrated countries like France, the U.K., Germany, Belgium, and many East European nations. How many more massacres like the ones in Paris, in Brussels, in Manchester do we need suffer?"

Others, like Marseilles attorney Herbert Lachapelle, have aggressively objected to defining the Muslim immigrant issue as a terrorism issue. "Islam does not radicalize and it does not create terrorists," Lachapelle wrote in his firm's blog. "But racism, intolerance, and poverty do. Islam means peace. Rather than French society — or European society for that matter — growing outraged and paranoid about terrorism, it should be outraged by its discriminatory policies and attitudes toward immigrant communities. They should be outraged at the unemployment rate among young people, particularly young Muslims, and consider why so many in those communities are so angry."

Lachapelle's firm had defended numerous immigrants against terror charges.

A DANGEROUS CATALYST

"Although this shootout ignited another immigration and terror debate in Europe, the completely unprecedented nature of the globe phenomenon might be the catalyst for a much bigger threat," said Dr. Edward L. Miller, a professor of psychology at Fordham University. "We are dealing with a yet unexplained event with these globes. It has baffled scientists all over the world. Since people fear anything they can't understand, the vacuum of knowledge left by science will quickly be filled with all kinds of spiritual and fringe belief systems. It's the fringe beliefs we must worry about."

The immediate aftermath of the Marseilles incident illustrates Miller's point. A statement posted on the web page of the Tunisian Kairouan Salafist Mosque, an Islamic fundamentalist group, claims that "It is obvious that these objects are the weapons of the devil and they are made to exterminate Islam, to perpetrate genocide against the Arab people. The world speaks of the first acts of violence as a result of these stones. These acts of violence are aimed at the word of Islam."

Iranian cleric Razmara bin Hussein told three thousand followers in a sermon that "The signs of Satan appearing all across the world must be the final call for all Muslims to unite and prepare for the final holy war."

Those who ignore the "obvious" threat of the globes, bin Hussein declared, are pledging themselves to the devil. All who side with the devil, bin Hussein added, must "suffer the punishment of the righteous."

"This sort of rhetoric is very frightening, obviously," says Dr. Martin Parkhurst, an International Affairs Fellow at the Council on Foreign Relations, "because the globe phenomenon has been embraced by so many people, particularly in Europe, as some sort of a positive sign. It's a lot like the American New Age Movement…the way many in Europe see this. You have the theories that they're signs from aliens or positive spiritual beings. So the point is that what do you have all of a sudden when you have one group of people seeing these things, these objects that science is at a complete loss to explain, as some kind of salvation and goodness, and another sees it as the work of the devil?"

CHAPTER 4

Dr. Gunderson's Meltdown. Reunion.
Road Trip. Villagers With Pitchforks.
Chase.

1.

"That son of a bitch," Rick Ballantine mumbled in the middle of the funeral service.

Almost immediately he felt Cornelia's elbow in his side. But he couldn't help it. The images on the small screen of his cell phone, the words in his ears from the ear-bud headphones, were just too frustrating.

When his gaze drifted to Cornelia, the look in her eyes was as sharp as her elbow.

"You're not going to believe this," he mouthed the words more than whispered them.

"...she would have wanted us to find our strength and to use grief for something positive," the voice boomed from the gravesite. "Sarah would have wanted us to rise above our grief and fight the evil that is pulling all of us down."

Rick nudged the volume on his phone higher and touched the triangular arrow on the screen. The YouTube video he had been watching continued to stream.

"I think it's a set-up," Dr. Marcus Gunderson spoke on the screen. "It's part of some anti-science plot...some, some ploy to return this world to the dark ages."

The video was shot by several Berkley journalism students, originally for their campus TV station. They had recently uploaded the segment onto YouTube. They interviewed Gunderson about the globes, the bomb threat, and the campus lockdown.

From what Rick could guess, the professor of engineering had been rattled pretty badly by the incident. The one-time voice of reason and advocate for measured, cautious scientific investigation now sounded like a demented loon. The man who only a day ago might have scoffed at the sort of rococo conspiracy theories Bill Canyon had regaled Cornelia with was now spinning his own yarn about a global cabal of fundamentalist religious fanatics concocting the globe "hoax" to destroy science.

"So there's a logical explanation, you mean?" a very youthful male voice came from off camera.

Gunderson's head snapped to his right. He threw a furtive glance out the window behind him. The interview might have been taking place in his office on the Berkeley campus. Nonetheless, Gunderson looked painfully ill at ease being there. Although the news had reported that the bomb scare was a hoax, perhaps, Rick thought, Gunderson was afraid of the "bombers" coming back and this time trying to kill him for real.

"I guess," Gunderson said, glancing out the window again. He had the unpleasant look of a terrified animal caught in a trap frozen onto his face. "I mean, there absolutely has to be," he said, his gaze darting back toward the camera. "No doubt about it."

"So what is it?" the student asked very calmly. Perhaps he, too, was getting worried about the professor's unhinged behavior.

Gunderson shrugged helplessly. "I don't know."

Although Rick had at first been angry to see this video— Gunderson promised the *Confirmation* team an interview first— he was starting to feel fortunate that *they* were not the ones having to deal with this scattershot meltdown.

"Well, Professor," said the interviewer, "Whoever is behind this somehow managed to pull off the greatest hoax in the history of the world, right? If it is a hoax."

Gunderson's eyebrows knitted together. "But of course it's a hoax."

"As a professor of engineering, how do you think the hoax

was done?"

Gunderson continued glaring at the camera without answering.

"I mean," the kid behind the camera said, his voice sort of tentative now. "Many other people have tried to guess how it was done, but no one could explain it yet. As an expert in engineering, how would you say the hoaxers pulled it off?"

Rick thought the students had been asking good questions so far. Now he hoped they wouldn't let the *esteemed expert* intimidate them into softball questions.

"I don't know how it was done," Gunderson said, a peevish, defensive edge to his voice. "Whoever did this must have spent enormous amounts of money on his — or their! — scheme."

How much money would it take to place dozens of these globes all over the world, you jackass? Rick wanted to yell at the screen.

"But what I do know," said Gunderson, "is the sort of insidious, dangerous effect it's had on the world."

"Can you talk about that?" the interviewer asked.

"We're just about on the verge of a holy war breaking out because of Islamic fanatics. We've had death threats against science professors. Bomb scares! I heard of a story where a man undergoing cancer treatment snuck out of the hospital to try and find one of the globes. He thought aliens were about to land, cure him, and fly him off to some sort of a paradise on the moons of Jupiter. Is that dangerous enough for you?"

"I think, Professor, that the process — you know, the mechanics of making these globes and putting them in the middle of a crowded city like they did here in San Francisco — just seems impossible to hoax."

That was a great point the kid made, Rick thought.

"At one time people thought crop circles were impossible to hoax."

That's not an answer, you asshole, Rick thought. *Come on, kid, you have to follow up if you ever want a job in the big leagues.*

"Well then, how are they doing all this?"

Rick was grinning now.

And then he would have sworn to God that he actually *felt* Cornelia's eyes on him. His eyes turned to her and, sure enough, she was glaring at him.

"I'll explain later," he whispered.

"Can't that wait at all?" she hissed more than whispered her reply. "Just a few more minutes, for Christ's sake?"

"Trust me."

"I don't know how they're doing it," Gunderson said. "But what's more important is what's happening. What this is doing to our world. People turning against each other. People turning against science and embracing all kinds of absurd, irrational, unprovable nonsense."

Of course, Rick considered, Gunderson himself was now making the same demand of *his* audience. He expected them to accept an unproven — and perhaps *unprovable* — assertion. Neither he nor any of the other militant skeptics could offer any plausible explanation for the origin of the globes. Sure, many of them made *probabilistic* arguments, claiming that the globes had to be made by an earthly source because there was no believable evidence to suggest that the supernatural existed. There was no evidence — or at least no evidence people like Gunderson or Pike or their likeminded colleagues *accepted* — that UFOs or ghosts or demons or elemental earth spirits were real. Thus, in all probability, whatever was behind the globes *had* to be something mundane. Like a hoax.

It reminded Rick of a sculptor in Vermont who also believed that the entire phenomenon was an epic, world-wide hoax. To prove his point, he went to work carving an exact replica of one of the mystery globes. In several interviews he gave during his project, he kept espousing the tenets of Occam's Razor to get his audiences to accept his hoax theory. All things being equal, Occam's Razor argues, the simplest solution to any problem is bound to be the correct solution. If he could replicate the stone globe, the sculptor argued ever more vehemently in each subsequent interview, then Occam's Razor held and the most logical explanation for the phenomenon was a hoax.

Except the sculptor's argument in this case was a bastardization of Occam's Razor. And replication did not necessarily mean a valid alternative explanation. That the globes had to be a part of a hoax because the sculptor could reproduce them was an erroneous argument. There were hundreds of conspiracy nuts all over the Internet, after all, who claimed that the moon landings could be perfectly replicated on sound stages on Earth. Certainly such replication was possible, but that did not mean that there was any serious reason to believe that the moon landings were government-orchestrated hoaxes. So, unless that sculptor could knock out dozens of globes in his home studio and deposit them in the middle of busy streets without anyone noticing, his argument had no weight.

And Gunderson's hoax rants rang just as hollow.

Except, Rick thought, *the crazy bastard does make one great point. What all of this is doing to the world is getting more and more disturbing.*

"So what was so important that it couldn't wait another minute?" Cornelia said, and nudged Rick.

He noticed people getting out of their seats now. He had been so focused on the video on his phone that he didn't even realize the service had come to an end. Sarah's casket was being lowered into the ground.

Rick quickly yanked the headphones from his ear and shoved the phone into his pocket. "It was Marcus Gunderson. He gave an interview to a couple of journalism students instead of us."

"I'm sure we can get something from him as well," Cornelia said as they got to their feet. "We're not airing our interviews immediately, after all."

"Yeah, you're right. And besides, Gunderson seems to have slipped the tracks."

"What?"

"I think that bomb threat freaked him out too much. He

sounded like a raving nut."

"How bad did he—?"

"Look, never mind," Rick cut her off as he scanned the funeral crowd. "You know, what I'm wondering about is how did that pastor manage to get set up to conduct the service here."

Cornelia shrugged. "I don't know. Pastor Prouty, was it...?"

"No, that wasn't Prouty. Remember what one of the people said when we got here?"

"No."

"Prouty had taken ill. But look, you said that Sarah was not very religious, and back at the hospital the other day the colonel certainly didn't sound like the type who was looking at all this like some great divine message or sign or something."

Cornelia didn't reply immediately, apparently mulling over the issue. "I'm not sure," she said at length. "Maybe it was Sarah's mother's wish. Or her brother, Jeff. He's in the air force, too."

"That would explain it," Rick said, looking around, hoping they could just drift away from the funeral but knowing full well they couldn't yet go anywhere. There was still work to be done here. They had to keep documenting the event. They needed to capture the human drama. They had to ask people questions on camera.

"Why?" Cornelia asked. "What's the problem?"

"It's just that I'm not in the mood for an old family reunion, that's all."

But it was too late for that, Rick realized, noticing the familiar face from across the crowd.

"Reunion?" But Cornelia caught herself. "You don't mean...."

"Yes, I do mean. The man we just listened to doing the service, Pastor Burke, just happens to be married to my ex-wife. And now I think they might say hello."

2.

At that moment, more than anything in the world, Rick wished that conspiracy-theory crackpot, Bill Canyon, could have been at the funeral services. Rick would have loved to have smacked him in the face and asked him if he still believed that there were no coincidences in the world.

Now the wildest coincidence stood right in front of him. His ex-wife, Lindsay, had come over to say a polite "hello" to Rick and to wish him well on his reality-show.

"So you're still sticking with show biz," Lindsay said her in usual soft, mellifluous delivery, a placid, beatific smile on her face. With that voice and that smile, Rick used to joke that she should have been cast as Mr. Roger's granddaughter and PBS could have kept its children's show going as *Ms. Rogers' Neighborhood.* Lindsay used to find it funny for a while, but once her regrets over having abandoned her acting aspirations turned into a festering resentment, she had taken to cutting Rick's comparison off with a sharp "Would you give that idiotic joke a rest already?"

"That's very interesting," she added a beat later.

Years ago those comments would have ignited one of their fights. Rick would have interpreted it as one of her accusations of infidelity, an accusation rooted in her disdain for Los Angeles and her resentment that he did not want to leave the city. Their problems had started with Rick's first brush with filmmaking, well before Wilt Kamen and two years into their marriage. Rick and several other patrolmen at his station had been approached to serve as extras on a film shooting in and around Santa Monica. Soon after their scenes started filming, however, they were given a few short lines to speak. The director liked to fancy himself as being "edgy." He usually cast a lot of cops and ex-cons in his films for authenticity. Rick's enjoyment of the experience, though, turned into a corrosive drop of poison in his and Lindsay's relationship.

Lindsay had been a drama and English double major at Tulane University, and moved to Los Angeles to try her hand at stardom after college. Less than a year later she was disillusioned with the brutal competition in the business and quit. She went back to earn a teaching certification from Cal State Fresno, and started a new career teaching English and social studies in a Tarzana elementary school.

Rick and Lindsay had started dating after being introduced by his first partner's wife. Louie and Elise DeFalco had a daughter in Lindsay's English class, and they met her at one of the parent-teacher conferences. Elise had often recalled how she took one look at the pretty young teacher and felt a "vibe" about her being right for Rick. Elise also usually swore up and down that she wasn't the "typical kooky new age type." But Rick and Lindsay *had* hit it off perfectly on their first date, and four months later they were engaged.

Shortly after they met, though, Rick sensed that Lindsay regretted giving up her acting aspirations too soon. But, he reasoned, was there really anyone out there who didn't regret not going after at least one outlandish dream? He didn't suspect, however, how regret tended to metastasize into bitterness in some people.

"It's a good gig," Rick said, making the effort to sound as mellow as he could. Although seeing the Gunderson interview had irritated him just enough to want to add "*So by interesting you mean you're regretting not sticking around a little bit longer?*" He also would have loved to have added, "*And was that vague email from you last month official notice that your lawyer was no longer suing me for that one missed alimony check from three years ago, from before you and Pastor Don were married?*" "So how come your husband's taking part in this?" he asked instead.

"Donald's a friend of Pastor Prouty, who's not feeling well."

"That's too bad," Rick replied, still stunned by the fact that Lindsay and her husband had ended up in the San Francisco area, and the coincidence behind their brush with the globe phenomenon. "Do you know Sarah?"

"Not personally, no."

"She was a friend of Cornelia's. That's one of my cohosts."

"Oh, I know," Lindsay said with another one of her thin, enigmatic hints of a smile. "Small world, right? You looked very close back there. Are you…?"

Rick almost couldn't believe what he was hearing. His blood pressure spiked. "What?" he said as evenly as he could.

"I'm sorry," Lindsay said, her smile more obvious this time, looking reconciliatory, apologetic. "Never mind, OK?"

Rick, though, *could* mind, no matter how much his better nature told him it was childish to keep dwelling on old slights. They had, after all, allowed their marriage to fall apart. But it frustrated him to realize that this line of dialogue was exactly like all the ones that had led to their explosive fights and sullen, sulking resentment of each other.

The fact was that in Los Angeles it could be hard to avoid the intrusion of show business into their lives. Besides of the gig as the speaking extra, Rick had also done several moonlighting stints on security jobs for film sets and at celebrity parties. Lindsay at first didn't want to know anything about the details, then conducted interrogations of Rick, wanting to know whether any women were hitting on him and how many women he talked to at the parties. The trouble in the marriage became obvious, and had come to the forefront of their everyday lives when Rick confronted her with a question about her insecurity. Was she really taking her regrets out on him? Was she unhappy with her life because she didn't have enough courage and fortitude to pursue her acting career?

But now Rick knew there was no point in going back to old, frustrating territory. There was information he needed from Lindsay, and he needed to concentrate on the job. "Look, what I'm wondering about is this ceremony. From what I understood, Sarah was not very…you know, very religious."

And he was but deluding himself, he knew, the moment the words came out of his mouth, if he thought this conversation was going to go anywhere other than back to old, painful places.

"Her brother, Jeff, requested it," Lindsay said.

As she did so, Rick's gaze had already darted away for a couple of moments. He was searching for sight of her husband.

That, too, Rick knew, was but some self-destructive impulse right now. He'd already had to listen to the man deliver the service. If Rick would see the Pastor Donald Burke anywhere nearby, he would get the old urges to slug him into insensibility.

"He knows Pastor Prouty." Lindsay's voice disrupted that vicious little thought slithering through his mind. "Jeff has been saved, and I guess he was able to persuade their father to listen to what Pastor Prouty and Don have to say about these globes."

Adrenaline surged through Rick now. "Oh?"

"That they're a danger. They're evil. My God, who would have thought Armageddon would be ushered in like this."

Try as he might, Rick was unable to separate the business at hand from their past. Maybe he had been a fool to think for even a moment that it was possible. It was Lindsay's "salvation" at the hands of the Pastor Burke that had ended their marriage, after all.

Lindsay, in her own way, was *exactly* like so many of the directionless, wannabe starlets, despite the fact that she had stopped pursuing roles less than a year after moving to L.A. She had gone through several phases while they were together. It appeared to be clear to Rick now in hindsight. Although Lindsay had stopped auditioning, she, too, had still quested to find an identity for herself. The first identity she had tried on was that of the dedicated educator. It was quite attractive, Rick had thought at the time, and told her often. He thought he was convincing when he said that he found an idealistic teacher more attractive than a glamorous TV or movie star. Nonetheless, the problem, Rick thought now, was that Lindsay hadn't become the teacher entirely out of idealism. She quit trying to make it as an actress because she had been intimidated by the business, and she reinvented herself as the first convenient thing she could think of.

Then Rick's brushes with Hollywood came and Lindsay's insecurities and regrets were unleashed. At that point, her feminist phase started and lasted very briefly. She had enrolled in a teacher-education program at a community college, taking a course in how to teach the critical examination of pop culture. As

Rick recalled her "media literacy" textbooks, the course seemed to blame everything but earthquakes on TV and advertising. She realized, she had said, that her acting career never really took off because she didn't have the right body type demanded by all the misogynistic male casting agents.

Nevertheless, the feminist media critic phase didn't hold Lindsay's interest for long either. After she had been invited to a Bible-study meeting by one of the teachers in her media-literacy class, she started her journey to "salvation." The Bible-study group led her to realize, she said, that she was trapped in a world of superficial, material distractions. Her soul, she explained, was withering away. She told Rick that they needed to get away from a place like Los Angeles. She wanted to move someplace smaller, slower-paced, a community where they could start a family and instill spirituality in their children while shielding them from all the amoral, vapid commercial values of Los Angeles. By that time, Lindsay had been regularly attending the Reconstructionist Faith Chapel.

How she could go from the feminist phase to the Reconstructionists Rick had a hard time figuring out for a while. He had attended a couple of services with Lindsay, and concluded that the group was like a collection of malicious Smurfs. They seemed charming and friendly enough on the surface — sometimes even overbearingly so — but you couldn't help but feel there was something threatening underneath. Moreover, one of the main tenets of their faith was the recognition of and respect for God's different plans for the genders. God had meant men to fulfill one role in society and the family, the group preached, and women another, and there were no two ways about it. Women, the Reconstructionists believed, were "blessed" to have been allowed by the Almighty to create life, and were entrusted to nurture children in the home.

Perhaps, Rick wondered in time, the group's committed hatred of the mainstream media in general and Hollywood in particular was what had swayed Lindsay so suddenly. But she had quickly turned into a devout follower and begged him to move away from Los Angeles and resettle in the small northern California town of Tulare. They could buy a house there, Lindsay explained, Rick could either get a job on the local police force or look for something else—she acknowledged that the Tulare Police Department might not have paid as well as the L.A.P.D.— and she would become a stay at home mom. When Rick told her that he was thinking of going back for a master's degree and pursuing a detective's rank, their strained relationship began to fracture. Pastor Donald Burke, however, running regular family counseling sessions at the church, had offered to be a friend and a confidant to Lindsay.

"Well, I hardly think there's reason to believe it's the Armageddon just yet," Rick said at length.

He said it with a light inflection, and when he saw the darkening look on Lindsay's face, he knew he had said it too lightly.

"How can you say that?" she replied. She had that wide-eyed incredulity in her tone that had so frustrated him back in the days when she was being sucked deeper and deeper into the Reconstructionist Church. It was the sort of incredulity marking her words when she used to ask him, "What do you mean you think my friends are insane when they say they're not sure that dinosaurs ever existed?" "Look at the deaths these globes caused. And there will be more, you can bet on *that*."

"This was an accident," Rick said more evenly this time.

"Come on! You're not one of these people grasping at straws about how there's a scientific explanation for this, are you? You can't possibly believe that it's all a hoax."

It was interesting how Lindsay reacted so strongly to the hoax theory. She had been eventually convinced that all the dinosaur fossils found around the world were a part of a massive conspiracy by scientists—funded by a global Satanic network— to discredit the Bible in a plan to pave the way for the coming of the Antichrist. "No, of course I don't believe it's a hoax," he said.

"So what *do* you believe, Rick? I mean, yeah, I didn't think you were trying to prove that this is all just some mass delusion, with this occult show you're participating in."

Oh, boy, the occult again, Rick thought. But that was exactly how she was bound to characterize *Confirmation* now. When Lindsay decided to devote herself to any one of these reimagined personas, she would commit one hundred percent. Shortly before their divorce, they had fought over whether or not to give candy to kids trick-or-treating. Participating in the Satanic holiday, Pastor Burke had concluded after years of careful scriptural research, was sure to sentence one to eternal damnation. Any interest in ghosts, psychics, fortune-telling, tarot cards, UFOs, Wicca, or new age music was occultic and thus Satanic.

"I'm after the truth. And I don't *know* what to believe. This is a mystery, and so far I haven't heard any explanation that seems to make sense, to be perfectly honest. And I sure as hell don't think that it's the Biblical Apocalypse."

Of course, before the last words came out of his mouth, he realized he'd handed Lindsay a perfect comeback.

"Sure as *hell*, Rick?"

"I don't seem to recall anything in Revelation about stone globes."

There was a smile on Lindsay's face now, but it was taut and bitter. "I'm impressed. You know where the Bible talks about the end of the world. You saw that in a documentary on the *History Channel?*"

"No. Saint Anthony's Catholic High School. The Jesuits told me all about it. Even though I'm sure you and Don don't take the Catholic Church seriously, because it's not medieval enough."

"Like *you* take it seriously...."

"Lindsay, look, what I'm saying—to answer your question— is that we have an unknown phenomenon on our hands. And so far, from what I've seen, the real danger is not in the globes themselves—"

"Come on—!"

"It's in *us*! Do you understand? In everyone's preconceived B.S. dogma they're trying to graft onto these things."

Lindsay shook her head and looked away in obvious disgust. "This is unbelievable."

"You can't believe what people are capable of doing to—?"

Lindsay's gaze snapped back onto Rick. "What makes these globes appear? Huh? What? What did it? What placed them all over the world? *What* is responsible? That's the evil at work here. What is the agenda behind all this?"

"What does that matter right now? It's *people* who are about to go at each other's throats. Go ask that magician, Pike. Go ask the people who thought they were justified in beating him half to death."

Lindsay's shoulders twitched in a dismissive shrug. "Well, they're obviously a bunch of crazed cultist fanatics. So what's that got to do with anything? Crazy people do—and always did—crazy things. What matters right now, for the whole world, is the supernatural, *evil* force that's behind these globes."

"No, it's not...."

"It's not?" Lindsay snapped.

Rick thought she was about to yell at him.

"Oh, for crying out loud," Lindsay said. "Would *you* open your eyes? Oh, and by the way, those new age or paranormal nuts who beat up that magician probably worship these ghost-hunting and UFO occultist shows you're filming right now. Have you ever thought about that?"

"Have *I* ever thought about that?"

"That's what I said."

"Have *you* ever thought about what's the big difference between you and them? You seem to be just as convinced that you're right and you're on the side of the angels, as your so-called occultist—"

"All right," Lindsay cut him off and took a step away from him. Aside from the anger in her eyes, Rick thought he could see something like...hurt? "I've just about had it with this."

"Lindsay," Rick said, trying to sound somewhat conciliatory this time. Of course, he knew it would do no good. "Can't you understand what you're doing—?"

"I understand what *you're* doing," she cut him off. "Attacking my faith just like you did during our marriage."

"Oh, come on! That's not quite how it happened, as I recall."

By the time the last words were out of his mouth, he no longer sounded conciliatory. And he no longer wanted to. At the same time, his eyes wandered the crowd, trying to see if Lindsay's husband, that little shit, was anywhere nearby. Had Don Burke seen his wife talking to her ex-husband? It was more likely that he was getting a rush out of rubbing elbows with the military people at the funeral. The Reconstructionist Faith Church loved the military, and tried pulling soldiers into the fold as much as the Scientologists loved celebrities. The U.S. military, they believed, had to be remade into literal "Christian soldiers."

"That's exactly how it happened," Lindsay said.

"No, what I was attacking, what I *objected* to, was the Pastor Donald Burke fucking my wife. That's what I objected to."

Rick would have been the first one to admit that there was a grotesque, comedic irony to the final breakup of their marriage. Lindsay ultimately embarked on an affair with her pastor, Don Burke, who at the time also happened to be married. A moralistic preacher who could sermonize a storm for hours about traditional family values, who decried America's moral decline, who believed contraception was a Satanic practice, wrecked two marriages because he couldn't keep his hands off Rick's wife. How this self-proclaimed "moral warrior" could justify his behavior, though, had its own unassailable logic. "God has a plan and a life partner for each and every one of us," Lindsay had explained to Rick when she told him that she wanted a divorce. "None of us listened to what God was saying—speaking to us in our hearts—when we married the people we did. Can you understand that, Rick? The fact that we had so many problems, that I wasn't comfortable in our relationship, that Don just knew in his soul that he had not married the right woman, is proof that we did not find our proper life partners in the very beginning. But try and believe, Rick, that in the end you will see that everything happens for a reason." That, in both Lindsay's and Burke's reckoning, had justified their cheating on their spouses for over six months.

After their divorce, the only time Rick ever got a piece of personal correspondence from Lindsay—everything else had come from her lawyer—was when she sent him a "words of encouragement" card in the midst of the Llewellyn Barclay fiasco. "One day you will see a reason for everything," she had written.

"I'm through," Lindsay said, recoiling from him. "Have a nice day, have a nice *life*, Rick. Go and enjoy yourself with your beautiful new TV star girlfriend. She's the woman of your dreams, I'm sure."

"For your information, she's not my girlfriend, OK?" Rick said, and if he wouldn't have sensed that near-palpable hatred radiating off Lindsay, he wouldn't have added, "But yes, I do like her a lot, and care for her a lot, and respect her hard work. That's where the two of us stand. I *respect* her as a colleague, and the way she's pursuing her dreams despite setbacks that would have defeated so many other people."

Lindsay stared at Rick before replying. Her hatred did not seem to subside. But, of course, Rick couldn't have expected it to. "You know what, Rick?" she said at length. "Fuck you!"

After Lindsay stalked away, balancing precariously over the grassy ground in her steep high heels, Rick noticed soft footsteps behind him. When he turned, he saw Cornelia. The awkward look on her face revealed that she must have heard a lot of the exchange. Especially the last parts.

"Well," Rick said, "I didn't handle that as well as I wanted to."

"I'm sorry I intruded on that."

"Like I said, I was curious about what…people like her and her husband were, you know, doing here."

"Oh?" Cornelia said cautiously.

"Let's just say their take on the globes is as disturbing as some of the weirdest things we've heard so far. I bet Jerry'll tell us to get them on the record too."

"No doubt. But look, Rick, I just came over to tell you that something's come up that you should know about."

"What's that?" he asked, a bit of relief flooding through him. It would have been nice to steer away from the uncomfortable topic of Lindsay Burke.

"Come on. We should go and talk to the other guys."

Rick gave her a quick nod.

As they started back toward their partners, Cornelia said, "Thanks, by the way. That's very nice what you said back there."

Rick noticed a tiny hint of a smile in the corners of her lips.

3.

"Dude, it's a standoff, man!" Ian called from the passenger seat behind Cornelia.

Rick took his eyes off the road for a moment, firing his glance at Cornelia next to him, then at Ian behind her. The two of them seemed to have a dueling-tablets competition going on, racing to find the latest breaking news out of the Noe Valley neighborhood.

"It's not *quite* a standoff," Cornelia replied.

"It's a bunch of people about to tear the whole block apart," Knight said from the seat behind Rick. "That's all anyone knows, and we'll know for ourselves in…what? How long 'til we get there?"

Rick wished they wouldn't keep asking him that. They would know as much as he did if they glanced at the GPS system on the dashboard. "I'm *not* from San Francisco," he replied as he gunned the engine again, darting through the yellow light of an intersection. "We'll get there as soon as we do."

"So then why are *you* driving?" Melinda called from the back seat behind Knight and Ian.

"The sixty-four-thousand-dollar question, ain't it?" Tony Griffin, wedged in between her and Matt Cooper, mocked.

Rick had the urge now to reach behind him, grab someone's tablet, and smack Tony in the face with it.

"Because he thinks having been a cop makes him the best driver on the team," Cornelia mumbled, still not dissuaded from scanning the online news sites on her own tablet.

Knight barked forth a derisive laugh from the back seat.

"You want to take the wheel, Doc?" Rick shot back, and couldn't help adding, "Maybe driving getaway cars was better training for this."

"I *know* it was," Knight replied, his voice sharp and challenging apart from just sarcastic.

"All right," Rick called through gritted teeth now as he hurtled the Ford F-150 SUV through another yellow light just as it turned red. "Could the comedy routine come to an end now, if that's quite all right? Anyone's more than welcome to walk."

"Yeah, good idea," Cornelia said.

The dead-seriousness in her voice made an impression on Rick. She was about to follow up with something crucial, so he said nothing.

"There are shots being fired out of the house and *into* the house," Cornelia said at length.

Out of the periphery of his vision, Rick could see Knight lean forward. He could feel the tension ratcheting up in the vehicle.

"OK," Cornelia went on, "so this seems to be the most complete information so far: This is the house of one of the guys involved in the start of the Powell Street chain reaction—"

"At the top of the hill?" Lacey called from the back of the SUV. "Where the globe started rolling?"

"Yes, that's right," said Cornelia, eyes and fingers skimming over the surface of her iPad. "There were two cars, remember? One hit the other. The other hit the globe and the globe went down the hill. So we're dealing with the guy who rear-ended the first car."

Rick, of course, had figured as much. When Cornelia dragged him away from the cemetery, she did say that some kind of an armed standoff underway in the Noe Valley might have been globe-related. It had to have something to do with Powell Street, he had reasoned.

"So get this…," Cornelia went on.

"Holy crap," Rick heard Ian say quietly. He, too, Rick thought, must just have come across the same information Cornelia was relaying.

"The guy in the middle of the standoff's a fugitive," Cornelia said. "Convicted sex-offender from Missouri. Statutory rape and child porn charges."

"This guy's toast," Ian mumbled. "They're gonna kill him by the time we get there. They're gonna mess him up."

"What happened?" Rick asked, glancing at Cornelia.

"During the police investigation of the crash, his criminal record turned up," she said. "*And* it leaked."

"His neighbors found out about it?"

"Yeah! And they're trying to evict him," Cornelia added.

"Evict him? Hell, they're trying to kill him," Ian said.

"Holy crap is right," Rick heard Lacy say.

He glanced in her direction in the rearview mirror. She was looking at Ian's tablet over his shoulder.

"This is a lynch mob," Lacy said. "Old-school horror movie shit. Villagers with the pitch forks."

"She's right," Cornelia said. "A group of neighbors tried to kick his door down and drag him out. Looks like he has a gun and started shooting. And some neighbors seemed to have guns, too, and *they're* shooting back."

"What about the cops?" Knight asked.

4.

"Cops got here in the middle of the whole thing," one of the neighbors, a forty-something man in an Oakland A's T-shirt, said. "Too late to stop *this*—"

The man's words were cut off by six rapid-fire pops that sounded like semiautomatic rifle rounds. Everyone instinctively ducked behind the SUV.

As Rick scanned the block, so did everyone else, all the locals already occupying covered positions behind the cars parked along the two sides of the street. But he noticed Matt and Tony aiming their cameras, respectively, over the hood of the F-150 and around its rear.

"Unreal," Matt gasped.

"Watch your head!" Rick warned as he flattened against the rear of the SUV and glanced through its windows and up the block toward the source of the police standoff.

Knight, Cornelia, Melinda, and Lacy were crouched beside the vehicle on its sidewalk side. The Ford faced nose upward on the steep one-way street, parked on the left side.

"The hell is that?" Knight asked, trying to peer up and toward the standoff at Rawley Heiser's—the unregistered sex-offender's—house. "Are the cops storming the house?"

Rick tried to figure that out, tried to get a glimpse around the police cars some one-hundred feet away as more shots rang out. They had to have been Heiser's shots, he reasoned. Rick couldn't see any of the patrol cops with automatic rifles. He wondered if Heiser had been planning for such an assault one day, and gotten ahold of a high-powered rifle like an AR-15 or M-16.

"No, I think he's coming out," the man in the A's T-shirt, who had also taken cover at the rear of the SUV, said.

Rick noticed him glancing around the rear of the vehicle and over Matt's shoulder. "Watch yourself!" Rick warned. "Get down."

The local did as suggested, crouching and dodging back toward the sidewalk.

"What's he got in there?" Lacy said. "An arsenal?"

"Naw!" the local replied. "All he had was a pistol."

"That doesn't sound like a—," Lacy started replying, but got cut off by another shot and the sound of cracking glass overhead.

"Shit!" Rick gasped, and crouched down. A round must have passed through the SUV's windshield and exited out its rear window.

"Watch your heads!" Dan Knight growled. "Get down! Forget the camera!" he yelled at Tony, who was still shooting over the hood of the vehicle.

"Jerry's gonna be pissed," Tony replied with a wild, weird, elated inflection.

His adrenaline kicking into overdrive, Rick guessed.

"Another messed up SUV," Matt said. "Jerry's not gonna be a happy camper."

"And that ding-dong up there's got more than a pop-gun," Lacy added.

"No," called the local in the A's T-shirt. "That was Manny Sifuentes' assault rifle." Rick and his group glanced at the man. "One of our neighbors," the guy said as more rifle fire erupted.

Then they all heard return fire from the cops. And more rifle shots answered in kind, dinging metal and breaking glass on the cars all around.

"Manny tried to rush the house," the A's fan explained, now almost flat against the sidewalk.

"Rush the house?" Cornelia said as more shots rang out.

Rick was sure he heard at least two rounds slice the air overhead. "Get down on the ground!" he yelled. "Everybody! Matt, goddamn it, get down before you get your head blown off."

Matt lowered to his knees, but kept his camera pointed toward Heiser's house.

"What in the hell was going on here?" Knight asked, looking at the guy in the A's shirt. "Why'd Manny...uh...what the hell his name, rush the house?"

"To take the son of a bitch out," the local said very matter-of-factly.

Two rounds broke some glass somewhere very close.

"Sick fucker," the local gasped. "The sick bastard had a pistol in there. He was waving it around. Threatening to start shooting people. Then he did. Just shot at the crowd—"

What sounded like the deep bellow of a police shotgun

blasted to life somewhere close to Heiser's house.

"The crowd...right," Rick heard Knight say with something of an ironic, deflated realization to his tone. "This all started," Knight added, "because the vigilante mob went to get some justice, huh?"

"Someone had to," A's T-shirt replied, that same matter-of-factness in his words. "Sick son of a bitch's been living here and no one's done a damned thing. But then we found out all about it. Thanks to that globe. Thank God for that globe — "

His words were cut off by an ear-drum-punishing blast of sound. Then the shock and heat waves followed. Glass was shattering, flying, spearing, tearing all around.

5.

As Rick started discerning individual sounds beyond the ringing in his ears, he was sure he heard the sounds of popping gunshots again. And they might have been getting closer.

"Holy Christ!" he thought he heard Knight saying. "They blew up the house."

As a matter of fact, aside from the noise of screams, cries, and car alarms blaring everywhere, they were all being assaulted by the acrid tang of smoke.

As Rick raised his head from the ground and glanced straight up, the blue, sunny skies were mottled by shape-shifting patches of black smoke. He wanted to get up, get his bearings and figure out what had happened, except the blasts of gunfire worried him.

"Is everyone OK?" he yelled at length. "Anyone hurt?"

He thought he heard random male and female voices calling "OK," "no," and "yeah," but couldn't be sure of who said what.

Someone screaming "Watch out!" cut through the rest of the din. Then he noticed Melinda beside him, slapping a strong hand on his left shoulder and pulling him back down to the pavement before he could stand up.

Once again, rapid-fire rounds struck their SUV. Then two more shots sailed overhead and hammered the wood and plaster of the brownstone behind them.

"He's making a run for it," Melinda said.

"Coming this way!" Matt gasped from his hiding place, still at the rear of the SUV. "Oh, shit! He's still got a gun...."

Rick pulled free of Melinda's grasp and glanced through the shattered remains of the Ford. What he saw in the direction of Rawley Heiser's house—or, rather, as they had found out from Cornelia's and Ian's in-transit research, his rented apartment on the second floor of a duplex—made little sense. The street up there looked as if it had been bombed. The far side of Heiser's building was charred black, its windows shattered, siding ripped off and strewn across the street, flames shooting out the windows. The police cruisers surrounding the area had been showered by debris, the cops dazed and either crouching or sitting on the ground.

Except one man up there still had his bearings, and he was still putting up a fight.

Rawley Heiser, I presume, Rick thought, seeing a short, blocky man in a pair of khakis and a blue T-shirt rushing away from the scene, approaching the *Confirmation* team's side of the street and clutching what indeed looked like an AR-15 assault rifle.

The words "gas explosion" trilled over the chaos.

Then a running woman on the other side of the street shrieked and tried to sprint away. Her movement, Rick noticed, caught Heiser's attention, spurring him to spin around and take three random shots at her. The woman disappeared behind one of the parked cars. She had ducked, Rick guessed, rather than been hit by Heiser's fire.

And then what felt like a body blow, followed by a searing wash of heat and near-deafening noise, came from up the street again. Debris sailed all around. What people Rick could still see standing, or in some form of a semi-crouch, must have been screaming or crying. He couldn't quite discern the sounds from the shock of noise.

But this time he did remain upright—or in a crouch beside the

SUV, precisely—to see a debris-outlined blob of yellow and black fire roil across the street on his left. The house next to Heiser's duplex had exploded. As it did so, it picked up two cars parked in front of it and flung them across the street. One of the vehicles, after spiraling through the air, slammed into a police cruiser.

Rick felt hands tugging on his shoulder again, urging him back down into a defensive position behind the F-150. It was either Melinda or Cornelia, he guessed, but didn't really pay attention. He tried to see what was going on in the middle of the street. What was Heiser up to? Could he, too, have been knocked down the by explosion.?

Gas explosions! Christ! The thoughts rushed through Rick's mind. The gas piping into Heiser's house must have been ruptured in the shootout. The first explosion probably spread the fire and the damage along the gas lines. *Will this spread? Is the whole block going up house by house?*

"We have to get out of here," he said, suspecting that no one would hear him. Everyone else next to him must likewise have had their hearing shot by the gas blasts. He had to communicate with the rest of his crew, Rick told himself, but he couldn't help but look for Rawley Heiser again. And he saw the lunatic rising to his feet in the middle of the street. Heiser still had his rifle in his right hand, but now it swung at his side.

"Get in the car!" Rick heard a shout that sounded like it came from the bottom of a pool of oil. Then a hand was tugging on his shirt. "The car!" Knight yelled.

Before thinking of doing so, Rick looked for Heiser again. What he saw sickened him.

The nutcase with the gun had rushed up to a man in a car parked on the other side of the street. Apparently others had the same fears about the gas Rick did. They were attempting to flee as quickly as possible. While most went on foot, though, this one man tried to escape in his car. Rawley Heiser, to the man's bad fortune, had other plans for him. Leveling the automatic weapon in both hands, Heiser shot his quarry in the face. Through the shattered glass on the driver's door, Rick could see the hapless man's blood and liquefied brain matter paint the inside of the car a grotesque crimson. Heiser then proceeded to drag his lifeless victim from the car.

"Get in!" This time Rick shouted as loud as he could, looking to make eye contact with each member of his team. Then he decided to lead by example and lunged toward the driver's door and got behind the wheel. "Move it!"

As he noted the rest of the *Confirmation* crew getting on the same page, he also saw Rawley Heiser swing his commandeered car out of its parking slot and send it speeding down the steep street.

"Is that the...?" Tony Griffin started to ask after jumping into the front passenger seat and buckling himself in.

"Yeah," Rick shot back. "The asshole that started all this."

But in the meantime, he, too, was firing up the SUV's engine and yanking the transmission into DRIVE. After throwing a glance over his shoulder to see that the whole team had piled into the vehicle, he urged the Ford out of its parking spot, swung it around to face the descent of the street, and took off after Rawley Heiser.

"Full-on reality TV!" Tony gasped as he aimed his camera out the front window.

From the right edge of his peripheral vision, Rick noticed Matt doing the same from the second row of seats.

"Yeah, and maybe we can stop that psycho before he gets anyone else killed while we're at it," Rick mumbled under his breath as he watched Heiser's stolen car reach the intersection at the bottom of the hill and slide into a sharp left turn.

As Rick threw the SUV into the same maneuver, he noticed that the fleeing crowd's worst fears were unfolding near the top of the block. Yet another fireball, propelling more wood, glass, metal, and aluminum-siding shrapnel into the air, across the street, and into parked cars, was bubbling skyward.

"Unbelievable!" Someone's voice, maybe Lacy's, Rick

guessed, sounded out from the back of the F-150.

"What's unbelievable is that guy's gonna get away," Tony gasped as Rick sped through an intersection, dodging around the rear of a car that had just barely cleared their path a moment ago.

What prompted their cameraman's pessimism, Rick noted, was the way Heiser managed to throw an inadvertent obstacle in their way about a half a block away. Overtaking a slower moving sedan, Heiser had veered too far into the oncoming traffic. Although he managed to correct his position quickly, dodging back into his lane, Heiser spooked an oncoming driver enough to urge him to swerve hard right…hard and far enough to plow into a parked minivan. Then, upon returning to his own lane, Heiser managed to clip the sedan he was overtaking, prompting it to spin out and block Rick's path.

"Oh, God!" Tony gasped this time, bracing both his legs as Rick took evasive measures, swerving around the sedan in front of them.

"Relax," Rick found himself hissing as he successfully cleared the obstacle. "Relax, we're good—"

"But he's not…." Dan Knight's voice sounded off from the back, assessing Heiser's situation up ahead.

Just as Knight concluded, Rick watched the fugitive's wild ride come to a sudden end at the next intersection. Heiser sped into the intersection which one moment was clear and the next blocked by a crossing vehicle. Heiser's car slammed into its nose, reshaping its right side into a crumpled mass of plastic and scrap metal. Unfortunately for Heiser's escape attempt, the collision also radically changed his car's forward momentum. Heiser's car also spun out, sharply enough to tip it over and send it into a corkscrewing roll through the air. Then the fact that the street dipped into a sharp descent past the intersection helped give the car more momentum, more airtime, and several more revolutions through the air before impacting into the pavement. The misshapen, disintegrating hulk of metal managed to bounce and slide as far away as the middle of the block.

6

ITALIAN GLOBE CONTINUES TO POLARIZE
By Arthur Kenneth Ashmore, *U.S.News and World Report*

For those who see a threat in the world-wide globe phenomenon, no steps seem too drastic in protecting themselves or attempting to warn the world. The town of Aquileia in Northern Italy found that out during the middle of the night on September 10[th,] when five sticks of dynamite were used to blow its globe apart.

A granite globe, exactly the same size and weight as all of the ones appearing around the world, made its entrance onto a small side street four days ago. But today it lies reduced to shattered, jagged slabs and rubble.

Three local men, Giuseppe Parlante, Francesco Bonucci, and Roberto Della Corte, have been taken into custody for the bombing. None of the men deny their role in the attack. In fact, they hope their act will inspire others around the world to do the same.

"These unholy things are an obvious threat to the world," Parlante told the local press. "Just look at how many people have been hurt as a result of them. Now we have this one in our town. How many more are coming? How many more people will be hurt or killed?"

"We were protecting our town, protecting our neighbors, our families," added Bonucci. "Everyone better wake up and start doing the same."

The three men also explained that they were hoping the world's military forces would start making plans for the systematic destruction of the globes.

But the only serious damage to property and threat to personal safety in Aquileia came as a result of Parlante, Bonucci, and Della Corte's attack on the globe. While the explosion broke the globe apart, enough of the blast was also diverted onto a nearby building, a small bakery, to cause damage totaling upwards of 3,700 Euros (or close to $5,000).

Ceasario Agostini, the owner of the bakery, who lives in an apartment above his business with his wife and two sons, suffered a ruptured eardrum as a result of the explosion. His wife, Teresina, had to be hospitalized briefly from a severe panic attack. Their son, Pietro, was cut by flying glass.

The Agostini family vows to file civil suits against the three bombers.

According to local police chief Giacomo Gagliardi, Parlante, Bonucci, and Della Corte were aided in stealing the dynamite from a local construction company by Bonucci's brother-in-law, Pascual Lazzari. Lazzari has also been arrested.

The bombing brought more turmoil to a town that had already been splintered into factions around the globe.

Some people, like Sylvia Balboni, support the bombers and their accomplice. "I'm sorry for the people who got hurt in that store, but I'm glad [the globe] is gone." she said emphatically. "I hope they remove its pieces and get them as far away from our town as possible. I know a lot of people will laugh at me [for saying this], but I think those things are evil. They're of the devil."

Others, like Maurizio Passerini, who came all the way from Rome to see the globe, couldn't disagree more. "Crazy people are the real threat. They should all be locked away for as long as possible. This place was special because of the globe."

Passerini represents a sort of pilgrimage movement across Europe, people flocking to the globes because they feel the objects have transformative powers.

"I could feel it when I got to Aquileia," Donatella Neri, who had traveled from Sardinia to see the globe, explained. "Even before I saw the globe. Like I was just ten years younger. I could feel a vibration of pure energy everywhere. Like this whole town was full of energy."

"Something important was going to happen here," Gabriella

Fiore, Maurizio Passerini's girlfriend added. "Now the only thing that has happened is a tragedy. The moment I heard of the bombing, I thought I would just cry for days. Like a piece of me had been torn out."

Marco Sebastiani, an Aquileia taxi driver who is also glad the globe is gone, could, nevertheless, not support the bombing. "Whatever powers, whatever dark forces put that abomination in our town…well, who knows what they might do now? This is not good for us. This is going to hurt all of us."

Afraid of some form of otherworldly retaliation for the bombing, Sebastiani is planning to move his family far away from Aquileia as fast as possible.

While the bombers await their day in court, debates about whether the globes truly have any physical effect on people and what the destruction of one of the objects will bring continue.

"These reported transformative powers of the globes are a form of mass hypnosis," claims Dr. Enrico Ungaretti, professor of clinical psychology at the University of Bologna. "People who want to believe in the power of these objects will experience these powerful reactions of well being, feelings of power, as they get closer to the globes."

Dr. Bonnie Whitcomb, professor of psychiatric medicine at the Yale University School of Medicine, agrees. "It's similar to the feelings of euphoria, possessions even, by divine forces, the kinds of things true believers experience at religious ceremonies."

Whitcomb, just like Ungaretti, points out that many people living close to the globes have never reported feeling any effects.

"People who want to experience feelings of power and euphoria around the globes do so," Whitcomb argues. "It's what we call a psychosomatic reaction. The mind is able to bring about the subconsciously desired physical sensations."

But just as in the case of most alleged paranormal or miraculous events, from so-called alien contacts to religious visions, those who truly believe will never be swayed by the kind of explanations Whitcomb is offering.

CHAPTER 5

Stunt. Fighting the Law. First Amendment.
Conspiracists on Twitter. Embedded. Lakenheath.
What Do You Know? Call for Transparency. Questions To Ask.

1.

"And now we owe you a big favor, Colonel," Dan Knight said as he followed Garret Robinson into his study.

Robinson, who'd had a placidly neutral demeanor since Knight arrived at his house on Travis Air Force Base, now gave him a very brief, but decidedly sharp, look before glancing away again. Robinson was going for the liqueur cabinet, aiming to do good on a fifteen-year-old Glendronach single malt scotch he had promised.

"I'm *not* complaining, of course," Knight said.

And he wasn't. It was better to spend the evening a free man than still fighting his way out of the legal and bureaucratic morass with the San Francisco cops, the District Attorney, Jerry Peretti's lawyer, and a passive-aggressive, suddenly bipolar Peretti himself.

"Don't worry," Robinson called over his shoulder as he started pouring their drinks. "This is not quite a done deal yet. The people from Washington are not happy with your group's little stunt...."

2.

(CNN) ...At what price blockbuster reality television? That's the question being asked right now in San Francisco as cast members of a yet unsold reality television program stand to face

139

charges of criminal negligence.

The stars of the in-the-works *Confirmation: Investigations of the Unexplained*, Professor Daniel Knight, ex-reporter Cornelia Oxenburg, and Richard Ballantine, the controversial host of the now-defunct CBS series *Hollywood Justice*, along with their technical crew members Melinda Rowland, Ian Durfy, Matthew Cooper, Lacy Anderson, and Anthony Griffin, have been arrested for their involvement in a high-speed chase in the Noe Valley.

"The freedom of the press does not give anyone the right to put innocent people's lives at risk," said Assistant District Attorney Charles Harper. "It does not give them the right to interfere with a police case or allow them to act as vigilantes and try and apprehend suspected criminals."

The *Confirmation* crew now stands accused of contributing to a chase with Rawley Heiser, a convicted sex offender involved in a shootout with the police. Heiser, now accused of shooting and killing three people in an armed standoff, including his neighbors Manuel Sifuentes and James Mead, and police officer Roderick Clemmons, attempted to flee the scene when the television crew gave chase. The chase resulted in three car wrecks.

The only serious injury in the chase was Heiser's, whose car rolled over several times after striking another vehicle in an intersection. He is now in a coma in the California Pacific Medical Center. The accident, said Dorothy Ferguson, a Medical Center spokesperson, left Heiser with severe head trauma, a broken back, two broken arms, and a crushed pelvis.

According to Assistant D.A. Harper, these accidents would not have happened had the *Confirmation* team not attempted to pursue Heiser.

"Make no mistake," Harper said, "this could have been much worse. There could have been more people getting caught in the middle of this chase. There could have been more injuries. There could have been fatalities."

Tanya Mancuso and Lloyd Peters, both of whom were driven to swerve out of Heiser's way and wreck their cars in the process, are considering civil lawsuits. Benjamin Fisher, whose car was struck by Heiser, is also reportedly consulting with an attorney.

The *Confirmation* group has garnered considerable media attention recently due to their involvement in the globe phenomenon. They were the first ones to find a globe in the outskirts of Mount Shasta City, California. Daniel Knight, Professor of Anthropology at Bakersfield State University and author of several books on paranormal phenomena, has been a prominent voice in the ongoing speculation about the nature of the globes.

Sources have also suggested that the *Confirmation* cast was about to be given access to the military's efforts to study the globes. How this proposed project will impact the car chase case remains to be seen....

From CNN's Victoria Marshall

3.

"They haven't committed fully yet," Robinson said, and tasted his scotch. "General Barrett's a stickler for by-the-book procedure. And right now, your people are out on bail."

Knight, too, tasted the Glendronach and found it exceptional. "That arrest was bogus," he said at length. "That psycho had a fully loaded assault rifle. There would have been a hell of a lot more shooting and more killing had he gotten away."

"Be that as it may," Robinson said coolly, "the law says it's not for you to interfere."

"We weren't interfering. We were covering the event. We *are* the press. *And* we have a right to document a shooting in the street."

Robinson grinned and took another pull on his scotch. "The press? By the loosest definition of the term."

"The First Amendment definition is pretty loose."

Robinson tipped his glass at Knight. There was a faint, amused hint of a smile in the corner of his mouth, but his eyes betrayed something else. Something crafty and challenging. "So I can assume the whole group is interested in working with us. You won't be too paranoid, I hope, about your...*journalistic* integrity being undermined by the government."

"Well, the government's not *going* to undermine it, will it?" Knight asked, his mind already turning over the bizarre set of Twitter exchanges Cornelia brought to his attention just after they split up following their release from police custody.

4.

NewWorldOrder Agenda Watch @NWOAgWatch
Latest out of S.F.: Govt & military/industrial/entertainment complex going to bed to bring U FAKE NEWS about #globes
867 Retweet 1023*

NewWorldOrder Agenda Watch @NWOAgWatch
Cast of @ConfirmationTV to document #NWO Govt's BOGUS investigation into #globes
705 Retweet 1053*

NewWorldOrder Agenda Watch @NWOAgWatch
#NWO & @ConfirmationTV investigating #globes: Let the coverup begin!!!
1001 Retweet 1237*

NewWorldOrder Agenda Watch @NWOAgWatch
#NWO + @ConfirmationTV + #globes = #brainwashing
1134 Retweet 1505*

Conspiracy Bob @BRadford
@NWOAgWatch I heard @ConfirmationTV is an #occult #Freemason controlled drivel. #Apocalypse #Antichrist #indoctrination
12 Retweet 9*

NewWorldOrder Agenda Watch @NWOAgWatch

All cast members of @ConfirmationTV have ties to the #occult, govt, #Freemason #conspiracy
1286 Retweet 1388*

NewWorldOrder Agenda Watch @NWOAgWatch
Dan Knight writes books about #occult #Magick
1250 Retweet 1410*

NewWorldOrder Agenda Watch @NWOAgWatch
Dan Knight teaches impressionable youth at school founded by a #Freemason. FACT!! #indoctrination
1465 Retweet 1637*

NewWorldOrder Agenda Watch @NWOAgWatch
Knight paving the way for #NWO #oneworldgovt. #indoctrination #antichrist
1403 Retweet 1655*

NewWorldOrder Agenda Watch @NWOAgWatch
@CorneliaOxenburg: a disgraced ex-Barbie Doll reporter. Killed career of whistleblower professor.
1522 Retweet 1566*

NewWorldOrder Agenda Watch @NWOAgWatch
Rick Ballantine: Brutal #LAPD cop. FIRED!!!
1611 Retweet 1653*

NewWorldOrder Agenda Watch @NWOAgWatch
@LacyAnderson: Military #insider. #Surveillance
1578 Retweet 1614*

NewWolrdOrder Agenda Watch @NWOAgWatch
@IanDurfy: Hollywood special effects tech. Expert in fake news, fake media images. #FalseFlag #MoonHoax #911Hoax
1787 Retweet 1823*

NewWorldOrder Agenda Watch @NWOAgWatch

@MelindaRowland: Ex bodybuilder. #Steroids DOD/DARPA #geneticgengineering
1643 Retweet 1704*

NewWorldOrder Agenda Watch @NWOAgWatch
@MattCooper: Very little govt connection. #coverup What is he hiding?
1602 Retweet 1793*

Conspiracy Bob @Bradford
@ConfirmationTV rotten to the core. In the pocket of the military, #NWO. Complete #MediaBias #FalseFlag
1863 Retweet 1892*

Freedom Crusader @PatriotJoe
RT @Bradford @ConfirmationTV rotten to the core. In the pocket of the military, #NWO. Complete #MediaBias #FalseFlag
30 Retweet 41*

Freedom Crusader @PatriotJoe
@NWOAgWatch Specifics about #globes & #Antichrist #aliens connection?

NewWorldOrder Agenda Watch @NWOAgWatch
@PatriotJoe #aliens are a misinterpretation of demonic interdimensional invaders. #globes are interdimensional
2004 Retweet 2163*

NewWorldOrder Agenda Watch @NWOAgWatch
#alien truth is that they're a govt #coverup
2105 Retweet 2348*

NewWorldOrder Agenda Watch @NWOAgWatch
#alien truth is that they're not from space. Interdimensional invaders. #demonic & hostile
2111 Retweet 2251*

NewWorldOrder Agenda Watch @NWOAgWatch
#occult connection of @ConfirmationTV & govt means a plot to
lie to the public & hide truth. #conspiracy
2345 Retweet 2417*

5.

Knight took a seat in one of Robinson's leather easy chairs and
drank more of the scotch. "We'll be…what? *Embedded* reporters
on the air force's globe hunt?" he asked, passing his eyes over the
aviation-themed decorations of the colonel's man-cave.

"Yes," Robinson said matter-of-factly as he, too, sat down
across the room from Knight. "Your group and probably a
few others. From what General Barrett said, the Pentagon will
get various media outlets involved. To keep it fair. Make it
completely inclusive and transparent. You're just lucky that
you're in a unique position, having asked to talk to us about the
globes before anyone else in the media did…and that the brass
originally said yes. *And* since your people were the first to find
one of these things." Now Robinson paused, staring into his glass
of Glendronach. "*And* because I know Cornelia and I could put
in a good word."

"Much appreciated."

"But you're really not feeling any kind of a coercion by the
military conspiracy, are you?"

From Robinson's sour tone, Knight wondered how much
perusing the colonel and at least his people here at Travis did
of the online conspiracy crowd. "No," Knight said, then, after a
beat, couldn't help but add, "not yet."

There was a sort of self-satisfied, inscrutable little smile on
Robinson's face. It was the smug, vaguely taunting look that
used to piss Knight off in another life. When people used to look
at a teenage Knight like that was when fists wound up being
thrown, perhaps weapons brandished, people forced to back
down, respect demanded lest things turn lethal.

"But I *am* curious," Knight said at length. *Let's see how open*

145

and cooperative these clowns really are, he thought.

"Aha?"

"What do you know about these globes?"

There was a long pause before Robinson replied. Knight noted how honestly baffled the colonel appeared to be.

"What does *who* know about them?" Robinson asked. "Me? The air force?"

"Yeah."

6.

(FOX NEWS) …The appearance of the latest globe in Suffolk, England, close to the town of Lakenheath and the Lakenheath Royal Air Force Base, has led to tensions between locals and the American military.

Charges of conspiracy and cover-up by the U.S. Air Force, which operates its 48th Fighter Wing out of Lakenheath, stems from the area's ties to the unexplained.

"I'm not surprised that thing would show up here," said James Bannister, a local mailman. "All the UFO and alien sightings and all that went on in the area here so many years ago."

The Suffolk area is still steeped in paranormal lore, with many UFO enthusiasts claiming that an alien spaceship made contact with American soldiers here in Rendlesham Forest in 1980. The alleged incident is still referred to as "England's Roswell."

Starting on the evening of December 26, 1980, airmen from the U.S. Air Force's 79th Fighter Wing, stationed at the time at the Woodbridge Royal Air Force Base, reported seeing strange lights descending toward Rendlesham Forest. The sightings continued for at least two more nights, with soldiers claiming contact with extraterrestrial spacecraft. Although the witnesses claimed the unidentified craft flew away, they said it left impressions in the ground, and levels of radiation high above normal were measured around the alleged landing site.

The Rendlesham Forest incident has been the subject of scores of books, articles, and documentaries about the UFO phenomenon.

This legacy of the unexplained in the area and charges of conspiracies now fuel new allegations of a much greater military knowledge of the mystery globes than the U.S. and British governments admit.

"That globe appears and now you have all the military activity going on all over the place…aircraft flying over the area day and night, yet the authorities are getting dodgy as usual. They claim they don't know anything after all," said Liam Norris, a member of a group of local UFO enthusiasts calling themselves the Aerial Phenomenon Research Center. "We think the coincidences are just too great to believe."

"They've lied to us before and they're lying to us now," said Bruce Alloway from the nearby town of Mildenhall. He, too, claims to have seen an unusual volume of low-level flights by American helicopters and fighter jets in the area, especially near the location of the globe. "Nothing but flashes of light from a local lighthouse or meteors or nonsense like that, they told us after the Rendlesham Incident. I believe there was something, you know, unexplained — an alien contact taking place in 1980 — and they lied about it. Now I think the Americans are behind this entire globe situation again, and they are trying to keep us in the dark. Our government, as usual, is going along and covering everything up."

The local consensus appears to agree with people like Norris and Alloway. Most people believe that the globe phenomenon is the product of some sort of secret American research project, and that at least the British government, if not most of the governments of the world, are conspiring to keep the truth hidden. The leading local theories range from time-travel experiments, experiments in creating interdimensional portals, to the globes acting as markers for an invasion force of alien spacecraft to land.

People who hold these views are also getting angrier by the day, and are starting to make their feelings known in ever more dramatic ways. An estimated six hundred people from the towns of Lakenheath, Mildenhall, and Thetford already held a protest rally outside the air force base. They are promising to not only keep the pressure on the base, but to take their movement to London and stage a similar rally outside the House of Parliament.

"We want answers, we want them now, and we will keep raising our voices to those in power, those who know full well what's going on here, until they give the people truth," said Georgina Easterbrook, an office manager from Lakenheath.

"There is something very big going on here, something that's probably putting all of us in danger," added Rufus Baines, a chef from Thetford, "and we're not going to sit by as the wealthy, the powerful, the well-connected are the only ones who can prepare for it."

This tension spilled over into an actual physical altercation on the evening of September 10 outside a Lakenheath tavern. American airmen Roy Malone and Eric Garcia were reportedly taunted by three local youths, Roger Craig, William Evans, and Bran Gedding, about the military's role in the appearance of the globes. Soon thereafter a fight broke out, sending Craig and Gedding to the emergency room and landing Evans, along with Malone and Garcia, in jail.

Lakenheath police chief Stephen Bailey insists, however, that the fight is not a true indicator of anti-American hostilities brewing among the general population.

"I would blame a little too much youthful machismo and the need to show off to a couple of girls for that fight rather than any kind of true hatred for the Americans," said Bailey.

He also added that the protests were the work of "fringe agitators."

From FOX's Raymond Miller.

7.

There was another thin smile on Robinson's face, but it, just like his glance, appeared distracted and distant this time, Knight thought.

As Knight's gaze flittered to a large framed picture of Robinson's two kids, Sarah and Jeff, on his desk, the distance in that look made sense. Knight was surprised the man could function as well as he did.

But Knight's thoughts were pulled in other directions as well. *What else will complicate matters here, Colonel?* he thought, noting Jeff Robinson's air force uniform in the picture. *So he's the "saved" member of the family, according to Rick's lovely and gracious ex-wife. And I wonder if she and her husband are still around, offering valuable spiritual advice to anyone who's willing to listen.*

"The *Man*? Is that who you mean, Professor?" Robinson asked. "What does the government know about the globes? The powers that be?"

"*Anyone*," Knight said, surprised by how forcefully the word came out. For a moment he wondered if the inflection came off as petulant, as desperately demanding as all of those conspiracy theorists out there, like the ones in England, shaking their fists and screaming and demanding that someone confirm their beliefs.

"I think that unlike all those yo-yos out there screaming conspiracy," Robinson replied, his attention refocusing on Knight, "*you* would realize that the military industrial complex is actually not quite as complex as Hollywood and a bunch of hack novelists would like everyone to think it is."

"*I* would understand?"

"Yes, Dr. Knight. Someone intelligent…oh, and I beg your pardon…."

That sounded odd, Knight mused. "For what?"

Robinson shrugged lightly. "It's not just because of Cornelia that I put in the word to have your people document our research efforts. It was because of you, too. We need the top minds working with us."

Knight wondered if the compliment was genuine to any degree at all. "I'm touched."

Robinson met his gaze with a rueful smirk. *Come on, Colonel, show me just how open you people are capable of being,* Knight thought.

"The president," Robinson said, "and his national security advisor have already met with particle physicists from Fermilab."

Knight had not heard of this in the news yet. "Fermilab. No kidding. Why?"

"Apparently," Robinson said, and paused to sip some scotch, "these are the people who can speak to the theoretics of black holes, dark matter, super strings…or some such thing. Multiple universe membranes…I don't know. *Wherever* these things might be coming from. There's going to be a meeting of the U.N. about all this. They'll be bringing in more scientists from Europe. Their brainiacs from CERN. People working their particle accelerators."

"Multiple universe membranes?"

"I guess they think the globes are coming from some alternate dimension…I don't know. But that's why they're getting the top people in the world together."

Knight turned that information over in his head and realized he didn't know what to think of any of it. Physicists looking at this made sense, but…. "Well, like I said, I'm flattered and all, but do they think I can contribute to alternate-dimension theories?"

Robinson gave him a long, probing look before replying. "Can you? Or since you're an anthropologist, can you contribute to communicating with whatever's on the other side? Inside the alternate dimension? Whatever sent these things over?"

Knight noticed how Robinson's look and tone sharpened as he spoke. There was a challenge in his words.

But Knight wasn't sure what an answer to that question might be. "Well," he said, knowing he had to choose his words carefully to come off sounding halfway intelligent…or to avoid sounding completely deluded and pathologically self-important. "I guess I wonder if whatever sent those the globes really wants to communicate. Or even cares what we have to say."

Robinson averted his gaze for a moment. "Yeah," he said very slowly. "Truth is…I wonder about that too."

The distant look in Robinson's eyes made Knight wonder about a lot of things. His thoughts, for one, skipped to his own family. For a second he considered his two ex-wives. They were, no doubt, frightened by the phenomenon. Amy and Margot were both just that type. They must have been holed up in their homes right now and living in fear, he was certain. They had to be looking at these globes as the harbingers of the worst. He thought about his daughter and his grandson in San Antonio, too. The sad truth of it was that Knight just couldn't be sure how they were reacting to all this. It had been that long since he had been in touch with them. He just didn't...didn't *know* them well enough to guess.

"I wonder what *I* would say to it," Robinson's voice startled him. The voice was dry, subdued, but not weak. It came from someplace cavernous and dark.

I bet you do, the thought ran through Knight's mind. All the while, he consciously kept his gaze from drifting back toward the picture of Sarah. *Would you want to say anything at all? Or just use whatever the air force has to blow it the hell back to where ever it came from? Blow it back in pieces.*

Robinson shook his head ever so slightly. "Fact is, whatever sent those damned globes did it for some reason."

"Yeah," Knight said simply, leaving it as neutral as possible.

"Maybe we'll get a chance to ask it."

Knight nodded and finally spoke when he felt he had his thoughts and his words for them in just the right order. Then, for good measure, he took a sip of the scotch to fortify himself. "Colonel. Look, I gotta ask you something and you need to be straight with me. Since I'll be this...what? Air force...*consultant?*"

Robinson simply raised an eyebrow in reply.

"Like I asked before. What *do* you people know about any of this? Are those globes really the first ones anyone's ever seen?"

Without his expression changing much, Robinson nodded his chin toward the window. "What? Like those people out there? Is that what you're asking me? Are we running some cover-up? Conspiracy? Did we get the globes from Roswell?"

"Roswell," Knight said, and chuckled. "OK. Just like all those people out there. The conspiracy, New-World-Order-nuts. That's what I'm asking. Is there any truth to any of the Roswell, Area-51, dead-alien-bodies stories? Do you people know what this is all about?"

8.

(Las Vegas Review Journal)...Nevada Senator Brandon Markwell called for a vigorous investigation of the globe phenomenon and the creation of a special Congressional subcommittee to make sure no part of the findings are kept from the public.

"The unfortunate situation since the start of this phenomenon has been a breakdown in the people's trust in our public institutions," Markwell said. "We need to be mindful of the national security implications of these objects appearing out of nowhere, on military bases like in San Diego, and the American people need to know what is being done to study this matter. What is being done to keep them and the country safe?"

Opinion polls, however, show a considerable percentage of Americans do not believe any type of government or military-led efforts to find the origin of the globes will be successful. Fifty-six-percent of the people, according to a Marist poll, believe the origin of the globes will not be found at any point soon. Thirty-five-percent say the government already knows more than it is admitting to.

"This fixation the public has with conspiracy theories is very troubling," Dr. Bentley Covington, a professor of communications at the University of Southern California, said. "It's not that our government is perfect, or that the military or big business and big corporations have not abused their power in the past. But believing that they could be behind something like the globe situation is giving them way too much credit."

Covington also agrees with Markwell that the public needs to be reassured that any efforts made to study the globes will be done honestly and openly.

"(Because) what becomes of a world where we believe anything we want without any proof? Where we pick and choose our so-called 'alternative facts' if we don't like the real facts?" Covington asked. "Where we believe our institutions are so corrupt and we are so powerless that there is no hope for any community action? In political involvement?"

Markwell also drew criticism from a large number of his own Nevada constituents when he said every possible explanation for the globes should remain on the table, even natural and man-made explanations.

"Just like CNN's Peter Rollins said a few days ago, there are incredibly talented illusionists out there who can make us believe we've seen the impossible," Markwell said.

He also proposed inviting several of Las Vegas's top magic acts to serve as consultants on any research efforts.

Jerome Pike was the last professional illusionist who criticized the paranormal explanation for the globes. He was the victim of a violent assault in Miami by supernatural proponents, the Church of the Universal Dawn.

"I don't know if Markwell is merely shilling for the Las Vegas tourism commission or if he's a part of an agenda to keep the truth hidden," Andrew Fullerton, the host of a popular conspiracy-oriented podcast in Las Vegas, quickly declared.

Most Americans no longer believe that a natural explanation for the globe phenomenon can be found. They do, however, support plans like Markwell's for a fully transparent research effort.

From Las Vegas Review Journal's Emily Harding

9.

"*You* people?" Robinson asked, his right eyebrow arching over a disappointed glance. "Really? Like I said, if you mean the government, the air force—"

"Yeah." Knight just had to cut him off, irritated by the way the colonel was attempting to slide around a direct answer again.

"I understand. It's all complex and it's not complex. So what's the truth? Does anyone really know *anything* about any of this?"

"Not about the globes, no."

Had he been sipping any of the scotch that moment, Knight was sure he would have choked on it at that instant. "Not about the globes?"

"From the seventies until ninety-six, the CIA studied whether psychics were for real. Inconclusive, by the way. And yes, there were the studies of UFOs. From the late forties through the sixties. And you can see shows about it all over TV. You understand? We don't know anything. What those things are. I mean yeah, there were lights in the sky. Radar signatures. What the hell's behind it, nobody knows. There are no aliens in Area 51, none of that crap." Robinson paused with a sigh and eyed his glass of scotch. "Basically, we're conspiring to hide our ignorance. The most technologically sophisticated military machine in history has no idea what's flying around in its skies."

"You know this for sure—"

"Know this for sure? No, not for sure.... Hell, I asked, OK? What they said sounded pretty much on the level."

"On the level...?"

Robinson gave Knight a tight look. "We've got people ready to kill each other over these damned globes. So we—the president of the United States, the Pentagon...*everyone*—we'd better get to the bottom of this real damn fast."

"There's no time for secrets?"

"No time for secrets," Robinson said with a tone, with a look that appeared to be real damned on the level.

"So what's the plan?" Knight asked.

"We'll know soon enough."

"You think they, your superiors in Washington, might want me in case we need to ask...them...it...some questions?"

"They thought it was a good idea."

"Well, I sure as hell can think of a couple of good ones."

There was a drawn-out moment of silence before Robinson

said, "So could I."

All the while, Knight's gaze was drawn back toward the picture of the colonel's daughter. "I know."

CHAPTER 6

Traffic Jam. The Hum. A Theory. Fired.
A Night at the Airport. Invitation to Travis AFB

1.

"His name is David Kwan," Cornelia said, looking into Matt's camera. "He's the manager of a Sunset District branch of Golden State Banking and Savings. The kind of...witness, the kind of experiencer, that makes us look closely at his claims."

Because he works for a bank? Cornelia wondered, considering how absurd her own script might have sounded right now. Then she scanned the faces of her colleagues, the rest of the team, plus Jerry Peretti, crammed into their bullet-riddled Ford F-150. With Doc Knight off at Travis Air Force Base, space was freed up for Jerry.

"This might be a man beyond reproach," Cornelia went on, sure her own words made about no sense now.

But she couldn't see any reactions from her team as Rick drove them west on Parnassus Avenue, heading for the Sunset District. Even Jerry, who had obsessively pored over her script, was too busy scanning emails on his phone. Did it really matter anymore how respectable anyone making a claim about the globes was? Scientists and college professors had been reduced to babbling cluelessness by all this. Rick had been right about Marcus Gunderson, their eminent engineer at Berkley, as well. The man had become a ranting, conspiracy-spouting wingnut, little different from a vagrant with a sandwich-board on the street screaming about the end of the world. How much more impressive was a mid-level bank executive like Kwan likely to be than a professor at one of the country's top schools?

So Cornelia had tweaked her script to read, "David Kwan risks a lot by going public with his claims. This could do irreparable damage to his reputation in an industry as conservative as banking. But he feels he has to tell his story." She had to break from the script at that point. "How did that come out?"

She looked at Jerry first, feeling her delivery came out sounding ridiculous.

Or is it more than the delivery? she wondered. It had to be more than that. It had to be more than Kwan…yet it was all of the above. It was the pointlessness of all this, Cornelia thought.

All of the above, she told herself.

They had almost gotten innocent people killed, her mind screamed. That's what all of her discomfort came from. It wasn't bad enough that one of the globes had killed Sarah. Now their pathetic, yellow-journalistic TV show was putting people's lives at risk. She felt as low, as unclean, as she had right after Sarah's death.

Rick was right, a voice in her head nagged, refusing her any measure of relief. He had been right when he argued with his ex-wife. *It's us. It's in us. It's on us. These globes aren't about to destroy the world. We are.*

More than anything, Cornelia felt like they were strapped onto a wild ride hurtling insanely toward oblivion. Yet no one around her seemed to realize it.

"Your script sounds fine," Matt said noncommittaly.

See what I mean? No one's realizing it.

"Yeah," Rick seconded, as cool as ever.

So what was keeping *him* together so well in the middle of all this? Cornelia knew Rick was capable of a great deal of introspection. How could he not be after all that he had been through over the last few years? Plus the things he had said to his ex-wife — *No, not just about me!* she wanted to tell herself, wanted to remain objective, but couldn't quite pull it off — had made her want to understand him, *know* him so much more than she had gotten to know him since they started working together a few short months ago. There was much more to him than the happy-go-lucky opportunist, the I'm-an-unlikely-TV-star-and-I-love-it façade he had created. But what was happening to him now? What was this stoic distance all about? Was it the cop thing? Did that chase put him back in his element?

But Cornelia looked back at her script instead of allowing all of these questions, all of the stress, to keep battering her.

"What if what he's about to tell us crashes the stock market?" Ian asked with an exaggerated deadpan.

And Cornelia almost laughed. *What the hell? It's as good a question as any.*

Jerry's eyes came away from his iPhone at last. "That's no joke, you know. The Dow's been taking a beating since this whole thing began."

Melinda looked at Ian and grinned. "You hear that? You afraid your portfolio's gonna get hammered?"

"Ian with a big stock portfolio? In his dreams," Lacy said, and laughed.

"No, seriously," Jerry said. "The market's been a disaster area. We've got these nutbags out there ready for fire and brimstone raining down...listen...." He paused and waved his phone around. "I mean, people are expecting the four horsemen of the Apocalypse to come down from the sky. Well, they've been riding up and down Wall Street. The markets are freaking out."

This time Matt turned his camera toward Jerry.

Cornelia thought she felt a wave of tension ripple through the SUV. The fact that they moved along Parnassus Avenue as slowly as they did helped add to that tension. She had seen Lacy and Tony's tight faces as they looked out the windows, contemplating the traffic jam. *It's not just Wall Street that's nervous,* Cornelia could imagine a hackneyed news comment saying, *but Main Street is scared out of its wits now.* People were leaving big cities in ever greater numbers. It was happening all over the world.

Places close to the globes were the worst. Cornelia and her group knew that the traffic they were mired in now was more than the usual evening rush hour. Many of these people were heading out of town. Traffic on the Golden Gate and Oakland Bay bridges was a bumper-to-bumper snarl as well. For a moment she doubted the wisdom of even doing an in-person interview with David Kwan. She knew they needed to get him on the record, but why couldn't it have been done via video conferencing? They would need to get up to Travis Air Force Base as soon as they could after talking to the banker, but Cornelia would have loathed to guess how long that could take, given the fact that the sun was about to melt into the horizon.

"So we've got enough gas in this clunker to make it out of town?" Lacy gave voice to Cornelia's concern, almost as if she was telepathic.

Cornelia looked at Rick for a reaction.

"Nope," he said.

"And I've seen some serious lines at three gas stations already," Melinda said.

Cornelia had an idea and thought there was no sense in wasting time bringing it up. She turned to Jerry. "How about we fly out of here when we're done?"

As she expected, Jerry looked less than pleased by the suggestion. In fact, Cornelia thought there was a slight flinch shivering through his features, almost as if he had bitten down on a painful tooth. "Uhm...look. We'll do just fine. Just because the world's panicking, there's no need for us to go to pieces too."

"And spend the extra money on a plane out?" Cornelia found herself snapping, her voice harder than she intended. It wasn't so much conflict with Jerry that she wanted to avoid as...well, as much as panicking.

Jerry didn't reply immediately. Cornelia saw the spiking anger in him beaming from his eyes. "We have to stay cool," he replied. "It's not the money."

"What was that about a network deal in the works?" Rick cut

in.

Jerry cleared his throat. "OK. Like I said, it's not the money. ABC sounds like they really want to make this happen. But the airport's likely to be jammed with people too—"

"Not like the Bay Bridge," Ian cut in this time.

Cornelia saw him looking at his tablet intently.

"People don't just want to get out of San Francisco," Jerry pressed back. "They want to leave the *state*. California's the only state that's gotten *three* globes. No concentration of globes like this anywhere else in the world."

"I heard that just about as many people are trying to get in," Tony said.

"I doubt that," Jerry replied.

"No joke," Lacy said. "I heard that the entire new age crowd of North America's flocking to Cali. For realz, guys."

"New age crowd?" Melinda asked.

Of course, it makes sense, Cornelia thought.

"Like those people in Mount Shasta City," Ian mumbled, still studying something important-looking on his tablet. "They think California's gonna be the epicenter of the Harmonic Convergence or the Age of Aquarius or some hippie acid-trip like that. I don't know...the UFOs with the Space Brothers will land at Haight-Ashbury or something...." Then his head snapped up. "OK, ladies and gents. We've got issues. The Bay Bridge's out of commission. Massive accident. Ain't nobody going nowhere on that one. In *or* out."

"Oh, good one," Cornelia found herself thinking out loud now. "That means...."

"All right, I get it," Jerry said.

"That we better fly out?" Lacy asked tartly.

"That we better fly," Jerry shot back. "After we get this Kwan guy's story. But get ready for a good time at the airport. You think it will be easy trying to get out?"

"Most people are probably going as far as they can," Lacy countered.

160

"Right," said Cornelia. "We only need a commuter flight north to Solano County and Travis."

"Wish us luck," Jerry said grudgingly.

"So in the meantime," Rick said, "What's Kwan's story supposed to be all about?"

2.

"I knew the globe was coming," David Kwan said.

It was the embarrassed look on his face that told Cornelia they had not made a mistake agreeing to talk to this man. When he gave his wife, Marjorie, a sideways, barely perceptible look of annoyance, Cornelia surmised that he would not have reached out to the *Confirmation* team would it not have been for his wife's prompting.

Cornelia had been sure until now that opening the *Confirmation* web page to invitations of anecdotes from globe experiencers had been a bad idea. She had told Jerry as much, but his was the final decision. It would be like opening a floodgate, she had told him, to every unbalanced lunatic in the world. They would drown in crazy, she had said.

Of course, she had been right.

Until David Kwan.

Cornelia still marveled at how Kwan had been found among the hundreds of emails from every conspiracy theorist, psychic medium, crystal-gazing new ager, everyone who claimed to have been told about the globes by aliens during an abduction experience, by angels, by Jesus Christ, by the spirits of Tibetan ascendant masters, by ghosts, JFK, Elvis, Michael Jackson's disembodied voice, and by renegade Freemasons.

Maybe Rick was right, she mused. Jerry probably had a collection of unpaid interns back in L.A. doing all the work. One particularly motivated college student must have come across Kwan's email. So now they sat on the deck behind the banker's house, surrounding him and his wife with lights and camera angles set up to catch the best of the orange-blue twilight horizon.

"I thought I was having a stroke at first," Kwan said, his gaze darting back and forth between Cornelia and Rick.

With Knight away at Travis, Cornelia and Rick pulled duty in front of the cameras.

"No, actually," Kwan added, "not at first. At first I thought it was my ear drums." He paused and glanced at his wife for a fleeting moment. Cornelia thought she saw Marjorie Kwan give him a barely noticeable nod of encouragement. "It was only when it started getting louder," David Kwan went on. "The ringing, I mean. OK, so that was the start of it. When I knew I was experiencing something strange. I had this...something I could best describe as a ringing in my ear. On and off, you know."

"Was this *like* a ringing?" Rick suddenly spoke up. "Or were your ears *ringing*?"

"*Like* a ringing," Kwan said after a moment's hesitation. "Not a clear ringing. That's what I told my doctor. It was more like.... It's hard to describe. Like a *hum* all around you. You feel like you're in the middle of some giant vibration. Like you're inside a giant engine. And I could feel it in my ears more than anything."

"So he went to the doctor," Marjorie Kwan added.

"Yes. Yes, I did," her husband confirmed. "At first I thought it was my ear drums. So he checked it and he finds nothing. Nice, huh? Absolutely nothing wrong with my ears. Well, I wasn't suffering any hearing loss. But then that damn hum would come and go. But I had no other ear canal related problems. No infection. No loss of balance. Nothing."

"And then the possibility of a stroke came up?" Cornelia asked.

David nodded with a rueful look. "Just the thought scared the hell out of me. Or worse yet, the possibility of a tumor."

Cornelia noticed the dark, tense look crossing Marjorie's face, and she could feel for what these people must have been through.

"So anyway, they had me undergo an MRI scan. Nothing. Didn't know if I should be relieved or scared. I didn't have a brain tumor *or* a stroke. But then the hum, the ringing, the whole thing would come back. What the hell was wrong with me? I thought I was losing my mind."

"Your doctors implied as much," Marjorie said bitterly. "Of course they won't say, 'well, we have no idea what's going on here and we have no clue what's wrong with you.' So they tell him he has a *psychosomatic* illness...."

"That I should see a psychiatrist."

Marjorie rolled her eyes in disgust. Cornelia couldn't blame her.

"The day the globe showed up, I was willing to see anyone!" David said. "It felt like a jackhammer was in my mouth."

"Whoa!" Rick exclaimed.

Cornelia noticed him shaking his head. "Exactly," she said. "So what did you do?"

"I had to take the day off from work, for one. Now mind you, the hum, as strong as it was, wasn't there non-stop. It came and went. Like in cycles."

"How long between the cycles?" Rick asked.

"Uhm...about an hour or so. I don't know. Maybe an hour. I didn't try to time it. Hell, I could barely think straight enough for that. But anyway, I called in sick. I couldn't deal with the office. But I needed to get out of the house. I just had this need to be on the move. It's weird, I know. I guess if I was doing something, it felt like I was trying to take control of some part of this. Yeah, look, I know how crazy this sounds."

"No, not at all," Cornelia replied, but cringed inwardly at almost the moment the words came out of her mouth. She realized how patronizing it sounded.

"So eventually I agreed to do lunch with this friend of mine, John Nicholson, who works on Powell Street. At a law firm." David paused with a shrug and something of an embarrassed look. "Yeah, you know, he tells me that if there's something really seriously wrong with me and none of these doctors can diagnose it, then I could have a case going...." He paused again with another shrug. "I wasn't seriously considering it. I just needed something to do. But anyway, the thing is that we were going to do lunch, right? So he mentions several places we could go to. Except the weirdest thing happens. I remembered a flier we once got to this new seafood place on California Avenue. It's right nearby. Close to John's office. So I just...I just *know* we have to go *there*. To that particular spot. And I don't know why. I mean, I don't even know how the hell I even remembered *that* restaurant."

"On California Street," Rick said coolly.

David gave him a knowing look. "Yeah. Where the globe shows up. And on the way there, as John and I are talking, the hum in my head is building up. I'm starting to really seriously consider a couple of malpractice suits at that point. What the hell do they mean there's nothing wrong with me? But all the while, California Street is drawing me like a magnet."

"But did you see anything?" Cornelia asked.

David shook his head. "No. Nothing. We were in the restaurant when it happened. I can't explain it. My head was ringing like a bastard, but no, I didn't see it. Why it didn't make me go out in the street, watch it appear, I don't know." After pausing and giving both Cornelia and Rick very intense, pointed stares, he said, "It was the globe. That's what caused the hum. I know it now. I'm sure of it. It all went away after the globe appeared. After it rolled down Powell. I heard, I *felt*, nothing since."

3.

"Eunice Stevens didn't say anything about a buzz," Rick said from behind the wheel. "Or a hum. Or *anything* like that."

Although his tone was still controlled, Cornelia's gaze kept wandering back to his fingers tapping away on the steering wheel in a fast, angry rhythm.

But she, too, was close to doing that any moment now. Sitting in the front passenger seat, she kept feeling the temptation to rest a hand on the dashboard and start drumming her fingers furiously. The SUV's slow crawl south along the 280 was starting to stretch her own nerves taut now. Their trip from David Kwan's house to San Francisco International should have taken no more than about fifteen minutes, but they had been on the road for close to an hour now, and were nowhere close to the airport. Their only stroke of luck had come when they were able to gas up the SUV at a Shell station without any serious lines to sit through.

"That's true," she replied. "But Kwan said it came to an end right after the globe appeared. I think he's right."

"Yeah. The two've gotta be connected somehow," Lacy said.

"But how?" Melinda asked.

"I don't know," Lacy replied. "Those things are...different. I don't know. Alien."

Ian Durfy, searching for something on his tablet yet again, called out "Alien? Really?" without taking his eyes from the screen.

"Look," Lacy said. "What I mean is they're not from around here...."

Rick chuckled now, not exactly with a derisive inflection, but...with a derisive *feel* nevertheless. "That's just a little *too* broad, don't you think?"

"I agree," Melinda said. "We have to be a little more methodical here."

"*Methodical*," Lacy said, drawing out the word and winking toward Tony, who was cradling his camera in his lap, trying to cover as much of the conversation as he could. "I like that."

Tony laughed in return, winking at Melinda. "You and the Doc hang out a lot, right?"

Melinda scowled at him. "Yeah, because this show needs some IQ points, too. Right, Jerry?"

But Jerry, just like on the trip to David Kwan's house, was back on his phone, tapping out text after text. "Yeah," he mumbled. "Uh, I agree with Melinda."

"See, I told you so," she said with a goodly tinge of mock

indignation.

"Well, you and Doc Knight need to form a *theory* now," Matt taunted from behind his own camera.

Their banter, however, didn't help Cornelia's agitation. "OK, so this is going to be a comedy show?" She hoped to catch Jerry's eye, but their producer's attention was still riveted to his phone.

"Well, Jerry?" she asked.

"Don't mind me," he said absently. "I'm still trying to get a hold of ABC."

"If we just come up with a major break in the case, I don't think we need to worry too much about one network or another," she replied.

"*If* we come up with a major break," Rick answered instead.

"That's what *I'm* saying," Melinda said before Cornelia could reply.

"What else can explain Kwan's hum?" Matt added quickly.

Cornelia was glad to hear it. "Sure."

"And that's what *I'm* saying," Lacy also interjected.

"Right," said Tony. "Even his doctors couldn't explain it."

"Except," said Rick, "we still need to remember Eunice Stevens. Until now she was the closest to a globe's appearance. And she said nothing about hums and vibrations."

Except for California Street, Cornelia wanted to yell out loud. "But that's technically not true," she said with what she felt was a very sensible tone instead.

"What do you mean?" asked Matt.

Cornelia looked at him, then looked into the lens of his camera. "That the block all around the Powell and California intersection was full of people. Along with David Kwan."

Rick nodded calmly. "OK, so they might have been closer. And do you think *they* all heard something?"

"All right…you have a point. We don't know if anyone heard anything. But we can't discount what Kwan told us."

"Do you really want to complicate this whole thing?" Lacy asked.

"Why not?" Melinda said, sarcasm well in place. "It's getting a little too dull for my taste."

After a beat, Lacy said, "What if only some people can hear it and not others? How's that for a theory?" Her tone, Cornelia thought, was surprisingly serious, considering the tense jocularity that had been possessing the group the slower and slower their commute got.

But what she said made perfect sense, Cornelia realized. "So it doesn't matter how close Eunice Stevens was to the Mount Shasta globe."

"Now that's a good point if I ever heard one," Rick conceded.

"And I'm on it!" Ian spoke up from the back of the SUV.

Cornelia looked in his direction. "Say what?"

"Stories of the other globe appearances. Any mention of *anything* about a hum, a noise, a vibration."

4.

"In plain English," Knight's voice came through the SUV's speakers, "what they're saying is we've been fired. The military no longer wants to do business with the show."

"We've been fired?" Jerry yelled, and for a moment Cornelia thought he would spring from his seat and lunge toward the F-150's overhead microphone. *"We've* been fired?" he yelled again, actually rising over the thunder of a jetliner passing low overhead and descending toward one of San Francisco International's runways. Given the fact that most of the SUV's windows had been shot out and they were next to the airport now, the volume of Jerry's tantrum was impressive. "You mean *we,* the team here. *Us!* Not you obviously, Doctor." When he sank back into his seat to plow his fingers through his hair in exasperation, Cornelia thought he was through. Except then his body tensed again, as if his seat had secretly been rigged as an electric chair and someone just blasted some near-lethal voltage through his body. "What the *fuck?*" he screamed, yet conveyed only powerlessness. "Fuck! Goddamn it!"

"OK, look, Jerry…," Knight's unperturbed voice came through the speaker.

"And what are *you* doing up there?" Jerry cut him off. "Come on! You're in the middle of it. So why aren't you fighting for the rest of the team?"

Before Knight could reply, Cornelia spoke up, trying to sound likewise sensible and low key. Yelling would serve no purpose here. "I don't understand. Why *are* they keeping you up there?"

"Yeah," Knight replied with an odd sort of nonchalance now. And Cornelia wondered if he was *trying* to antagonize Jerry this time. "Well, they haven't thrown me off the base because they think I can help them."

"*You* can help them?" Jerry snapped.

The peevishness in those words, the condescension, Cornelia thought, was not the right way to go. As she had learned since Knight had been added to this team, the biggest egos in show business paled in comparison to the egos of academia. Knight enjoyed needling Jerry every time the producer tried to let it be known that he was the true alpha male of the group.

"Jerry, you need to control yourself," Knight said, and now Cornelia could have sworn she could *hear* the smirk on his face. "All right? We all need to be constructive here. The fellowship has to hold."

Cornelia could see Jerry's chest heaving. She wondered what he was about to yell back at the professor. Instead, he merely said, "We must have an entire team to document this professionally."

Cornelia guessed that that must have taken an epic amount of self control for Jerry. At the same time, she was frustrated by his solipsistic remark. If anyone would have wanted to mock the stereotype of Hollywood self-importance, they couldn't have come up with a better line than that. As much of an egomaniac as he might have been, Cornelia also thought Jerry was quite bright. Trying to spar with Knight when the old man had the upper hand was a dumb thing to do. If Knight wanted to, he could make sure this instant that *Confirmation* would never get anywhere near government inside-information again.

"Yes, Jerry," Knight said, "they seem to be under the impression that a doctorate in anthropology might be more important right now than having produced *Terror from the Fifth Dimension.*"

Jerry was predictably nonplussed by that, his chest heaving again and veins rising along his forehead. But Cornelia was happy to see that common sense prevailed in the producer and he kept his mouth shut.

"All right?" Knight's voice came through the speakers again. But this time the attitude, Cornelia thought, might have been dialed down just a notch. Knight had gotten his shot in, had scored a good hit into Jerry's ego, the proper testosterone hierarchy had been established, and now it was time to do serious business. "So calm down, Jerry. I'm trying to help you. I am trying to talk them into letting you stay a part of the media team documenting all this. But maybe you can help out by —"

"I don't understand," Jerry sputtered.

"What's that?" Knight asked.

"Yeah, me neither," Lacy spoke up this time.

"This shutdown," Jerry fumed. "Them shutting us out of this. *Firing* us! What the hell is this all about? Why now? They were going to talk to us. Give us access. Robinson was authorized to talk to us. What happened?"

"Yes," Cornelia couldn't help adding. "That's an excellent question."

"Some of the people in Washington seem to think your show's too tabloid," Knight said very calmly.

Perhaps too calmly, Cornelia thought. She noticed Jerry clenching his fists.

"*My* show?" Jerry replied. "So now you're —"

"And the car chase didn't help things," Knight continued. "But look —"

"I thought you were going to explain that we saved lives," Jerry snapped.

"I tried. But, Jerry, would you just listen to me? Just calm down. All right? Just be cool. Now listen to me! What happened with your network contacts? Washington still wants to work with the media. They're still talking transparency. They want to convince everyone that they're not the problem. Especially now that we have protests outside of at least five military installations across the country. Including Travis. It's getting nuts up here. So, once again, what's going on with the TV deals you had in the works? Can't any of your contacts pull strings? If you can tell me that we'll be backed by a major network player, I can make a stronger case and they'll let you guys join the press team."

Cornelia saw Rick shaking his head. "Yeah," he said with a smirk on his face, "explain that we're a better choice to cover this than Diane Sawyer."

Another plane coming in for a landing shrieked overhead.

"No!" Cornelia thought it was wise to pull the *Confirmation* team's strongest card from the deck. "We're a better choice because we figured out how to tell where a globe will appear."

"Come again?" Knight's startled voice came over the speakers.

"You hear me?" Cornelia asked. "Tell them that! Tell them that we've got a breaking story. We can predict when and where a globe will appear. I'm not kidding here! That's the truth!"

5.

"Does that help?" Cornelia asked as she lowered herself to the floor and leaned against the wall next to Melinda.

Melinda had been squeezing and releasing, squeezing and releasing a Grip Master exercising mechanism for at least five minutes as far as Cornelia could tell. Maybe the exercises helped take the mind off the noise of the teaming masses circulating all around Terminal One of the airport at five in the morning. Maybe it helped ease the stress of frustration, the annoyance over being stuck in this holding pattern, camped out at San Francisco International with nowhere to go.

Melinda grinned while she continued watching one of the TV sets suspended from the ceiling nearby. "To deal with the stress? Not really. Helps keep the wrist strong so I don't injure it again lugging all of this stuff around.... Oh my God! Can you believe these people?"

Cornelia followed her gaze to the TV. One of the CNN talk shows was in the middle of one of the myriad globe debates dominating all of television.

"...It's the guns! You want to start curbing all of the violence, you get rid of all the guns anywhere near any of these globes," one of the guests, a woman wearing a blinding-bright lime-green jacket, argued vehemently while gesticulating with both hands. "Globes and guns don't mix! Period! End of discussion!"

A man wandering by and texting furiously on his phone nearly tripped over Cornelia's feet.

"Want to try it? Maybe it'll work for you." Melinda looked at Cornelia and offered her the hand exerciser. "Has everyone else been on a full walking tour of the airport again?"

In fact, Matt was the only one slumped on the seats nearby at the moment. He was fast asleep, Cornelia could tell. Six other seats next to him were reserved by the video gear. To Jerry's credit, just as he had predicted, the airport was now an immense waiting room. Teeming crowds of thousands had overrun San Francisco International, including the people attempting to catch booked flights, the frustrated, the depressed, the surly, the defeated waiting on delayed flights, and all the hopeless who just camped out and prayed for a standby seat and a cancellation. The *Confirmation* team, in contrast, was waiting for a true miracle. Not only were they waiting for Knight to get back to them about how they were suddenly in the good graces of the military, but with word that some kind of a special flight from Travis Air Force Base was on its way to pick them up.

Cornelia took the hand-expander and started squeezing it as she glanced at CNN overhead. The hand gizmo was quite tough to work, and she knew she wouldn't be able to keep it up for much longer than a minute. But, then again, she didn't have Melinda's thick, muscle-corded forearms either.

"...Sure, disarm the people like we're in some police state!" a man with the lean, wiry features of a long-distance runner, wearing a brown suit and a glaring orange tie, offered a rebuttal on screen. "We don't know what's going to happen next, what kinds of...things will make themselves known—things that put those globes all over the world, and we can't even defend ourselves—"

"Whatever put those globes will be immune to guns," the woman in green cut in.

"Excuse me, please, but let me finish—"

"You're not going to lead the world-wide resistance against the space invaders—"

"May I finish?" the gun-rights advocate raised his voice.

"One at a time, please," the voice of a host from off-screen instructed.

"Nobody knows what's behind all this," the gun advocate, now identified by a caption as Lane Perkins, said. "And people have a right to defend themselves. They have the right to peace of mind."

The woman in the lime-green suit, identified as Susannah Nash, replied with, "No one will have any peace of mind with trigger-happy crazies running around and taking shots at people!"

"Well, I want to defend myself if any of Ms. Nash's crazies threaten me and my family."

"And you'll have nothing to worry about if sensible gun laws would finally take the weapons away from the crazies, Mr. Perkins."

"And you don't think crazies and criminals will get guns even if you make them illegal? We've got plenty of cocaine and heroin addicts out there, and both those drugs are illegal. There's this thing called the black market—"

"Feel better?" Melinda asked as Cornelia struggled to

complete another repetition with the grip-exerciser.

Cornelia couldn't help laughing. "Surprisingly...yes."

"Have at it," Melinda said and chuckled, blowing an errant lock of hair from her eyes.

"Wow! You do this enough and you can go back to competing again."

Melinda shook her head with an exasperated look. "If *Confirmation* goes nowhere — no air force help, no network deal — I might need to get my mind off things. Never could sit around and do nothing."

After resting her hand for a moment, Cornelia gave the strength device three more quick squeezes. The pump burned through her hand and up her forearm. "I know what you mean. This could be addicting. I should have gotten into bodybuilding after I lost my job in Florida."

"Sure," Melinda said, and nodded enthusiastically. "I got into it after a knee injury in college. After I couldn't swim anymore. Lost my scholarship."

"That stinks."

Melinda shrugged with a more intense sort of contemplative look in her eyes. "I always wanted to believe that if stuff doesn't turn out right, you know, you can get stronger as a result."

Cornelia recalled Melinda's exchange with Knight in New Jersey now. "So there's a reason for...."

Melinda returned a tight, rueful chuckle. "Yeah, well, I'm not so sure about that anymore." Her gaze panned across the chaotic mass of people circulating all around. "All of this...." She pointed her chin toward the TV set, where a graphic now filled the screen reading, "*Up Next: The Globes. The Future. The Threat.*" "I don't know what kind of a purpose can be behind any of this."

Cornelia had no idea what the answer was either. She had absolutely no idea at all. "Despite the craziness we've seen...the fights, the Heiser shootout...."

She could almost literally feel Melinda's eyes on her, looking at her for an ever-elusive solution, guidance, a theory that tied up and explained everything elegantly.

"Maybe," Cornelia said, "we can still somehow change for the better as a result of this?"

She hated the way her statement turned into a half-hearted, tentative question on the end.

"I hope so," Melinda replied, her voice stronger, more resolute.

"So do we know anything to back up our bluff?" Rick's voice suddenly called over the noise.

Cornelia saw him weaving his way through the crowd, carrying a bag in one hand and a tray of coffee cups in another.

"My hero!" she called, and rolled her eyes in mock elation. "When things are at their bleakest, Rick always comes through with what matters the most. Coffee!"

"I do what I can, ladies," he said, studying them on the floor. "Anything wrong with the chairs?"

"Nothing much," Melinda said. "If we hadn't been sitting in them all night long."

"Shut up and hand over the coffee," Cornelia said, and patted the floor next to her.

"Sure, why not," Rick said as he lowered himself to the carpet and leaned against the wall. "And how about a sugar rush to go with the caffeine?"

And Cornelia noticed that the bag he was holding came from a donut shop. Except the inscription and picture on it looked odd. "I can't believe it."

"Oh, believe it!" Rick said. "What good is a world-changing supernatural event if no one can cash in on it?"

"You gotta be kidding," Melinda said as Rick held up the bag.

On its side, a cartoonish drawing depicted three people looking in astonishment at a mystery-globe-sized donut ball with a giant bite taken out of it. The enormous donut was supposed to be sitting on a pavement of some sort that was too weak to support its weight. Cracks and fissures were drawn extending in all directions from the bottom of the donut.

"They're mystery donut holes," Rick said as Cornelia opened the bag and fished out one of the pastries.

It looked to be coated in cinnamon and sugar. To approximate the appearance of granite, Cornelia guessed.

"See, they all look alike on the outside," Rick said, "but when you bite into them, they all have a different mystery filling."

Cornelia popped the one she held into her mouth, tasting a rich chocolate cream inside.

"Jerry has the wrong idea about how to make money from these globes," Melinda said. "Here, give me one."

"So, what's going on?" Rick asked as Cornelia and Melinda helped themselves to more donut globes and coffee. "And do we have anything to make good on that bluff of yours?"

"Nothing yet on the bluff front," Cornelia said, and sipped some coffee. "Been looking at every globe story we can, but no one like David Kwan's turned up anywhere."

Rick's gaze drifted toward the TV. "Not even with all those *experts* analyzing this thing day and night?"

"Nothing's changed," Cornelia told him. "One guess is as good as the other. Except now they're getting crazier and crazier. And I didn't think that would be possible." Which made her think of the donut globe in her hand. *Cashing in.* "It's pure ratings and theater now. So I supposed if the air force shuts us out, we can just go digging up all the crackpots we can."

"Some pundit," Melinda said, tipping her coffee cup toward the TV, "argued that we should detonate nuclear bombs in the Pacific *and* the Atlantic at the same time."

Rick's eyebrows shot up. "Are you serious?"

"'Fraid so," Melinda said.

"So we can show the globe-makers that we mean business," Cornelia added.

"I want to crack a joke right now," Rick said, and shook his head. "Except I'm not sure I can. Let me get back to you, though."

"The speculation about them," Melinda said, "you know,

the origins and who put them all over the world and why. Well, it's getting more and more colorful. Like there's one about them being time-transported in from the future by Nazis hiding at the South Pole. Then one guy said it was all because of the gays—"

"What?" Rick blurted out, and Cornelia thought he would drop his hot coffee in his lap. "Nazis brought the globes from the future because of the gays?"

"No, those are two separate arguments," Cornelia corrected. "One conspiracy theorist thinks it's Nazis that brought the globes via time machine because…you know, they're *Nazis,* and this is their weapon of global domination."

Melinda chuckled. "Get it? *Global* domination."

"Oh, God," Rick groaned. "And someone else thinks this whole thing is because of *gays?*"

"Well, naturally," Melinda said. "It's a punishment from up high."

"Why am I not surprised?"

"Your ex-wife and her husband would be on *that* bandwagon, wouldn't they?" Cornelia couldn't resist asking, although she started regretting it almost as soon as it came out. She hadn't intended to hurt him by dredging up bad feelings. But given that exchange at the cemetery she had overheard, perhaps all the bad feelings were still on the surface.

Rick sipped his coffee, then allowed a half smirk as he said, "They probably are."

"On that note," Melinda said, and took another mystery donut from the bag, "did you ever find out the deal behind how come they were at that funeral?"

That, Cornelia thought, was a good question. She and Rick had, after all, been wondering about it before the Heiser incident spun everything off into the land of total chaos.

"It's Sarah Robinson's brother," Rick said. "Apparently he's been converted into the Reconstructionist way of seeing things."

That was a surprise, Cornelia thought. "Wow! I didn't see that one coming. Now I wonder who else in the family's in the fold."

"Not their father," Melinda said after biting the donut in half and studying its red cream filling.

"From what we saw at the hospital, definitely not Garret," Cornelia added.

"Except there's something about the Reconstructionists," Rick said, and paused.

Cornelia took note of the caution in his voice. "What's that?"

"They're big fans of the armed forces. *Very* big fans."

"That's just what we need," Cornelia couldn't help thinking out loud. Almost immediately she noticed the sideways glance coming from Melinda. "People who think this is the work of demons—because of gays, mind you—palling around with people who control the nuclear arsenal."

Rick quickly cocked an eyebrow. "No need to get panicky just yet. The air force doesn't decide what's done with nuclear weapons. Civilians in Washington do."

"Yeah, well," Melinda said with somewhat portentous tones, "you know what I said about this making us stronger?"

Cornelia looked at her. "Yeah?"

"Forget it!"

"Forget what?" Jerry's characteristically edgy, high-strung voice startled them.

"What is it, Jerry?" Cornelia asked.

"Want a cup of coffee, boss?" Rick said with what must have been his most laconic tone, Cornelia guessed. But he *had* brought four cups of coffee on that tray. "It's still nice and hot."

"Keep the coffee," Jerry snapped. "I'll have some at Travis."

"Say what?" Rick asked.

"Got a call from Knight. They're giving us a chance. There's already a plane on the tarmac."

6.

Although the Gulfstream V jet that had been sent to pick the *Confirmation* group up from San Francisco had just reached its

177

cruising altitude, Cornelia knew it was only a matter of minutes before it would start its descent into Travis Air Force Base. The short flight time was a problem, and the entire team knew it. So she, along with Rick and Lacy, crowded around Ian as he kept furiously perusing his iPad in one of the seats near the back of the plane. Glancing over her shoulder, Cornelia was glad to see Jerry distracting the two air force men at the front of the plane while Melinda, Tony, and Matt worked their video and audio equipment in between the two groups.

"So what's going on?" Cornelia asked Ian as quietly as possible.

Carrying on a private conversation in a small aircraft like this, its class most often used as a private toy for corporate titans or millionaire celebrities, was not easy. The interior of the Gulfstream was, Cornelia guessed, perhaps as large as a spacious drainage pipe.

"Can we tell the air force brass anything true?" Rick added. "Or are we getting booted out of Travis the moment we land?"

Ian nodded. "I think we have a good chance of staying."

"What did you find?" Cornelia asked quietly.

Ian glanced toward the front of the plane first. "References to vibrations and hums," he said at length. "*Feelings.* In some of the stories about the people who found globes. Not in all of them, though. Remember that woman in the bookstore back at Mount Shasta? The one talking about the globes being made by earth spirits? Lois Mackenzine? She said she felt a *vibration of positivity.* In Italy, in that town where they blew up the globe, one of the people also talked about feeling a vibration of energy. It looks like the reporters missed what was right in front of them. Thought they were talking to a lot of touchy-feely new age yo-yos."

Cornelia had to grin at yet another Ian Durfy crack at the "new age yo-yos." With his long locks held back in a ponytail, he would have been the first member of the group to be accused of meditating with crystals every morning.

"The reporters weren't taking any of it literally," Lacy said.

Ian looked up from his tablet. "Exactly."

"Good," Rick nodded with a smile of his own, and stepped back. "Excellent! So now we really have something to take to... well, whoever's trying to make sense of this."

"Sure," Lacy said, but Cornelia caught something in her tone and noticed a distant, tense look in her eyes. "And let's hope they keep their word and let us stay involved."

"Well, now we know what we know, right?" Ian said, and glanced at her. "If the G.I.'s don't want to let us play, I'm sure we can go to any number of scientists at any university. Am I right?"

"Maybe," Lacy said under her breath.

And what she was hinting at was already dawning on Cornelia.

"What do you mean?" Ian asked.

"We can go anywhere we want to with this information," Lacy almost whispered. "If they don't lock us up first. They could declare this is nothing but empty speculation that can cause more panic and disorder, and have us detained as a national security threat."

Ian looked out the window. "Aw, crap," he said softly.

Lacy threw a glance toward Jerry at the front of the plane. "Maybe we should have thought of this before rushing on this plane. But stardom beckoned, didn't it?"

"All right," Rick said just as quietly as he leaned back toward the group. "Let's everyone chill. We're here now and we need to see how it plays out. And remember, we're not the only media who will be at the base. Let's just all stay cool for now."

When no one replied, Rick backed away and took one of the seats by a window. It was quite a characteristic move and attitude, Cornelia thought. And she hoped he was right. There was nothing to do but wait now until they got face to face with Garret Robinson and whoever he was reporting to at Travis Air Base.

So she took the seat right next to Rick.

"Nice job keeping it together back there," she said at length.

179

Rick glanced at her with a distant little grin before looking out the window again. "I guess I have you fooled."

"No, you don't."

"I'm not ready to shoot someone who disagrees with me over all this, yeah. But that's hardly being Clint Eastwood."

Other than wanting to know how Rick could stay "Mr. Cool" when things were at their weirdest, his quip did make her curious about something. "Well, who *is* disagreeing with you?"

Rick looked at her without the smile this time. "Say what?"

"Who do you think is wrong? About the globes. About everything."

"Probably everyone," Rick said very matter-of-factly. "I mean Nazis? Come on!"

"Yeah, that's pretty stupid."

"Or the wrath of God over gays? Or Atlantians from Mount Shasta…."

"Remember, it's the alien citizens of the Kingdom of Lemuria that come from Mount Shasta," Cornelia cut in. "But that stuff about Atlantis is kind of cool."

Rick raised an amused eyebrow now. "Really? Cool?"

"It kind of is, yeah. It's different."

"Yeah, I guess it is…*different.*"

"All right, Professor." Cornelia had to press the issue now. "If we're all wrong, then what are they? What are these globes?"

"Oh, I'm not the professor in our little team," Rick said with an easy shrug. "And I have no idea what the globes are. About the time the second one showed up, the one in New Jersey, well, I decided I probably am not going to be the one figuring this out either. So I might as well sit back and enjoy the ride and not stress too much."

"Actually, that does sound a lot like Doc Knight," Cornelia said, surprised by what he'd said. She couldn't quite put her finger on it, but she was certain that she had sensed a tension between Knight and Rick since very shortly after the *Confirmation* team had started working together in Mount Shasta City.

But Rick shook his head immediately. And quite resolutely, Cornelia thought. "Knight?" he said. "I don't think so."

"Oh, I think so."

"No way."

"Why not?"

Rick glanced out the window for a beat before looking at her again and replying. "When the Doc's thinking of any higher power, I don't think he's willing to sit back and just roll with the punches."

"Really? How do you think he feels?"

Rick looked Cornelia square in the eyes. "I think he hates it."

And she was impressed by the certainty in his voice. They did say that effective cops needed to be very good judges of character, didn't they? Although she was intrigued by Rick, Cornelia was now just as intrigued by his take on their crusty, hard-living professor. "You think he hates the globes?"

"He hates whatever made them. Whatever's interfering with the world."

"Why?"

Rick shrugged, and with a lighter tone he said, "I guess we could ask him, but…." Then after a pause, he added with a harder edge, "Because they're interfering with the world."

Perhaps he was right, Cornelia mused now. If she wanted to know what made Dan Knight tick, all she needed to do was ask him. But now, and ever since she had overheard him arguing with his ex, Cornelia was much more interested in understanding Rick. "But you, on the other hand," she said, "*are* willing to roll with the punches."

"As long as I can," he said lightly, but he did give her a quizzical look.

"I mean, how long will this go on? Globes appearing one after the next? What's all this leading up to? What's the reason for all this?"

"I have no idea," Rick said with no flippancy, no sarcasm, no levity, and no worries either. Then he added, "And getting

181

an ulcer over it's not going to change anything. Except give me an ulcer." After the last word, however, he did allow a sly little smirk. "And *that* would really ruin my day."

"I guess that makes sense," Cornelia replied.

A beat of silence hung between them as she thought she noticed the plane slowing and dropping altitude.

"Yeah," Rick said, and cast a quick glance out the window. "I've just been the type to keep calm and go with the flow since... since Llewellyn Barclay back in L.A. That's been my philosophy since, and I think it works. You don't turn on your body-cam one time...and, well, here I am, on a TV show and in the middle of the investigation of the century."

"Well, that was a hell of a turn of events," Cornelia had to admit. But she also had to add, "But the flow right now — out there — all over the world...I think it's going in the wrong direction."

Rick looked her in the eyes, and somehow it seemed to put her ill at ease. He said nothing, just waited for her to go on. The silence seemed to ask her to offer a solution to the problem she posed...but one she didn't have herself.

"It's not just going in the wrong direction," she spoke at last, feeling that her words were somehow awkward. "It's insanity," she added, but felt no more effective.

"Well," Rick replied slowly. "If Dan gets us hooked up with the military now, we can find out the truth."

"You think so?"

"Unless Lacy's right." Rick seemed to be switching back to the light deadpan again. "And we get used for our information and then locked away in a rendition camp in Albania."

"That's not funny!"

"Sorry. I know."

"I don't want to sound like the cynical journalist, but I don't want to put too much stock in the sensibility of the government. Even with our information on the.... What? The hum? The vibrations?"

"What I mean," Rick said, more evenly this time, "is that we're not going to find anything—with or without our Eureka moment here about hums and vibrations—and neither will the government. Even if they *are* brilliant. We'll find out whatever the thing behind all this decides to let us find out. So we might as well enjoy the ride."

For a second Cornelia wasn't sure if the unpleasant sensation in her stomach was caused by Rick's statement or the plane's fast descent. "That sounds kind of like resignation," she said after a beat.

"It's being realistic. About the globes *and* the flow."

"I don't know. I think sometimes caring and making something happen is worth the try."

"Oh, of course it's worth a try," Rick said.

And Cornelia was so glad he sounded sincere about it.

Even his smile looked reassuring this time. "Probably won't work," he quipped, but did it with a kind of "I'm pulling your leg" wink. "But it's worth a try."

"That's the spirit—"

Before Cornelia could finish, the plane banked so violently that she was thrown against Rick. And she noticed the ugly thumping sound of his head striking the window.

7.

INCURSION OVER TRAVIS AIR FORCE BASE
By: Dennis Crenshaw, *The San Francisco Chronicle*

A hot air balloon flown by protesters was shot down by snipers over Travis Air Force Base in the early morning hours of September 12. Stanley Dorner, Eugene Babbit, and Helen Lasky, members of a protest group that has been picketing in front of the base, were piloting the balloon when it was brought down. The three were able to walk away without injuries after sniper fire deflated their balloon and brought it to a gentle landing inside the base. All three have been arrested and are now facing federal charges for trespassing.

The balloon, according to the base's Public Affairs office, nearly collided with a Gulfstream V jet flying in from San Francisco.

Dorner, Babbit, and Lasky have been camped out by the base for the past four days in order, they claim, to bring attention to the military's role in the creation of the globe phenomenon.

"This military installation, just like the ones in the San Diego area, if not many more across the country, have a clear hand in the appearance of these globes," said Roger Lutz, one of the organizers of the event. "We want answers and a full disclosure of what goes on behind the gates of these bases."

Lutz's group, along with a network of likeminded conspiracy buffs, has accused the government of using alien technology, invisibility devices, time-manipulation technology, and interdimensional doorways to create the globes. All of these devices, the protesters allege, are highly dangerous.

"Imagine the power of three nuclear weapons going off all at once," said Lisa Engelhardt, a protester and student from the University of California Berkley. "That's the sort of damage the technology in use at this base could do. Millions of people's lives are at risk here, and we need to put a stop to this."

"They're doing highly dangerous weapons research in there and they claim they're doing it in the name of the American people," said Zoe Miller, an Oakland resident and mother of three who joined the protest on the morning of the balloon incident. "Well, they're not doing it in *my* name. They're not doing in in the names of my kids. Nobody asked me if we wanted to be any part of their dangerous experiments."

According to Martin Scoggins, however, the base's chief public affairs officer, the protesters are ill-informed about what goes on at the base and the entire U.S. military's role in the globe phenomenon.

"Despite what many people might have read on the Internet or in the supermarket tabloids," said Scoggins, "our base—or *any* military installation—does not have the sort of technology that could make these globes appear out of thin air. The air force, in a joint program with the Pentagon and some of the top scientists in the world, will begin an extensive investigation of this phenomenon. But we are certainly not the ones causing it."

Scoggins added that Travis Air Force base is open to the public. His office gives guided tours every Thursday.

"We certainly wouldn't be running tours," he said, "if we had alien technology or any such thing bringing granite globes out of the *Twilight Zone*."

As far as the protest movement is concerned, however, the air force's attitude is patronizing and offensive.

"How dare they make light of the situation like that?" Benjamin Green, one of the protestors, replied. "It shows how much contempt they have for the American people. Well I, as a taxpayer and a Vietnam veteran, intend to sit out here and make my voice heard until these people come clean about the cover-up. If they want to shut me up, if they want me to leave, they'll have to drag me away."

"Like we're going to accept anything they say at face value," added Harry Lombard, an electrical engineer from Vallejo and avid conspiracy blogger. "After everything the government's lied to us about, they're guilty, you know, until proven innocent. Liars until proven truthful. The truth is right in there. Right inside Travis Air Base. Hidden from the people."

As for the balloonists, they could face up to six months in jail and fines up to $10,000.

According to Scoggins, no one on the incoming jet was injured as a result of the evasive maneuvers it had to take to avoid the balloon.

CHAPTER 7

The Skeleton Crew. Knight's Offer.
Goodbye To Lindsay. Can't Roll With the Punches.
Watching the News.

1.

A bolt of pain lanced through the side of Rick's head as he tried to scratch an itch as gingerly as he could. Getting his skull bounced off the side of Gulfstream's bulkhead as hard as he had, he was surprised he couldn't feel a larger swelling. It did hurt like hell, though. The ibuprofen tablets he had been given shortly after arriving at the base were not doing their thing yet either.

The atmosphere in the conference room didn't help matters much. Most of the people sitting around the enormous table looked either befuddled, hopeless, or irritable. Mostly irritable, Rick surmised from the pinched, sour expressions and the flinty, suspicious glares with which everyone sized up everyone else.

The most befuddled and irritable was Jerry, despite the fact that the *Confirmation* team was the only representative of the media sitting in on what had been described as a "skeleton crew of the U.S. government's investigative response to the globe crisis." David Kwan's claims did indeed seem to make their team the most valuable to the government, but *Confirmation* had not yet been given permission to film anything. Jerry, in turn, looked like a little kid who had been promised an enormous slice of cake, only to have it taken away from him in the last moment. "Would they try and push George Stephanopoulos around like this?" Rick had heard him grumbling shortly before the meeting. So far, his continuous reminders that ABC News was negotiating a deal with him had not born much fruit in terms of getting permission to electronically document anything.

"So we still have to come up with a workable plan to even approach this whole mess, ladies and gentlemen," Colonel Michael Franciosa, the base commander and the man doing most of the pacing, said. With Franciosa's distinguished, almost patrician features and studious eyes, Rick thought he looked more like a business executive than a hard-charging warrior. "And with three of these globes all clustered in California, we better do some serious approaching before the rest of the people from Washington show up. We need result right *now.*"

"Obviously we need to round these...*people* up. If we really do have more than one. And do it right away," an attractive yet severe-looking woman in her mid-thirties, wearing an air force class A uniform and the rank of major in the medical service, a Dr. Kristine Murakami, replied. Her eyes flicked little glances of condescension toward every member of the *Confirmation* team. "We'll start with this Kwan individual and go from there. If the CDC will be sending their people too, maybe we'll have something valuable to share with them."

Rick thought she sounded as if she had swallowed another previously intended comment. Maybe something along the lines of, "So we don't look like idiots taking our cues from a reality TV production crew."

"Dr. Murakami's right. We need Kwan and others like him right away," a marine corps lieutenant colonel with a name tag on his uniform reading "Rutkowski" seconded. Rick thought he remembered the man's first name as being Sam from the fast initial round of introductions. His short, dense-looking physique reminded Rick of the way the Wolverine character was drawn in the *X-Men* comics.

Since the globe investigation was going to be a joint-services effort, on top of all the scientific and medical consultants Washington was promising to round up, this meeting included representatives of the navy and the marines as well, given the fact that the second California globe appeared next to their installations. Rutkowski's home base was the Marine Corps Recruit Depot in San Diego. But he had shared a flight to Travis with Lieutenant Colonel Frederick Graham from San Diego's Coronado Naval Amphibious Base. Graham, a light-complexioned African American, had, much like Franciosa, the reserved and cerebral bearing of a business executive or a college administrator.

"If there's anything to this buzz and vibration theory," Dr. Murakami said, "*and* somehow only a few handful of people can hear it, we need to see what makes them tick." After a quick beat during which she appeared to be weighing the pros and cons of another statement, she added, "As skeptical as I am."

Her barbed delivery of those last words reminded Rick of Lindsay's style of verbal combat during the worst moments of their breakup. Lindsay was always fond of the well-timed final word, a little coup-de-grace after her most potent insults and recriminations.

As his pulse quickened for a split instant, Rick's attention automatically drifted toward Cornelia. And it worked, he realized. It worked perfectly. What stewing anger a memory of Lindsay could ignite in him, a glance at Cornelia instantly smothered.

"This Kwan guy's for real!" Jerry snapped. His eyes darted not just to Murakami but the rest of the people in the room. He had obviously taken the doctor's little jab as a personal affront.

"So what do we do? Go and grab him off the street?" Melinda spoke up.

"Yeah," Ian added. "Like is that even legal?"

"You remember that collision you almost had with the hot air balloon?" Colonel Franciosa said.

Graham, the navy man, rolled his eyes and said, "Jesus Christ!" in the discrete tones of a country club patron stunned by a particularly inferior vintage of port.

"People are about to start killing each other all over the world because of this," Franciosa continued.

"Three of our embassies have gotten credible threats already," Rutkowski interjected, with the tense body language of someone ready to wrestle an opponent to the ground.

"The point is," Franciosa continued, "getting ahold of Kwan and others like him *will* be legal."

It made sense, of course, Rick knew. It was the whole point of his team being here. Kwan, and presumably others who had the same experience with the hums, were the one true break in this mystery so far. The only problem seemed to be the doctor's carelessly worded phrase of "we have to round these people up." Rick wondered about her bedside manner now.

"I'll believe that when I have a theoretical explanation for what makes his...*powers* work," Murakami came right back at Jerry with a sharply focused, challenging glare.

Rick couldn't help chuckling now. "Powers? Doctor, you make him sound like some kind of a superhero."

Murakami gave him the same kind of stare. "No, *you* do. And, Mr. Ballantine," she said, infusing "Mr. Ballantine" with the voice of a middle school principal about to deliver a sentence of a week-long detention, "my line of work requires me to be skeptical until I have some solid proof of something. I'm not your villain here. I'm not implying that you and your friends concocted this story to gain access to the government's investigation. But I...but *we* need some facts. Some data. And that's why I want Kwan and others like him."

But Murakami's fire-breathing delivery implied exactly that she suspected Jerry and his whole crew of fabricating a grand piece of flim-flam.

"All right! Let's all focus here!" Garret Robinson spoke up at last as he raised a hand. "We *are* all on the same team. There *is* something compelling to this David Kwan's claims — "

But Franciosa cut in as he took a seat now. "And Dr. Murakami is also right. We need *some* scientific data before we draw any conclusions. Since we pretty much have squat so far and dozens of globes seem to be inspiring people all over the world to act on their most paranoid impulses."

"But a theoretical framework?" the one other civilian in the room beside the *Confirmation* team said all of a sudden. "Without which all of this phenomenon is bogus and a pseudoscientific pipedream? That's what I used to say when all of this started. Before all of my students dropped my classes. Before my car was keyed."

It was Vincent Rafferty, a physicist from Cal State Fullerton with a specialty in something having to do with high-energy physics that Rick was incapable of recalling. He did remember Knight mentioning, however, that the young professor was not only brilliant—short-listed by some academic trade paper as one the new physics whiz-kids to watch before he even finished his Ph.D. at Princeton—but quite untenured and having somehow run afoul of his school's administration as a result of the globes. It must have made the call for help by Washington suddenly very attractive.

"I mean, that's the whole problem," Rafferty continued. "There *is* no theoretical framework here. It's what makes unexplained phenomena, you know, *unexplained*."

"And our job, ladies and gentlemen," Murakami snapped right back, infusing "ladies and gentlemen" with that middle school principal tone again, "is to *explain* it." She then looked at Franciosa and Robinson, *demanding* more than asking, for a measure of backup. "Am I not right? And we can't do that without some sort of a theoretical framework to start from."

"OK, you're right," Cornelia suddenly spoke up.

Rick noticed that it seemed to surprise the military people and the two scientists the most. But none of them appeared to be bothered by her.

"*People* will help us get to the bottom of this phenomenon," she continued, "and we need to find them. And hopefully we'll find most of the right ones." Pausing, her gaze swept the room as she attempted to make a sort of conciliatory eye contact with everyone. She held Murakami's gaze the longest. "But for that,

190

you might need another specialist in here as well."

"Like who?" asked Franciosa.

"A media specialist," Cornelia replied.

When she said that, Rick noticed Murakami stiffen. He wondered if she might have done something more obnoxious like roll her eyes or say something cutting had Cornelia not just come to her defense. The doctor, Rick surmised, did not believe the social sciences had anything to contribute to the management of this crisis. And he also wondered with some amusement — the sort of amusement that allowed him to enjoy the mayhem of a good *Three Stooges* episode and the violence of professional wrestling — about how Murakami was going to get along with Knight.

"You mean to say —" Murakami began.

But Cornelia cut in. "Yes. The only way to find these people is through analyzing media coverage."

"No offense," Murakami said with a shake of her head and a rueful little smirk, "but I think we're doomed."

"We don't need the hyperbole just now, Doctor." Colonel Robinson came to Cornelia's defense with a harder edge to his voice.

"Or we could put out another invitation," Jerry exclaimed with the tight, unstable sarcasm of an offended, egocentric child. "Everyone who's heard sounds and vibrations, please come down to Travis Air Base for the full, free, taxpayer-provided checkup."

More condescending impatience than anger flashed in Murakami's eyes, Rick noticed. She looked as if she was thinking that she would never embarrass herself by losing her cool on account of this inconsequential little man.

"Like the colonel said," Knight spoke up, moving in to extend good will and rein in the most troublesome member of his team the way Robinson had just done. "We all need to stay cool." His words were aimed squarely at Jerry.

Rick could have sworn there was an embarrassed look on Knight's face, an unspoken request for allowances, his acknowledgement of the indignity that an intellectual of his stature was feeling, having to associate with an unsophisticated show-business oaf like Jerry Peretti.

Jerry, of course, still not over their argument from the previous evening, gave Knight a seething look, but said nothing.

"All right. So let me understand this," Murakami said in well-controlled tones. "Our process for predicting where these globes will show up will now include sitting and watching the news and browsing the web."

Put in those terms, Rick not only recognized but understood the unease on the faces of the soldiers in the room.

"We need to try anything we can," Rafferty said in a sort of whatever-the-hell, we-might-as-well tone.

"And no, I don't have any better ideas," Murakami replied. "*Yet*. But we are going to find those people who might have a link to this phenomenon—a *predictive* link—based on what some reporter chooses to write in order to make a news story sound snappier and sell papers? And get more hits online? Oh, and once that reporter made sure the whole story's written to engage the intellectual level of a third-grader. No offense to our friends from the mass media, but please excuse my skepticism." Her final words regained some of her earlier sarcastic snap.

"It *is* the best idea we have to work with," Robinson came back immediately with a dry, equally uncompromising retort.

"Exactly," Knight seconded. "It sounds strange. I grant you that. And we all do. But we have to try something."

"Yeah," Rutkowski said, "the barbarians are at the gates."

"Quite literally," Graham tagged on. "With their hot air balloons."

"Like Dr. Rafferty would agree," Rick spoke up, "militant skeptics aren't too popular out there right now."

Rafferty merely nodded with what looked like a cross between a wistful, defeated grin and a wince of pain.

"Of course," Murakami came back with a much more conciliatory, yet intensely unhappy, tone, "this country—this *world*—is slipping into the Dark Ages again. Aren't we glad to be living in the twenty first century?"

Rick would have liked to have added, "Maybe because the skeptics insisted that this was nothing but an elaborate hoax and a mass delusion for a bit too long," but chose to keep it to himself for the sake of peace in the room.

"Yes, it's unfortunate," Franciosa said, and shifted in his seat. "And all beside the point right now. What is, *is*."

"And Washington's not getting us all together to fight amongst ourselves," Robinson added. He paused and looked at his superior for a moment. "So let's get a hold of David Kwan, shall we?"

Both the representatives of the navy and the marine corps nodded.

"And someone will start going over every single word ever written or spoken about anyone being near those globes and feeling vibrations?" Graham asked.

"Whoa," Ian said quietly, exhaled, then added, "we got some work on our hands."

Franciosa looked at Cornelia. "So tell me what kind of a media specialist you need."

2.

"What do you think? Should I tell her to go to hell?" Knight asked as Rick finished guzzling the last of the water in his sports bottle.

He really wished the professor would stop bombarding him with questions as he tried to catch his breath and recover. It was bad enough that the run had felt a lot worse than he thought it would after....

Aw, crap! After just over a year! Rick's inner voice berated him. *Is it against your religion or creed to do some cardio once in a while?*

But the fact of the matter was that running and cardio work were always easy to let slip by the wayside. This had been especially so since his involvement with the *Confirmation* project.

He always lifted weights, even on the road, but the cardio work always betrayed what he supposed was one of his character flaws. It was just too boring.

But now the base running-track was next to the temporary housing unit he and the *Confirmation* crew had been stuck in, so he'd decided to give a three-mile run a shot. Things didn't go as smoothly as he anticipated.

"Telling her to go to hell might not be necessary just now," he replied as he hoped to walk another lap around the track.

Knight chuckled as he walked beside him. "Sure. You mean you want to tell her yourself, right?" Another irritating chuckle followed.

"No, I think the high road will do," Rick replied, really hoping Knight would just go away. "But I can't believe Lindsay's still here."

"Yeah, it's weird, isn't it? Well, she and her husband are weird people—"

"I mean *here*. At the base."

"It's nuts, I know."

Rick glanced at Knight, wondering what insult he was about to aim at Lindsay. He knew the old man considered his ex-wife a lazy sponge, a gold-digger who had hooked up with the wealthy Pastor Burke because his Reconstructionist dogma justified a family structure where a woman wasn't required to have any identity aside from that of a wife and mother. Knight also thought Rick was just as weak for not taking more of a scorched-earth approach to their divorce. "A divorce," Knight had lectured, "and take it from someone who has plenty of expertise in the matter, is a World War II, blitzkrieg, total-war situation. I'm talking original *Karate Kid*, Cobra Kai, 'an enemy deserves no mercy,' 'sweep the leg' total annihilation."

"I'll tell her to go to hell if you say so, Chief," Knight said, apparently intent on following Rick around the track. "That'll be a nice touch. You don't even have the time for her to—"

"No," Rick said firmly. "I'll handle this."

"OK," Knight said, and laughed. "Go to hell might be too much. How 'bout...you're sending a message that you and Cornelia are all tied up with something and you don't have the time. Since Cornelia never, you know, needed to take *years* to figure out what her life was all about."

Rick was irritated when he felt a grin wanting to slip into the corner of his mouth. The old bastard really knew how to bring out the worst in him.

"That's fine," he said at length. "I'll get rid of her myself."

Knight nodded. "Aha," he mumbled, and swaggered off the track. "Oh, by the way," he called over his shoulder. "I think she's waiting for you by the visitor center." Then, after taking another three steps, Knight turned around again. "And one more thing!" he called. "They're bringing in David Kwan. We have permission to shoot some footage of him arriving at the base. You might want to hurry up for that."

Rick nodded and tried to picture the layout of the base in his head again. What was the shortest distance to the visitor center? But it wasn't the David Kwan news that prompted him to want to get through whatever Lindsay had to say. He wanted to see Cornelia again.

3.

By the time Rick arrived at the visitor center, he was close to regretting that he hadn't sent Knight to meet with Lindsay. Sure, he kept telling himself that he would have given the professor express orders to be on his diplomatic best behavior...but what did that matter now? What he would say to his ex kept turning over in his head. Would he tell her that he didn't mean what he said about her affair? No, the fact was that he did mean it. And he was still bitter about it, and he still resented both Lindsay and Donald Burke for it.

Wouldn't want me to lie to you, would you, Lindsay? a thought streaked through his mind. *A lying tongue is an abomination, isn't it?*

Or that he didn't intend to hurt her with that jibe about Cornelia? The one about respecting Cornelia more because she could pursue her dreams and career under the greatest adversity whereas Lindsay couldn't? That he admired Cornelia because she was strong whereas Lindsay was weak and indecisive? No, he told himself. He could not deny those feelings because they were true.

So instead he simply said, "Lindsay," as they stood face to face again. Then, realizing how he looked in his sweat-stained T-shirt and shorts, he added, "Sorry about that. Bad timing."

"No, Rick," Lindsay replied immediately. There was a sort of vehemence in her eyes, Rick noticed immediately. "*I'm* sorry. You were right. Last time. Oh my God, you were *so* right."

That caught him off guard. He wasn't about to complain about what Lindsay had just said, but it was quite a curveball. "What do you mean?" was the only thing he could think of asking.

"I've been glued to the news since the other day. And thank God you're all right. I'm so glad you weren't injured in that chase."

"Thanks," Rick heard himself say awkwardly. "Really, Lindsay, I appreciate that."

"But as I'm watching the news and reading about everything that's going on—what happened right here with that balloon—everything, all this craziness…well, it made me realize that you were right."

Lindsay paused and looked Rick square in the eyes. Her probing, animated glare, her odd delivery, made him wonder if this was her strange, roundabout way of apologizing for coming on so strong the other day, apologizing for *something*. But he wanted her to get to the point as soon as she could, wanted to understand exactly what she meant, so he said, "I'm not sure I get what you mean."

"What you said about the globes and *us!* All the people in the world. All of us. The real threat is inside of *us*."

This surprised Rick since Lindsay—or at least the version of her he was most familiar with, the one he had been married to—was not one to backtrack or apologize for a lot of things.

"You had it right, Rick. *We* are the threat." She then took a step closer to him, leaned in, and with a conspiratorial tone said, "Because that's the real power of the globes. They bring out the worst in us. The sin, the evil that's in all of our hearts. *That's* what the globes do. They're like a...what? Trojan Horse? Can we compare them to that? Like, they look harmless. They're a mysterious gift from beyond. Oh, I think a lot of people believe these things are from some benevolent force. Some friendly alien or earth goddess or something like that. That they're some gift. But they're not. They have the power to unleash the worst inside all of us. Until we kill each other."

Wow, Rick thought. *How does one argue with that?* He honestly didn't know, and didn't want to get into any sort of analytical discussions with Lindsay about it. Because she *had* been right; her words did mirror his own assessment in a way.

He started nodding slowly, and that, in turn, prompted Lindsay to add, "Is there no more of a potent weapon the devil can use against us?"

"I really don't know," Rick said quietly.

Lindsay returned a thin smile. "I know you don't. I know you have a hard time believing. But you believe your eyes, don't you?"

"Sure."

"And you believe all the sick, destructive, hateful things people are about to do to each other as a result of these globes. Those are facts you can hang on to."

Rick nodded.

"Then the answer to all of this is obvious. These things need to be destroyed."

Lindsay's customarily placid, inscrutable smile was still in place, but her words, Rick realized, were forged in steely determination.

197

"I have no control over that," he replied.

"But your opinion is valued. That's why you're here. Working with the military."

That comment brought up another important matter, something Rick had to know. "Look, Lindsay, just curious about something."

"What's that?"

"What are you guys doing on this base?"

"Don held a service for some of the airmen. Many on this base, like Sarah Robinson's brother, as you know, have been saved. They just needed words of encouragement and guidance with this coming storm."

"I see."

"That's what it is, Rick. You know as well as I do. A storm. We *must* get rid of these things before we all perish." Then Lindsay paused for a deep breath. "But unfortunately, I *do* have to go. Don and I will try and drive home. As fast as we can on these roads, I suppose."

"All right. And, yeah, be careful on the roads."

Lindsay was about to back away, but paused for a moment. "Oh, and Rick.... Do go back to Cornelia. I think you two would be wonderful for each other."

Before Rick could reply, she turned and walked away. He was glad that she did and he didn't have to say anything else. The problem was he was feeling unspeakably low at that moment. Lindsay had wished him well and encouraged a relationship with Cornelia...just moments after he admitted to himself that he had enjoyed hurting Lindsay the other day.

He felt he needed to take a shower right away. But it wasn't just the run that had left him feeling unclean. Could some soap and water, he wondered, scrape away the taint of self-disgust?

4.

Rick was surprised to run into Cornelia as she walked away from the row of guest apartments set aside for *Confirmation*. With what Knight had said back at the track, he couldn't imagine what she would be doing here. She *was*, after all, the chief interviewer of their show.

"Hey," he called to her as she lifted her gaze from her phone and whatever news site she was perusing on it. "What's going on? I ran into Dan back at the track. Don't they want you for the shooting with—?"

"With Kwan here? Nope. And Jerry's not happy."

"What's going on?"

"The news broke. Kwan and the hums and vibrations he's hearing. The rest of the press got ahold of it."

Now *that* was a surprise. "What happened?"

Cornelia pocketed her phone. "His neighbor happened. After we talked to Kwan, he repeated everything to his neighbor who, by the way, is a globe blogger."

"Globe blogger?"

Cornelia returned a weary kind of what-is-this-world-coming-to smile and a shrug. "Why not? Some people blog about food, others blog about cats. Kwan's neighbor blogs about globes. And hums and vibrations and photos of air force people coming to meet David Kwan. And Kwan arguing with them. And Kwan's lawyer showing up, too. And everyone leaving their house. Oh, and a few of said air force people staying behind and making the mistake of trying to tell his neighbor—Andy Michener, by the way—that he should keep quiet about what went on there."

Rick couldn't keep a little guffaw of laughter tumbling from his mouth. "And these people are supposed to be hiding back-engineered UFOs?"

Cornelia laughed too. "Maybe the local members of the air force couldn't. You know these California types. Too mellow and laid back."

"Now the secret's out? The rest of the media picked up on it?"

"Yeah," Cornelia said lightly. "And some of our friends in uniform are not happy about it. Especially the medical service's answer to General Patton."

"Oh, her—yeah. Murakami's just not quite sure, I think, that we're not a bunch of con artists. That we're not working with Kwan on some sort of a scam to get access to the government's globe investigation."

"Anyway, you remember what you said about, uh…."

"About what?"

"You know, rolling with the punches. It's probably right."

Except Rick had been having second thoughts. "I'm not sure anymore."

"Oh?" Cornelia, looked genuinely taken.

And Rick wondered just what kind of an image she had of him. "Yeah," he said, something prompting him to infuse that word with as much gravitas as he could. "The thing is…I just had a…well, a bit of a disturbing experience."

"With Lindsay?" Cornelia replied without a beat.

And that really caught him off guard. *So, someone has been talking.*

"Dan told me," Cornelia added quickly, noticing Rick's surprise.

But of course he did.

"Sorry," Cornelia tagged on quickly. "If it was something private…."

"Oh, no," Rick replied, noticing how fast and how unequivocal his own words were. "Definitely nothing private. As a matter of fact, Lindsay wants to warn all of us."

"About what?"

"Only that the world is coming to an end."

Cornelia looked puzzled for a moment, as if trying to figure out how serious he was.

"For real," he said. "That's her message to all of us." Although he wanted to sound serious as he spoke, an impulse to smile almost sunk into the corner of his mouth as he thought of Lindsay's other bit of advice.

"Well, it sounded to me the other day like she and her

husband are always prepared for that."

Rick couldn't help chuckling now. "I think they are. But she also said something that might be on the money."

"Oh yeah?"

"That it's not the globes that will do it. But *we* will."

Cornelia hung on those words for a moment, her gaze very graven now. "That might be true."

"And you can't just go with that. Sure, Lindsay and her husband are. Probably getting ready to be raptured away or something."

Cornelia gave him a crooked, humorless little grin.

"But this is the time to try and do something about it."

"How?" Cornelia asked, her tone almost a whisper.

"I don't know yet. But we have to start working hard at figuring it out."

"That's funny," Cornelia said after a beat, "because I was starting to seriously doubt that anything *can* be done."

Before Rick could reply, he felt the fingers of her right hand tentatively moving over his left. As he moved to hold them, she took a firm grasp of his hand and pulled him closer.

"Maybe we can...with people who are used to fighting the odds," Rick replied, staring into her eyes as her lovely face came closer to his with the passing of each word from his lips.

When Rick kissed her, Cornelia took his other hand as well, holding him tight, holding him closer to her, encouraging it.

And suddenly she pushed away. "Do you think...?"

"What?" Rick whispered, wanting to kiss her again but distressed by her vacillation. "You don't...?"

"I do," Cornelia said, "but is this the right time? I mean, we don't even know what will happen to us from day to day."

"Maybe that's why it's the right time. We need something to live for."

Cornelia's hands tightened on his and she kissed him again with renewed vigor and passion.

Except Rick noticed a problem. "I'm kind of a mess," he

whispered a moment later, embarrassed, conscious of his sweaty running clothes.

"Then let's get you cleaned up."

5.

If Rick had seriously entertained the idea that the tide of chaos could be controlled, entering the base's command center would have made him rethink that idea. The installation's communications nerve-center, loaded with rows of computer consoles on the floor-level and towered over by nearly monolith-sized monitors on three walls, was now relaying a flood of breaking news to the air force personnel crowded into the room, and the *Confirmation* team hovering on the periphery of it all.

After having been led inside, Rick tried to read the body language all around as much as the images flickering away on the myriad of screens. Was all this something good or something pushing the world to the brink of whatever apocalypse Lindsay and Don Burke must always have been preparing for?

Or maybe it's neither, Rick thought as he felt Cornelia brush against him. At first he felt the impulse to reach for her again, to find her hand and hold it, except this was not the right time. She, too, must have realized the same thing, he guessed, because she was not reaching for him either.

Maybe it's time for business first, his mind called to him, commanding him to focus on the tumult in the room and all of its possible implications, instead of the profound way his relationship with Cornelia had just changed.

The first implication he noticed was cameramen Matt and Tony panning, pausing upon, then panning their cameras yet again at the command center personnel. So something must have happened to let Colonel Franciosa and his globe study group allow them full access and documentation privileges.

Catching a glimpse of Jerry standing nearby, studying everything with steely intensity, Rick also noticed that their producer looked elated. Despite the fact that Cornelia had been under the impression that Jerry was not happy with the leaked news of Kwan, something had finally gone his way and he was relishing it.

Before he could ask anyone what was happening, Rick saw Kristine Murakami glaring at him and Cornelia. The doctor sized him over the way he would have expected her to had he still been in his running clothes instead of cleaned up, shaven, and in a fresh pair of khakis and a polo shirt.

"Did you two get lost?" Murakami asked.

"What's happening?" Rick asked instead.

"This hum phenomenon of Kwan's is suddenly infecting people all over the place."

"All over San Francisco?" Cornelia asked. She seemed as stunned as Rick felt.

"All over the world," Murakami replied immediately. "That's what we're monitoring. News reports from around the world that have anything to do with anyone claiming to hear hums and buzzing and vibrations."

"I guess we won't need a media analyst," Rick thought out loud.

"Yeah, guess not," Cornelia seconded.

But Rick was too curious to not broach another subject, no matter the reaction it would get out of the temperamental Murakami. "So, since we were right about Kwan, we get to stay on the investigative team? By the way, what *is* his condition that he can feel the vibrations…?"

"We don't know what his condition is," Murakami replied, much more coolly than Rick had thought she would. "Of course it would have helped if we could have started on his examinations sooner rather than later. If we didn't have to argue with his lawyer. And *you* get to stay a part of the team for now because one of the networks wants to follow a scientific expert consulting with the government on all this. And Washington agreed."

"What? Dan Knight?" Cornelia exclaimed.

"Yes," Murakami replied flatly. "They want to show complete

transparency to the world and foster international cooperation. All in light of stuff like *that*." She nodded toward one of the overhead monitors.

On the one hand, what he saw made the populist part of Rick's nature soar. Here they stood in the heart of a major defense facility's command center, and the people in charge were watching broadcasts of CNN. The screen Murakami brought their attention to was displaying live shots of from CNN's *The Situation Room* program. *An informed press is the soul of democracy*, he almost said in the most droll tone he could muster. But, unfortunately, the report was also about a violent demonstration in Madrid.

"What's going on?" He asked as he watched the scenes of an angry, bottle and rock throwing mob, riot-police trying to keep them under control, protesters being dragged away in cuffs, and shots of broken windows on stores and vandalized cars.

"Everyone with their pet paranoia around the world coming out and using all this as an excuse to throw rocks and set things on fire," Rick heard Garret Robinson's voice from behind him.

"That's about it," Murakami concurred.

"And why all of this investigative project will go international," Robinson said, "and keep the media informed. To try and get some control over all this lunacy. You got just about every fundamentalist religious sect out there believing these things are the work of the devil. Every radical nut—right-winger, left-winger, anarchist, anti-corporatist, eco-terrorists, skinheads, what have you—is trying to overthrow whatever government is in power."

"What about them?" Cornelia asked, staring at the monitor of the Madrid riot.

"Who the hell knows?" Robinson grumbled with a shrug. "And does it really matter? They want to bring down the government because it knows more than it's saying about a local globe, and they think the strings are being pulled by the American government and their conspirators."

"And more and more of these people hearing the hum now

is going to be a break?" Rick asked.

"We'll find out," Robinson said, then looked at Murakami. "Right, Doctor?"

"We'll try our best, sir."

"But how?" Cornelia tore her fascinated, repulsed gaze away from the riot monitor. "You don't even know what makes people hear the hum."

"Well," Murakami started to answer, and Rick noticed how tense she looked doing so. She obviously wasn't happy speculating about something as exotic as the hum-sensitives. She probably didn't even have a clue about where to start looking for a root of the affliction. "We're going to run every test on Kwan we can think of. And we'll get in touch with as many people as possible who are hearing the hum."

"Exactly," Robinson cut in, sounding much more enthusiastic. "We're going to our nearest concentration of hum-experiencers."

"Concentration?" Rick asked.

"Yeah," Robinson replied. "There seem to be places where an unusually high number of people have reported this affliction."

"And where's the nearest concentration?" Cornelia asked.

"Hawaii," Robinson said.

6.

VATICAN AND SCIENTISTS CALL FOR PEACE AND RESEARCH
By: Arthur Gates, *Los Angeles Times*

In the wake of the world-wide protest movements and the outbreak of violence, the Vatican and an American scientist have called for open-minded investigations of the globe mystery and a refrain from the vitriol and violence that have come to mark the entire phenomenon.

"No matter how scared people might be, hate and violence will not solve anything," said Monsignor Leonardo Anzalone in a press conference held at the Vatican Observatory in Castle

Gandolfo.

Monsignor Anzalone, a Jesuit priest and astronomer, is a member of the Curia of the Roman Catholic Church.

During the press conference, he was joined by Dr. Duane King, an astrophysicist from the Steward Observatory at the University of Arizona in Tucson. The University of Arizona is a host institution for the Vatican Observatory.

"This sort of aggression we are seeing all over the world," said King, "is antithetical to all religious faiths, and it's antithetical to all reason and scientific inquiry. It must simply stop right now before it escalates into a territory we can't come back from."

When asked about so much of the controversy and ill will being fueled by what many see as a chasm between science and religion, Monsignor Anzalone insisted that such a chasm need not exist. He pointed to the Catholic Church's strong support of scientific inquiry.

"We must use science to solve this dilemma," he insisted, pointing at the Vatican's own observatory program as one of the bridges between faith and reason. "God's truth is reflected in all of nature and in all phenomena in the world around us," Anzalone said. "We need to study this [globe] phenomenon to find out if it is a natural phenomenon, a true miracle, or if it might be something demonic."

Although the monsignor did make a controversial acknowledgement of a possibly demonic source of the globes, he called for more rigorous scientific research before any conclusions were reached.

"The answers to the globe mystery need to be found in this world," he said. "The globe mystery needs to be explained from within itself. For this reason, scientific research and overall scientific progress is very important."

Anzalone also reminded that although it is not an official Vatican position, he had long advocated for the study of parapsychology. Parapsychology applies scientific investigative methods to seemingly supernatural phenomena.

"These globes," he argued, "are a phenomenon originating in nature, as they are certainly material objects. But they are from a realm in nature we do not understand."

The monsignor compared the globes to unexplained phenomena like telekinesis, UFO sightings, or telepathy.

Dr. King also urged the world to look at the globe phenomenon as a positive opportunity.

"Instead of fear and violence," he said, "we need to look at these globes as perhaps the most exciting time to be researchers and scientists. We know the phenomenon is real. There is no disputing it any more. So now let's take up the challenge and study it. Let's understand it without any preconceived notions."

The very nature of the phenomenon, King believes, could possibly change the world in ways no one can imagine.

"This is going to lead us to an entirely new understanding of reality," he said. "This will make us see the very laws of nature, physics, the entire universe in a whole new light. Let's embrace all of this instead of closing our minds and fighting each other."

What impact these suggestions will have remain to be seen as violent clashes between globe-related protests and police have broken out in Greece, Portugal, Spain, and in Rome.

Catherine Buchanan contributed to this report from Rome.

CHAPTER 8

The Pattern. Coincidences. A Test of the First Amendment.
Weighing a Man's Character. Rumors of Impatience. Attack.
Chase. Helicopter.

1.

Cornelia decided that she would not turn to one of their cameras and reflect on her mix of emotions any time soon. At least not without a script.

The truth would be such a cliché anyway, she mused. *Well, OK, maybe not entirely a cliché.*

She was in the middle of the story of a lifetime—the lifetime of any journalist anywhere in the history of journalism—and her mind kept wandering to Rick. To his guest apartment back at Travis.

No, definitely not for the cameras, she decided.

Some TV critic would lambast *Confirmation* for perpetuating a negative sexist stereotype. "Why does the strong female lead have to be hung up on a romantic dalliance in the middle of the story of the century as she sits in the macho, metallic confines of a transport plane at thirty thousand feet over the Pacific and on the way to Hawaii?"

Maybe because the strong female lead is also a human being, she retorted in her mind as she stood by one of the windows of the ironically named Boeing C-17 Globemaster, and studied the green-blue ocean below melting into the cloudless horizon.

And because Rick, the strong male lead, is also hung up on the same things, she added as she felt a hand at the small of her back. It touched her just momentarily, but she could sense it was Rick.

She thought it felt clandestine, yet self-assured and firm.

And, indeed, he moved to stand next to her a moment later, a light crease of a smile in the corner of his mouth. "So have they solved the mysteries of the universe yet?"

"They think they're close," Cornelia found herself saying with very dry sarcasm.

Since the last news reports they saw in the command center back at Travis had offered no good news from around the world, the mood inside the plane had settled on full-bore apocalyptic.

"Let's check it out," Rick said.

They might as well, Cornelia thought, and stepped away from the bulkhead. Once again, there was the welcome feel of Rick's hand on her shoulder for a moment as they headed toward the gathering closer to the front of the plane.

The cavernous cargo-bearing aircraft had become the mobile headquarters for the Travis-based branch of the government's globe-phenomenon study unit. Since the military had somehow concluded that Hawaii was a hotbed of globe-sensitive individuals, they wanted to dispatch a team with as much equipment as would possibly become necessary to use in the field. That equipment turned out to be two Humvees, a UH-60 Blackhawk helicopter, along with pallets full of medical testing equipment.

As for the personnel, Kristine Murakami had been tasked with selecting a group of doctors to go with her—mainly neurologists, as Cornelia recalled—and provide enough hands and sharp minds to try and get to the bottom of what afflicted people like David Kwan. Along with the scientific team, they were matched with a Navy SEAL platoon and a team of the air force's special operations troops, the Combat Controllers. And if their plane wasn't loaded tightly enough with their crew—leaving only the sidewall seating as the rest of the belly of the C-17 held the hardware—a small and carefully selected press pool from the four networks and CNN also crowded the plane.

As she and Rick made their way further forward, Cornelia

noticed that the serious discussion about the latest globe developments around the world took place next to the helicopter. That was the section of the cargo hold that afforded the most space between the bulkheads and the hardware.

"…This is classic. I'm telling you," she heard Knight's voice among the gathering. "It's easy to see the pattern."

"What pattern is that?" asked a female reporter.

Cornelia couldn't recall which network she was with. But each representative group of a media outlet, Cornelia saw—including their very own techies, Matt, Tony, Lacy, and Melinda—were recording the discussion from every possible angle.

Of the study unit's leadership, only Sam Rutkowski and the navy's Frederick Graham had joined this away team. Colonels Franciosa and Robinson stayed behind at Travis, coordinating operations with the Pentagon and the Chairman of the Joint Chief's of Staff.

"It's a test. And it's a part of a pattern," Knight said.

"But there is no precedent to this *anywhere* in history," one of the other reporters said.

"In a way there is," Knight said with an intense glare.

"Like what?" a voice asked from the crowd.

"I think this is *testing* us," Knight said. "*And* provoking us."

"I can see that perfectly," Cornelia heard Ian say, and saw him elbowing his way closer to the nucleus of the gathering. As a special effects technician, he might have had some strong opinions, Cornelia surmised, about perceptions being manipulated and audiences being provoked.

"Is this the conclusion they reached?" Cornelia heard Rick's voice close to her ear.

"Apparently so," she replied.

"Look," Knight said, "just ask yourselves how far people would go if surrounded by chaos and anarchy."

"How violent they are willing to become?" a reporter from NBC News asked.

"No," Knight said. "Just the opposite."

"What do you mean?" the reporter asked.

"How far they are willing to go for peace and security? What are they willing to do to make all the anarchy stop?"

The group around Knight appeared to be stumped by the question, because no clear, determined response came from the professor. There were murmurs of quiet discussion and speculation all around, but no one was willing to offer any self-assured theory to match the question.

But Cornelia knew why. She knew why the taut fear had settled over the group. Maybe what Knight was proposing was even more disturbing than the chaos rising all around the world.

"What are we willing to give up to make the riots stop?" he asked, and probed the people around him with a flinty glare. "It's classic, isn't it? What was Germany willing to give up in the 1930s? The Russians after the collapse of communism, when the crime and chaos swept in?"

"After 9/11?" Someone among the reporters said. "Patriot Act anyone? NSA spying. Warrantless wiretapping?"

"So take all that to the hundredth power," Ian now spoke up forcefully.

Cornelia noticed Rick shifting uncomfortably beside her. Then she felt his hand take hers and give it a quick squeeze.

"You know what this sounds like, don't you?" he asked.

Eyes and a couple of cameras shifted in his direction.

"Every conspiracy theorist's hard-on!" Rick said.

Cornelia thought she heard some snickering in the crowd.

"Come on, we can't put 'hard-on' on network TV," a voice spoke up.

"Oh, yeah," Cornelia heard Jerry's voice now. "The end of the world is coming but we need to censor TV. So we don't corrupt the impressionable youth. You can put it on your web page, can't you?"

"Look, people!" Rick's voice rose. "The point is that this is exactly what all the conspiracy theorists—those people out there in their balloon, the ones throwing rocks, setting fires—this is exactly what they are saying. Do you want to confirm their paranoia?"

"It's not quite the same thing," Knight replied.

"It's real close," Rick insisted. "There are enough people out there already pointing at every government in the world, claiming this was done as some kind of a grand plan to enslave everyone. Who else but governments have something to gain from this?"

Cornelia could imagine all those protesters around Travis wanting to launch rockets at their plane instead of blocking it with a hot-air balloon.

"But what I'm asking," said Knight, "is what if we can prove one-hundred-percent, we can prove without a doubt, that all of this is coming from somewhere else? Just look around the world. At all the insanity people are capable of doing. Who has any faith in humanity left?"

"We're all nuts," Ian exclaimed. "We're a bunch of animals. This is humanity at its worst. We've just been exposed for what we are."

"Now just consider how long this might go on," Knight said. "How many more days of this? Weeks? Months? When is the chaos, the anarchy going to stop? So now suppose whatever *Wizard of Oz* is behind all of this steps out from behind the curtain...."

"You mean like an alien or something?" Melinda asked.

Cornelia noticed Knight wince at the word "alien."

"Maybe," he replied evenly, however. "At this point aliens are as good a guess as any."

"And the point *is*," Ian said, "that what if the...alien, this *whatever*, this *thing* offers to help us put an end to all of the insanity?"

Knight nodded, looking at Ian like a prize pupil who had done his professor proud.

"Why don't you get a load of this?" a young female reporter in the crowd waved her iPad around. "Listen to this! This is coming off of a blog." With all eyes and cameras on her, she proceeded to read, "'Humanity doesn't even deserve a chance any more. We're killing ourselves because we're so stupid. First it was concentration camps. Then nukes. Then terrorism. Then we destroy the environment. Now we have these globes show up, and what do we do? We fight and kill each other. I can't wait for whoever created these globes to come and clean up this world.'"

"Need I say more?" Knight asked.

"We can't ignore this," Ian added with grim determination. "And I mean everybody. The world. All of us. This is the real threat, and we have to bring attention to it." He paused and nodded at cameras. "With everything we have."

"So you seriously think," said Rick, "that this is some kind of a...what? False flag operation? Isn't that what the conspiracy nuts call it?"

"Someone setting this up on purpose just so they can profit— so to speak—from it?" Cornelia heard Lacy's voice rise from amidst the gathering.

There were a lot of nods to her question.

But she shook her head. "I think that sounds far fetched. I'm with Rick on this. I think we're trying to force our own...you know, *behavior*, our way of thinking, onto something that's totally out of this world."

"Yeah, I think she's right, too." Cornelia found herself more thinking aloud than adding her voice to the discussion.

"Maybe yes, maybe no," a youthful-sounding voice joined the conversation.

Cornelia quickly noticed it was the physicist they had met at Travis, Vincent Rafferty.

"You're completely right about the out of this world part," he said. "However, I don't think that rules out the possibility of us trying to figure out its reasoning."

There was a general inarticulate grumbling rising from the gathering, and Cornelia found it hard to guess who was taking which side.

"Whatever is behind the globes," Rafferty continued, "has to be intelligent enough to know what sort of an effect all of this is having on us."

"You think so?" Lacy replied, already skeptical of Rafferty's position.

"I think it's a reasonable guess," Rafferty said.

Cornelia noticed Knight nodding his head in definitive agreement.

"I think," said Rafferty, watching Lacy closely, his inflection almost sounding sheepish, "that whatever force is behind this is watching us, monitoring us, our culture and our reactions, and probably calculating its own reaction to our behavior right now."

"So we have aliens out there monitoring our broadcasts? Our Internet?" said one of the reporters. "And coming up with more ways of manipulating us?"

"Maybe," said Knight with a glum matter of factness.

"But I'm having problems with that," Lacy said.

"I think I do, too," Cornelia said, making the effort to speak louder now and insert herself into the conversation.

Knight glanced in her direction.

"Yeah," said Lacy, "I think you guys are bringing the globe maker down to our level. Do you know what I'm saying?"

"What if the globe maker doesn't even consider humans any sort of noteworthy creatures on this planet?" Rick added.

Knight shook his head with a look that was somewhere between a smirk and a wince. "I think you're *way* overselling the globe maker. And completely underestimating the human race."

"Now wait a minute," Rafferty replied. His glance somewhat brightened, Cornelia noted, as he shot a look Lacy's way. "I do think Lacy has an interesting point of view. You know, the physicist Michio Kaku once said something similar about how aliens would behave if they could come to Earth. You know the old question: if all those UFOs are space aliens, why aren't they landing on the White House lawn? Well, he said that we probably can't figure out the aliens' motives any more than ants in an anthill could ever understand what that highway construction a

214

few feet away is all about."

"Thank you!" Lacy said. "Exactly! And said much better than I ever could."

A smile crept onto Rafferty's face and Cornelia would have sworn that he was blushing. *So the boy genius has a thing for our tomboy?* she thought, feeling herself smiling inwardly. *And in the middle of all this craziness, why not?* she told herself as she looked at Rick.

Except Rafferty's look quickly turned to what looked like a shade of disappointment. "But, the thing is...I'm not sure if we can apply the same principles here," he said, very obviously studying Lacy's for any reactions.

While Lacy's glance remained completely neutral, Cornelia noticed Knight's face lighting up with an intense sort of vehemence. "And ants don't have nuclear weapons," he said quickly.

"Unfortunately...see, the thing is...," Rafferty said, all the while looking at Lacy as if he was in a private conversation with her, "I don't see how the violence, all the chaos this world is spinning into, couldn't be grasped by anything advanced enough to create those globes." His words sounded apologetic. He even punctuated his last sentence with a sad shrug.

"I don't know...," Lacy replied quietly. "Maybe."

"What I think," Knight said with a shake of his head, "is that whatever created these globes knows exactly what they're doing and the kind of responses it will elicit. It wants to create chaos so it can look like a savior when it shows its face."

Cornelia could tell that Lacy, no matter what she might have said to Rafferty, still appeared to be unconvinced. Rafferty himself was somewhere on the fence, and extremely uncomfortable about it from the way he kept glancing at Lacy. The rest of the press people just looked baffled and scared.

"I don't know about you," Rick said, leaning closer to Cornelia, "but I don't think I can listen to that debate for another five hours."

"Neither can I," she replied. "Let's get out of here."

As they walked toward the aft sections of the cargo hold to sit and relax in a couple of sidewall seats, neither of them hesitated to hold hands all of a sudden. Just as the unknown had given them the best reason in the world to give in to their attraction back at Travis, so it now made perfect sense not to keep their new relationship hidden. With everything that group had been debating, with the tension passing through this plane, there was no sane reason to keep love out of these cold, fearful confines.

Cornelia just hoped Rafferty and Lacy might realize that too.

2.

The first thing Cornelia did after stepping onto the stairway leading out of the C-17's forward side-door was to look into the distance, to try and spot the perimeters of the airfield and see any signs of trouble.

"No hot air balloons," Rick said before she could as he stepped in behind her.

Before they had taken off from Travis, Cornelia heard that the base was about to suspend its public tours out of security concerns. She wondered if the same was the case here at Hickam Field.

The air base, officially called the Joint Base Pearl-Hickam, shared its runways with both the Naval Station Pearl Harbor and Hawaii International Airport. In the state's capital and on its most populous island, the base, Cornelia reasoned, could be a super-high-powered magnet for chaos now that the world press was blaring headlines about people being able to somehow predict the appearance of the next globe. But as far as she could see, everything appeared completely serene as of yet.

"They're too busy trying to spot the next globe to be bothering with us," Cornelia soon heard Colonel Lloyd Brubaker, base commander, tell Lieutenant Colonels Rutkowski and Graham, as well as Kristine Murakami, as the globe investigation group was led across the flight line. The blunt-faced, crew-cut Brubaker walked with a slightly noticeable limp, but moved with long, quick military strides nevertheless.

While the airfield might have been peaceful upon their arrival, efficiency and heightened caution were the order of the day. The local man in charge apparently wanted them on their way and doing their hunt for the globe-sensitives as fast as possible.

"And how's the local population holding up under the circumstances?" Murakami asked, raising her voice to compete with the sound of one of the commercial airliners approaching its runway nearby.

"On edge," Brubaker, too, shouted over the noise of the aircraft.

Cornelia quickly noticed the press entourage picking up its pace, trying to get as close to the base commander and the head of the procession as they could. Luckily, she thought, the *Confirmation* team was in a slightly advantageous position in the pecking order of the guests because of Dan Knight. His scholarly credentials still got them all more attention from the military leadership.

"The situation," Brubaker continued, "is, I suppose, much like in San Francisco. I read the stories about the protesters at Travis. The insanity of all the people trying to get out—"

"And get in?" Knight spoke up as he increased his strides, making sure he stayed as close to Brubaker as he could.

Journalist's instincts still honed, Cornelia quickly lurched toward him to make sure she moved in his wake and advanced as quickly as he did toward the head of the power structure in the group.

"What's that?" Brubaker asked.

"Getting in," Knight repeated. "What about getting in? Do you have all the globe pilgrims coming to Hawaii?"

"From what I heard," Brubaker said, "airline reservations both in *and* out of the islands have completely been jammed. Everything's overbooked. So yeah, since the press got a hold of the stories of people hearing this buzz, thousands of people either

SAREBARNA WILLIAM DONOVAN

want to run or want to be on the next plane in."

Then a thought occurred to Cornelia, something that had been an inarticulate shade in the back of her mind until now. "Any of the people who've talked about hearing the hum," she exclaimed quickly. "The local experiencers," she continued when Brubaker cast a look over his shoulder and made eye contact with her. "Any of them military personnel?"

For a moment Brubaker seemed to be stumped, but replied, "No. Actually, no. No one here reported anything like that."

Then Cornelia noticed the contemplative look in Kristine Murakami's eyes. "That's right...," the doctor said quietly, apparently unnoticed by Brubaker or anyone else.

"As far as we know, they're all civilian reports," said Brubaker.

"The island has a large military population, right?" Murakami raised her voice.

"Statistically—" Cornelia began, but was cut off.

"Someone from the local bases," Murakami interjected forcefully, "from Hickam or Pearl, should have been among the experiencers."

"And the reports that have been coming in so far," Cornelia said quickly, and stepped closer to Brubaker, not appreciating Murakami's pushiness. "Where has it fit in the population so far? I mean, were they truly all locals, or were any of them from the tourist population? Just so we can guess if the phenomenon is entirely in the location, or something having to do with the experiencers alone."

These were questions Brubaker had obviously not considered until now, because his face looked ever more quizzical.

"Entirely in the location alone?" Murakami replied instead, and Cornelia noted the disapproval in her voice. "I think it's obvious that we're dealing with some aspect of the location—"

"Not entirely!" Cornelia shot back. "If we did, everyone in San Francisco would have been going crazy from phantom humming in their ears. Including us!"

"All right," Murakami replied, obviously irritated and impatient now. "And it's also obvious that there is something about specific individuals. So what?"

"Wouldn't it be strange if only locals heard the buzz in Hawaii? In a place with so many tourists? And again, if no military personnel heard it? With such a significant number of the local population being in some way connected to the military?"

"Statistically," Cornelia heard Rick say behind her, "those *are* interesting questions."

Cornelia barely suppressed a satisfied smile as she noticed his strong inflection.

"And I don't have any of the answers to that," Colonel Brubaker replied quickly. Before either of the bickering women could, Cornelia thought, amused. "I suppose your group will be able to figure that out. But let me warn you about something first."

With that, Brubaker paused and let a theatrical beat of silence hang in the air.

"What's that?" Cornelia asked, glad she got the question out before Murakami could.

"There might be more experiencers out there than we're aware of."

"Oh?" Murakami did get the follow-up question in.

And Cornelia understood its simplicity. The doctor must also have been suspecting the answer.

"Yeah," Brubaker said. "Because we have reasons to believe many experiencers are actively trying to avoid us."

"And let me guess why," Knight said, snark and attitude well loaded into each of his words.

Brubaker gave him a rueful look and nodded. "Right. Check some of the local radio shows. The podcasts. Social media."

"People are being told to stay away from the government, aren't they?" Knight asked.

"They're afraid they'll be locked away. With the military's mad scientists doing experiments on them forever," Brubaker said.

Cornelia noticed Murakami giving her a quick glance.

"Well," the doctor said, "what if we use the press corps to try and counter all the conspiracy-theorist propaganda?"

"You certainly can try," Brubaker said. "And you'll have your work cut out for you. We've got a couple of real rabid ones doing their podcasts from the islands. They've got some people convinced the government's got concentration camps for the experiencers all across the country, and that aliens are running the Pentagon."

"Wait a minute!" Rick spoke up.

Cornelia, of course, suspected what he was about to say.

"Can't anyone talk to these bloggers and podcasters?" Rick asked. "Find them and—"

"And what?" Brubaker replied. "Two problems with that. Number one is the finding part. We don't even know what island they're on. They went, as they say, off the grid some time after 9/11." When Rick rolled his eyes in frustration, Brubaker added, "Not that we didn't try already. Local FBI office gave it a shot, from what I heard. Tried to find the source of the podcasts and their web pages. Got traces routed all over the world. Conspiracy theorist computer geeks tend to be smart bastards. They know how to hide in cyberspace.

"Now, of course, you also have to consider something else. Should we be able to find these clowns, there's the little matter of the First Amendment to deal with. They have the right to say and tweet and podcast whatever they like."

Rick nodded before Brubaker even finished his last sentence, a crooked grin on his face. "Come on, Colonel. You guys are the air force. Don't you have a whole cadre of men in black that can find anything and make anyone disappear?"

"They're all at Area 51," Brubaker said, then glanced over his shoulder toward the press people trailing behind. "Our good friends in the news media," he said with a grimace, "they know how this is a joke, don't they?"

"I'm pretty sure they do," said Cornelia.

"Speaking of Area 51," Brubaker continued. "If it all goes south, we might even get harassed by a Nevada senator who's vacationing here. Been asking questions already. But anyway, you ladies and gentlemen are about to have an eventful stay in the Aloha State."

"Where are we going first?" asked Knight.

"I suggest King's and the Kaiser Permanente Moanalua Medical Centers. Some of the people who've heard the hum are there. The ones who came in voluntarily. We thought it would put them at ease if they didn't have to come into a military facility."

3.

"I've always been a knee-jerk First Amendment purist," Cornelia said, surfing the local conspiracy web pages Lyle Brubaker had recommended, "but this is going too far."

"Some of this stuff seems to be inciting criminal behavior, if not violence," Lacy Anderson said from the seat behind her.

The Travis globe-study team, minus the air force special operations commandos and the SEALS, had been loaned several GMC Yukon SUVs at Hickam field, and the *Confirmation* group had taken two of the vehicles. Cornelia now rode in the same car with Rick, Melinda, Matt, and Lacy. Rafferty, not surprisingly, sat next to Lacy. The two of them, Cornelia was glad to note, just seemed to gravitate together naturally.

And every time she noticed these details, Cornelia's attention first drifted toward Rick sitting behind the wheel, then she felt the most incredible exhaustion. It was more than just their six-hour flight from Travis, of course. The two of them had let their guards down, given in to their attraction, had given themselves to each other for an hour in California, but it had been nothing but business ever since. It was draining, frustrating, and depressing, Cornelia thought. Only the fact that she knew Rick felt the same — the stolen glances, hands held, a word of affirmation when they got a moment away from all of these people — allowed Cornelia to stay focused on the job at hand.

"…the implication of violence is *so* subtle." Rafferty's voice snapped Cornelia's attention away from her drifting thoughts. Her glance first shifted toward Rick, then toward the palm-lined, high-end real estate, shops, and scenery of Waikiki as their convoy of SUVs rolled down Ala Moana Boulevard. She had been to Hawaii on spring break once in college. She remembered wanting to come back again when she was a successful journalist breaking world-changing stories every day, and when she was accompanied by the love of her life. *So how did the plans turn out…?* she wondered before Lacy's voice demanded her attention yet again.

"Isn't that right?" Lacy called.

"What's that?" Cornelia replied, forcing every other thought from her mind.

"You don't need to specifically say, 'go kill people,' or 'blow stuff up,' or 'go overthrow the government' to incite violence, do you? It's not covered by the First Amendment, right? It's just like shouting 'fire' in a crowded theater, isn't it?"

"You have to be *real* clear in what you're inciting people to do," Cornelia replied. "I mean real, literal, crystal clear. There should be clear intent in your words. And there should be a real likelihood of imminent violence coming about as a result of what you said or wrote."

"And that's where I think the posts don't quite meet the legal requirements," Rafferty said. After a pause, though, he quickly tagged on, "Although I could see a lawyer making a convincing case."

He cast a quick glance Lacy's way after his last words. The conciliatory tone in his voice made Cornelia want to smile.

"So what do *you* think?" Melinda asked.

"Yeah," said Rick. "You're our media law authority."

"I'm hardly an authority," Cornelia replied. "But I think the people who write this stuff online know how to skirt the law."

"You think so?" Matt asked as he filmed their conversation.

"This is the kind of stuff white supremacists and survivalists and all those fringe anti-government fruitcakes write every day. I don't think it qualifies as causing imminent violence."

"Well, one of the fruitcakes was tweeting about how all the people who have voluntarily contacted the authorities about their hum symptoms have already been placed in chains and flown to FEMA detention camps on the mainland," said Lacy. "That's a clear lie."

"But will it, without a reasonable doubt, make people commit violence?"

"It's doubtful," Rick said, and made a turn onto Punchbowl Street.

"I think so too," said Melinda.

"God, some of this stuff is just off the wall," Rafferty said a moment later. "What the hell is the matter with people?"

Lacy chuckled now. "A web page by the—get this!—the Conspiracy Kahuna, says that the hums had been beamed into the minds of a select few people to hasten the New World Order's declaration of global martial law."

"Hmm," Rick mumbled a moment later.

"What's that?" Cornelia asked.

"Just...hmm," he replied.

"Oh really? Just hmm? Meaning what?"

Cornelia caught Rick's glance flick to the rearview mirror, as if he was interested in the reaction of the people in the back. Or *some* of the people in the back.

"I just thought," Rick said, "that it sounds a bit like what Doc Knight said back on the plane."

Or what Vince Rafferty was somewhat, half-heartedly agreeing with? Cornelia wondered. *As long as it didn't offend Lacy?*

"Oh, he doesn't think the government is doing this," Rafferty said quickly.

"I don't think so either," Rick replied. "But it's the same kind of reasoning. That something is causing all this for a personal gain. And I mean gain as in a dictatorial takeover." A heavy beat of silence hung in the car. "It does make you think...," Rick added.

"Makes you think about what?" Cornelia asked.

"The kinds of things you asked Brubaker about back at the air field. Who exactly hears all this stuff? And why so many all at the same time? Why just now?"

Those were questions with no clear answers. Not even clear, logical guesses, Cornelia considered. That, of course, was why another heavy, awkward beat of silence sat in the car, like a miasma oppressing everyone.

"Because David Kwan's condition went public?" Melinda said at last.

"What?" Lacy asked.

"David Kwan?" Melinda said, her voice very tentative now.

"That's an excellent point," Rick said.

"And I think I agree," Rafferty seconded.

"Speak! Speak!" Matt said, swinging his camera back and forth from Rick to Vince Rafferty.

"Why do so many people," Rick obliged, "suddenly become globe sensitive so soon *after* Kwan's story hits the airwaves? I mean, suppose the air force's clumsy visit to Kwan's house wasn't seen by his neighbor. The globe-blogger, mind you!"

"Yeah!" Lacy cut in. "Then the press would never have caught wind of the whole hum sensitivity."

"Or they wouldn't have put two and two together the way Ian did about some of the other hum-sensitives," Cornelia added.

"Exactly!" Rafferty said. "But still the point is that until the Kwan story broke...." He let his voice trail off, reminding Cornelia of Knight's occasional pedantic impulses, when he spoke as if he was lecturing students and urging them to participate in class and come to conclusions on their own.

"Until the story broke," Lacy said, looking at Rafferty with a beaming smile, "all these other places—Mount Shasta, that Italian town, even San Francisco—had at most one person talking about hums."

"All right," Melinda said. "So this is something important—"

"Oh, I think this is something potentially huge," Rafferty blurted. "I mean really, *really* significant."

"Like what?" Melinda asked the obvious when Rafferty appeared content to let his statement hang in the air.

"Well...," Rafferty said, and paused. "I don't know."

Melinda rolled her eyes in frustration.

"I know, I know," Rafferty said, and nodded vigorously. "This is really frustrating."

Lacy giggled at the whole exchange.

"But look," said Rafferty, "it's still a step in the right direction...."

"On, come on!" said Melinda.

"No, I think he's right," Rick agreed. "It's better than nothing. At least we noticed a problem. Now we know what needs to be investigated."

"We're grasping at straws," Melinda said, still unsatisfied.

"I think it's a pretty big straw we just grasped." Cornelia had to agree with Rick and Rafferty.

But before any more could be said, her cell phone rang. When she glanced at its screen, she saw Kristine Murakami's name and number displayed.

"Oh, God," Cornelia couldn't help letting slip. "What does *she* want?"

After she finished talking to the doctor, her good mood was immediately knocked down a couple of notches. And the others could sense it immediately.

Matt's camera was immediately aimed at her. She could imagine her face framed in a tight close-up.

"What's up?" asked Rick.

"I should have realized this back at the base when Brubaker told us about the Nevada senator."

"What about him?"

"He is very concerned with the globe crisis and, as a member of the Armed Services Committee, he would like to talk to us. To gather some facts. Our good doctor, Kristine Murakami, of course, somehow manages to dodge all this, and *we* get nominated to brief the senator."

"OK," Rafferty said, sounding somewhat baffled. "So what's the problem?"

"Have you ever heard of Senator Bling?"

4.

"...and *this* guy is Washington's most outspoken advocate for transparency in studying the globes." Cornelia explained. "This is just *so* wrong."

"Like things couldn't get any weirder," Lacy said.

"He's the first one on Capitol Hill who took the whole thing seriously," Knight said, and started to count points off on his fingers as they walked past the King's Medical Center atrium and into the sort of maze-like, confusing corridor system Cornelia had always hated in hospitals. "And *this* guy is the only pro-military flag-waver who actually stands with the soldiers when it counts," he said. "Not just throwing them into combat like cannon fodder, but *consistently* voting for more benefits, more VA spending...."

"Been censured by the Ethics Committee," Cornelia shot back, tired of listening to the Brandon "Senator Bling" Markwell fan club.

"Ethics Committee? Gimme a break! Prostitution's legal in the county where, you know—"

"He was caught...!"

"He wasn't *caught*," Knight insisted with that smarmy soft-pedaling tone. "Where the alleged liaison—"

"No, not *alleged*. It happened. He admitted to it. *After*, mind you, after it was clear he couldn't keep denying it any longer."

"It was perfectly legal."

"Then why didn't he come out and admit to it? Why lie to the press? Why not say, 'these are the values I live by, take it or leave it,' and be honest? You think prostitution should be legal, just own it."

"No politician can say that."

"I completely disagree" Cornelia exclaimed, shocking herself by the way she almost yelled those three words.

"And I agree with you, Cornelia," Melinda's voice came from behind them.

"Why, thank you!"

"Do we need to take it as a matter of course that *politician* is synonymous with duplicitous scumbag?" Melinda asked. "I think not."

"Why, thank you again."

"What he did hurt no one," Knight countered.

"Unlike the time he was accused of putting campaign donations to personal use?" Lacy said. "And that, by the way, is the military point of view," she tagged on with sharp, mocking sarcasm.

"Charges dropped. Not a thing proven," Knight crowed.

"On a technicality, if I recall," Lacy insisted.

"No, that's not true. It was *not* a technicality. And come on! Think about this logically! Why would a man worth some one hundred and fifty million dollars misappropriate a lousy ten thousand of campaign donations? Get real! And that's a *personal* fortune of one hundred and fifty million dollars, if I may repeat. *One fifty mil,* aside from his wife, who's got something in excess of thirty or forty million dollars from her film production company."

"I think you're getting a bro-crush on him, Doc," Lacy said.

"Yeah, that's a good comeback," Knight said with the weirdest petulant inflection. "All I'm saying is that—"

"It's not a victimless crime," Melinda interjected.

"Say what?"

"The sex industry dehumanizes and objectifies women, and—"

"Says the bodybuilder posing in her little string bikini."

"That's not even the same thing!" Melinda snapped, and Cornelia would have been willing to put down some money and bet that Melinda was aching to hit Knight at that point.

227

"Bodybuilding is empowerment."

Knight rolled his eyes.

And although she was no longer in competition shape, Cornelia was certain that Melinda could still pack a wallop of a punch. For his safety's sake, Cornelia thought, not unamused, that Knight, no matter the street brawler he might once have been, was wise to control his derisive mannerisms and sarcasm.

Knight started to say, "The fact is that Markwell wasn't even married when he was with the hookers, and—"

But Rick's measured and reasonable voice suddenly cut him off. "Look, the fact is that Senator Bling Markwell somehow managed to spend three terms so far in Washington, despite the fact that he spends as much time pissing off both sides of the aisle as most other politicians claim they try to reach *across* it. And now he's going to want to start injecting himself into *our* investigation."

"And I'm sure that in this case that's not a good thing at *all*," Lacy said. "I mean, come on. The guy's just a creep."

Cornelia couldn't help chuckling now. Both Rick and Lacy were right, she realized. Markwell's political survival skills were almost supernatural, as was his ability to get himself into trouble on a weekly basis due to his penchant for a fast-living, high-spending lifestyle. Exactly as Knight had said, Markwell was a supporter of the military, especially spending on healthcare and benefits for veterans—a former army national guardsman himself—yet his weekends in a Mineral County bordello were made public a week after he received an endorsement for his reelection campaign by the League of Women Voters. While the revelations about his sex life might have cost Markwell not just the League's support, but the local Republican Party's nomination, he soon ran on his own newly formed High Desert Libertarian ticket. He took advantage of the way a pair of unpopular Republican and conservative-Democratic candidates split a sizable right-leaning Nevada electorate, and barely squeaked back into office with the independent/libertarian support.

"He's carrying way too much controversial baggage," Cornelia said quickly before…before, she supposed, Rick could have said something in support of Brandon Markwell that would have really disappointed her. With no comment from Rick forthcoming, she added, "I really don't think our work now needs that kind of a distraction."

"We might not have a choice," Kristine Murakami said over her shoulder.

Leading their party toward a conference room where a group of the local globe-sensitives had been gathered, Murakami had, until now, been ignoring the debate about Senator Bling.

"From what I heard," Murakami said, "he's about to fly in from the Big Island. He's playing golf down there at the Four Seasons Resort with some showbiz people. He still seems to think that his Vegas magicians will help solve the globe mystery."

"They don't call him Senator Bling for nothing," Lacy quipped. "The Four Seasons' got some ten-grand-a-night suites."

"Well, once he gets here, maybe Doctor Knight can chat with him."

5.

"Doctor Murakami, look," Sam Rutkowski said, and Cornelia thought that Frederic Graham, standing next to him in his crisp tropical-white navy uniform, was about to nod in enthusiastic agreement any moment now. "Here are some hard facts. Unless we get these people to cooperate and get some solid answers— that hard data *you* have been talking about since we found out about all this hum and buzz and vibration business—well, the word could come down from the Pentagon that this is still a national security issue, and we have the right to take whatever steps are necessary to get more cooperation."

Kristine Murakami's entire countenance clouded, and Cornelia couldn't blame her. You couldn't force the impossible, no matter what kind of military-style bullying, demanding, or bureaucratic pressure you attempted to throw at it. Murakami and the rest of the air force doctors she had brought along from Travis had just spent over an hour in the fifth-floor conference room with four of the local globe-sensitives, and emerged no wiser as a result.

"Cooperation, Colonel?" Murakami replied in the measured tones that best illustrated that novelty T-shirt slogan and Internet meme favorite, *Stress: the overriding impulse that keeps you from beating the crap out of someone who desperately deserves it.* "These people have come down here of their own free will. They've undergone a battery of tests that tell us nothing more than—"

"And now you told them they can go home?" Frederick Graham cut in. "How do we know they will come back when you want to run more tests?"

"We know where they live."

"And if they go into hiding?"

"Do we want to turn these people into our prisoners now?" Murakami shot back. "Like I was saying, there's nothing at all to indicate there's anything out of the ordinary about *any* of them. I mean, just look at their files! They're just like David Kwan. Nothing unusual. One has high cholesterol. Another's blood sugar is too high, for God's sake. He's already been told to lay off the candy bars or he'll have a nice case of Type 2 diabetes. Then we have buzz-sufferer number three. Nothing more than an old college football injury to his left knee. The fourth one had kidney stones removed when she was thirty-two, does yoga three times a week, and she's on the pill because her husband's been feeling frisky a lot lately and they can't afford a third child. In other words, completely normal, average people with normal, average health issues."

"And they can all hear something no one else does," Rutkowski replied, unmoved. "Or at least something the *majority* of the people can't hear."

Cornelia noticed Murakami breaking eye contact with Rutkowski, letting her impatient, frustrated gaze sweep over the lobby outside the conference room.

"And they can hear something, *Doctor*," Rutkowski pressed, the edge of his voice sharpening, "that's tied to a phenomenon that has people at each other's throats all over the world."

"I haven't forgotten why we're here, *Colonel*. And I know full well that we need to keep doing every test and try to find anything we can. But you *can't* force scientific results by yelling and threatening the way you would with boot-camp recruits."

"And are you ready to explain that to some idiot senator in about a day?" Graham asked. "An idiot senator who, by the way, just happens to be on—"

"On the Armed Services Committee, I know."

"And now he wants to know everything we're doing about this," Rutkowski jumped in. "Maybe because he's up for reelection. Maybe he's had another bimbo eruption. Maybe he was caught saying something stupid again about legalizing drugs, or prostitution, or enjoying a threesome, or God knows what, and he wants to divert attention away from another budding scandal."

Cornelia choked down a laugh now, but her near guffaw caught Rutkowski's eye. He, Murakami, and Graham acknowledged her with brief eye contact. What almost made Cornelia laugh was the marine lieutenant colonel's up-to-date knowledge of Washington gossip.

"If we can't show any progress," Graham said, "the Pentagon will be after us." Then his voice lowered, but he made eye contact with Cornelia. "And then we might be told to round these people up...and start turning off the cameras and stop being so concerned with diplomacy and transparency. And it doesn't matter what this senator says about transparency, you mark my words."

"All right," Murakami replied. She, too, looked at Cornelia for a moment. "I get it...." Except her voice faded out as her gaze drifted toward something on the far side of the lobby. "All of these floors are carpeted," she then said.

What? Cornelia thought, and followed her gaze.

Apparently what had caught Murakami's eye was a man in

a custodian's gray-green overalls moving a wheeled bucket and mop. On one side of the lobby—the side opposite of the one they were looking at—stood the bank of elevators for the hospital's general staff, patients, and visitors. Where she and Murakami were looking, however, ran a corridor toward a corner that led off to the service elevators.

It made sense, Cornelia thought, since that was the area where the custodian had emerged from.

But what is he doing here? a voice in her head whispered. *Murakami's right. It's all carpeting here. What do you mop?*

"What's that?" she heard Rutkowski asking now.

Cornelia, too, had noticed another newcomer. Aside from the custodian, the globe study-team in the lobby was now joined by a man in a white lab coat, a stethoscope around his neck and a clipboard in his hand. Although standing about five feet and ten inches or so tall, he was of a slight, unexercised build with an uncombed thatch of frizzy red hair and a pasty, freckled complexion.

The stethoscope…the clipboard…exactly what you'd expect a doctor to look like.

And no one else in the lobby took notice of him.

What's wrong with this picture?

"What floors did that man come to wash?" Cornelia heard Murakami ask.

"What are you talking about?" Graham replied. "Maybe he's going to do the bathrooms."

"I've been to the bathroom. It's been freshly cleaned."

But Cornelia's own unease was fed by the man who looked so much like a doctor. She kept studying his appearance, his movements, as he was about to pass the spot Lacy milled around, talking with Vince Rafferty, Melinda, Matt, and….

Where is his name tag? Cornelia wondered to herself as the stranger passed within three feet of Lacy. *And why did he come out of the service elevator?*

The full realization hit Cornelia and sent a shock of adrenaline through her body.

A doctor in a lab coat like that would have something identifying him. A name tag pinned onto the coat or embroidered on it. But this guy did not....

And he was making eye contact with Cornelia. In a split instant he knew that she knew.

His left hand let the clipboard drop while his right one went into the lab coat's pocket. As he withdrew a scalpel he lunged toward Lacy, snaking his left arm around her and slashing the scalpel at her throat.

6.

"Let the hostages go!" the phony doctor screamed, brandishing the scalpel wickedly close to Lacy's throat and face. "We know what this is all about. The people will know! You can't hide the truth. These people know where it will happen next. You won't make them disappear."

"What the hell?" Cornelia heard Rutkowski growl nearby. His voice was just about the only one among the various gasps, curses, and pleas for the hostage-taker to calm down and let Lacy go.

Cornelia saw Rafferty just about paralyzed by terror. Melinda, Matt, and Ian were all trying to steady their voices and implore the attacker to put his weapon down.

"You won't get away with this," Lacy's assailant yelled. "The government can't silence its people."

"The experiencers," Cornelia now heard Rick's voice nearby.

When she glanced in his direction, she noticed him return her look.

"The hum. The experiencers," he said. "He thinks we're here to silence them."

"Stay back!" the attacker yelled, apparently aiming his words at anyone within earshot and anyone getting heroic ideas. "You let the people go and I won't hurt her!"

Except the attacker was so focused on everyone else in the

lobby that he neglected the potential problem he held with his left arm. He had apparently gone after Lacy because she was a target of opportunity—close, within arm's reach, one of two women, and her petite build a better choice than the muscular, formidable-looking Melinda. But he could not have known about Lacy's military training and apparently very-well-honed hand-to-hand combat skills. One moment he was standing upright, clutching Lacy against his body, and the next his height and weight had been turned against him. With staggering speed, Lacy used her lower center of gravity to pull her attacker off balance, flip him over her head as she dropped to one knee, and plow him into the floor. As she did so, she twisted his elbow and wrist into a vicious-looking lock, forcing him to give up his grip on the scalpel while at the same time, no doubt, snapping his joints and tearing cartilage and ligaments.

The disarmed attacker's shrieks of pain rang across the lobby.

As blood-curdling as the stranger's cries of excruciating agony and pure helpless rage were, the people in the lobby were relieved the threat had been neutralized. Cornelia certainly was. She, as everyone else must have, lowered her guard and took a breath of relief.

But it was a mistake to do so.

"Let him go! Get back!" a man's voice howled over the din of the lobby, drowning out even the cries of pain ululating out of Lacy's attacker.

Then a gunshot thundered across the hall, followed by screams.

The custodian! Cornelia realized and, just as she predicted, saw the man in the overalls wave a large automatic handgun around. But if he was the partner of the man in the lab coat....

"Lacy!" Cornelia gasped, looking for her teammate.

Where had that shot been aimed?

But relief followed a moment later. Lacy was still crouching next to her attacker, still gripping his arm and twisting it in a grotesquely unnatural angle. She was, just like everyone else in the lobby, thankfully, unhurt.

The fake custodian, in the meantime, kept waving his gun around, clutching it in both hands now, a wild-eyed look of adrenaline-fueled frenzy and fear contorting his features.

"I said let him go!" the gunman screamed, haphazardly waving the pistol in Lacy's general direction, and squeezed off a shot.

While Lacy remained unhurt—the shooter looked inept with that gun, Cornelia recognized—waves of screams and shouts trilled across the lobby and people hit the floor. Lacy, Cornelia was glad to see, was smart enough not to stand her ground but let go of her captive's arm, hit the floor flat, and attempt to roll away.

Then, as the shooter got his wish—his partner freed from Lacy's grip—he seemed to hesitate, unsteady, unsure of what to do. The redheaded man in the lab coat had been released but he was apparently still delirious from pain. He still lay on the ground, writhing in pain, completely disconnected from reality.

The gun shifted in the shooter's hand nervously, and Cornelia's heart managed to hammer even faster than it had before. Spiked on adrenaline and in the grip of fear, her mind was still capable of clear and logical reasoning. The gunman's twitchy, panicky movements and his unsteady command of his weapon signaled an amateur. And that, Cornelia decided, was potentially more dangerous than if had they been accosted by some highly trained assassin. This guy was a complete live wire, unstable, unpredictable, and deadly.

A second later something happened that had Cornelia wondering if they were about to all escape this madness or if their death sentences had just been signed. An alarm *whooped* through the lobby and, Cornelia guessed, throughout the hospital.

This guy's either going to run for it or he's about to take down as many people as he can.

The shooter shifted back and forth on his feet and steadied his grip on his pistol.

Oh no! Oh no! Cornlia's mind screamed.

But then the gunman spun around and bolted, sprinting toward the service corridor. Moments later Cornelia could hear the slamming of a metallic door. The guy had retreated into the stairwell.

What happened next Cornelia would never be able to explain.

There was a blur of movement on her right and when she turned to examine it, Cornelia saw Rick jumping to his feet. "Son of a bitch!" she heard him hissing as he ran after the gunman.

Perhaps his previous cop identity had taken over, Cornelia realized as he darted around the corner of the service corridor. Running after a fleeing gunman was what Rick would have done when he was still on the L.A.P.D.

And back when she was still a reporter, Cornelia would have run after a cop chasing a gunman. Now her old instincts took over as well, and she ran after Rick.

7.

Cops and reporters were supposed to charge into the thick of the action, Cornelia knew, but now she wondered what made Lacy follow them. She had been in the Signal Corps in the army, a techie behind a computer. Perhaps she was just pissed at having been shot at by this guy, and seeing him trying to escape was stoking her ire. The fact that Vincent Rafferty followed Lacy made sense. He was, more than likely, going nuts over seeing her in the line of fire again, so he stoically ran up the stairwell after them, trying to help the woman he was falling for. Military men Rutkowski and Graham coming along made some sense. They were the ones ultimately responsible for the globe study-group and the colonels might have been, Cornelia ventured a guess, regretting not bringing along the SEALS or the Air Force Combat Controllers. But bringing up the rear behind the military brass were Dan Knight and Tony Griffin with his camera. So eight unarmed people were chasing the gunman up the stairwell now. The direction of the chase itself was something else Cornelia couldn't quite understand.

A nerve-jangling clap of gunfire rang out overhead, then echoed throughout the stairwell.

Ahead of her, Cornelia saw Rick flinch and flatten against the wall. Seeing her behind him, he gave her a look of murderous intensity. "Get out of here, goddamn it!" he said through clenched teeth. "You'll get yourself killed." When he saw the entourage in his wake, he let out a string of particularly imaginative curses.

Another shot rang out somewhere overhead. If they didn't get killed, Cornelia reasoned, they would surely go deaf.

But her ears hadn't been punished enough not to notice the trample and echo of running feet several floors below. So was the entire globe team on its way up? Was Murakami down there? Jerry Peretti?

Cornelia made the mistake of leaning toward the edge of the stairs, trying to see down the well to catch a glimpse of who was coming up. For a moment she was glad to see what appeared to be uniforms. Hospital security —

And then a shot rang out again.

She felt a grip on the back of her shirt yanking her back and slamming her against the wall. She could hear the whine of a bullet whizzing by, ricocheting off the concrete.

"Are you *trying* to kill yourself?" Rick hissed at her as he let her go.

Pain radiated through the back of her head where she had been knocked against the wall.

"Now stay here!" Rick ordered, and bolted up the stairs.

In the other direction, Lacy sprinted toward her, taking the stairs two at a time. "Are you OK?" she asked.

"Yeah," Cornelia gasped, and listened to the running feet echoing through the stairwell overhead. "Come on!"

As she and Lacy continued upward, two more shots rang out.

Cornelia thought the adrenaline surge was knocking her heart against her ribcage now. Then another shot blasted out, and she thought she heard a bullet rebound off of metal. Moments later another jarring metallic crash sounded out.

There was silence after the gunshot, a stillness in the shaft, but then....

Air? Cornelia's mind raced.

She was sure she felt a draft now.

"Come on," she said to Lacy over her shoulder. "I think they reached the roof."

"Corner that bastard," Lacy replied. "I wanna throw his ass to the street below."

"Yeah, me too."

"Not if I do it first."

When they reached the top of the stairwell, they were looking into yet one more set of stairs. These ones, Cornelia noted, were made of metal grating. They appeared to rise toward some kind of a metal structure.

"We're on top of the hospital," Cornelia thought aloud as she looked toward the top of the stairs. She could see Rick crouching up there, the bright blue tropical skies above him.

"What's that?" Lacy asked.

"Hey, wait a minute!" a male voice came from somewhere below. Cornelia thought it sounded like Rafferty.

"I think that's a helicopter landing pad," Cornelia said.

"Yeah," Lacy replied, ignoring Rafferty. "A nice wide place for that psycho to be exposed."

"And for us to be exposed, too. He has the gun, remember?"

"And a limited number of rounds," Lacy said, and sprang past Cornelia.

This time taking the steps three at a time, Lacy went up to join Rick at the top of the stairs. As Cornelia followed, she noted the fury in Rick's eyes as Lacy crouched beside him. When Cornelia had nearly caught up to them, she heard something new. It was a rhythmic, steadily increasing sound from overhead.

"It *is* a helipad, isn't it?" she asked as she tried to squeeze in between Rick and Lacy.

Neither of them replied. When Cornelia took stock of the

situation on top of the building, she realized why.

Just as she'd suspected, they had been led to the hospital's helicopter landing platform. Except the gunman was not standing in the middle of the structure alone. He was waving his pistol at a woman in light blue scrubs. A doctor perhaps, Cornelia surmised. Off to the left of the stairwell she also noticed a structure on the edge of the platform. It appeared to house an elevator shaft leading off the roof, its opening wide enough to accommodate teams of doctors and nurses and gurneys to move patients in and out. And right now the opening to the elevator was crowded by what looked exactly like a collection of doctors and nurses.

So Cornelia's gaze went to the sky. She looked for the source of that rhythmic sound, because a team of medics on a hospital's helipad meant only one thing.

8.

The medevac helicopter made its approach to the landing platform with no awareness of a problem. How that could have been, Cornelia couldn't imagine. There must have been radio communication between the aircraft and the hospital, even if the pilot couldn't have guessed that there was something amiss below. For some reason, its landing gear extended, the helicopter touched down in the middle of the platform.

"Or maybe because the emergency's bad enough that he can't turn away," Rick yelled over the roar of the helicopter's turbines and the blast of air all around. "Or he was told to land or people start dying down here."

As the helicopter settled on the platform, its left side-hatch slid open. Cornelia could see the EMTs inside huddled around a figure on a stretcher.

"He's gonna trade the patient for the chopper?" Lacy hollered.

Except Cornelia couldn't be sure of that since none of the hospital personnel by the elevator made any moves. The gunman, however, did. He ran straight for the chopper the moment its hatch was wide open.

Cornelia felt vibrations on the metal stairs beneath her. The other team members must have been bringing up the rear. For the moment, though, her attention was riveted on the helicopter and the gunman.

"I don't believe it!" Rick yelled as the shooter reached the helicopter. "That miserable bastard...."

Apparently there was to be no trade, Cornelia realized in horror as the gunman leaped into the aircraft. Or was he just going to throw the patient out and force a takeoff before the hospital staff could leave the elevator? But a moment later the answer to that question became obvious as well. The helicopter started to shift, lightening the load on its landing gear.

"He's making them take off!" Rick shouted.

Cornelia, of course, understood...except she didn't understand what Rick did next. He sprang from the stairs and bolted across the landing platform, moving straight for the helicopter's open hatch.

Cornelia, as well as Lacy, remained speechless as they watched Rick dive into the aircraft as it lifted about a foot off the platform.

"What's happening?" a shout came from behind now. It was Rafferty pushing his way to the top of the stairway.

He was ignored, however, as both Cornelia and Lacy lunged upright, moving forward in some shared unconscious gesture of futility. Rick was already inside the helicopter, and the aircraft was moving higher and higher into the air.

Except the chopper didn't continue on any kind of steady and controlled departure pattern. At about thirty feet off the ground it paused in a brief hover, then went into two wild rotations, drifting all the while lower and lower again and closer to the elevator structure.

The medics around the elevator bolted in all directions, not unreasonably fearing that the out-of-control aircraft was about to crash into them.

They're fighting, Cornelia's mind screamed in realization.

However, she didn't realize the full extent of the danger until someone was tugging on her shoulder, urging her to start backing away.

"Come on! Move!" Rafferty screamed now, tugging at both Cornelia and Lacy.

And the scientist was right, Cornelia recognized a moment too late. The helicopter's erratic movements changed direction again, this time lurching to its right—straight toward Cornelia, Lacy, and Rafferty's position—its nose dipping, then bolting forward.

"Move!" Rafferty and Lacy howled at the same time.

And Cornelia did so.

The helicopter, Cornelia's panicked mind just realized, was so low now that as it moved forward—its nose lowered—its blades actually stood a chance of instantly pureeing her and her companions in a matter of seconds. They had to run faster than they had ever run in their lives, and they needed to get off the platform. To do so, they bolted for the platform's edge, leaping over the threshold and plunging to whatever awaited on the roof-proper some twenty feet below.

Cornelia now knew full well what they meant about time slowing down at the moment of an absolute life-altering catastrophe. She could feel herself hanging in the air, drifting through space, imploring gravity to take hold and pull her down to the roof as the medevac helicopter was upon her. She could sense the individual blades slice the air at the precise spot her head was at just fractions of a second ago.

The helicopter zoomed overhead and past the edge of the building as Cornelia, Lacy, and Rafferty pounded into the roof. Pain racked her body and the air left her lungs, but Cornelia couldn't help looking toward the edge of the building, trying to find the out-of-control aircraft. Rick was inside that thing, fighting with a gunman, and apparently the pilots had a tenuous hold on the aircraft's controls in the middle of it all.

Rising to her feet and staggering toward the edge of the roof,

Cornelia caught sight of the chopper at last. The machine halted in midair again, this time its nose rising upward, then spun into a wide, wobbling rotation.

Cornelia felt as if all the blood circulating through her body had turned to ice while her heartbeats thundered in her ears. She saw movement by the chopper's open hatch, then a figure plummeting out, tumbling toward the ground hundreds of feet below, arms and legs flailing in useless near-death reflexes.

"No!" she heard Lacy gasping beside her.

But the helicopter's wild movements stopped soon after one of its passengers was ejected. The aircraft's rotation ceased, the machine gaining altitude and coming back in for another approach of the platform.

"The stairs!" Cornelia exclaimed. "Where are the stairs?" She needed to get back on top of the platform immediately.

As Lacy helped Rafferty—who'd either broken or sprained an ankle—stand, Cornelia lunged into a sprint, circling the perimeter of the helicopter platform, desperately looking for a stairway or a ladder to the top.

She eventually found a metal-grate stairway next to the elevator structure and scrambled to the top as the besieged helicopter touched down. Fighting the buffeting winds of the rotor blades' downdraft, she struggled closer and closer to the aircraft as Rick stepped from the open side-hatch.

9.

SITES OF LOCAL LEGENDS OVERRUN BY GLOBE-WATCHERS
DESPITE HOSPITAL VIOLENCE
By: Nancy Akiona, *Hawaii Tribune-Herald*

Since the Hawaiian Islands have been identified as having one of the highest concentrations of people with a special sensitivity to the globe phenomenon, crowds have been flocking to sites connected to local folklore in ever greater numbers. Even the shooting incident at King's Medical Center has not deterred these globe pilgrims. Some, however, are concerned about the impact on the local ecology and the safety of these historical sites.

"The Hawaiian islands have a particularly rich history of spirituality and legends," explained Maxwell Kekumano of the Polynesian Cultural Center. "So many people are asking if our historical sites might explain the unusually high number of people who have been experiencing the hum and vibration phenomenon of these mystery globes."

Stories of people who report hearing a low-frequency hum near the appearance of a globe were first reported in San Francisco. Although the doctors and various scientists working for a newly formed study group run by a joint military task force announced that it does not yet understand what makes people hear these noises, what the government calls an "unusually high" number of people have come forward in Hawaii and claimed to be suffering this same affliction.

To date, other high concentrations of hum-sensitive people have been reported in Sweden, in Tanzania, in Ghana, Uzbekistan, and Austria.

On the Hawaiian Islands, just as in the other highly afflicted areas, many people are wondering where the next globe will appear. Many have been flocking to places like the Temple of Mu and Mahaulepu on Kauai, Nahuma Point on Maui, or the Kazumura Cave on the Big Island, hoping to see the appearance of a globe.

"This is a world-changing phenomenon," said Cynthia Reynolds, who traveled all the way from Baraboo, Wisconsin, in hope of seeing the next globe, "and I believe it will be a life-changing experience for me if I get to witness one appearing. This trip was worth everything for me. And sure, I was frightened by what happened at that hospital, but this is just something I need to do."

"Peace will always win out over hate and violence," Rudolph Metz, a visitor from Philadelphia, Pennsylvania, said. "We can't

CHAPTER 9

A Brief Escape. Senator Bling. Game Changer?
Emergency Powers. On the Beach. In the Philippines.

1.

"…and they have what that we don't? Little Timmy, come on! I mean, seriously, can you explain it to me, dude? One of these globe things appears in the Pacific…and it's in the Philippines? Come on! What kind of B.S. is that? The Philippines?"

Rick was snapped out of his deep, restful sleep by the sort of radio programming he despised the most in the world: the Wacky Morning Personality Show. He was about to slap his palm on the snooze bar except the gears in his brain fell into place quickly enough, and he was able to pick out the key phrases of the shrill, obnoxious rant on the nightstand radio.

Globe thing?

Philippines?

"What the hell is this?" he mumbled, and tried to focus all of his attention on the radio.

"…Dude? Little Timmy? You gotta help me out with this, brah!" the star of whatever show the radio was tuned to kept haranguing some obligatory sidekick.

As much as he wanted to make sense of the material on the radio, Rick's complete attention could not focus on the show exclusively. Something was missing, and that was a major problem he could not ignore at the moment. Namely, Cornelia was not in bed beside him.

"Yeah, man! I don't like that either, man!" The obligatory sidekick had the obligatory moronic slacker dude inflection. "The

Philippines? That's just not right, brah. Like, you know, we're the U.S.A. and everything, and we're number one. You know what I'm saying?"

A woman's cackling joined in the festivities of the morning madness on the radio...or whatever this cretinous show was called. In Rick's experience, wacky morning shows, no matter where in the U.S. they aired, were invariably called "Morning Madness," or "Morning Madhouse," or "Morning Zoo" or some such iteration on the phrase.

"Little Timmy for president!" the woman's voice on the radio said.

"For real!" said the star. "Eileen, you're a genius."

"But yeah, brah," said Little Timmy. "This is like total bogus, you know what I'm saying? We like saved the Philippines during World War One...you know?"

Eileen howled with laughter.

"I heard about this big granite ball showing up in the jungle in the Philippines last night," the star of the show said, "and, you know, it just makes my blood boil."

"It pisses me off, Jazzy Jim!" Little Timmy said.

"We have far superior jungles to anything they got in the Philippines," Eileen opined with mock graven seriousness.

"And we've been hearing all this stuff about people all over Hawaii hearing vibrations and everything," the star, Jazzy Jim, said, "and we still don't get a granite ball of our own. So what's that all about? And, you know, those douches in California've already gotten three balls."

"I hate California!" Little Timmy blurted out.

"Tell me about it," said Jazzy Jim.

"I want balls right here in Hawaii," Eileen added. "The Philippines are like in the big-ball club now, and we still got nothing."

"I feel for you because you really love balls, don't you, Eileen?" said Jazzy Jim.

Little Timmy let out a round of lascivious, snorting laughter.

"What can I say, Jazzy Jim?" Eileen replied. "I totally love balls. Great big, massive balls. I can't get enough of 'em."

"All right, so if the aliens or whatever are monitoring the airwaves now, we demand our own balls right here in Hawaii, in the U.S. of A. For Eileen's sake."

"Pleeeeeze!" Eileen whined.

"All right," said Jazzy Jim. "So how about we send a message to the aliens from AC/DC with an oldie but a goodie. What else? 'Big Balls'...."

Rick turned the radio off upon the opening bars of the *AC/DC* song.

As his gaze swept the hotel room, he ran his fingers through his hair, rubbed his eyes, and fingered the tender spot on the left side of his jaw. It was a reminder of a punch courtesy of Cornelia yesterday afternoon.

The fight in the helicopter yesterday was more akin to a wrestling match, with the gunman—since identified as Maury Wexler, a contributor to a local conspiracy web page—refusing to give up his weapon, trying his best to blow Rick away, or shoot the car-wreck victim strapped onto a stretcher on the helicopter, or, failing either of those options, to kill a pilot. Wexler managed no more than the minimal damage a couple of elbow jabs to Rick's stomach and chest could deliver. But after Wexler departed from the helicopter following a shove from Rick a moment before Wexler would have been able to shoot one of the pilots, Rick thought the last threat of physical assault had been neutralized. The helicopter returned to its landing pad, to be greeted by most of the globe team and, taking point on the pad, Cornelia. Before saying anything, though, she clocked him on the jaw.

"What the hell were you thinking?" she had shouted over the racket of the helicopter. "Huh? Are you mentally deranged?"

Still high on adrenaline, Rick had almost burst out laughing. "Remember what we said at Travis?" was all he could reply, noting how Cornelia was balling her fists again.

"About not just sitting by and doing nothing?" Cornelia had

yelled. "Getting yourself killed is *not* an acceptable alternative!"

Before she could hit him again, Rick had made his move, seizing her by both shoulders and embracing her in a long, deep kiss.

By the time they had finished, the helicopter's engines had powered down. While the rotor blades continued their revolutions overhead, their speed decreasing with each turn, it was quiet enough for them to notice some of the laugher, hoots, catcalls, and applause from the people on the platform.

"What a start to the morning, huh?" Rick heard Cornelia's voice at last and noticed her lithe, naked form step out of the shadows on the far side of the room. She held a can of soda in her hand, something she must have retrieved from the ridiculously overpriced mini refrigerator.

Studying all the lines of her stunningly beautiful body, Rick had already tried to push any thoughts of the globes out of his mind. He wanted to care about none of it for as long as he could.

"It's the *perfect* start to the day," he said as she arrived at the bed and stood over him. He ran his left hand over her thigh, up her buttocks, then caressing her stomach, sliding his fingertips down, questing between her legs.

The pop of the soda can opening cracked across the silent room. After taking a sip, Cornelia offered him the drink.

"A caffeine and sugar rush for some energy?" she whispered.

"Naw," Rick replied, slipping his hand to the small of her back and pulling her closer still. "I've got plenty of energy."

Cornelia reached down and tossed the sheet off him. "Good," she said, and straddled him quickly and smoothly.

He had, of course, reacted long before she was on top of him, and now their rhythm, their passion, their breathing and pounding heartbeats had them become as one again....as they had the previous evening, just after leaving King's Medical Center and after Cornelia decided to give up on trying to punch him again. Except for the two of them, an oddly uniform and apocalyptic group-think had bonded all of the members of the globe-study team together. From the soldiers to Kristine Murakami and her doctors, the *Confirmation* group and the rest of the network TV press corps, a consensus had emerged that the globe phenomenon had just thrown the world into the very final and soon to be very short countdown to something utterly cataclysmic. Doc Knight had especially creeped Rick out. His warning about the dangers of the globes, and the even greater dangers of the "witless, brain dead, new age assholes getting ready to march all of us down the throat of the wolf at the door" made Knight sound like he would now have been at home with Lindsay and the Reconstructionists. Rick needed to get away from all that, needed to have those people out of his life as completely as he could, even if it was only for a few hours. Cornelia felt the same way.

"It's like a different group of people came out of that hospital," Cornelia had said yesterday afternoon.

That was when she and Rick had been allowed to ride in one of the SUVs without anyone else tagging along. It was after they had left the Honolulu Police Department's Waikiki substation. The police, naturally, wanted statements on every moment of the attack at the medical center, except the military and the local FBI office were able to wave "national security" around vigorously enough to get everyone released within an hour and on their way back to Hickam.

"And I can't even stand being around them right now," Rick had replied. With a quick couple of turns through traffic, he had lost the rest of the procession heading back to the air base and drove up to the valet parking lot of the nearest and largest hotel he could find on Waikiki Beach.

As high-strung and paranoid as the rest of the team had gotten, Rick was glad to see that they were still willing to leave him and Cornelia alone for at least one night. The SUV had, of course, its GPS device and could be tracked anywhere. Since they were on an island, how far would they be able to go? But no calls, no hassles came after Rick and Cornelia had decided to strike out on their own.

They wound up at the Ilikai Hotel on Ala Moana Boulevard and booked an ocean-view room for the night. One of the hotel's claims to fame, they had been told, was the fact that its penthouse balcony had been zoomed in upon during the opening credits of both the old and new versions of the *Hawaii Five-0* TV show, introducing main character Steve McGarrett. By the time Rick and Cornelia stood on their own balcony, the sun had almost completely set, leaving the horizon a darkening indigo against the black silhouette of Diamond Head volcano a few miles away, and leaving them to marvel at the brilliant city lights of Waikiki below.

Oddly enough, it felt as if neither of them had ever seen a city nightscape as captivating as this before in their lives.

But not only had the sun risen now, not only had that idiotic morning talk show on the radio forced another globe development into Rick and Cornelia's blissful, lovemaking solitude, but now the room's telephone blared to life with its harsh electronic jangle.

And it refused to stop.

From within the depths of the pleasure created by their entangled, perspiration-slickened, overheated bodies, Rick tried to will the phone into silence.

"Someone's refusing to go away," Cornelia whispered into his ear.

"I'm going to kill whoever that is," he moaned in reply.

"You need to find out who it is first," Cornelia said, and kissed him on the cheek.

"A little lower," Rick teased in reply.

"What?"

"Where you hit me yesterday. It still hurts."

Cornelia playfully bit him there instead. "Get the phone!"

"Yeah? Ballantine," he growled into the receiver at length.

"Mr. Ballantine," a woman from the front desk addressed him. "There is a call for you from a couple of gentlemen here in the lobby. They say it's extremely urgent and related to the...," the woman cleared her throat, "the work you are doing with the

250

air force. They say they're here on behalf of Senator Brandon Markwell."

2.

On their short drive over from the Ilikai Hotel, Rick had told Cornelia that perhaps they had read Senator Brandon Markwell all wrong. Whoever would elect to stay at the much smaller Moana Surfrider, the oldest hotel on Oahu, dwarfed by the enormous modernity of steel and glass edifices of all the new hotels crowding Waikiki, could not have been all that bad.

"A preference for a historic building over the flash and size of these new hotels speaks to character," Rick had said, watching for some signs of agreement on Cornelia's face but not really finding any.

That was just before they were told that the senator and his wife were not actually staying in the historic section of the Moana Surfrider. Located on Kalakaua Avenue, a five-minute drive from the Ilikai, the Moana consisted of three segments. The central building was the oldest part of the hotel, originally constructed in 1901. Since then, however, the establishment had been expanded with the Tower and Diamond wings added on to its west and east sides. The modern architecture tagged on to the hotel proper's Hawaiian Gothic style looked wildly incongruous. Of the two additions, the Tower, where the Markwells now resided, had the hotel's most extravagant lodging, the Penthouse Ocean Suite. This sort of instinctive and very public gravitation toward the ostentatious, the flashy, and the overpriced kept building Markwell's reputation as someone incapable of keeping controversy at bay.

When criticized by a Carson City newspaper for a trip to New York where he tallied hotel and entertainment bills in excess of three hundred thousand dollars, Markwell had started off on the right foot in deflecting the bad press by claiming he would pick up the tab for the various Broadway plays he'd attended and treated his massive entourage of staffers to. However, when offering to spend "no more than a dime" over the travel budget allotted to each member of the Senate, he made headlines by tagging on the quip, "I don't understand why anyone would think I would bankrupt the treasury or anything. My wife and I have more money than even any grandchildren we might ever have could ever spend. I can more than pay my way where the law requires that I do."

The press, political bloggers, and both Republicans and Democrats pounced on him, accusing him of everything from "fleecing the American people for even using a single dime of public money for any sort of travel if he and his wife are so rich, while so many American families are struggling to stay afloat," to "fostering a cultural atmosphere of waste and overconsumption," and "showing an open disdain for the traditional family by hinting that he and his wife might not have children." Markwell's own response to the controversy was the reminder of both his and his wife's working class roots. He had worked his way through college holding down two jobs, he reminded, before his eventual success in the dot-com boom of the nineties. His wife had likewise struggled at one point as a none-too-successful child actress before her sudden prosperity as the producer of a series of low-budget, direct-to-video slasher films. Then he added the somewhat boilerplate declaration that, "I am very proud of the fact that my wife and I have been successful, and I devote all my energies to public service to make sure that the American dream and the same success is within the reach of all Americans." But the Nevada press also pointed out that Markwell's pro-environment rhetoric and voting record quickly increased in the wake of his "New York-gate." "At least Senator Bling knows how to keep his friends close and happy," The *Las Vegas Sun* remarked after the controversy.

"Mr. Ballantine. Ms. Oxenburg," Brandon Markwell's mellifluous tones greeted Rick and Cornelia as they were ushered toward the Penthouse Ocean Suite's balcony. "I'm so glad we are able to meet." While politicians of the media age were all impeccably trained for public speaking, Markwell's voice was somewhere on the level of a star radio announcer or voice-over artist.

The senator was waiting for them in the living room, a glass of what might have been either water or vodka in one hand and an enthusiastic — yet not really insincerely so — bearing. In a pair of white silk slacks, a blue and white Hawaiian shirt, and crisp white loafers, he looked more like the sort of leisurely celebrities whose company he enjoyed so much rather than a legislator about to delve into the government's response to a world-wide crisis in the making. Physically, however, Markwell looked exactly like the man every political handler and P.R. professional would ever dream of. At fifty-two years old, he looked like a former college track athlete or baseball player who was still in the same fighting shape he was over a quarter of a century ago. His trim, broad-shouldered, narrow-waisted athletic physique, along with his impeccably coifed salt-and-pepper hair and handsome face, made Rick think of a man in a low-testosterone-treatment commercial explaining how his new regimen of wonder drugs gave him the energy and stamina of a man half his age in the boardroom and the bedroom.

"Our pleasure, Senator," Rick replied after Cornelia said "hello." "Have you already met with the team at Hickam?"

"No. Since you were in the neighborhood, I thought we should meet first. And, by the way, this is my wife."

Glancing in the direction of the room the senator pointed to, Rick, almost on cue, heard the clicks of a pair of high heels upon tiles as Devon Markwell entered. The nearly robotically timed entrance reminded Rick of every quip and one-liner he'd ever read about the "android couple" and the "nip-and-tuck couple" from Las Vegas. Standing about five feet eight or nine inches tall, Markwell's wife looked like a former model who might have been put through a marine corps boot camp by a drill instructor with an obsession for weight training. Devon Markwell didn't so much as walk or move as she flexed. Outfitted in a tight, short white skirt and sleeveless light grey shirt, she was a stunning, angular specimen of muscle and sinew.

"Thank you for joining us," she said, and shook hands with both Rick and Cornelia.

Devon's attractive yet enigmatic smile, with lips that were slightly turned down in a perpetual pout and a strong-chinned face, framed by her very light blonde hair cut in a pageboy, reminded Rick of the "icy blondes" favored by Alfred Hitchcock in so many of his films. Although Devon had the similar light complexion Cornelia had, there was a natural warmness and an inviting glow that seemed to emanate from Cornelia. Devon Markwell made an instant impression of hard formidability.

"Would you like anything to drink, by the way?" she asked. "It's early in the morning. Any coffee, maybe?"

"Thank you," Cornelia said.

"Excellent!" Devon replied before Rick could say anything.

"Sure," he added a beat later.

Before Devon left the room, Rick noticed how her gaze seemed to linger on Cornelia for a moment.

"Senator," Rick said to break the silence that hung over the room as Markwell's wife sashayed out. "Were you just staying down on the Big Island?"

"Yes," Markwell said with a toothy, campaign-trail smile, "and hopefully I'll get to go back, too. There's a former eighties hair-band drummer vacationing there, and I'd like the chance to win back some money he took from me on the golf course. But, first of all, let's set down some ground rules, all right? It's Brandon and Devon."

Cornelia nodded and smiled.

"Sure," Rick seconded. "But I'm curious. Why us?"

"Come on," Markwell replied. "Let's go out on the balcony." But as Rick and Cornelia complied, he said, "It's because you two were in the thick of things, Rick."

"Unfortunately," Rick said as they took seats around a circular, glass-topped table.

"Hell of a thing it was, jumping into that helicopter," Devon's voice sounded off before her husband could say anything.

She joined them with a very pleasant smile, but not coffee, and took a seat between Markwell and Cornelia.

Room service, Rick surmised, would be serving them shortly.

"Well," he said, in answer to Devon's comment, "that guy was going to take that chopper hostage. Now that's bad enough in my book, but that was a medevac bird. Someone needed to get to that hospital right away."

"You're a hero, Rick," Markwell said with a firm, appreciative nod.

"It was instinct," Rick said, and rubbed his jaw where Cornelia had hit him.

She sent a little mock scowl his way when he glanced at her. "It was reckless," she said.

"Heroes often are," Markwell said with proud smile. "But this is what I would like to ask you: What is your impression of people like those attackers?"

"Other than those two trying to kill us, I didn't get much of a chance to form an impression."

Markwell didn't reply. Suddenly, Rick noticed his hail-fellow-well-met mask slipped. Markwell's brown eyes seemed to bore right into him, commanding him to try his best to form an impression and answer the question. The impression Rick did form on the spot, in turn, was of Markwell himself. The man's oddball, hedonist image seemed to be concealing something very tough and, most importantly, *smart* about him.

"They were obviously disturbed," Rick said, "and there are probably a lot more of them out there. These are the moon-landing-was-a-hoax people. The 9/11-was-an-inside-job people. Osama bin Laden is still alive and the theme song of *Mr. Ed* reveals Satanic messages when you play it backward. They make up their minds about what they want to believe and selectively interpret the world to fit those beliefs."

"Interesting," Markwell said evenly and with an appreciative nod. "People with all kinds of strong religious and spiritual beliefs do the same."

True enough, Rick thought, but said, "Except the Catholics or Buddhists or Orthodox Jews aren't trying to shoot up hospitals. For that matter, neither are the believers of most mainstream religions. You know, I kind of liked that stuff the spokesman from the Vatican Observatory said a couple of days ago."

But now he also wondered what it was that separated people like Lindsay from Murray Wexler and his redheaded buddy, who'd tried to slash Lacy and got his arm broken for his effort.

"But we've been talking to people like the two at the hospital since this whole thing began," said Cornelia. "We talked to one back in San Francisco. He thinks the government made the globes with time travel technology—"

There was a faint audible ring from the suite's front door, and a minute later one of the Markwells' aides glanced through the balcony door. "Room service," he said simply, and Markwell gave him an easy nod.

"But like we were saying," Devon said as the room service man came out and set a tray with a large coffee carafe and cups on the table. "Time travel technology? Made by the government?" She swept her gaze over everyone at the table and showed a thin, amused little smile.

With that pouty set of her mouth, Rick thought she made the time-travel assertion sound so howlingly absurd that it would have required no more words to deride the idea.

Nevertheless, she added, "Since whatever made these things obviously works, it was *obviously* not made by us. Not putting down the ingenuity and know-how of the American technology sector, of course."

"Of course you're not, honey," her husband said with the perfect deadpan.

"Of course she's not," Rick couldn't help adding with a grin now.

Everyone chuckled at that as they poured cups of dark-roast

Kona coffee.

As Rick did so, the thought skittering through his mind was, *Either these people are the world's biggest bullshitters, or I'm actually starting to like them.* How he would tell Cornelia this would be another matter.

"But here's what I'm getting at," Markwell said, again with deadly seriousness. "If the local cops and the FBI and Homeland Security — not to mention your little globe group and the people at the Pentagon —"

"Like General Barret?" Devon cut in with a roll of her eyes. "Our Chairman of the Joint Chiefs of Staff?"

Markwell nodded with a thin, knowing smile. "If they all think these people are a threat...," he said, but let his voice trail off, all the while studying Rick with that piercing, intrusive glare. He was, Rick knew, asking him to confirm or deny the statement.

So Rick said, "They do."

"Then what do you think all the other Wexlers and their little playmates all over the islands will do next?"

"These people are not just in Hawaii," Cornelia replied quickly.

"I know," Markwell said.

"Well," Cornelia said, "*I* think — and you might want some psychiatrists and psychologists to give you real data — but I think some people don't have any sort of purpose to their lives unless they think they're surrounded by enemies."

"I agree," Rick said. "The late Murray Wexler's pals are those people."

"Clinical paranoids?" asked Devon. "Bordering on schizophrenia?"

"Maybe," Rick replied. "And to answer your question, if the cops and the FBI and the military start running around trying to apprehend these people — just to tell them to tone down all their New World Order time machine Illuminati bullshit — it will be like confirming their worst fears."

Markwell gave a grim nod. "Like the raid on the Branch

Davidian compound in ninety-three."

Rick knew he'd pegged Markwell correctly. This was not a stupid bumpkin who'd stumbled into politics *Mr. Smith Goes to Washington*-style, despite the tawdry image he was incapable of shaking. "Like Fonzie used to say on *Happy Days*, 'Exactamundo.'"

"That's what I was afraid of," Markwell replied. "I never liked the idea of cracking down on civil liberties. Not even in times of national emergencies. Our country's strong enough to weather an emergency *with* our freedoms intact. But there's never been an emergency like this."

At first, Rick almost smiled. For one thing, Markwell sounded like he was in full politician mode. However, his staunch civil liberties stand almost made Rick blurt out, "Senator Markwell will always fight for your right to party. People with a penchant for a wild, unconventional time in the bedroom will love those civil liberties." However, Markwell did end on a note that was open for all sorts of sinister interpretations.

A heavy silence hung in the air before Marwell added, "And I will *never* support any curtailing of Americans' freedoms."

"Good, Senator," Rick said with all sincerity. "I mean, Brandon. That's really good to hear."

"You know," said Cornelia, "the funny thing is that yesterday the heads of the globe team were worried that *you* might take steps toward a heavier government hand in this."

"They must have been thinking of the wrong Brandon Markwell."

Not if you're known as Senator Bling, Rick thought with an inward smirk.

"So what about those so-called globe-experiencers?" asked Devon.

Rick said, "You'll have to talk to the group's head doctor, Kristine Murakami. Real interesting woman. But as far as I know, she's found nothing extraordinary about any of them."

"Wow," Markwell said simply. "No kidding."

"And how about the story out of Nebraska?" Devon asked,

throwing Rick for a loop.

When he glanced at Cornelia, she appeared to be just as confused by the question.

"What story?" Rick asked.

Devon replied, "Someone claims a very sick fifteen-year-old girl was healed after seeing a newly arrived globe on the island of Crete."

"I haven't heard about that."

"Well," Markwell said, "the Internet—and even the mainstream press—is full of all kinds of crazy noise. It's easy to miss."

"And you're sure this isn't a bit of noise?"

"This is an American kid," Devon said.

"Her doctor swears it's true," Markwell tagged on.

3.

"If it's true, it could be a real game-changer," Rick said as he drove their borrowed SUV west on Ala Moana Boulevard and toward Hickam Field.

The information Devon Markwell had dropped in their lap had Rick and Cornelia grappling with its implications rather than comparing their impressions of the slick-glamour of the Nevada power couple. Just before they left the Markwells' suite, the senator had invited them to a show their Vegas magician friend, "The Mindbending" Alexander Dorian, also staying at the Four Seasons on the Big Island, was putting on every night. Rick would have been game, just for the sake of seeing how another professional illusionist was dealing with the globe phenomenon. Maybe "The Mindbending" Dorian even knew something about how "The Astounding" Jerome Pike was doing these days. The last Rick heard, Pike had completely disappeared from the public eye after his assault in Florida.

"For the better or the worse?" Cornelia asked, not looking up from her iPad as her fingers quickly slid across and tapped away on its surface.

"I don't know."

"Or it could be a wild goose chase. Like David Kwan and all the globe sensitives."

"It could be that too," Rick had to concede.

Cornelia suddenly looked up from her tablet for a moment. "All right, listen to this!" she exclaimed, then went back to studying the information she'd just found. "Her name is Sally Foster. She's fifteen, just like Devon Markwell said. She lives outside Lincoln, Nebraska. The family's originally from Kansas City, Missouri. They moved to Nebraska because of her father's telecom-executive job. Everything was going perfectly for the family until a year ago, when Sally was diagnosed with a particularly aggressive form of brain cancer. Three months ago the doctors told the family she had less than a year. Maybe five, six months at most."

"So what were they doing in Crete?"

"Recreating a family trip to the Mediterranean from three years ago. There's a grandmother in Greece. It was one of Sally's happiest memories visiting there. And now was her last wish that they try and go back to the Mediterranean before she died."

"And they happen to run into a globe."

"Exactamundo."

Rick couldn't help grinning at that. "Could it have been a natural remission?" he asked, despite the fact that he doubted the possibility, and the question caused some troubling implications to start bubbling up from the depths of his mind. "I mean, a remission can happen on its own...can't it?"

"I don't know. All this says is that her doctor doesn't think so."

"So what are the reactions to this so far?"

"Mixed."

And Rick suspected as much, explaining that uneasy feeling that had been haunting him ever since they left the Markwells' penthouse. "Oh really?"

Cornelia's fingers worked the iPad. "Some think it's a miracle.

Others that it's a fraud."

"Miracle?"

"Oh yeah. Take your pick. It was from Jesus, from the earth spirits and globe makers, angels, or aliens. Whatever people already happen to believe in."

"Remember back when all this started? There was somebody somewhere dying of cancer who left his hospital and treatments to be cured by a globe. There's no word of whether he got better, is there?"

There was silence from Cornelia for about two minutes. "I can find stories about it," she mumbled as she kept searching the web. "Mainly scientists railing and ranting about how this is all a hoax and making people do stupid things. You know, giving up on science and reason and putting their faith in superstition and pseudoscience. But nothing more. If he would have been cured, I'm sure we could find something. The way the Markwell woman heard about this girl. Actually, I think if we wouldn't have been so focused on every news story about people hearing hums and vibrations, we probably would have heard about Sally Foster by now, too. There's been quite a bit about her on the web."

In his gut, Rick had suspected as much. "Strange that only one person gets healed so far, isn't it?"

"Yeah," Cornelia said with a rueful tinge to her voice. "The nature of the unexplained and the paranormal, isn't it? Reminds me of this one story I covered as a rookie reporter. The owner of this diner in Gainesville said the face of the Virgin Mary appeared on one of her buttermilk pancakes. She said she felt in her heart that there was a purpose to it all. Whole bunch of people flocked to see her from all over Florida. Even as far away as Georgia and Louisiana. They wanted to, you know, hear what the meaning of it all was."

"So did she reveal what it was all about?" Rick couldn't help blurting out.

"Oh, yeah, she did. She said the Virgin wanted us to love each other."

"That's it?" Rick asked, knowing how disdainful it might have sounded, even though he didn't intend it like that.

"That's it. Although you did have a lot of people who said they felt feelings of good will and euphoria after their pilgrimage."

That bit of information actually gave Rick a sinking feeling. "Nobody said anything about feeling a *buzz* of positivity or feeling like they were *vibrating* from love and good cheer, did they? Because if they did, we better keep that to ourselves."

"No, not that I recall."

"Good."

"I know what you mean. Kristine Murakami would be back to calling us a bunch of con-artists."

"You know it."

"Well, I should add one more thing. As I recall, the whole thing didn't turn out so well for everyone. There was this one guy who walked off his job—can't even remember where he worked—to make the trek to see the miraculous pancake. Left some big project or something that was on a tight deadline. Real serious stuff, you know. Worth like, I don't know how many million dollars to his company."

"To witness the miracle and have his life change."

"Yeah," Cornelia said with a painful wince. "And he was told that we should love each other."

"That must have been disappointing."

"His life did change, though."

"It did?"

"Unfortunately. He was fired."

It figured, Rick realized, not helping at all his growing sense of dread and foreboding. "Maybe we just need a little solid scientific data about this Nebraska girl," he said, noting the unsteady tone in his own voice.

"Sure. Tell Murakami and the rest of the military brass that we should jump back on their big plane and fly to Nebraska."

4.

"As a reporter myself," Cornelia said, "let me just put it out there that the senator would not be happy with this kind of small meeting and the clampdown on information."

Rick and Cornelia's meeting with Markwell had prompted this immediate meeting with the key personnel in charge of the globe-study group, but everyone else was excluded. Base Commander Lloyd Brubaker gathered Rutkowski, Graham, Murakami, and Knight, but the conference room they were in was locked down and two of the Navy SEALS they had brought from California were guarding the doors.

Via a massive high-definition screen on one of the walls, Garret Robinson was able to add his input from Travis Air Base. But that input right now was a derisive chuckle. "Yeah, the senator who just crawled out of whatever orgy, or swinger's club, or whatever sleaze pit he and his wife usually enjoy spending their time in."

"Never let it be said that I like to tell others how to live their lives or what kinks to indulge," Dan Knight said, planting his elbows on the conference table, aggressively leaning into the conversation. His posture reminded Rick of a sumo wrestler leaning forward and getting ready to ram his opponent. "*And* I've defended Markwell before, but given everything that's happening, *and* his take on this whole conspiracy theorist situation, I don't think Brandon Markwell's qualified to have anything to do with the phenomenon *or* this project *or* this group."

So Rick had the impulse to shove back. "And, as *you* pointed out a few days ago, someone who's been pretty damn successful back in Nevada. Reelected to office three times?"

"As they say, that was then and this is now," Knight snapped.

"And I happen to think he makes some sense here," Rick shoved right back.

"But on the ground right now *we* make the decisions on this," Brubaker jumped between them suddenly.

"I'm just warning you," Rick said, "he's going to want to come down here and talk to you."

263

Knight leaned back in his chair and threw his hands apart with a shrug. "National security. Can't we just shut all of this down? Classify everything?"

"Aren't we getting a little extreme here, Doc?" Cornelia replied.

"Are we missing some part of the big picture, Cornelia?" Knight answered her.

"What big picture?" Cornelia asked. "That we had another globe appear somewhere? At least it was in the Pacific."

"Hey...Hawaii? Philippines? We were in the same ballpark," Rutkowski said with some mild snark in his voice.

"But it's not the end of the world yet, is it?" Rick said.

"Except," Knight replied, as deadly serious as ever, as tightly wound as he had been since the King's Medical Center incident the day before, "people are acting like it. All over the world. You mark my words, we're gonna have more attacks like the one at the hospital."

"I don't doubt it," Robinson said from the teleconferencing screen.

"Are you ready to see a van full of explosives drive up to the gates of this base?" Knight asked.

Rick noticed everyone shift uncomfortably in their seats all of a sudden.

"Look," Kristine Murakami said, "the uncomfortable fact is that it *could* happen. We need to recognize that."

"I completely agree," Brubaker seconded immediately.

"So what about the rest of these assholes?" Rutkowski asked grimly, appearing to first chew up, then spit out each word. "Like the ones at the hospital? That nutcase they have in custody...."

Graham shuffled through some papers in front of him. "Moloy," he said, taking and skimming one of the sheets. "His name's Gary Moloy. His friends all over the Internet are screaming that he's being tortured. That civil liberties are being suspended all over Hawaii, and the military will soon be rolling the tanks down the streets."

"Yes, that's exactly what I'm talking about!" exclaimed Rutkowski. "What *are* we going to do about it?"

Cornelia turned to Brubaker. "Colonel, remember what you said yesterday? About their First Amendment rights?"

Before Brubaker could say anything, Robinson replied, "Cornelia, look, we know how you feel about that. But the fact is that this is a special circumstance."

"The First Amendment has survived much bigger emergencies," Rick interjected.

"No," Robinson came back, "I really don't think so—"

Before he could recite his fears of the apocalypse, Rick couldn't contain himself from adding, "So what do you all propose? That we start arresting anyone who's written some stupid, paranoid rant on Facebook about the globes and conspiracies?"

"No," Knight said, "just the maniacs like Moloy and Wexler and the rest of their kind."

Rick almost shook his head in melodramatic dismay. "Oh, God. I can't believe that the sleaze ball politician's the only person who's making sense right now."

"By proposing to do nothing?" Brubaker asked, impatient disgust well planted on his face.

"No," Cornelia said, "not by proposing to do nothing—and right now I'm just feeling really unclean agreeing with the sleaze ball politician—but if we overreact, we could be doing more harm than good."

Rick noticed Knight rolling his eyes. Before the professor could reply, he said, "Look, Doc, approach this as an anthropologist. You got all these paranoids out there. Hiding in their basements, out in some hole in the jungle, *wherever.* If you try and round them up…hell, if you just try and talk to them, they're going to take their insanity to the next level."

Knight shook his head. "Rick, they're already there."

"No, they're not! And this is what Markwell said, and he's one-hundred-percent correct: It's going to be just like Waco in ninety-three. They believe the war with the government is coming, and if you try and interfere with them in any way, they will see that as a confirmation of all their paranoia."

"*Then* you better start putting up barriers against car bombs," Cornelia said.

"*Exactly*," Rick said.

But Knight still appeared to be committed to standing his ground. "Somebody out there," he said as portentously as he probably could muster, "is no doubt putting that car bomb together right now. People like Moloy and Wexler are off-the-rail psychos. They don't need anyone pushing them any further."

Rick noticed Brubaker massaging his right temple. "Perhaps a point can be made for prudence. For now at least."

"How about prudence and identification?" asked Robinson. "Can we have these lunatics under some kind of surveillance?"

"I guess we can try," Brubaker said.

There was a long beat of silence in the room.

At length, Murakami asked, "And the next item on the agenda?"

All eyes gravitated toward her.

"Maybe," she said, "we should make sure we don't lose our globe sensitives. Does Senator Bling have any suggestions for that one?"

This time, all gazes drifted to Rick and Cornelia.

"Not really," Rick had to reply.

"I say we keep track of them," Rutkowski said with a stiff nod.

"I agree," Robinson replied quickly.

"Why?" Brubaker asked, looking at Murakami now.

"Because they're still our only connection to this phenomenon," she said.

"So *now* we should bring them all in, Doctor?" Rutkowski asked, not hiding his surprise over her change of heart from a day ago.

"Yes!" Murakami said strongly. "*Now* we should. Because now we know for sure they could bolt, go into hiding."

266

Knight shook his head slowly, but Rick noticed how he was drumming his fingers violently on the conference desk.

"*Now* I think it's pointless," Knight said, and paused. He swept his gaze around the room, as if challenging everybody to make eye contact. "Look, folks, whatever's doing this just said 'Fuck you' to us. That's exactly what all the globe sensitivity was. It just sent us a message with its middle finger. It says, 'I'm in charge and not you. You can't figure me out. You can't predict what I'm about to do, so don't even try.' This sensitivity cluster here in Hawaii, all the other ones in the world.... *Meaningless!*"

"But David Kwan felt it and the globe appeared in San Francisco," said Murakami.

Garret Robinson shook his head on the screen overhead. "No," his grim voice came from the speakers embedded in the walls, "Doctor Knight is correct. All these sensitives, they were like radar chaff. You throw out false signals to hide the real one."

Murakami's eyes drifted off to some point on the surface of the table unseen by anyone else. "Oh, God," she said at length. "Of course. That makes sense. David Kwan might be the real thing, and there might be other real sensitives out there."

"Except," Robinson completed the thought, "no one's going to pay attention to anyone else again who hears sounds and buzzes."

"Well," Knight began, with a sound to his voice that was an unpleasant kind of a cross between self-satisfaction and disgust, "depending on where in the world you are, you better keep your mouth shut if you think you're hearing any hums or vibrations. An experiencer in Ghana got stoned to death because they thought his hearing of the hums was a sign of witchcraft. Nice, huh?"

Murakami pinched the bridge of her nose and shook her head. "This is spiraling out of control."

"And there's nothing we can do to control it," Knight said. "Except to prepare—and given the state of the world we're living in, I don't know how that's going to work—to prepare for whatever comes next."

"What do you think is coming next?" Graham asked.

"Nothing good. A takeover. Total control. A demand for total obedience. I'm telling you all, this will get a lot worse. And like I've been saying before, then *something*, whatever made all these globes, will make itself known and it will demand that we worship it."

There was a comparison Rick just had to bring up for Knight now. "You know, Doc, my ex-wife would probably agree with you right now. Except she'd call it the Antichrist."

Knight gave him a sharp look. "There is no such thing as the Antichrist...but she probably has the right idea."

So here's someone else going through a perfect one-eighty switch along with Murakami, Rick thought. *The incident at the hospital must have done a real number on him.*

"I agree," Robinson's voice came through the speakers. "This is a threat."

"And the nuts are already flocking to the Philippines," Knight said, "They want to commune with the globe spirits ushering in the new age. Idiots!"

"Was there a buzz in the Philippines?" Cornelia asked.

"Probably not," Brubaker said, and shrugged.

And now Rick noticed Cornelia looking at him, attempting to make eye contact.

"By the way," he said at length, knowing full well where the line of conversation he was about to open up would lead, "how about we add another item to the agenda?"

"What's that?" Brubaker asked.

"This story out of Nebraska...."

5.

Rick's eyes took in the expanse of the stunningly beautiful stretch of beach, sand, and surf, a brilliant cloudless sky overhead. It was the sight millions of people paid a lot of money to visit or yearned to visit at least once in their lives. He watched the beachgoers all around, the crowds that appeared to be unconcerned with the madness metastasizing out of control all around the world. He wondered about why they all looked so calm. Had they all dreamed of, planned for, saved for this trip to Hawaii for such a long time that now they refused to let the globe stories dominating every form of mass media bother them? However they were dealing with it all and managing to look as carefree as they did, Rick envied them. He wanted to be one of them right now.

"You know," he said, and turned to Cornelia as they walked in the water along the edge of the beach. "I like it out here enough that I might not want to go back to the base again."

"You want to quit?" she asked. "After what you said back in California? What are you going to do then?"

Rick simply shrugged.

"Jerry's not going to be too happy," Cornelia said. "Neither will your agent."

"Everything we're doing...and I'm not just talking about us, the show. I mean *them*. Robinson, Rutkowski, Murakami. This entire circus. It's all pointless. We're running around in circles here. Knight was actually correct. You know that? He was right. The globe-maker just told us to go fuck ourselves. Coming out here was a waste of time."

"Look, Rick, I was annoyed too that they're not taking the Nebraska kid seriously," Cornelia said with a calm, agreeable tone.

"Self-important fools!"

"That they are. But look—"

"Do you know what I'm gonna do?" Rick felt himself blurt out. As much as he wanted Cornelia to calm him down, as much as he wanted to blow off steam by coming out to this beach, it still wasn't working. "Huh? Do you know what I'm gonna do?"

"What?"

"I'm gonna take the senator up on his offer. I want to fly down to the Big Island, play a round of golf, and watch his magician friend put on a show."

Even before the last words left his mouth, Rick noticed Cornelia's eyes cloud over.

"If I were you," she said at length, "I'd watch my back around your new BFFs, Brandon and Devon. I think those two people only take part in whatever they can personally profit from."

"Yeah, well, so far they've said more things that make sense that anyone on this little globe-hunting study group of ours. Can you believe what Brubaker and Knight and Rutkowski are proposing back on the base right now? They want to hunt down anyone writing anything about conspiracy theories. They want to put the island under martial law."

Cornelia nodded with a distant, thoughtful look in her eyes. "Yeah, that's a little extreme. I agree."

"And Doc Knight? I mean, holy shit! I think he's lost his mind. He really is worse than Lindsay now."

Cornelia chuckled at that with a quick nod. "You might be right there too."

"So yeah, what Markwell said about civil liberties…hell yeah. He's right. Forget the hookers and the bling and all that B.S. He's actually the sanest person here."

Cornelia shook her head and looked away from Rick. Her expression was more akin to disappointment with him now, rather than anger.

So Rick quickly said, "Look, what really matters is that I've just heard the U.S. government's top-flight globe investigators say crazier things than Markwell ever has in his life."

After a beat, Cornelia said, "All right, Rick, maybe that's true. But I think there's still some advantage to staying here a little longer."

This time, though, there was something else in her voice. Something tense and nervous. There were bigger things to worry about, she seemed to concede with her tone alone, than the odd private lives of the Senator and Mrs. Markwell.

"What's that?" Rick asked.

"If things go bad, being with the military might be the safest place."

"If things go bad, it's probably because *they* will make it go bad," Rick said, almost immediately realizing that he had missed Cornelia's meaning.

"Or maybe not."

"What?" he asked her worries dawning on him. "You think aliens will attack?"

"I don't know," Cornelia said strongly. "OK, Rick? I don't know what could go wrong. But we're not just dealing with human stupidity. There's *something* out there...."

Rick took a heavy breath before replying. It had felt good to rant until now, but he couldn't ignore Cornelia's fears. And she did have point. "I know —"

Before he could say anything more, he felt his cell phone vibrate in his pocket. He quickly fished it out and glanced at its screen. *Oh, crap....*

"What is it?" Cornelia asked.

"A text from Jerry. He says to check the news. There's fighting in the Philippines."

6.

Cornelia had told him that she felt ridiculous, but Rick thought that was still better than feeling chafed and uncomfortable. Since a second text from Jerry said they had less than fifteen minutes to get back on the base if they wanted to remain a part of the globe-hunt team before the installation would be locked down, they sprinted out of the water, up the sand, and to their SUV as fast as they could. Rick had made the mistake of sticking his wet, sand-covered feet back in his sneakers, whereas Cornelia remained barefoot. Now, walking toward the base's command center with shoes full of sand — the cuffs of his jeans still rolled up to look ridiculous as well — it felt as if someone was trying to take his skin off by making him wear stockings made of abrasive-paper. Padding along the corridors barefoot might have been embarrassing Cornelia, but she should have been appreciating the comfortable choice she'd made.

So I guess I couldn't leave it all behind after all, Rick thought as they entered another chaotic command center. *Cornelia called my bluff.*

"State Department's telling all Americans to stay away from the Philippines." Sam Rutkowski got them caught up on the news immediately. "And they're putting all our military bases in the Pacific on alert. Some terror cell out there...." He paused, looking like he was grappling for a name as Kristine Murakami appeared behind him. "What the hell's their name?"

"Abu Sayyaf," she answered immediately. "They're active in—"

Rutkowski cut her off, though. "Yeah, in the same general location the globe showed up."

"Southern areas of the country," Murakami forcefully inserted the information.

"Where a group of these spirit-power new age nitwits go stumbling into," Rutkowski said, with the expression of someone who had just bitten into a rotten piece of meat. "Remember when some Iranian cleric said this whole thing was about Satan's plan to exterminate Islam?"

"Don't tell me," Rick replied. "These Abu Sayyaf people are big fanboys of his, right?"

"How'd you guess?"

"Newsbreak, ladies and gentlemen," Frederick Graham exclaimed as he strode over. "Reports are coming in about a hotel bombing in Manila."

"Hotel?" Cornelia gasped.

"Look at that," Murakami said with the same stunned, breathy voice, and pointed at one of the command center's larger screens.

It was showing a lot of shaky-cam images from some type of a newscast. A rapid-fire edit of flames shooting out of the windows of a tall building, a billowing wall of smoke enveloping the establishment, running people, dazed people milling around, and frantic paramedics and various first-responders moving bloodied and soot covered bodies filled the screen.

"They're waiting to confirm which hotel it was," Graham said. "Big one, though. Fancy. A lot of Americans. They're also promising to shoot down American aircraft next. There will be a press conference from the White House soon."

Rick felt Cornelia next to him. "I think a trip to Nebraska's pretty much not happening right now," she quietly said into his ear.

"Yeah," he muttered and started backing away from Murakami, Rutkowski, and Graham, who were paying no attention to either him or Cornelia anyway. "Unless we go to Plan B and ask for some outside help."

"Help?" Cornelia asked. "From who?"

"My new BFFs."

7.
U.S. PREPARES FOR HOSTILITIES AT HOME AND ABROAD
By Trevor McSweeney, *The Washington Post*

In the wake of the terrorist attacks on the Philippine islands, the United States is experiencing a state of heightened alert not seen since the aftermath of the attacks of September 11, 2001. As warships deploy to the Philippines, many in the U.S. are preparing for the worst.

In an effort to boost security on U.S. military installations in the Philippines, the Pacific Fleet's Carrier Strike Group Nine deployed its flagship aircraft carrier, the USS Ronald Reagan, along with the guided missile cruisers USS Chancellorsville and USS Cape St. George to Manila.

"Our objective is the security of military bases and personnel that might be targets for further attacks," explained Rear Admiral Connor F. Stevens, Commander of the Pacific Fleet stationed at Pearl Harbor Naval Base in Hawaii. "Should the situation on the islands change, we are prepared to support the evacuation of civilians and aid in assisting counterterrorist efforts."

Many Americans, however, have been left unsettled by the violence in the Pacific because of the added unknown of the globe phenomenon.

"Everything until now we could understand, you know?" said Neil Horton, a software engineer from Bethesda, Maryland. "The political situations, the religious situations until now were something we knew about. We understood...I guess we understood as well as [you can] what was behind 9/11, behind everything going on in the Middle East. However, this whole globe situation just keeps changing every day."

Horton also added that he has been taking special precautions protecting his family.

"I was never the survivalist and gun-type person until now," he said. "But now I'm ready to move my family out of the city and to start stocking up on everything we need stay safe...to have enough to eat in case of any type of an emergency, and to protect ourselves. It's just the unknown. It's not knowing anything that's so terrifying."

Despite the gun control debate heating up once more, sporting goods stores and gun stores have reported record sales of firearms and ammunition.

"The next threat could come from anywhere," said Louise McClaren, a single mother of three children ages six to fourteen in Lawton, Oklahoma, who purchased two shotguns and a handgun following reports of the hospital attack in Honolulu. "I mean, I could not believe that craziness in Hawaii. What if some disturbed person comes and attacks you because of something you said about a globe? So I'm going to do whatever it takes to defend my children. You can believe anything you want about globes or aliens or whatever, but you will stay away from my family."

A commission of mayors, however, issued a statement that the best defense against any globe-related threat on U.S. soil is to keep a level head and stay calm.

"Aside from one accident, no globe has hurt a person," said Senator Brandon Markwell, who was vacationing in Hawaii at the time of the King's Hospital shooting in Honolulu and who supports the mayors. "Only people driven to violence out of fear and unfounded panic have hurt others. At this point we need to heed the words of President Roosevelt. All we have to fear is fear itself."

CHAPTER 10
Secret Conference

Dan Knight sat in the conference room again, doors closed and locked, two Navy SEALS outside and making sure no one could enter. Except this time he was alone. He was looking at Garret Robinson on the teleconferencing screen ahead of him, trying to read the man's face, trying to interpret his intentions. Was Robinson, he wondered, acting as a grieving father in the decisions he made, the course of action he was recommending to the Pentagon? Had he been converted to a new way of seeing things by his "saved" son? Or was he what he had always been and acting for the same reasons; a military man convinced that what they were about to do was the best possible tactical move?

But it didn't matter, Knight decided, because it was the right thing to do. What the Pentagon was about to embark on was the only chance the world had of surviving what lay ahead.

"Peretti wants to stay put," he told Robinson. "He thinks this is where the action is, and he wants to be where the rest of the media are."

Robinson nodded. "Good. It's best to keep him out of it."

"All right, I understand what the next step has to be, but you need to give me details now. What exactly will *it* be?"

"First of all, you're going to listen to Ballantine and go along on this trip he's proposing. If Markwell is willing to fly him and Cornelia to Nebraska, let him. But go along with them. Keep us informed of what's going on in Nebraska as we're planning the second phase of this operation."

"All right. So can I get some information about where exactly this second phase will take place? And why you think it has a chance of working?"

Knight had a rough, theoretical idea of what the "second phase" was supposed to be, but so far he couldn't imagine why it made any more sense than all the wild-assed plans they had so far for rounding up people who heard hums, or going out into the middle of Nebraska to find one fifteen-year-old girl.

He saw Robinson take a deep breath on the screen, as if gathering all his strength to go plowing through a long, complicated story.

"You know what I told you about those old study projects," Robinson said, "Into understanding unexplained phenomena...."

"The UFOs?"

Robinson shook his head. "The *unexplained.*"

Why am I not surprised after all? he thought, then said, "It figures. So you do know —"

"Oh, no!" Robinson said very emphatically. "No, we *don't.* This isn't us. We're not behind it. It's not back-engineered UFOs, Nazi flying saucers, any of that crap. And we don't know why it's happening."

"So what *do* you know?"

"We think we know where it might be coming from."

"Where?"

After a beat, looking thoroughly uncomfortable, Robinson said, "I take it you've heard of the Taos Hum."

Of course Knight had heard of it. Starting in the early 1990s, a few people near the town of Taos, New Mexico, started complaining of a persistent low-frequency humming sound bothering them. Much like David Kwan and the other hum experiencers in Hawaii, they compared the sound to the vibration of a distant motor. Also like Kwan, the Taos hum-experiencers all told tales of distress and suffering from this inexplicable affliction, not to mention the skepticism of doctors they sought treatment from. Although various hypotheses tried to account for the Taos hum, everything from cell phone transmission and seismic activity to electrical power lines and high-pressure gas lines, not one had so far been conclusively proven to be the source of the hum.

"I did an article about it for a New Mexico magazine years ago," he said.

"You went out to Taos."

"Yeah."

"Did you hear the hum?"

"No...."

Robinson nodded again with a knowing look. "Only some people do."

"Like these globes," Knight said, the significance of Taos dawning on him. "People like David Kwan. And you think Taos is where all of this is coming from?"

"Maybe one of the places."

"Yeah, there are several places like that all over the world," Knight said. As a matter of fact, similar hum phenomena had been reported from England as well, from the towns of Bristol and Leeds, for decades now. In Scotland, some people heard the hum near the town of Largs. In Windsor, Ontario there had also been documented hum incidents, as well as in Bondi, Australia. "And these have been studied by...what? The air force? The Pentagon?"

"Both air force and NSA," Robinson said. "But, just like the whole UFO thing, we found nothing. We had no idea what it could be. Written off by most as some sort of a psychotic episode these people had. Psychosomatic for some. Mass hysteria. They heard things because they were expecting to hear hums and vibrations. Recently, unless you wanted your career to start hitting some road bumps, you didn't insist on having anything to do with hums and vibrations in Taos. The prevailing attitude in Washington's been that it's all a waste of time and money... well, until now that is."

"So the people here in Hawaii...?"

"Like I said earlier: radar chaff. Nothing but decoys.

Whatever's doing this is playing with us. But now we have an idea for sending the bastard a message."

CHAPTER 11

Alexander Dorian. Loaner. The Foster House.
Henry Roberts. Rescue. Taking Sides. The
Encounter. Clash. Confirmation. Reunion.

1.

"Now you see it," Alexander Dorian said as he smoothly placed the red rubber ball on the glass-topped coffee table with his thumb and index finger, all to the rapt interest of his jet-black cat, "Now you don't." In a blink, Dorian swept his hand over the ball, seemingly making it disappear.

"Amazing!" Dorian gasped, and the cat apparently thought so, too, because it quickly started pawing the spot where the ball had been just a moment ago.

"What's this?" he asked a second later, snapping his fingers, reaching behind the animal's little head and producing the ball seemingly out of thin air.

Flashing a raffish stage smile, he tossed the ball to Lacy.

"We all feel like that cat, don't we?" she asked, snatching the ball out of the air.

"And we have as much chance of figuring it out as that cat does," Brandon Markwell said, and sipped some champagne from the flute in his hand. He took a seat on the cream-white sofa across the table from Dorian. "But the best of us soldier on despite the odds," he added, and offered a toast with the champagne Rick's way.

The cynicism was off-putting, Rick thought, no matter how true it was.

"I think our situation's much worse than that," Dan Knight

said, and joined them. "You, Mr. Dorian, love that animal, I take it. As all pet owners do. He's your *companion animal*, isn't he?"

"Absolutely, Professor," Dorian said.

"So you would never actually take pleasure in tormenting that creature. Our globe-maker, as I think it's all too obvious by now, *does.*"

"Well, let's hope that's not the case," Cornelia spoke up now as she walked over. "In Nebraska we do have a fifteen-year-old kid who was healed by a globe."

"And let's hope the healing is exactly what we think it appears to be," Devon Markwell said, and sat next to her husband. "Can I have a sip, baby?" she said in a stage whisper, and he gave her the champagne flute.

"We'll know soon enough," Rick said, glancing toward one of the airplane's windows and noting how the sky outside was fading into a burning orange twilight glow. Flying east after their refueling stop in San Diego, it felt as if time was speeding up. While Rick wouldn't speak for anyone else on the plane, to him it felt as if they were hurtling uncontrollably into some sort of an overwhelming destiny.

They were traveling on Alexander Dorian's private plane—or mobile home, as he liked to call it—a Boeing 737-800 that had been tricked out in every luxury accessory one would want in a home away from home.

Dorian also boasted that he had as much communication equipment on board the plane as the president had on Air Force One. On the one hand, that was helpful at the moment. They could keep abreast of world events in light of the violence in the Philippines. But, on the other, the information carried by all the news services was too depressing. A part of Rick felt that if he could wish for anything, he would want to stay aboard that plane and keep flying around the world indefinitely, cocooned in all that garish luxury, high above and removed from the rest of the craziness on the surface tens of thousands of feet below.

And thank God for high-concept seventies crime shows, Rick thought. When the air force at Hickam blew off his proposal to investigate the Nebraska miracle-kid, Brandon Markwell was able to secure their immediate passage off the island courtesy of his friend, "The Mindbending" Alexander Dorian.

Part of the 737's luxuries included a tail end that had been converted into a garage for a bright yellow Lamborghini Huracan sports car. A hatch had been installed under the tail, able to descend into a ramp. It was his childhood fantasy, Dorian had explained, to be able to live on a customized plane he could drive a car into. It was just like a plane owned by his childhood inspiration, a crime-fighting illusionist in the early-seventies TV show *The Magician*, starring Bill Bixby. Dorian had been six-years-old when he saw that show, and he had been captivated by magic since. Once he made his millions in his Vegas act, Dorian had decided this plane was his ultimate homage to his inspiration.

"Tell me, Mr. Dorian," Cornelia said, "Did you—?"

"Please," the magician cut her off. "It's Alexander."

"All right, Alexander," Cornelia obliged, although Rick noted the embarrassed look crossing her face. He suspected he knew what she was about to ask.

Since a sly smirk crept onto the chiseled visage *People* magazine once referenced when declaring Dorian one of the one hundred most attractive entertainers in the world, Rick suspected that the magician knew what Cornelia was getting at as well.

"What I was wondering about," said Cornelia, "was whether you thought the globes were a massive hoax back in the beginning."

Dorian made another rubber ball dance around the fingers of his right hand before it seemed to vanish again. "Like my obnoxious colleague, the Astounding Pike did?" he asked, and lifted his left hand, the ball seeming to pop into existence at some point as he waved it around with a nimble flourish.

"Yeah, just like Pike," Knight said, and sat down on one of the plane's deep, decadently comfortable recliners. "Poor bastard. I do honestly miss those great debates we used to have."

"I assume he was good for your work," Dorian said, making the double meaning in his words came through loud and clear.

"Yes, he was," Knight said very bluntly. "The villain to my hero. The rationalist wet blanket out to rob the world of its magic and wonder."

"I'm sure it worked the other way around, too, Professor," Dorian said, and Rick noted how that attitude, that challenging cockiness never left his voice.

"Of course it did," Knight replied quickly. Rick was sure the old man did so to deprive Dorian of the pleasure of landing his little verbal barb. "I was one of the superstitious barbarians. Threatening a world of scientific enlightenment and progress. A real menace, I was."

Dorian just continued smiling genially with a little tip of his head. "But to answer your question, Cornelia, yes, I did. For quite a while. And Brandon here still won't let me forget it."

"Oh, you bet I won't," Markwell said.

"And I'm not going to let him," Devon said. "For as long as I've known Alex, I never imagined he could act like such an arrogant prick until these globes showed up."

"Oh, yeah," Dorian replied enthusiastically. "Guilty as charged. Magicians are world champion pricks."

Rick thought the last three words out of Dorian's mouth had the most curious, indescribable inflection. It was either Rick's imagination, or it hinted at dimensions to the relationship between Dorian and the Markwells that he didn't care to contemplate.

Who am I to judge people who are helping me? he told himself. *After defending Brandon Markwell's unwavering commitment to civil liberties.*

"We're party-poopers and obnoxious skeptics," Dorian said. "There's nothing so fantastic, otherworldly, or miraculous you can imagine that I can't fake on a stage."

"Except for these globes, darling," Devon said, and took a healthy swallow of her champagne.

"In a way, I still say they're a hoax," Dorian insisted, with the sort of confidence that surprised Rick.

"Come on, Alex," Markwell said. "Just give it up."

"No, no, wait a minute!" Dorian insisted.

"What?" Lacy asked. "You're gonna say it's a government conspiracy or something?"

Dorian let out a dismissive, contemptuous snort of laughter. "The government? Like the military you've been hanging out with for the past couple of days?"

"Well...," Lacy began, but her voice trailed off.

"No offense to a fine public servant like the senator here, but the government's a collection of bureaucratic clowns," Dorian said. "Just look at what they're doing right now. Putting all their focus on the Philippines. Trying to harass those hum experiencers all over Hawaii. What a joke! So no, it's not a conspiracy. But as Arthur C. Clarke tells us, any sufficiently advanced form of technology will be indistinguishable from magic."

That was, Rick reflected, in fact the reason for only half of the *Confirmation* team going to Nebraska. Even Jerry Peretti thought the real story was in the Pacific. He even wanted most of the technical crew there to get the best footage in case anything more happened in either the Philippines or on Hawaii. He was so angry at Cornelia for going with Rick that he told her Melinda could do just as well on camera as she could.

"Meaning what?" asked Cornelia.

"That whatever's doing all this is some kind of a flesh and blood being. Or whatever passes for flesh and blood for a being with sufficiently advanced technological capabilities."

"Oh really, Alex?" said Devon. "But then what is really the point? What's the difference?"

"Well, we're not dealing with any sort of a god or spiritual being behind all this," Knight replied quickly.

"We're dealing with something," said Lacy, "that's, you know, related to us the same way Alexander relates to that cat."

"Aha," said Dorian.

And Rick caught the distant look in Lacy's eyes. "Like Vince said," she continued, "like the construction workers next to the anthill."

Not only had Rafferty broken his ankle on the hospital roof, but the military brass had ordered him to stay put in Hawaii. Since Cornelia had told Rick about the budding relationship between Rafferty and Lacy, he felt sorry for the way she wound up having to be separated from him. But Rick was also impressed with the way she was committed enough to getting some answers to this phenomenon that she insisted on coming along after she decided those answers were in Nebraska.

"Yeah, well, like you said, Devon," Knight replied. "I'm not sure it matters if whatever's doing this is intent on deceiving us or intent on making us think it's some kind of a god."

"That's why we have to make sure we find out the truth and tell as many people as we can," said Dorian with a sort of earnestness that surprised Rick.

"Tell people?" Lacy asked.

When Rick glanced at her, he was taken by the surprisingly distant and hard look in her eyes.

"The truth, you mean?" she added.

Dorian nodded. "Yeah."

"Good luck."

An awkward silence hung over them for a moment.

Rick was wondering when a politician like Markwell would speak up and express his faith in the American people. But he wasn't surprised when the senator sat quietly for another moment.

When Markwell did speak, it was after glancing at his watch. "We'll find some answers to all this very soon."

2.

Dorian's 737 touched down in Lincoln, Nebraska, leaving its passengers in something of a predicament. The sun had already set, no one in the group knew their way around the area, and they were unable to get anything other than voice-mail at any of the phone numbers the plane's communication center—no matter that it was supposed to rival that of Air Force One's capabilities—was able to dig up.

"So how about you wait until tomorrow morning instead of renting cars and stumbling around in the darkness now?" Devon Markwell suggested.

"On God-knows what kind of crazy, confusing backroad these people are living on," her husband seconded.

Rick couldn't help smiling at that. The comment could have been construed as being elitist, he wanted to tell Markwell. Rick was sure Markwell had enough constituents in Nevada who lived on confusing backroads.

"I ran into a globe on a backroad not that long ago," Rick quipped.

"There you go," said Markwell.

"Except something doesn't feel right," Rick had to insist.

"What do you mean it doesn't feel right?" Dorian asked.

"Why can't we reach *any* of them on any of those phone numbers? Some of those must be cell numbers."

"I don't know," Cornelia said. "It's late. Maybe they don't believe in letting technology intrude on family time."

That was an interesting way to grasp at straws, Rick thought. "Do you really believe that's the case?"

Cornelia returned a rueful smile. "No."

"I don't think so either."

"But here's what I believe," said Knight. "If we try and get a rental car right now, we might not even get one with a GPS. And I'd rather not be trying to make sense of a map in the middle of the night in…. Where the hell do these people live, anyway?"

"Between Lincoln and Palmyra," Rick said.

"Of course," Lacy jumped in, her sarcastic tone suggesting she was squarely in Knight's camp. "That really narrows it down."

"Sure," Knight added. "Because I come to Nebraska all the time. Know this place like the back of my hand."

"Forget the car rental," Markwell said with an uncharacteristically hard and resolute voice. "You've got something right here that'll get you in and out of any off-the-map place. Day, night, or in the middle of a snow storm."

It took Rick a moment to catch on, but he did so by recognizing the ashen look on Dorian's face.

"I don't know about that," Rick had to say, not wanting to abuse the magician's hospitality.

"Yeah, I don't know either," Dorian said. "I mean off the beaten track…. That's not quite so good…."

"Take Alex's Lamborghini," Markwell insisted.

Cornelia let out a thin whistle.

"Right," Rick said. "I've never even laid my hands on a car that costs that much, let alone taken it out for a spin in the middle of the night."

"This is urgent," Markwell pressed. "And that car's got one of the best navigation systems you're likely to find anywhere in the Midwest." Then Markwell paused and gave Dorian a hard look. "Alex! Ask not what your country can do for you…and you know, all that good stuff."

"Well, I suppose," Dorian said at length with a wavering voice.

"You're a great American, Alex," Devon added.

"And when we find out something history-changing tonight," Markwell said, "and when the cameras start rolling, Alex and I will be right there next to you."

"Of course," Rick said.

Dorian had a look on his face that said, "I'd better be." But out loud he said, "Can you drive a manual transmission?"

3.

Rick could drive a manual transmission quite well, and the Lamborghini, powered by its six-hundred and ten horsepower V10 engine, had left Knight and Lacy's rental Honda Accord well behind, no matter how much Rick tried to make sure they could keep up. Cornelia, giving them directions by phone, tried to assume they would not get lost on their way out to the Foster homestead.

As Rick had predicted, the Fosters' quite prosperous-looking, sprawling property was hardly on the end of a network of country dirt roads. It was merely secluded.

"And it looks completely deserted," Cornelia said as they rolled up to the house's front drive.

The lights all around the property were indeed out, except something was still off as far as Rick's cop's instincts were concerned. "But the gate to the driveway was still open."

"Come on, Rick. This is middle America. You know, people here leave home and leave their front doors unlocked."

Rick stopped the car on one side of the stairway leading up to the Fosters' porch. "Not in a world," he said, "that's very violently divided between people who love the globes and the ones who think they're Trojan Horse gifts from demons." After they got out of the car, he added, "And right now no one loves the globes more than the Foster family—"

But Rick's words were cut off by a sound that chilled the blood more than perhaps any other sound for a person having even a passing familiarity with firearms. The metallic snaps of a shotgun pump-action slide getting racked no more than a few feet away stopped him and Cornelia dead in their tracks.

"And just which side of the divide are you on, my man?" a male voice called out with a mild Midwestern twang.

4.

"Believe me, Mr. Ballantine, when I tell you that there was a time when I would take a piece of paper and very, *very* gently push a spider out of my house. The thought of taking any form of life was just completely abhorrent to me," said the leader of five men holding Rick, Cornelia, and the Foster family at gunpoint in the middle of a spacious living room. "My name, is Henry Roberts," he said, somehow surprising Rick by the fact that even his name was as prosaic as his appearance. Maybe, a crazy thought skittered through Rick's mind, he was expecting his captor to be called something like Billy Clyde, or Buford, or Big Enos. "And believe me how sorry I am that circumstances have brought me to this."

With his jeans, sneakers, and a brown windbreaker, the middle-aged Roberts looked like he could have been a small-town car salesman taking a long weekend to relax in the country. The big problem, however, was the M-16 assault rifle he appeared to be quite adept at handling. A hunch also told Rick that the weapon was, more likely than not, converted to full automatic mode.

"What circumstances?" Rick asked as neutrally as he could. As he did so his eyes darted once again to the Foster family—parents Charlie and Rosemary and kids Sean and Sally—each of them seated in rattan chairs in front of the large fireplace on the left side of the room and held at gunpoint by four of Roberts' partners. The fifth gunman was back outside on sentry duty.

"Haven't you been watching the news lately?" Roberts asked, his voice betraying something akin to dismay—disappointment, even, with the unread ignoramuses that had stumbled into the middle of his assault on the Fosters—rather than any true menace or rage.

The looks coming from Roberts' compatriots, on the other hand, told a different story. Their looks belied the small-minded cruelty of petty thugs Rick had seen enough times on the streets of Los Angeles. Whatever this attack on the Fosters was all about, Roberts was definitely the mastermind of everything, a man with some sort of a grudge that could no longer be contained, and he was smart enough to command the respect of and somehow control a group of men who were capable of the sort of violence he might not have been up for on his own.

But Rick couldn't help shaking his head at Roberts' question. "Reading the news? You wouldn't believe me."

"All those debates going on and on and on, day after day,

one show after another saying the same things, making the same arguments over and over again," Roberts said, almost as if he was oblivious to Rick's words. "They're good. They're evil. It's something great. It's the end of the world. I swear to God, I could just sit there with the sound off and say every single line that would come out of their mouths."

When Roberts paused, a thick pall of silence hung over the room. Except for a tiny metallic rattle that caught Rick's attention. The noise lasted no more than about two seconds, but Rick could have sworn it sounded like a thin piece of metal of some kind being jostled by a vibration.

"All talk," Roberts went on, oblivious to the vibration. His eyes appeared to be searching some distant points in the room as he spoke. Again, the signs were all ones Rick had seen numerous times before, had read about in countless police reports, and had seen in interrogations. Henry Roberts was typical of most people doing time for murder. This was a crime of passion unfolding here. Something had been stuck in Roberts' craw for a long time, and now something had at last set him off. He had probably never committed a crime before in his life, except one festering little grudge had finally boiled up into something toxic, something he could no longer control. This monologue was his way of airing all of his grievances. "All talk all the time. Everyone trying to sound so intelligent and rational and poised and in control. Planes of reality, they say. Hyper space. Alternate dimensions. Quantum string, whatever the hell. And what no one is willing to admit is that *we* are dealing with some evil, cold-blooded *selection* system. Do you realize that?" At last he paused and shot a tense, angry look at Rick and Cornelia. "It's a *selection* system. That's why it's here. To select some and let others die—"

"Mr. Roberts," Cornelia said very softly.

Rick wished she wouldn't have done that as one of Roberts' henchmen, a heavyset, bearded man in some type of a hunting jacket and cradling a shotgun, flinched.

"Mr. Roberts," Cornelia went on. "I know what you're talking about. This selection system that you think is—"

Roberts' look darkened, and Rick noticed the M-16 shift in his hands. "What the hell do you think you're doing? Trying to talk your way out of this? Because you're not doing it well."

"*Please*," Cornelia insisted. "Just listen to what I have to say—"

"Do you remember those stories out of San Francisco?" Roberts cut her off. "That globe going down that hill and—"

"I know," Rick cut in, hoping to divert Roberts' focus from Cornelia. "We were there."

Nonetheless, she said, "One of the people killed there, Sarah Robinson, was one of my best friends from childhood."

Roberts raised his voice in indignation now. "I'm sorry to hear that, because my brother also died. Except my brother wasn't crushed by a globe. He got some damn fool idea in his head...." As Roberts paused, his gaze skipped to the Foster family, beaming ferocious hatred at all four of them. "Had some idea that the globe would save his life. All those TV shows put on one earth spirit-power hippie asshole after the next about world transformation and a new age and how we will all live forever. Live forever, huh? Is that what you want to tell a man who's in the hospital with cancer? That he should leave his doctor, his medication, and try to get to the spirit mountain in California where the first globe appeared because he will be healed?"

I guess we found what we were looking for, the words screamed through Rick's mind. When he shot a quick look Cornelia's way, he could see comprehension dawning on her as well.

But someone else replied to Roberts' rant first.

"Mr. Roberts, I am truly so very sorry for your loss," Charlie Foster spoke in what sounded like a strangled wheeze. "But please—"

"*You* shut the hell up!" Roberts hissed, and briefly swung the barrel of his rifle in his direction.

"Look, Mr. Roberts," Rick jumped in, "this is *not* their fault."

"*No,*" Roberts replied, contempt searing his voice. "His

daughter was just selected to be saved while others get to die."

Rosemary Foster now whimpered, "Please! I beg you...."

What again no one else seemed to notice was the tin metallic rattle from somewhere in the house. Rick's eyes darted about as he tried to remain still, but he saw nothing that could have been making that sound.

"What the fuck is that?" one of Roberts' thugs, a guy in a woodland camouflage overcoat, sounded off.

And Rick couldn't be sure whether he was glad to hear his words or not. Someone else had taken note of the noise apparently.

"Nothing!" Roberts snapped as his underling before glaring at Rick again. "So now you people tell me what it is exactly that makes *her*...," he stabbed the barrel of the M-16 toward Sally, "special. What makes her *better* than everyone else."

Rosemary began sobbing now, her body heaving and convulsing.

"Why does she get healed while others deserve to die?" Roberts raged.

"It's not about deserving to die...," Rick tried to answer.

"Oh no!" Roberts cut him off. "You mean there's some selection process here that makes sense? That's fair?"

"Believe me," Cornelia said, "I asked myself that a million times after Sarah died. What's the purpose behind this? Why? But I *don't* know." She paused and pointed toward Sally. "And she doesn't know either."

"She's a kid, for God's sake," Rick tried to implore Roberts, hoping there was still some chance of talking him out of this frenzy, this hatred that had been bottling up inside him, ready to burst. "What are you going to do, kill her? Are you going to kill a little girl because she lived while...?"

"A kid?" Roberts asked. But instead of the roiling anger in his voice, there was the slight halt of confusion. Rick wondered if that little pause was something significant enough to offer hope. Maybe Roberts didn't have it in him to either kill, *or* allow his goons to hurt, anyone. "So maybe that's it? She's an innocent kid, and that's why the globes chose her to live? Well, guess what, friend? How many other kids do you think are out there? In hospitals! Suffering and dying right now!" Roberts' glare darkened again as his delivery was getting more and more vehement. "Kids whose families don't live in big fancy houses like this. Ones who don't have a big fancy Cadillac SUV in the garage. So is that it? Huh? Are they all better than everyone else? If you don't live in a big house you deserve to die? Huh? My brother fixed copy machines for a living. So I guess that means he's not as good."

"Look," Rick said as he heard the clatter of something metallic resonate from what must have been the entrance to a kitchen on the far side of the room. "I don't pretend to understand *any* of this. But this is not *her* fault. She is not making any of this happen...."

"Oh no?" Roberts spat. "But what is *she*, what are *they*...," he waved his gun at the Fosters again, "doing about any of this? Do you know? Do you know what they've been doing since their daughter's been miraculously healed? Going to all the hippie globe earth-power gatherings, talking about how all of this is all so wonderful and the globes will heal people, that's what. Just have faith, that's all." Roberts paused for a long beat, his nostrils flaring almost as if he was trying to suck all the oxygen out of the room, before he bellowed, "*Lying*! That's what they're doing."

"No!" Charlie Foster cried. "I swear! Please understand...I swear to *God* that—"

"Oh, you can swear to God all you want," Roberts yelled back. "Your globe god, you mean. Isn't that right? The one who's making the selections."

"Whatever those globes might be doing," Rick, too, raised his voice, hoping there was still a chance of calming Roberts before he spiraled completely out of control. "It is *not* that little girl's fault. Do you understand? Do you think she asked for this...?"

"I think she," Roberts continued raging, "I think *they* know how the selections are made. They know how it's decided. Who is good enough, who gets to live and who gets to die. And I'm going to make them talk. They've deceived the world for the sake of some bloodthirsty—"

Except Roberts' word froze in his throat as the entire living room was bathed in light.

5.

A moment after the room was flooded by lights, it was assaulted by noise; flooded by the noise of a revving engine, a gunshot, then the sounds of wood tearing, disintegrating, glass obliterating, the scream of a man knowing his life was about to blink out in an instant.

As Rick spun toward the sound of the noise and the lights, he saw the front end of a car barreling toward the Foster house. At first the vehicle hit the stairs to the porch, began crushing it, yet at the same time getting its momentum deflected upward as if by a ramp.

Rick dived through the air, his arms grasping for Cornelia as an oncoming car slammed into the front door of the Fosters' home, tore it to shards of wood and glass, instantly killed one of Roberts' gunmen who had taken a shot at it, then skidded across the living room, ran over a second gunman, and went ramming into the wall on the far side.

As he and Cornelia slammed into the hardwood flooring, Rick's glance shifted toward the spot where Roberts used to stand, finding him sprawled on the ground as well. But, unfortunately, Roberts was not on the ground because he had been hit by the incoming car. He was down because he, too, had dived out of the way.

And another unfortunate sight was that of two remaining gunmen still on their feet, unhurt. One of them, in fact, was raising his own M-16 now, searching for the nearest target of opportunity. The target he seemed to have settled on was Rick and Cornelia.

Except he didn't get a chance to take the shot. Three ragged holes burst open on his chest as semiautomatic gunfire thundered through the house. Roberts's goon staggered backward, exit wounds spraying blood all over the Foster's fireplace and mantle, eventually losing his footing and melting to the floor.

Before the last standing thug could even get as far as aiming, gunfire battered his upper chest, drilled into his face, and a final round caught him in the right temple and removed the left side of his skull.

Rick would have liked to have known who their saviors were at that moment, but first Roberts had to be dealt with. The leader of the assault on the Fosters appeared unhurt, about to rise to his feet and go for the M-16 only about a foot or two from his grip. So Rick reacted by springing upright and lunging for Roberts.

Rick connected with Roberts in a battering tackle, having invested all of his strength in hitting the man as hard as possible and moving him away from the assault rifle. The hit, however, turned out to be so hard—and Roberts's body weighed much less than Rick anticipated—that they both hurtled farther backward than Rick had thought they would. Their bodies crashed into a picture window on the left side of the living room, obliterating it into a crystalline spray, then they caught on the window sill, flipped over, and exited the house.

Still tangled up, Rick and his opponent landed on a section of the porch that wrapped around onto the side of the house. After plowing onto the glass-covered wood flooring, though, they both made the effort to rise to their feet first. Roberts was going to run for it, Rick surmised, as the unhinged man had probably just figured out that Rick outweighed him by great deal of lean-muscle bodyweight. But after everything that had gone down back in the house, there was no way Rick was going to let him do that.

Except Roberts thought he could buy himself a little lead-time in his escape by taking a swing at Rick's head...and doing it with an improvised weapon. Just as Rick was almost completely upright, Robert's right hand flew toward his face in a wide haymaker swing, a brief flash of moonlight glinting off something in his fist.

Glass! Rick's mind screamed, urging him to duck before at least one of his eyes could have been taken out. Roberts had apparently taken hold of a glass shard and tried to cut him with it.

But Rick's evasive move worked and his attacker's hand flew less than an inch over his head. Then, before Roberts even completed the full swing of his arm, Rick went on the offensive, launching a fist into his midsection and doubling him over with pain. Exploiting his on-target assault, Rick hit Roberts again, sending him staggering backward toward the porch railing, then striking yet again with a fist smashed into Roberts's face.

The battered would-be assassin fell against one of the posts supporting the roof above the porch. Blood now gushed from his misshapen nose and split lip, yet he still remained upright. As he stared at Rick, there was still a frenzied energy behind Roberts's eyes, no matter how bleary and dazed they might have appeared.

Something in that look made Rick lash out again, grabbing him by the throat and holding him fastened against the post.

"More...," Roberts wheezed at length, despite the pressure Rick kept on his throat. "There will be...more...," he groaned, blood and spittle flying from his lips and nose. While back in the house he had still kept some semblance of a grip on sanity, now the energy radiating out of Roberts's frenzied glare spoke only of completely implacable madness. When Rick let up the pressure of the choke hold, Roberts hissed, "The deceivers will be killed!"

"Think again," Rick spat, and tightened his fist as hard as he could, crushing Roberts' throat. Then, as a grotesque, rattling gurgle rose from the man, Rick grabbed his belt with his left hand and hoisted upward. Suspending Roberts in mid air only for a moment, Rick slammed him back down with as much force as his muscles could expand.

The back of Roberts' neck slammed against the porch railing, snapping instantly.

Then Rick turned around and staggered back to the window he had just come crashing through. Aside from the Foster family, a distraught Charlie and Rosemarie attempting to comfort and shield their children from the sight of four dead men bleeding out onto their living room floor, he found Cornelia and Lacy approaching him.

"You know," Lacy said, reaching the window first, a stainless steel Beretta 9mm handgun at her side, "you couldn't have done this with your fancy little Italian sports car. But what I can't understand is why you two didn't stick around and ask if the Mindbending Dorian didn't have any weapons on his plane." Then she lifted the Beretta and winked at him. "Would have saved you some stress."

"There was another one of them out in the woods," Rick replied flatly.

"*Was*," Lacy said with another wink.

Rick heard footsteps on the porch a moment later. Turning to see who it was, he found Dan Knight approaching, tucking what looked like a massive Desert Eagle .44 magnum into his belt.

"So," Knight said evenly, "anyone mind telling me what the hell happened here?"

6.

Rick, Cornelia, Knight, and Lacy were sitting on the benches inside the little gazebo next to the Foster house. It was a quiet spot to let some of the adrenaline burn off. Inside the house, they saw, the Fosters had their lights back on. In fact, Rick noted, it seemed like every single light must have been on. He wondered if the family had called the police yet.

"And the kicker is," Knight spoke up at last, a couple of prolonged moments of silence having passed since he and Lacy were given the full story of Henry Roberts and his gun-wielding friends. "The thing is," he said, a distant, angry, disgusted look on his face, "that I think he was right."

Rick saw Cornelia reacting to those words as if she had been given a backhanded slap. "What?" she asked. "Coming in here and taking these people—"

Knight shook his head with an annoyed glare. "Taking them hostage and trying to kill them? No! Come on! Of course not...."

"But his take on all this," Lacy said, "is right on the money." She cast a quick glance toward the house as she paused. "Why her? Why that kid? What makes her special? Better than everyone."

"I don't know," Rick said, feeling like his receding adrenaline rush had given way to a bone-deep exhaustion and a slowly pulsing headache. All that and frustration. These were valid things Knight and Lacy were saying, except he didn't know how to respond. The person who'd dragged them out here, talked them into flying in from Hawaii, was now clueless as to what kind of sense to make of Sally Foster. "It makes no more sense than the rest of this whole globe phenomenon, but—"

"But it's something new?" Knight asked bitterly.

"But it will get us dragged down to yet another police station and held until God knows how long?" Lacy asked.

"Remember, we have a U.S. senator on our side here," Cornelia replied. "He's still out there at the airport."

"And yes," Rick said, "this is all something new. It's some kind of a direct interaction between people and the globe. At last! Something we've never seen before."

Cornelia nodded vigorously now. "Yes, I think that's what we need to hold onto now and—"

"And just look at it the right way?" Knight cut her off. "Go and study that kid? Call Murakami and her doctor friends in here to run every test on her find out that...Surprise! We have no idea why she was healed while these globes have no effect on anyone else in the world."

"Maybe she heard a buzz," Lacy said with a tone of angry sarcasm.

And Rick heard something again. A creaking. Something metallic and vibrating.

"This is a wild goose chase again," Lacy said, and shook her head. "This thing is jerking us around. Except last time we got to go to Hawaii. If we would have stayed there at least we could have caught some waves, worked on a tan while we learned absolutely nothing new and had gun and knife wielding crazies trying to kill us."

"No!" Cornelia insisted. "Wait a minute! Maybe it's a progression of some sort. First the globes, then the people experiencing the hum, and now it's a physical effect."

Rick thought he felt the vibration all around now. As if something was affecting the gazebo all around them. "Do you hear that?"

The look that came back from Knight was openly contemptuous. "What? Are you hearing a buzz too?"

Lacy replied with an equally derisive chuckle.

Except now one of the M-16s that had been taken from the Roberts gang, the weapon leaning against the bench Rick and Cornelia sat on, started to vibrate. Had Rick not grabbed it, the weapon would have fallen over.

"Yes," Cornelia said. "I hear it too."

"It's probably the wind," Lacy said, and shrugged.

But as Rick held the M-16, he thought he felt the slight snap of electricity against his fingers, the kind of sting created by a static charge picket up from a rug.

"No," he whispered.

"It's something else," Cornelia said, looking around now.

Knight's hand went to the gun in his belt, and Rick definitely saw him flinch when he touched it.

"Can you smell that?" Cornelia said, and got up. She quickly wandered away from the gazebo. "It's all around. Like ozone."

"Yeah," Rick said, and followed her. "It's like everything around us is electrified."

"What's happening?" they heard a yell coming from the direction of the house. Turning around, Rick saw Charlie Foster approaching. "It's like the house is shaking apart," he said, the look of stressed bewilderment melted onto his face. "Like all the nails...you know, all the metal things, everything holding it together is shaking."

Behind him, Rosemarie and the two kids rushed from the house.

Then, as soon as they all climbed down the wreckage of the smashed stairway, Rick noticed Sally stop dead in her tracks and point to the sky.

"Look!" Cornelia's voice called out, and when he turned to her, Rick saw her staring and pointing in the same direction as Sally Foster.

What they were both looking at appeared to be a glowing orb of some sort coming closer and closer from the horizon. Moving in complete silence, it grew somewhat in size, except it was hard to judge just how large it actually was or how far away.

When he reached Cornelia, Rick heard her say, "It's coming here," very quietly. Then he felt her hand against his, her fingers quickly slipping around his hand.

But a moment later, as it indeed came to slowly hover almost directly over the Foster property, the orb split in two. Then it divided yet again, then once more, and once more again. Five identical points of light formed a ring in the sky straight overhead.

"What *is* that?" Rick heard Lacy gasp behind him.

"Maybe another progression?" Cornelia whispered.

Indeed, yet another change in the spectacle took place, with zigzagging bolts of what looked like lightning flashing from the orbs, zigzagging across the sky, arcing between the orbs.

Then, less than a minute later, a concentrated field of light spread across the area ringed by the five orbs, growing in intensity, spewing its own lightning bolts through the air, toward the ground, toward the orbs. From within this brightening inner zone, they all watched in stunned silence as what appeared to be an enormous globe of some swirling, light-pulsating, somewhat metallic, somewhat transparent, material slowly floated toward the ground.

*Hard to tell...hard to estimate...hard to characterize...*the thoughts shot through Rick's mind. It was difficult still to estimate how high up the object was, especially since it soon stopped its descent. *Five, six hundred feet, perhaps?* It was also impossible to guess what it was made out of. *How can I guess what something that's capable of this would be made of...?* or even decide if the thing was solid or some kind of a phenomenon of pure energy.

Except for the light. One thing that was certain was the brightness of the object kept glowing, bathing everything all around, until Rick thought that every pore on his body, every cell inside of it, was being shone through by light that felt like a solid, tangible form now.

He tried to turn to Cornelia, but he wasn't sure if he was capable of movement. He wasn't sure if he even felt like he had a body. All around him now was nothing but that intrusive, all-consuming light.

7.

Rick thought he was inside some type of an enclosure, a hall of some sort, a physical place, yet his awareness of it came from some sensory input other than his eyes and ears. The most accurate description he would ever be able to give of the experience was that it felt "dreamlike." Nothing more concrete than that. Only "dreamlike." He knew there was solid ground under his feet, that there was a roof over his head—somewhere high above, but how far away was impossible to tell—and even the fact that this space had borders all around, at some unknowable distance. Yet all of these physical, solid things were made of bright white energy. Rick just *knew* it.

And he heard a voice with crystal clarity.

"You did well," the voice spoke. "You came and you did well."

The voice was surprisingly youthful, Rick noticed. Clear spoken, loud, apparently human...but with a voice like that of an adolescent male.

"You and your friends came as I...I hoped you would. I'm glad I was right."

And then Rick saw the speaker.

Indeed, he appeared to be a perfectly average-looking youth of about seventeen, perhaps eighteen years old. His face was, in some odd way, unremarkable in every possibly feature. Aside from the fact that his hair appeared to be a light brown color against all the white energy all around, there was nothing about him that Rick thought would ever be in any way memorable. He appeared to be dressed in some type of a body suit that was just as white as everything else Rick's mind registered.

So average...so why is he so familiar?

"What are you?" Rick mouthed the words, and he was glad to be able to hear his own voice.

"One who wants to warn you," the...*kid? The stranger? The being...?* spoke. "And, most of all, to apologize."

"What is this all about?" Rick had to ask immediately. He had to get to the point quickly, he knew, before he would lose all his faculties and have some kind of a breakdown.

Is a nervous breakdown even possible here?

The being's—for some odd reason a part of Rick's brain wanted to process this thing speaking to him by referring to it as "the kid," but he knew that would not have been accurate—facial expressions took on something akin to the look of sheepish, regretful embarrassment. "A mistake," it said, sounding again exactly like a deeply contrite human eighteen-year-old. "A mistake has been made. By me. But now the people of your world are about to feel its full ramifications."

Oh, only now *we will feel the full ramifications?*

"The globes!" Rick said quickly. "Are they about to hurt people?"

The being shook its head. "No. Your people are about to make the next mistake. And it has the power to...."

"The power to what?" Rick blurted out, an irritation spiking through him as the thing in front of him let his voice trail off. There was that quality to his voice again, Rick realized. Like a kid who knew it had screwed up and now tried to find the best way of explaining. *Human!* the next thought coursed through Rick's mind. *He has an effect on me the same way a real person would.*

"To cost millions of lives," the being said, this time with a level of firm conviction. Again, like a human who knew there were no more ways of dancing around the truth and knew it could earn points by being honest. "You have to stop them."

Wherever he was, whatever state he was in, Rick could still feel the sensation of an adrenaline spike, of panic. "Stop who? From doing what?"

"Please believe me that all this was not my intention when...."

"When what? When you created the globes?"

The being nodded, again looking contrite. "Yes."

"Why?"

"First you must save your people."

"Save them how?"

"You must tell your companions that locations in...New Mexico, in Taos, in Bristol and all similar places must not be attacked."

What the hell is he talking about? "Attacked? Who's attacking what?" Rick asked, another frightening realization dawning on him. Since leaving Hawaii, he hadn't been keeping track of world events. Had the situation in the Philippines escalated into something much worse?

"Your companions know," the being said. "They have been communicating with your military. People you have been working with."

"My companions...Knight?"

The being that looked like an average college freshman nodded. "Yes. This should not have been. It has all been a mistake. But my...*people*? Others wouldn't have approved. But I felt your world needed it. I was wrong."

Rick's mind kept reeling. "Your...*people*?"

"That's the phrase you would use."

"So there are more of you?"

A slight nod again. "Yes. Always have been."

"What?" Rick found himself saying, growing ever more

certain that perhaps a nervous breakdown was very much possible even here, whatever this place might have been. "What are you...?" he mumbled, about to say "people." "Aliens?" he said very tentatively instead.

There was a look of confusion on the being's youthful face. "In a way," he said at length. "We have been called so many things over time. We have looked so many ways."

Unbelievable, was the only thought that formed in Rick's astonished mind. "So *this*...it's not what you look like?"

"No. This is what I...what I *made* myself look like to you."

To put me at ease? Rick thought. But this bit of information also made sense. It explained that feeling of familiarity Rick had. The being created an image to register in Rick's brain, acting almost like some sort of a composite-sketch program, something that could choose among various facial features, creating something that registered a reaction in the viewer. He also wondered if this otherworldly thing could access his mind, his memories, perhaps drawing on his subconscious recollections of people he had seen throughout his life—people he had been friends with, people he liked—and created this composite creation.

But Rick had to shake his head. "You need to make me understand," he demanded. "What was all this, the globes, those people hearing the sounds...the...the hums? What was it all about?"

"A sign," the being said. "It was supposed to be a sign...but it never should have been. You should not be going to Taos. My... *people*...my companions, can do irreversible damage to your world if the military's plans are carried out. I tried to correct the mistakes. I created the false experiencers of the signals...."

"All these other people who can hear the hums," Rick thought aloud. "Radar chaff. So that was correct. To hide the real experiencers."

"You must stay away from Taos."

"No!" Rick wanted to insist as strongly as he could. "Wait a minute! You owe me some clear answers."

"At another time."

And, once, again, all that Rick cold see, hear, feel all around him, inside of him, was formless, brilliant energy.

8.

"This is...it's incredible!" Cornelia gasped. "A progression. It doesn't make any sense to me. But...but one step leading to the next."

She, actually, was the first one to speak. Knight and Lacy, along with the Fosters, sitting around the gazebo—where Rick was told he had reappeared—were all dumbstruck by his disappearance and reappearance almost as much as they were by his story.

As Rick looked around, he wouldn't have been able to even take a wild guess at who would be the next one to say anything. Expressionless, frozen stares studied his every movement. In a way, it was a good thing that they were still the only ones on the property, that the local police could not be summoned by the Fosters from the house. As it turned out, Henry Roberts and his gang had cut the telephone landlines and smashed all of the Fosters' cell phones when they attacked. In the shock and confusion of the aerial light show and Rick's disappearance, Cornelia, Knight, and Lacy hadn't yet gotten around to using any of their phones to call anyone out to the property. But one thing Rick was quite sure of, though, was who he *wanted* to do the talking next.

"What's in Taos, New Mexico, Dan?" he asked.

As there was little reaction from Knight, Rick shifted his gaze to Lacy.

"Taos?" Cornelia asked.

"Yeah, Taos," Rick said, but kept watching Knight and Lacy.

First there was the look of recognition from Lacy and her effort to avoid eye contact. Then Knight ran a hand over his head and gave it a slight shake. When he did make eye contact with Rick, his focus seemed to have the intensity of a laser that could cut through steel.

"Maybe the real answers," Knight said quietly.

"So it's true," Rick said.

"Well, if your little glowing friend told you," Knight replied, his voice carrying both weariness *and* menace at the same time.

"What's true?" Cornelia asked, the astonishment and confusion ringing through her words. "What's going on here? What about Taos?"

Rick stared at Lacy, as if by force of will he could compel her to look at him and come clean. "You know about it."

"Yeah," at length she met his gaze and said.

"I just told her before we left Hawaii," Knight said.

So that was why she'd left Rafferty behind, Rick guessed. In a way, she *did* believe in the importance of this trip to Nebraska. Except she believed in Knight's and the Pentagon's plans for what needed to be done next.

"I'm confused," Charlie Foster spoke now.

Rick noticed the fear in his wife's eyes as she tightened her grip around their two children.

"Taos," said Rick, "and some of these other places are where our military friends think they can attack this...these...*things.* Whatever they are."

"*Attack* them?" Cornelia said. "So...oh, my God! Have those people, those...?"

"The conspiracy nuts?" Knight cut in. "Have they been right all along? No! Nobody knew. They first put two and two together after people like Kwan. After the hum."

"Yeah, I get it," Cornelia replied as Knight's voice trailed off. "The hum sensitives. But put *what* together?"

Knight took a deep breath. "These places, like Taos and Bristol and the others, well, they've had a history — *long* history — of some people sometimes hearing an inexplicable hum. Hell, it's been studied for years. With the same results Murakami got from Kwan and all the others in Hawaii. Absolutely nothing. So they made a guess that Taos might be some kind of...I don't know.

OK? Nobody actually knows. They're all guesses." Knight paused and gave Rick a hard look. "What did your little glowing buddy tell you about them? What *are* these places? Portals to where ever they come from? A gateway to their alternate dimension? But it was one hell of a good guess, wasn't it?"

"Yeah, it was a good guess," Rick said. "And now you'll have to contact them—who is it? Robinson? The Pentagon?—and tell them to call it off, whatever they're planning. Is Markwell a part of this too?"

Knight laughed and shook his head. "Do you think Markwell would be let in on this? You can *not* be serious. As much as I defended him, now I'm sure there's at least *one* thing those holy rollers got right, trying to force him out of office."

"*That's* the one thing they got right, Dan?" Rick shot back. "It seems they'd want to destroy these beings as much as you do."

"Wait a minute!" Cornelia cut in. "Just wait a minute."

Both Rick and Knight looked at her.

"Destroy them?" she asked. "How exactly do they think they have any chance of destroying this?"

"If places like Taos are portals," Knight said with a shrug, "the portals must be opening a lot. And if they open, we can send things through. Like weapons. Missiles. A nuclear warhead."

"I don't believe this!" Cornelia almost yelled.

"Yeah," Charlie Foster gasped. "That's…that's…."

"Completely insane?" Cornelia completed the thought.

"And it can't happen!" Rick said.

Lacy was the first to reply, even though Rick could see Knight about to come back with a retort. "Why not?"

"Yeah," Knight said with a bitter, rueful little smile. "Why not?"

Rick was stunned that a man he had been working with so closely for the last several months could go off the rails to such an extent. "Because there are more of them, that's why. And you *can't* destroy them. It wouldn't work. Except to piss them off and force a retaliation we won't soon forget."

"How do you know?" Knight interjected suddenly. "Did that thing tell you so?"

Rick saw the knowing, crafty look on Knight's face as he stumbled into giving an instant reply. "Come *on!* Just listen to yourself! And whose insane idea *was* this? To try and attack even if Taos and these other places *are* portals to their world? Does anyone seriously think they have a chance in hell of succeeding? Can they imagine the technology it takes to put these globes here? Do we stand any kind of a chance against that?"

"I'm actually more and more convinced that we do," Knight said.

"*You* can not be serious."

"If these things are all-powerful," Knight came back, "why are they even *asking* you to call off the attack anyway? Why don't they — I don't know — make all the missiles and weapons fall out of the sky harmless?"

"And why do you want to provoke them?"

"And why don't I accept their good will? Here, come on, trust us! Trust our good intentions. That we'll treat some of you special and give them favors and save their lives. And we'll treat others like dirt. Let them die. Let them suffer."

With each word out of his mouth, the fury built inside Knight. Rick could see the ferocious set to his eyes, veins thickening along his forehead and neck.

At the same time, Rick also noticed Rosemarie Foster's posture stiffening, her hold on her children tightening.

"Because it's all a part of something much bigger that you can't understand?" Knight continued spitting one angry word after the next. "No! No way! I won't do it."

"Then what's the alternative?" Rick demanded, his voice also rising.

"To make a stand," Lacy said. "He's right. I won't wait for these…*things* to just put us under their thumbs —"

"There's no reason to believe that at all," Cornelia added.

"You honestly don't think so?" Lacy asked, her voice getting as hard as Knight's now. "Come *on!* Let me do what I want to you, and in the end even the hardships will have some deep important meaning…except you will never be able to understand it. *Bull! Shit!* I've heard that line with every flag-draped coffin coming back from Afghanistan, from Iraq…with everyone I knew who died. No more!"

"And you're willing to sacrifice the world for your suffering?" Rick asked, his voice hard, angry, but feeling at the very same time like a hot, searing blade was being shoved into his chest. It was Lacy's pain he was feeling, he knew full well. He understood her, knew the fury driving her, yet he knew how wrong she was in the stand she was taking.

"I won't let this sadistic, cold-blooded *thing* that treats our lives like some kind of a game excuse my suffering," Lacy hissed.

"Well, thank God it's even asking. It's giving us a choice," Rick replied.

"Exactly," Cornelia asked. "We're given a chance to end all this."

"And then what?" Knight asked.

"That's right," Lacy said. "And what comes next? Did they tell you that?"

"Yeah," Knight fired off a question before the last word even left Lacy's mouth. "What's all this leading up to?"

Rick couldn't help shaking his head. "Look, I *don't* know…."

"Because he didn't say, did he?" Knight answered. "Well, I'm calling bullshit on his good intentions."

"Things like this don't have good intentions," Lacy said.

"I can't believe you two," Cornelia cried, and sprang to her feet now. "*Look* at what we're up against," she yelled, and waved her hands toward the now-empty sky. "You *seriously* think beings like this can just be fought…?"

"And what's the alternative?" Lacy replied, her words acidic with anger and condescension.

"*Exactly*," Knight said. "And can't *you* two realize what this is all leading up to?" He, too, stood up now and pointed at the

Fosters. "*That's* what! That girl. People like that. Just have faith. Don't question."

Then he turned and stalked out of the gazebo. As Rick also sprang to his feet, he was sure Knight was going to march over to Dorian's Lamborghini and attempt to leave the Foster property immediately. Out of the corner of his eye, Rick noticed Lacy rising as well.

Except Knight spun around and stopped. With his right hand he reached into his jacket and pulled out a bulky-looking object. "Satellite phone," he said with a nasty, leering defiance. "This connects us back to Travis. Back to Robinson. Back to the fighter squadrons and bombers on alert now and ready to head to Taos. And that call your best pal from the *Twilight Zone* wants us to make is *not* going out."

"Robinson, all the others, they trusted you to come with us and find out what's going on, didn't they?" Rick yelled at him. "So you're going to lie to them?"

"No. Because they want the same thing."

As Rick approached Knight, he saw the old man's knees slightly bending, his center of gravity just ever so slightly lowering. It was a fighter's stance, Rick knew. "You don't know that," he said. "You're withholding vital information here. They're trusting you to tell them *everything* that's happened here."

Knight shook his head, the look in his eyes still defiant. "I'm not telling them shit about any of this, do you understand? The call is *not* going out."

So Rick dropped his gaze and shook his head. His entire posture loosened, he hoped he telegraphed a look of exasperated defeat....

Until he balled his right fist and lashed out at Knight with as much speed as he could. The punch connected with Knight's face, stunning him, but not quite throwing him off balance. So Rick struck again with a second right jab, this time making the old man catch a few steps backward to keep from spilling onto the grass.

"The world...," Rick hissed as he followed up the two right jabs with a left one. "Is not...," he spat as he attacked with two right jabs again, this time to Knight's midsection. "Going to end...." Two left shots to the midsection again. "Because little Danny Knight...." A hard right hook to Knight's cheek that snapped his head to the side, forcing him to spew ropelike gouts of saliva-mixed blood through the air. "Is angry at life's hard knocks!" Then a left hook that snapped Knight's head back and finally threw him off balance.

Dropping the satellite phone, Knight reeled backward and sprawled onto the ground.

Gasps of surprise, revulsion, and random shouts of "Are you insane?" "Jesus Christ!" and "Stop it!" came from behind Rick.

On the ground, though, Knight stirred surprisingly soon. In fact, he was attempting to elbow his way upright within seconds of going down.

"Oh, shit...," he gasped after rolling onto his side, then pushing upright, and spitting out more blood. "You feel strongly about it, don't you, Junior?"

Rick looked around, trying to find where the phone had been tossed in the darkness. "Make the call...," he began, except Knight's recovery really was *much* faster than expected.

Knight had pushed off the ground and lunged at Rick like a football player making a tackle. Getting Knight's head and left shoulder rammed into his midsection, he stumbled backward, then went down on the ground hard. Knight, in turn, was following up on the attack immediately, keeping him pinned down while driving his fist into his abdomen and chest, one vicious blow after the next.

As hard as Rick fought to tighten his abdominal muscles, he knew he would be winded very soon, all breath beaten from his lungs if Knight got the chance to land a few more of his battering-ram punches. So Rick kicked against the ground and twisted his body, rolling over Knight, then rolling over him once more, grappling, pushing, and clawing to free himself from the old

311

man's hold.

Once the hold was broken, it was a race against Knight to get upright first. But it was a race Rick won, giving him the chance to lash out again, taking a swing at Knight's face but catching him only on the side of the head.

Blinding pain, in turn, shot through Rick's right hand. It reminded him of why the boxing glove was invented and why old-time bare-knuckle matches used to go on for dozens of rounds. Hitting someone in the head or face tended to cause more pain to the puncher than the one on the receiving end of the blow.

Knight, in fact, barely reacted to the punch, coming back with a lightning-fast swing of his own. The strike angled from down to up, an attempted uppercut to Rick's chin. It was a shot that, nevertheless, missed its mark, glancing off his cheek.

"You can bow down and obey," Knight rasped as he came at Rick again, throwing a hard left jab that hit him in has chest. "Do what this damned thing tells you. Back down like you always do."

When Knight attempted a right-handed swing at Rick, he was able to block it with his left forearm and retaliate with a jab to Knight's midsection. What Rick had hoped for was an upward blow to Knight's abdomen, a shot which, if placed at just the right spot, would knock the old man's diaphragm upward and force the air from his lungs. That would, Rick hoped, stun him enough to end the fight.

Except that Rick, too, missed his mark, delivering a useless punch to Knight's chest.

Indeed, Rick's mistake earned him a left hook that had him seeing a field of stars and expanding splotches of light shower across his field of vision. The effects of the shot were nearly blinding, but not completely so. He could catch the blur of Knight's right fist coming at his face and was able to duck it.

With the shot evaded, Rick went on the attack again, battering Knight with a round of punches to his chest, abdomen and sides, driving him backward. Rushing after him and seeing Knight's legs start to sag and wobble, Rick hoped to take him out of the game with one well-aimed fist to his face. As he was about to lunch his last assault, though, shouts and screams from somewhere behind him, somewhere perhaps close to Cornelia's position, distracted him just for a fraction of a second long enough to mistime his strike and make it land just far enough off target to compromise its effectiveness.

Pain bolted through Rick's right hand again as he caught Knight on the forehead. Although the hit staggered him, Knight was able to fight back with a right fist to Rick's midsection, then a left one to the face, then a winding series of blows to the abdomen again that completely robbed Rick of his advantage. In fact, the game-ending shot to the diaphragm had suddenly become Knight's, exploding into the middle of Rick's body and staggering him so hard that all air, all oxygen departed his lungs. Gulping, staggering, struggling for any amount of oxygen to replenish his exhausted, battered body, Rick had become completely ineffective in the fight. Knight could actually hold him, pull him upright, then deliver a head-butt to his face that was close to a complete short circuit, then reboot, of his brain.

When the reboot was complete, however, Rick found himself flat on his back. At first he saw the field of stars of the night sky in front of him. He could feel—and almost choked on—blood in his nose flowing back through his sinuses and down his throat. More blood trickled out the side of his mouth, and his right hand hurt so much that he was certain more than one bone had to have been broken. And then the field of stars was blocked.

Dan Knight suddenly blocked Rick's vision, towering over him, his hands raised, clutching something, and a fiendish, revenge-crazed glare in his eyes.

"Die, you bastard," Knight seemed to whisper through a raspy, subhuman hiss. Blood dripped from his own lips, nose, and the lacerations on his lips, cheeks, brows.

And Rick recognized the object in Knight's hand. It was a

313

rock, about the size of a soccer ball and painted perfect white. Rick had seen them lining the driveway. And now Knight was going to use one to kill him with it.

"Die.... Die.... All of you...," Knight kept wheezing, but his body seemed to be frozen in place.

Then, as he kept still, glaring at Rick, the maniacal focus in his eyes slowly gave way. Something like recognition and horror took the place of hate and rage. It was almost like he was waking up, Rick recognized. He looked, Rick thought, like a man who had allowed his own demons to run rampant for a while, and now was frightened, ashamed of the thing he had temporarily become.

But as Knight's posture loosened, his arms shifted as if he was ready to throw away the rock, a gunshot cracked across the night.

Knight appeared to be startled by it so much that he looked like he lost his grip on the rock. The object shifted and wobbled wildly in his grip.

No! Rick's mind screamed. *He's come to his senses, but now my brains will be bashed in because he was startled.*

He invested his last ounces of energy into shifting to his right, and managed to move just far enough to evade the plunging rock by one lucky split instant. The massive object impacted the ground exactly where his head had been a fraction of a second ago.

Then Knight melted to the ground, wheezing and gasping for air.

Has he been...?

Knight spat out another mouthful of blood. "You're good, kid," he stammered. "No street fighter, but you're OK for a cop."

So he wasn't shot, Rick thought with some relief, and pushed off the ground, looking around frantically, trying to figure out what happened.

Back at the gazebo, he saw Cornelia gripping Lacy's hands and forcing them skyward. Lacy held the stainless steel Beretta.

314

Soon enough, though, she dropped it. Then, as Cornelia released her, she melted to the ground and soundlessly sobbed.

"So everyone's come to their senses," Rick mumbled, spat blood, then fell back down into the grass.

When the field of stars in front of his eyes vanished, it did so because it was overtaken by a flood of burning white light rather than the figure of anyone bent on murder.

9.

Rick could see the abrasions on his knuckles, tasted the blood in his mouth, smelled it, and felt the cut on his lip. Yet the pain itself had diminished. As he moved the fingers of his right hand, all he felt was something like a dull, throbbing ache.

"Is it healing me?" he mumbled as he looked around, trying to discern anything in that white plane of energy he had been transported into again.

"It can help you somewhat," the being's voice sounded in Rick's mind more than in his ears. It sounded the same, however. It was still as youthful as it was before, with that self-effacing quality hiding behind its words.

"*Somewhat?*" Rick asked as he looked around, left to right, then started spinning around trying to find the thing that looked like a kid. "You brought that girl back from the brink of death. All I get is *somewhat?*"

"I'm sorry," the being said, and as Rick turned once more, he found himself standing face to face with it again.

"Sorry, huh? So is this when the answers come?"

"I thought you understood."

Rick shook his head, a sharp little prickle of anger passing through him. "No. Actually, I don't. But how about this: let me ask you a couple of questions."

"Of course."

"When you said we did good, what was that all about? Those men, those crazies about to hurt that whole family, did you do that to lure us out here?"

315

The being shook his head with a sad look in his eyes. A look, Rick considered upon second glance, that was almost wounded. "The child was healed because I did need *someone's* attention. The signs…the globes have been so badly misunderstood, their existence abused, that the world's attention needed to be shifted away from…."

"From what?" Rick snapped. "From a reason for people to kill each other?"

The being nodded. "And you were the only ones who took notice."

If you only knew, Rick thought. "Thank God for Senator Bling's perceptive wife," he muttered.

"What is that?"

"Never mind. And, uh, what then? We're coming out here, and you appear to me because you got *lucky* that we had a connection to the military, on top of seeing your little sign with that girl."

"Yes," the being said with that soulful look again.

"I don't believe this," Rick said, all the while his mind tried to grapple with another problem he felt was right in front of him, yet something he was ignoring. *Maybe Doc Knight's shots to the head's slowed me down.*

"All right," Rick said at length. "So…so this is what I don't get. Why contact me now? Why the sign? Why the girl? Why not make yourself known?"

"You rather that the girl's life wasn't saved?"

"What?" Rick blurted out, again that anger coming back and stoking him. "Of course not. I mean…shit…*yes*, I *am* glad she is safe and she's OK and she won't die…. She won't die, will she?"

"No, she won't."

Rick nodded vigorously. "Good. OK, good. But what I don't understand is why these…*signs* that we could just as well have missed?"

The being took a deep breath—or, Rick considered now, it made a motion that appeared to look like what a human would do before plunging into a complicated narrative, a narrative of something he wasn't too proud of — and looked Rick in the eyes. "It is forbidden for any one of us to interfere with the free human will. But...."

"But what?"

The being waved its right hand through the air and the white eternal expanse all around seemed to fade into a bleak, pitted landscape of some place that appeared to have been burned and bombed beyond recognition. The sky overhead was an oppressive, sickly brownish-black ceiling of corruption. Along the horizons, Rick thought he could vaguely see spires of some sort struggling to stand upright. They could have been anything in this weird, utterly ugly and alien landscape, but somehow he just knew they had been artificially constructed.

"This place used to be like your world," the being said. "A paradise."

"What happened?"

"They destroyed themselves," the being said in a hollow, matter of fact tone.

Rick found himself at a loss for words. Was there a point in asking how or why? After everything that had been happening since people found the globes....

No, not found them, a voice in his mind corrected him. *Since we tried to* figure out *what they were.*

"They destroyed themselves," the being said, "because they had no hope that there was something better lying ahead in the future. With all their differences, if they could have just believed that there was something better to come."

"Is that what the globes were for?"

"That is what I hoped they would do. To give you... Confirmation? Isn't that what your people are yearning for? Why they watch what you do?"

"What I do? The show, you mean...."

The being nodded. "They want a sign of something greater. Something beyond."

"So you give us the globes."

"Yes. And now I understand why I shouldn't have."

"Because people forced their own beliefs on them? Trying to bash in the head of anyone who disagreed?" Rick almost whispered, the full implications of the entire phenomenon dawning on him now.

"Yes."

"But why so vague? Come on! Why not something more concrete?"

The being gave a thin, embarrassed smile. "Something more concrete than a twenty-ton globe of granite?"

"Oh, come on!"

"What more, Rick? More people like Sally Foster?"

"Exactly!" Rick snapped. "Yes! That's what I'm talking about. Heal more people like her."

"And how many more? And how many more illnesses and tragedies can we avert? We can't avert them all. We can't avert man-made tragedies. Tragedies people choose to inflict on each other. But tragedies nevertheless. But we can't stop them. We can't interfere with human will."

"But...." Rick was about to retort, but realized he couldn't think of a way to do so.

The blighted landscape all around faded away, and the field of white returned.

"I thought the globes would be enough of a sign."

"Right. Except they weren't."

"They were a mistake."

"Oops," Rick said as facetiously as he could. "And all the damage done as a result of...of your *mistake*, because you couldn't predict this would happen—"

"It pains me. It pains all of us."

"Well, that's good to know."

"I...taking this form...taking this human form...I can feel human feelings, human sensations. I can understand your anger and pain."

318

"So what next? Will there be any more globes?

The being shook his head immediately. "No. No more."

"Well, that's good. The mess they made, though, can't be helped, can it?"

The being shook its head with less enthusiasm now. "No, it can't."

"Well, hopefully," Rick said slowly, thinking of that hellish landscape, "we'll manage somehow."

"I...I'm certain you will," the being replied, except Rick caught the hesitation in its voice.

You little bastard! Rick wanted to scream. *Not only did you make a mess of the world because you couldn't plan ahead, but now you won't even come clean, fully own up to it.* "So this is goodbye, then?" he asked instead.

The being opened its right hand, as if initiating a handshake.

"Tell me something again," Rick said suddenly. "You said you feel our human sensations in this form."

"Yes. We do. And I feel what you do. The anger and...and I hope...."

"You hope there will be no hard feelings, right?"

The being gave a thin, beatific little smile. "Yes, Rick, no hard feelings."

"All right," Rick said, and extended his own hand, taking the being's in a firm handshake. Except suddenly he gave the hand a hard yank, seeing the being stumble forward, just like a physical human would. He greeted the being's forward momentum with a hard left-handed punch into its face.

The being, again just like a human, staggered backward, completely disoriented. Rick was sure his face even contorted in pain. And he was glad.

"No hard feelings, pal," Rick managed before a bright burst of light took him from this place forever.

10.

Rick found himself knee deep in thickets, weeds, and

overgrown grass all around. The place didn't look familiar at all. Despite the fact that the sun was coming up, he could recognize nothing around him.

"No hard feelings, huh?" he mumbled as he tried to negotiate the wild brush, noticing what looked like a paved rural highway some one-hundred feet away. "Except this time you don't take me back to the Foster house. Asshole."

Looking at the brightening horizon, Rick thought that it made sense that he was still in Nebraska. If that being—and whatever other companions he referred to so vaguely—wanted to settle the score for that punch by depositing him in the middle of Kazakhstan or some such place, the location of the sun would have been different.

"Probably an abandoned road going nowhere," he whispered to himself again. "Good luck trying to get back to Lincoln."

When he patted his pockets, looking for his cell phone, he found it missing. Whether he had lost it in the middle of the fight with Knight or if he had been relieved of it in—*relieved of it where? The damned* Twilight Zone—would be an interesting question to ponder for the upcoming few hours.

Except he wouldn't need to do that, he realized a moment later. His mind reeling at the promise of the sound he heard in the distance, he trampled and sprinted through the brush as quickly as he could, pushing himself like a madman to get to the road.

I don't believe this!

At first it sounded like a car engine in the distance, but a few moments later Rick knew this wasn't the sort of car that usually ran the back roads of Nebraska. It's deep, rumbling engine belonged to a very specific car.

"I do *not* believe it!" he couldn't help himself from shouting as he reached the road and saw the low-slung body of Alexander Dorian's Lamborghini Huracan approaching.

"I definitely do *not* believe it!" he shouted again, and started waving frantically.

As the car came to a stop in front of him, its driver-side door was already opening. A moment later Cornelia was getting out, a smile beaming off her face, springing forward and rushing into his arms.

"What happened?" Rick could barely gasp between their kisses.

"What happened?" Cornelia asked with astonishment. "*You're* asking *me* what happened? You just vanish into thin air again and you're asking *me*? I mean, where did you go? Back to the...you know...?"

"Yeah, actually yeah...but wait a minute. Where am I? How did you know to come here?"

"The Fosters' place is just around that bend," Cornelia said, pointing back in the direction she'd come from.

"Oh," Rick could merely exclaim. "But how did you know...?"

"You would show up here? Look at the sky! Do you see any thunder clouds anywhere?"

This made little sense, so Rick just said, "Thunder clouds?"

"Yeah, thunder clouds. There are no clouds of any kind anywhere, are there?"

As a matter of fact, there weren't, so Rick just shook his head as he looked around.

"So it looked a little strange with like, dozens of lightning bolts lighting up this area for about two minutes. Don't you think?"

That made sense, Rick realized.

"And you won't believe what else's happened," Cornelia said enthusiastically.

"I probably won't."

"The cops who showed up—you know, to take care of the bodies in the house—well, they're telling us that news is coming out of Scotland—Edinburgh actually—that the globe there is gone. It's disappeared! The news all over the world is picking up on it now. Just heard it on the radio too."

"Yeah, it figures," Rick mumbled. "Not that it really makes any difference at this point."

"What…?"

"Knight and Lacy? Are they all right?"

Cornelia's look darkened for a brief moment now and she shook her head, eyes rolling. "Yeah, they're still getting ready for the end of the world, though. Going on about how they're not going to bow down and worship anything."

Rick couldn't help expelling a crazy, relieved little bit of laughter at that. "Good. Let's tell them to keep fighting the system."

"Rick?" Cornelia asked, her voice getting a little more grave. "Did…*it* tell you anything else? Is it over?"

"I think so."

"So…uh, so what was this…?"

"What was this all about? Well, let's just say it was about the importance of learning to plan ahead."

Cornelia looked utterly puzzled. "I don't understand."

"There's a lot less to understand than you might think," Rick replied, looking around again, feeling like he had grown really, truly tired of Nebraska. "Do you know what I want to do now? Go back to Hawaii and do nothing but play golf for the next three days."

"Rick, come on!" Cornelia said as Rick took steps toward the Lamborghini's passenger side door. "What was all this about?"

Rick thought about the most succinct way he could summarize everything he had just heard in a place his mind could still barely process. "Let's put it this way," he said at length after opening the car's door. "You know that story you told me about the Virgin Mary on the pancakes?"

"Yes," Cornelia said, still sounding and looking understandably baffled.

"Made you ask the question, if we get miraculous messages from the other side, why does it come in such a lame form as a face on a pancake?"

"Sure, I guess. That's the obvious question."

"If God wants to send a message, why does he do it on a

pancake?"

    "Yeah."

    "Maybe that's the best he can really do."

THE END

About the Author

Barna William Donovan, a professor of communication and media studies, is a graduate of the film school of the University of Miami and he earned his Ph.D. from Rutgers University. His books on film and fandom include "The Asian Influence on Hollywood Action Films," "Blood, Guns and Testosterone: Action Films, Audiences, and a Thirst for Violence," and "Conspiracy Films: A Tour of Dark Places in the American Conscious." His commentaries on film, television, and popular culture have been quoted in media like the BBC, Variety, LiveScience, Forbes, Yahoo News, HLNTV, and various publications from Europe to Latin America.

WITHDRAWN

Sanibel Public Library

CPSIA information can be obtained
at www.ICGtesting.com
Printed in the USA
LVHW02s1800020918
588936LV00004B/349/P

9 781629 899510